THE LAST NAZI

A Joe Johnson Thriller

ANDREW TURPIN

The Write Direction Publishing

COPYRIGHT

WELCOME

Thank you for buying *The Last Nazi* — I hope you enjoy it!

This is the first in the series of thrillers I am writing that feature Joe Johnson, a US-based independent war crimes investigator. He previously worked for the CIA and for the Office of Special Investigations—a section of the Department of Justice responsible for tracking down Nazi war criminals hiding in the States. The second book in the series, *The Old Bridge*, and the third, *Bandit Country*, are also for sale on Amazon.

I am keen to build a strong relationship with my readers. As part of this, I intend to send occasional email updates containing details of forthcoming new books, special offers, and perhaps background information on plots and characters. For example, I sometimes join with other authors for promotions where we offer a selection of our books at a discounted price—or even free.

If you would like to join my Readers' Group and receive the email updates, I will send you, FREE of charge, an ebook 'box set' containing the first five "taster" chapters of *The Old Bridge* and *Bandit Country* (it includes *The Last Nazi* which you already have).

To sign up for the Readers' Group and get the free box set, go to the following web page:

www.BookHip.com/HGFSHT

Andrew Turpin, St. Albans, UK.

To my brother Adrian, for all his help with this project.

"The passage of time has in no way lessened the gravity of the crimes, and the perpetrators ought not be rewarded for their success in evading detection or concealing their misdeeds. And perhaps most important of all, justice must be sought in order to send an unmistakable message of deterrence to would-be perpetrators, namely: if you dare to commit atrocities, you will be pursued, however far you run and however long it takes to apprehend you."

— Eli Rosenbaum, director of the Office of Special Investigations, United States Department of Justice, 1994–2010, writing in *Jewish News*.

PROLOGUE

Monday, December 18, 1944
Nazi-occupied Southwestern Poland

The tunnel roof collapsed with no warning. Tens of thousands of tons of dirt and rock fell almost as one, triggering a shock wave that threw all the men to the floor.

The flickering lights that lined the tunnel wall went out instantly.

Then came a series of smaller rockfalls, which clattered and rattled down like minor landslides over the impenetrable mountain of rubble that now entirely blocked the route back to the entrance.

Finally, there was utter silence.

Jacob Kudrow groaned and clawed at his face in the blackness.

He propped himself up on his elbows and spat out a mouthful of sand and soil.

Then he coughed and gasped, trying to suck in air.

But this only brought in yet more earth and dust, dry

particles that clogged his nostrils and stuck in the back of his throat.

Then he realized he could no longer hear.

No, not again, he thought.

A wave of panic ran through him. It was the same sensation he'd had when he was ten years old, underwater and fighting for his life in the freezing Vistula River in Warsaw, long before the Nazis had marched in and changed his life.

It's over, it's over.

Jacob ripped open his filthy blue and white striped shirt and clasped the corner of the material over his nose and mouth. He coughed violently, then sucked in again, this time through the cotton.

Now, at last, a fraction of oxygen came through. Again he coughed, again he sucked, his entire focus on his own survival.

More air reached his lungs. "Breathe through your shirt," he shouted to the others, unable even to hear his own words.

Jacob turned to where he knew Daniel had been standing and reached out his hand, then stretched a little further. He found a shoe, then a leg, which moved and then moved again. His twin's hand touched his.

Thank the Almighty.

Gradually, the dust settled, allowing Jacob to breathe more easily, and he began to hear again, too. First there were the grating coughs of those around him, all battling for air, and a few thuds as more rock fell from above.

Finally, Jacob saw faint pinpricks of light coming nearer and nearer down the tunnel toward him. There were voices, quiet at first but getting louder.

The first words he heard through the darkness were the unmistakable tones of the SS first lieutenant talking to one of the other guards in German. "The Führer will go *mad* when he finds out what's happened here," he said.

Jacob immediately knew why. An hour earlier, he wouldn't have. But now he did.

"Get these damned prisoners down to the far end, away from this rock," the first lieutenant shouted to the guards. "Make sure all the boxes come too. Go on, move. There should be twelve more boxes, so count them carefully."

The flashlights were now above Jacob, shining down on the prisoners on the floor. Jacob surveyed the damage. *A miracle*. The group of twenty-one prisoners, who had been standing less than forty meters from the roof fall, were covered in filth, faces black, but they had all survived.

"Up, up, lift your boxes, then walk, single file, follow me," the guard yelled.

Jacob reluctantly got up and strained to lift the heavy wooden box lying at his feet.

"Quick," shouted the guard. At the second attempt, Jacob hoisted it onto his shoulder and got into line behind his brother.

"Are you okay?" Jacob whispered. Daniel nodded.

They all shuffled to the end of the tunnel where the first lieutenant, his thin face and SS uniform also now covered in grime, stood and watched, hands on hips. The prisoners placed their boxes on the wooden pallets with the others they had stacked neatly earlier in the day.

Other than the first lieutenant, there were only two guards now. The others must have been buried under the rockfall or left on the other side of it, where the Nazi train stood.

Jacob heard the first lieutenant mutter to a guard about the tunnel engineers. "Damned amateurs, always cutting corners, taking too many risks, going too quickly." He swore loudly and hobbled around the stack of boxes, counting them as he went.

When he finished, the first lieutenant whacked his riding

crop hard on the final stack. "Two hundred. Okay, get these prisoners down there and out. Move," he ordered, pointing toward the back of the main tunnel.

"The escape tunnel," Jacob murmured to himself. "Of course." In his panic, Jacob had almost forgotten the nightmarish eight weeks he and a large group of other prisoners had spent digging it earlier in the year. Less than half of them had survived to see it completed.

A guard led the group into an opening at the back of the main tunnel and down a much smaller tunnel, barely high enough to stand in, with few roof supports, uneven walls with protruding tree roots and a narrow rocky floor covered with large puddles.

The men carefully made their way for around a hundred and fifty meters along the tunnel, with only the two guards' flashlights for illumination. They were forced to crawl for the final short stretch, where the roof was too low to remain upright, until they emerged into a dry concrete sewer.

"Thank the Almighty that the sewer's unused," Jacob said to Daniel. They continued to crawl along a short section of the sewer before finally emerging through a snow-covered metal grill into the freezing blackness of some woodland. Daylight had long gone.

The guards led them by flashlight to a narrow road that was blanketed in ice and snow and marched them down the valley to the Ludwikowice Klodzkie village railway station, where they had arrived early that morning.

As they had been every morning and night for the previous few months, the prisoners were herded onto railway cattle cars that were still ankle-deep in pig and cow dung after being procured from a local farmer. Ten of the group were pushed into the front car, the remainder, including Jacob and Daniel, into the rear one.

A guard climbed in and began to tie the prisoners' hands

behind their backs to a horizontal steel rail that ran along the inside of the car.

He was about to tie Jacob when the guard from the front car called through, asking for more rope. The guard jumped out, and when he returned, Jacob had his hands ready on the rail.

But the guard, whom Jacob noticed was sweating profusely but also shivering, his face ashen, moved straight to Daniel and tied him, missing Jacob.

After he finished securing the others, the guard sat on a stool at the back and rested against the wall, his eyes closed, one hand on his sweating forehead. The train began to move up the valley toward Gluszyca, where the Wüstegiersdorf concentration camp lay—part of the Nazis' Gross-Rosen complex.

After a few minutes, the guard's head nodded forward. He was asleep.

Jacob inched his hand to his left until he touched his brother's bound right hand. Daniel, who was sitting with his eyes shut, his head bowed, jumped as if he had been touched with a live power cable but recovered quickly. Jacob kept his eyes fixed in front of him, but in the gloom he began slowly to unpick the knot that held Daniel's hands to the metal bar, his fingers struggling in the cold.

Finally, the bindings came free.

Jacob noticed a length of wood lying almost buried in the excrement on the floor, halfway between him and the guard. As the train crawled toward a bend, Jacob stood, his legs wobbling with fatigue and the motion of the train, and made his way toward the rear of the car. He picked up the wood and, with what remaining strength he had, slammed it into the sleeping guard's temple.

The guard opened his eyes just before impact but too late. He collapsed unconscious on the floor.

Jacob beckoned Daniel, whose eyes were now wide with fear, and moved to the open door at the back of the car. As the train rounded the bend, Jacob made eye contact with the other prisoners.

All of them, without exception, looked silently at Jacob.

How he wanted to liberate them—these men with whom he had shared some of the most horrific experiences a human could possibly endure. They had spent months as slaves, digging endless underground tunnels for Hitler's Project Riese in the Owl Mountains.

Jacob's friend Konstanty gazed at him with dark, shrunken eyes. There was Stefan, who had two children; Bronislaw, taken by the SS only a day after his wedding; Berek, Janusz, and the rest.

But Jacob knew he had no time to untie the knots, no knife to cut their bonds.

They knew it too. Konstanty just nodded, almost imperceptibly.

Jacob turned, took Daniel by the hand, and they both jumped into the darkness.

They landed on a pile of snow-covered gravel, then rolled over and flattened themselves to the ground. "They're going to come back, they'll come back," Daniel said and buried his head in the snow.

But they didn't come back. The train kept going, around another bend and behind the silhouette of some trees.

Jacob lifted his head. A short distance away was a narrow river. "Over there, the water," he said. "We can walk up it. It'll stop the dogs from smelling us."

The brothers removed their striped pants and wrapped them around their necks, then shuddered with shock as they waded into the icy river.

The riverbed was slippery and muddy and the brothers had only walked a short distance when they heard gunshots echo clearly down the valley. The blasts went on and on, a few seconds between each.

Jacob stood still for a couple of seconds. The bastard had shot them. Every single prisoner.

He met Daniel's eye, but neither of them spoke. They already knew what they had both escaped from. Speaking the words aloud would change nothing.

He shook his head and looked up to the sky for a few seconds, then back at Daniel. "Come on, quick, before they bring the dogs."

They continued to wade through the knee-high water, legs now numb, until thick rushes finally made the stream impassable.

"I know what's in those boxes, up in the tunnel, and it's not dynamite," Jacob said, as he helped his brother out of the water and onto the snow.

Daniel turned to him in the near dark, the whites of his eyes contrasting with the grit that still covered his skin. "You *know*?"

"Yes. Konstanty tripped, not long before the tunnel roof fell in. He dropped his box and a plank splintered off. I helped him fix it before the guards came, but I saw inside."

PART ONE

CHAPTER ONE

Tuesday, November 8, 2011
Washington, D.C.

Joe Johnson strode past a row of parked Cadillacs, Buicks, and Lincolns, most of them black, stretching almost the entire length of Benton Place Northwest, a tree-lined street in one of Washington, D.C.'s smartest suburbs, nestled amid an array of embassy buildings.

Halfway up the street was a three-story brick home, a grand affair with a fifty-yard frontage, three short flights of steps leading to the broad front door, and a porch bookended by stone pillars.

A hint of drizzle fell from dark clouds that scudded in from the west and left water dripping from the ornate black metal fence in front of the property. It was only just after one o'clock, but the light from chandeliers in the downstairs rooms cut a clear swath through the gloom.

Suited businessmen and women in navy cocktail dresses

or cream pantsuits hurried in, all of them greeted by a tall man in the doorway.

There he was: Philip M. Pietersen, the man who had invited Johnson. He was a bit thicker around the middle, without a doubt, and had a few gray streaks in his black hair, but otherwise was as he had been a decade and a half ago.

Johnson walked up the steps and raised his hand in greeting as the man spotted him. "Philip, hello. I decided to come after all."

Philip held out his hand and they shook.

"Been a long time, Joe," Philip said. "Fifteen years or more, isn't it?"

"About that. Nice little place you've got here." Johnson ran his hand across the short-cropped semicircle of graying hair that surrounded his bald patch.

"Thanks. Go on in, we'll chat later. I've got someone who's keen to meet you to talk about your war crimes lectures," Philip said.

Johnson nodded and walked through the door into the vast hallway.

An array of blue banners hung from the walls, all proclaiming the same slogan: David Kudrow 2012: Reviving America.

Republican Party officials ushered guests into the ballroom and handed out fund-raising leaflets. Johnson took one and stepped to one side to read it.

"David Kudrow: Your Best Chance of a Republican in the White House" it proclaimed in large letters, above a picture of the candidate.

There was a brief biography and a reprinted *New York Times* editorial headlined "Kudrow Set to Sink Romney and Take GOP Nomination."

Flipping it over, Johnson noticed a small photograph of a

smiling Philip at the bottom, captioned "Confident: Campaign Manager Philip M. Pietersen."

Johnson shook his head, crumpled the leaflet into a ball, and tossed it into a nearby bin.

He accepted a glass of champagne from a server and meandered into the ballroom, which was furnished with rows of seats and a small platform at the front, bedecked with more Kudrow banners and the Stars and Stripes.

He made straight for the back row, but before he could sit down, he felt a tap on his shoulder. "Joe, I thought it was you. What are you doing here?"

Johnson jumped and swung around to find a familiar face. It took him a moment to find some words. "Fiona, hi . . . um . . . I didn't know journalists were invited today. How's things?" Johnson hesitated, unsure whether to shake her hand, kiss her, or do nothing.

They both made awkward half-movements before Fiona inclined toward him. He bent down and pecked her on the cheek.

"Me? Oh, I guess I'm okay, sort of," she said. "I'm still at *Inside Track* doing political stuff. Head down, you know, getting on with things. Trying to pay my bills, stay out of financial trouble with the bank, with very limited success right now I have to say," she said. "I miss the *Times* occasionally, but the website is quicker and they're breaking more stories, so I enjoy it." She put her hand on the back of the chair beside Johnson. "I'll sit here next to you. How are you doing?"

"Usual routine, working away, still doing private investigations. Kids are doing fine—you know, growing up scarily fast," Johnson said.

They looked at each other for a second, but she didn't reply and they sat down at the end of the back row.

Johnson studied her. Fiona Heppenstall's hair was longer

and her jacket a little sharper than they were the last time he had seen her back in 2006, when she was still at *The New York Times.*

Johnson said, "I'm only here because I had an invite out of the blue from Pietersen. I used to know him from years back at Boston University. Runs his own software company now. Bit of an asshole but he's obviously a top dog in the party. I thought this might be interesting, as I'm in D.C. lecturing. A party fund-raiser. Won't get any money from me, but I thought it had to be worth a visit."

She turned to him. "Yep, Pietersen's definitely an asshole. He also invited me. I think I'm the only journalist here, which is a bit unusual. But you, lecturing? Since when? I thought you just did the investigative stuff?"

"Yes, that's the bulk of my work, but I've done ad hoc lecturing for years down at the College of Law, the War Crimes Research Office. I'm speaking on the Nazis this afternoon. I do know a bit, so I get roped in once a month or so."

"Of course, your doctorate. I forgot." She became distracted as the chatter in the room died down and the speeches began.

David Kudrow took to the podium, looking energized. Johnson scanned the ballroom. There were at least four hundred people in there, all looking appropriately rapt.

"Obama and his Democratic Party cronies have presided over huge historic debt levels and a deficit that has become eye watering, while proving they are no friend to business and no friend to those who are trying to make an honest profit out of commercial endeavors," Kudrow boomed.

The room erupted in applause.

Fiona whispered in Johnson's ear, "This guy's got a real chance against Romney, and then maybe Obama. Who knows? His family's loaded; he's apparently got a $100 million fund lined up already. They're Polish, you know, originally."

Kudrow continued, "We've seen Obama pump a trillion dollars into bailouts, gimmicky jobs initiatives, and failed attempts at stimulus, all for nothing. Did you know that one in six Americans is now on food stamps? We've lost two-and-a-half million jobs.

"Instead, we need an environment that will support business, create jobs, grow the economy, and allow us to balance the books. I want to see us start by hugely reducing the size of government and cutting federal spending. We need to repeal Obamacare, which is nothing more than government taking over our national healthcare system, and we must cut corporate taxes and increase exports. That's just for starters."

Kudrow moved on to give more detail on his health-care and education policies. There seemed to be genuine passion for the message that was being delivered. The man on the podium was striking a chord with his audience, most of whom were middle-aged, well-dressed business people. Next to Johnson, Fiona scribbled away in her notebook.

"Now let's turn briefly to foreign policy," Kudrow said. "I'm a friend of Israel—goes without saying, you know that. My father survived a Second World War concentration camp. Without his courage, I wouldn't be here today. But what's the greatest danger out there for Israel? It's Iran, the biggest sponsor of terrorism we've seen. The ayatollahs are a massive threat to Israel, a massive threat to the whole of the Middle East, and a massive threat to the United States. I tell you, I'm going to hunt them down, smoke them out, and pull their terror ring down.

"I promise I'm the man to deliver all of this and more, and I thank you all for attending," he said as he concluded his fifteen-minute speech to another thunderous round of applause.

Members of the audience rose and made their way to the

reception rooms, where catering staff stood ready, their trays laden with more champagne.

Fiona led Johnson to a large living room. As they walked, he got a glimpse of Kudrow at the end of a corridor leading off the ballroom in an animated argument with another man, at whom Kudrow was gesticulating with a clenched fist. After a few more heated exchanges, the other man pushed Kudrow in the chest, waved his hand dismissively, and walked off. As he did, an older white-haired man wearing black-rimmed glasses intercepted him, whispering fiercely.

"Who was that man there, Fiona, who just argued with Kudrow, and the one that seems to be scolding him for it?" Johnson asked.

"The one he was arguing with is his brother, Nathaniel. I met him a few times before, but I'm not sure what he does, party-wise. The white-haired guy wearing the glasses is their father, Daniel," Fiona said.

The noise level rose as the real business of the afternoon began: networking, both social and political. Champagne glasses clinked, people laughed, and business cards were exchanged.

Fiona put her notebook back into her bag. "I've got to chat to a party official over there before he leaves. Don't you dare go without speaking to me." She squeezed Johnson's forearm and smiled, a familiar twinkle in her eye. "You're looking good, Joe. I've been missing you a bit."

Uh oh, thought Johnson. He couldn't deny feeling a little pleased, though, as he watched Fiona disappear into the crowd. He did try and stay fit, even if going out for a run or lifting a few weights seemed increasingly hard now that he was into his fifties. If he could find a way to resist sneaking in the odd cigarette and cut back on the wine he would probably feel better still.

Johnson turned around to see Philip bearing down on

him, accompanied by the man he now knew to be Nathaniel Kudrow, a tall, dark-haired, slightly stooped figure in a black suit and a tie, holding a glass of champagne.

"Joe, let me introduce you to Nathaniel, David's brother," Philip said. "He's been to a couple of American University's war crimes lectures at its law college, which is where you're teaching later, is that right? He's interested in talking to you about all that. In fact he was the one who suggested I put you on the guest list."

Johnson shook Nathaniel's hand, relieved to see Philip move away toward the bar.

"Good to meet you," Nathaniel said.

"And you. Thanks for suggesting me to Philip. I'm curious about why you did, though."

"Well, I've heard a lot about you," Nathaniel said. "I gather you not only lecture on war crimes, but you were a Nazi hunter as well. Your reputation precedes you. People still talk about that California senator who had to quit the presidential race a few years back after your investigation."

Johnson sipped his drink.

"Yes, that was one of my jobs. You could say Nazi hunter, I guess. I spent a long time working for the Office of Special Investigations, if that's what you mean. That's going back a few years. I run my own private investigation business these days and do part time lecturing."

"Let's find somewhere to sit," Nathaniel said. "I stood for all the speeches through there—no seats left." He steered Johnson toward an antique maroon sofa, where they sat down.

"So, why are you interested in war crimes?" Johnson asked.

"The main reason is my father and uncle are Polish; both were in concentration camps," Nathaniel said. "That's partly why I've been going to the lectures."

Johnson sat up. "Polish? Where were they from and which camp were they in?"

"They were from Warsaw. It was one of the Gross-Rosen camps. I know they had a tough time. They dug out miles of tunnels in the Polish mountains for Hitler so he could build his missiles and weapons safely underground, out of range of Allied bombers. A safe place for the Nazis to store their plundered treasure, gold, artworks—and for Hitler himself to use as an emergency bolt-hole if the war went up in flames. You name it." He stopped and sipped his drink. "They don't talk about it much."

Johnson was surprised but, out of habit, didn't show it. "Gross-Rosen? I know a bit about that network of camps. They were horrific. They did well to survive, that's for sure. Most Jews didn't."

"How do you know about it?"

Johnson hesitated. He could tell the man about his mother later.

"I just have a strong interest in what the Nazis did. I wrote a Ph.D. thesis on that era, years ago. So your father and uncle, they're clearly survivors. Must be old now?"

"Yes, in their late eighties. They're twins. They ended up in London after the war, and my uncle Jacob stayed there. I was there not long ago visiting him. He's got a grandson now, Oliver, who's at university. But my father, Daniel, moved in the 1950s over here to Los Angeles. He's done all right and the family jewelry business thrives. He's happy to see David do so well. Unlike me."

"What do you mean?"

"Well, David's on a roll, career-wise. Different than me. I'm the black sheep," he grimaced. "I'm just helping him between jobs. You lose one job, and it takes a while to find another. It's been like that since Lehman Brothers went under, and that was what, three years ago? I was a trader and the whole sector bombed out." He drained his glass.

Johnson nodded sympathetically. "I'm sure something will turn up. I was laid off from a job back in 1990 and thought it was the end of the world. But I enjoyed my next job at the OSI more, in some ways."

"Who did you work for previously?" Nathaniel asked.

"CIA, actually, in my late twenties," Johnson said.

Nathaniel glanced at him obliquely. "You were CIA?"

"Yes, I worked in Pakistan and Afghanistan," Johnson said. He didn't want to talk about that. It was time to change the subject. He thought back to what Fiona had said about the Kudrow family's wealth. "I was going to say, it's tough out there, but how *do* you raise political funding given the economy these days? Can you fall back on family funds?"

Nathaniel shrugged. "David's own business does okay, but generally, yes, you're right, the funding comes from my father and my uncle. But I'm sure that plenty of these people here," he said, gesturing around the room, "are happy to dip into their pockets."

He took another drink. "Then David's got the Polish trust fund of course." He gave a forced laugh.

Johnson pursed his lips. "Sorry, a Polish trust fund?"

Nathaniel's eyes roamed around the room, and he wrinkled his nose. "Not a trust fund as such," he said, lowering his voice. "Although the Polish goose does keep laying its golden eggs, so to speak." He signed what looked like a swastika in the air in front of him with his forefinger.

Johnson quickly decided Nathaniel wasn't trying to make a joke. "Sorry, is there something you're trying to tell me?" he asked.

Nathaniel sipped his drink. Johnson saw Fiona looking at them from the other side of the room.

"Some other time, if you like?" Nathaniel said. "Not here."

Johnson fingered the nick at the top of his right ear. He could see Nathaniel peering up at it.

"Yes, that would be interesting," Johnson said.

He watched as Fiona walked across the room toward them, and he slowly came to his feet as she arrived.

"Hello, gentlemen, sorry to interrupt." She shook hands with Nathaniel, who also stood to greet her. "I'm Fiona Heppenstall. We've met before. Nice to see you again."

Johnson checked his watch. "I'm really sorry, but I need to leave, or I'll be late for my lecture. Can I leave you both to chat?"

He nodded at Fiona, who was frowning slightly, and promised to call her, then exchanged business cards with Nathaniel. "I'll e-mail you," Johnson told him. "We can arrange to speak again."

Nathaniel nodded. "Let's do that. Good to meet you."

Interesting, Johnson thought on the way out. *So the father and uncle of a Republican front-runner were in the same concentration camp as my mother.*

But Nathaniel appeared to have more to say than that. Johnson resolved to contact him the following day.

* * *

After Johnson's exit, Fiona found herself feeling momentarily disappointed. She'd been looking forward to a good catch-up with him, and maybe a drink or two afterward.

"I think I'd better go too, Nathaniel. Nice to see you again."

"Oh, don't you have time for another quick glass? I thought it would be good to chat for a while, you know, with the campaign coming up."

She flicked back her long dark brown hair. He would

almost certainly be a useful contact to cultivate for the future given his brother's rate of progress.

"Okay," Fiona said, "I can stay for a little while. It's been quite a year so far for your brother."

"Yes, it has. David's setting the pace, and I, we, are trailing along in his slipstream. I've been taking a real interest in some of your recent investigative pieces. They're good. What's coming next?"

"I'm thinking of writing something on the Republican newcomers and the struggles they and their families have had to succeed," Fiona said, touching Nathaniel's arm briefly.

They sat on the sofa. "The question is," Fiona said, "how can candidates like David compete with the likes of Mitt Romney, and then, if that hurdle is overcome, Obama?"

Fiona had been fascinated by David Kudrow for some time, not least because of the funding he had amassed.

Her website *Inside Track* had recently published a long story headlined "Companies Channel Millions into Secret Campaigns." Other news organizations had jumped on the bandwagon with pieces about the political action committees, supposedly independent, that supported candidates.

A few days earlier, *The New York Times* had run a headline screaming "Secret Money Fueling a Flood of Political Ads." And *The Huffington Post* had gone with "Super PACs and Secret Money: The Unregulated Shadow Campaign."

Just that morning on her way to the event, she had received a text message from her news editor, Des Cole: *Fiona we need good background on funding, super PACs, where is cash coming from. Get what you can.*

Fiona had a gut feeling she should try and push Nathaniel while she had the opportunity. Normally she found relatives of high-profile politicians were wary of journalists. She shifted forward.

"I'd like to look at how billionaires can more or less buy

elections, whereas other less well-off families can't," Fiona said. "It's obviously all relative, and your family is very wealthy, but not as wealthy as, say, Mitt's."

"You're right," Nathaniel said, "and it raises all kinds of questions. Fairness, honesty. Should politics be for the rich only? I sometimes think we're playing a dangerous game. And if that's happening, who's representing the underclass? Their numbers are rising since the financial crash. They're hidden and often angry. Is their voice being heard in Washington? I don't think so."

Fiona sat back in her chair. "That's not the usual line you get from the Grand Old Party. Refreshing to hear. How does your brother fit into that, then? And how is he being funded?"

"A good question," Nathaniel said. "We've got a few sources of money, between my father and his twin brother in London. They can donate to both David and to some of the PACs we think are worth supporting."

Maybe it's time to flirt a little, Fiona thought. It usually loosened tongues, especially with middle-aged men.

She stretched out her legs in front of her, knees at right angles, so her black dress rode up her thighs a little, just as Nathaniel turned toward her. As he did so, she ensured that her knee caught his.

It was amazing what proximity could do to a source, particularly when she was wearing a cocktail dress like the one she had on right now. Which was, of course, exactly why she'd chosen it.

He said, "You know that if a PAC's contributing directly to a candidate's campaign, then people aren't supposed to donate any more than $5,000."

"Look, I write about that stuff just about every day," Fiona said.

"Of course, sorry. But the point is that if the PAC's going

to campaign independently, then there's no limit. So that gives my father and uncle plenty of scope." He paused and said slowly "Of course, that's as long as they don't coordinate directly with what David's doing." Then he stared hard at Fiona.

Did he just raise his eyebrows a fraction? she asked herself. She felt Nathaniel was reading her expression.

He shrugged. "I'm not sure I always agree with it personally. It's a minefield. Perhaps we could have a chat about it another time, just not here."

She nodded and decided to change tack. "I knew your family was Polish originally, but I didn't know you had an uncle in London." She had only three weeks earlier interviewed David Kudrow and he hadn't mentioned anything about his father having a twin brother.

Fiona bent toward him and made sure their knees brushed lightly together once more.

"Yes, the two of them work very closely together even now, despite the distance. They are twins, after all," Nathaniel said.

He looked at her. "By the way, just to be clear, this is all off the record, isn't it? I don't want to be quoted on any of it."

"Absolutely, you have my word."

Nathaniel nodded. "Wasn't it you and Johnson who finished off that California senator several years ago? The one who was running for the Republican nomination. What was his name, William Marsh? The Nazi sympathizer."

Fiona glanced sharply at him. "Yes, that's right, back in 2003. He was a U.S. senator. We did collaborate on that story. You've got a very long memory."

In fact, it had been one of the stories that had made her reputation. Marsh, on the right wing of the party, had been forced to resign from Congress and pull out of the race for the nomination against the incumbent George W. Bush.

Fiona ran a front-page story in the *Times* revealing that he had for more than two decades sheltered and employed a senior ex-Nazi Auschwitz prison camp guard, Heinz Waldmeister, at his forestry and timber business outside San Francisco.

Johnson and she had worked together on the investigation after both were tipped off by the same source, an ambitious younger party official who was aiming to supplant Marsh, although he ultimately failed in that objective. Johnson had then led the initiative to have the eighty-five-year-old Waldmeister deported and successfully prosecuted at a court in Munich for a series of brutal murders at Auschwitz.

Nathaniel nodded again. "I remember it well. A notable scoop for the *Times*." He hunched over and looked at Fiona steadily. "It pays to have good sources, doesn't it? We should chat further."

Then he stood up. "I'd better go now, but I'd definitely like to meet again. Do you live in D.C.?"

"I do," said Fiona. "It would be great to catch up again very soon. I'd like to talk about what you've been discussing in a bit more depth, if possible. I'll give you my details." She reached into her small brown leather handbag as she stood and gave him a card.

Fiona shook Nathaniel's hand and watched as he walked across the white oak floor toward the entrance hall. Her reporter's instinct told her he had something more to say but was holding back.

CHAPTER TWO

Tuesday, November 8, 2011
Washington, D.C.

Fiona exploded.

"Absolutely not, Des. I am not doing that damn story. I haven't stopped since I came back from that fund-raiser. I've had no dinner, nothing to eat. If this company can't hire enough people to cover the workload, that's not my problem. I'm meant to be an investigative reporter, not a hack."

She was almost spitting across the desk at Des Cole, her boss, both hands on her hips and her face starting to turn the same color as her crimson cardigan.

Des, a gray-haired Englishman and chief news editor at *Inside Track*, just stared at her.

"Apart from going out to the fund-raiser, I've been in here since ten this morning and it's now what, half past nine? And you're asking me to write another piece," Fiona said. With that, she pressed the off button on her laptop, slammed the lid shut, grabbed her coat, and headed across the newsroom toward the elevator.

"Look, Fiona, come back here a second. I just need to discuss—"

But Des wasn't given the chance to finish his sentence.

Fiona drummed her fingers on the side of the elevator as it ground its way down from the fifth floor, then walked swiftly through the revolving door at the front of the building.

Muttering a volley of expletives under her breath, she veered left and continued up 15th Street Northwest toward her apartment, a fifteen-minute walk away on the same road.

By now, the street was almost deserted, with most office workers well ensconced in their homes and apartments.

Glancing to her right, back in the direction of her office, she caught a glimpse of a figure ducking behind a wide pillar outside the entrance to an underground parking lot a block or so behind her. Pausing, she checked again, but then turned away.

In that moment, she decided. She didn't feel like cooking and didn't want to spend the evening sitting alone in her apartment. Instead, she would dump her bag at home and go to the wine bar around the corner, enjoy a quiet glass or two, and choose something from the menu.

Fiona walked briskly northward across L Street Northwest. She felt calmer now and realized she had gone over the top with Des. She made a mental note to text him later and apologize.

As she waited for the green light at the junction with Massachusetts Avenue, she glanced behind her and again thought she saw the shadow of a person, this time moving behind a tree. She felt the same sensation she sometimes had when someone was eyeing her in a bar or a restaurant, as guys often did. But pivoting around once more, she could see nobody.

A few minutes later, she was home, fumbling in her handbag for her key to the main entrance of her large, nine-story apartment building, grandly christened Miramar Apartments.

She had lived in her fourth-floor, two-bedroom apartment, overlooking Rhode Island Avenue, the Holiday Inn on the corner, and the Doubletree Hilton, for two years, since she had split up with her boyfriend and they had sold their house, at a large loss.

One attraction of Miramar Apartments had been the short walk into work, rather than suffering the long commute some of her colleagues endured.

Fiona opened her front door, threw her bag into the hall-way, and headed immediately out again, around the corner to her favorite restaurant, B Too, on 14th Street Northwest. A cozy modern Belgian bar with wooden decor and a long wine list in addition to the beers, it was expensive but worth it. Fiona had become almost a regular, especially on evenings such as tonight, when she finished work late.

A waiter greeted her at the door with a smile. "Good evening Fiona. Would you like your usual table?"

"Thank you, Alex, I would. And can you bring me a bottle of that Spanish tempranillo? I'm desperate for a drink."

One hour, one venison fillet, and half a bottle of wine later, Fiona was feeling much more at peace with herself. She glanced out the window at the passersby and the traffic, which was still busy.

Then someone tapped her on the shoulder.

"Hello, Fiona, I hope you don't mind. I just noticed you sitting there and . . . "

She whirled around, startled. "Nathaniel! Where did you come from? At this time of night? Do you live around here?"

Fiona had been enjoying her solitude and initially felt quite annoyed. *Is he the one who followed me up the street?*

"No, no, sorry. Maybe I shouldn't have . . . It's just that I'm staying at the Greenacres Hotel down the road and I happened to notice you sitting here when I went past. I actually meant to get in touch today, because I'm heading back to LA tomorrow afternoon, but I ran out of time. Look, I'll leave you in peace. I can see you're chilling out here."

She calmed down. "So you just walked in. You're not actually eating here, I presume?" He shook his head and straightened his coat, making as if to leave.

Fiona hesitated. "Okay, seeing as you're here, would you like a glass of this?" She pointed at her bottle.

"Are you sure?" Nathaniel asked. "Maybe you'd prefer to be by yourself?" But she was already signaling to the waiter for another glass.

"Okay, then, thanks," Nathaniel said. "I just thought, you know, you might like to chat through some of the stuff we were talking about at the fund-raiser earlier. It's probably easier here."

The waiter arrived with a second glass, waited until Nathaniel sat down, and then poured wine into it for him.

Fiona sipped her wine and surveyed the restaurant. There were several other diners: a middle-aged Latino who had just come in and was sitting by himself two tables away, studying the menu, a British couple talking excitedly to each other, an old lady, a group of four businessmen—nobody who seemed to be a rival journalist, she was relieved to see.

She brushed her hair back over her shoulders.

Then she had a quick thought, reached inside her bag, and took out her phone. She tapped the screen a couple of times, as if she were just checking her text messages, and put it on the table. It was always useful to record such conversations, in her experience.

CHAPTER THREE

Wednesday, November 9, 2011
Washington, D.C.

Nathaniel woke up in his hotel room. His head throbbed and his tongue felt dry. He groaned and put his hand on his temple, then sat up in bed.

What was I doing last night?

He glanced at the red glow of the digital clock on his bedside table, which told him it was quarter past six. He felt for the bottle of water and pack of aspirin he had put next to the clock.

Nathaniel's memory of much of the previous evening felt a little hazy. Having followed Fiona to B Too, he had left her at around quarter past midnight and headed back to the Greenacres Hotel.

But instead of going to his room, he had gone to the bar.

There he had sat on a stool and ordered a local beer. What was it called? Ah yes, of course, The Corruption. He recalled looking at the bottle label and chuckling to himself. After drinking it, he had ordered another.

Shortly afterward, he had gotten into a conversation with a woman who was waiting for a friend. When the friend had turned up, the three of them had ended up sharing two bottles of shiraz followed by a couple of double whiskies each. By that stage, Nathaniel had been well and truly drunk.

Both women, slim, good-looking blonds, were political researchers who worked for different Republican senators, so they had mainly talked politics.

He had optimistically suggested they come back to his hotel room for a nightcap, but the two of them had looked at each other, giggled, then mumbled something about needing to get to bed and had left.

Nathaniel groaned again. *It was all just too embarrassing.*

He was still wearing the same clothes as the night before, and a feeling of nausea was starting to swell in his stomach.

Have I done the right thing?

"Ah, screw it," he said out loud into the darkness, which was broken only by an eerie orange glow that seeped into his bedroom through a slight gap between the curtains. "They can't carry on like that any longer. *Somebody's* gotta put a stop to it."

Nathaniel removed two aspirins from the pack and washed them down with some of the water.

Then he picked up his phone and tapped out a short message. *Job done. Please make the first transfer now.*

He selected a number from his list of contacts and pressed send.

There was the sound of a siren wailing as a police car sped down the road outside the front of the hotel. A hint of its red and blue lights strobed in through the bathroom window.

Now Nathaniel really was feeling sick. He could feel the

bile rising in his throat, and he broke out into a cold sweat, a clammy, damp sensation that spread across his forehead.

Long experience of dealing with the after-effects of overindulgence told him he wasn't going to be able to ride this one out. Better to vomit up the contents of his stomach and get it over with. He slid out from under the duvet and staggered into the en suite bathroom, battling to retain his balance as he went. There, he got to his knees in front of the white toilet bowl and began to retch.

He heaved three or four times before the cocktail of wine, whiskey, and food from the previous evening finally reappeared, leaving him feeling weak and wretched. Nathaniel kneeled on all fours, feeling drained and utterly sorry for himself.

It was then that he heard a noise behind him. He twisted his head and caught sight of a black, hooded silhouette standing in the doorway to the bathroom.

Through his alcohol-induced haze, Nathaniel felt his bowels turn over. The skin on his scalp tightened like a drumhead. "Hey, who's that? Who are you?" he said, his voice rising sharply.

The dark shadow moved toward him, one arm raised in front.

Nathaniel couldn't make out who it was beneath the hood, which was pulled down over the intruder's face. But there was no mistaking the flash of silver from a long, wide-bladed knife the person was holding.

"As you said, somebody must put a stop to it," a vaguely familiar man's voice said. "I warned you to keep your mouth shut. But like your politician brother, you can't stop talking, can you, my friend?"

Nathaniel instinctively yelled out, his voice now jabbering in fright. "No, no, I haven't told anyone, I never said . . . please, don't . . . no, no . . . "

They were his last words.

The man, whom Nathaniel now recognized, rushed toward him and shoved him hard to the floor. His chin hit the white floor tiles, crunching his teeth together. Then he felt a hard blow in the center of his back.

At first he thought the man had hit him with his fist and flattened him. His first instinct was to somehow haul himself back up into a kneeling position. But as he did, he looked down. There, protruding from the left side of his chest, was the sharp, silver point of the man's knife.

That was when Nathaniel Kudrow's world went black.

* * *

Portland, Maine

The unusually warm November had allowed many trees in Portland to keep some of their red, yellow, and gold finery in a last stand before the assault from strong winds and overnight frosts finally finished them off.

But Johnson's mind wasn't on the fall colors outside.

His lecture at American University had gone well, but he hadn't arrived home until after midnight because his evening flight back to Portland, some five hundred miles northeast of the capital, had been delayed by more than an hour. Then he had been up at half past six to fix breakfast for his children before they left for school.

Now, sitting in his home office, he clasped his phone to his ear. "No, Mrs. Richardson, you've called me four times in the past hour about this and it's not really helping. As I said to you before, if we're going to stand any chance of finding your husband and the girl, we'll need to think where he would be most likely to take her."

"Yes, I know that." Mrs. Richardson, a high school assistant principal's wife, was a nervous woman with a high-pitched voice. She had called Johnson a couple of days earlier, after her forty-eight-year-old husband had failed to return home after work.

One of the man's former pupils, a striking blond girl whom he had recently been assisting with special Spanish-language tutoring to bolster her college applications, had also disappeared.

"The thing is, given that the girl is eighteen, it's a difficult one to involve the police with," Johnson said. "I've had checks done on his credit cards and bank cards, but they've not been used. He must be using cash. His phone seems to be switched off, so we can't trace that—not easily, anyway. But you said he's a creature of habit, likes routine—so can you do something for me? Just make a list of the places you have been to on vacation with him and the family in recent years—hotel details, everything—and e-mail it to me. Go back, say, over the past ten years."

"Okay, I'll do that."

"Good. I'll speak to you later, Mrs. Richardson. Thanks."

Johnson ended the call and stood behind his desk, hands clasped behind his head, pen clenched between his teeth.

To deal with the Richardsons, Johnson had temporarily dropped another case, which involved a search for a professional baseball player who owed a lot of money and had vanished.

Johnson sighed. He sympathized with the woman, but it was just more of the same type of work: phone call after phone call, trawling through search engines, social networking websites, census archives, libraries, company accounts, and birth, marriage, and death records.

It really felt like small-town stuff.

He checked his watch. He hadn't even had time for a

second cup of coffee or to listen to the news. Now he needed to drive down to South Portland for a meeting with another client.

As Johnson pulled on his jacket, the family dog, Cocoa, a three-year-old, chocolate-colored Labrador, jumped up from his prone position on the floor and began wagging his tail. "Sorry, boy," Johnson said, patting Cocoa on the head. "Your walk will have to wait today. Later."

He climbed into his blue Ford Explorer, then drove his usual route over the Casco Bay Bridge. The blue expanse of Casco Bay lay to his left, and to his right the Fore River and the white tanks of the Turners Island oil terminal glinted in a low wintery sun.

His phone rang and he glanced down at the screen. It was Fiona.

Johnson hesitated in answering. He still felt uneasy about the brief fling they had in 2006 after his wife's death, during the months before he had moved from D.C. back to Portland. It had happened too soon, for all the wrong reasons, and Fiona had been hurt when he had ended it.

He felt it was a bad idea to reignite that particular flame, or to inadvertently seem open to reconnecting in that way, but he wasn't sure what Fiona was thinking, especially given her comment at the fund-raiser that she'd been missing him. Then again, Fiona hadn't actually said that was what she wanted either.

Johnson let the phone ring for several seconds, but then eventually pressed the green button.

"Hi, Fiona, I'm driving. How are—"

"Joe, have you heard?"

"Have I heard what?"

"About Nathaniel Kudrow?"

"No, what's happened?"

"He was found dead, stabbed, in his hotel room first thing this morning, not far from my apartment."

Johnson cursed. "Oh, shit. No. You've got to be joking."

He swerved a little, almost sideswiping a van that was passing him.

"Unfortunately I'm not. It's all over the news, radio, TV. We're running a long story on it. I've just finished writing a piece for our website; that's why I didn't call you before. It's a big story."

Johnson exhaled. "Unbelievable. Do you know what happened?"

"A maid found him in the en suite bathroom. A huge knife wound straight through his chest, in at the back, out at the front. He'd been sick in the toilet and was supposedly attacked immediately afterward. Police already have a theory that whoever did it hacked the hotel door lock with some electronic tool. Nobody heard or saw a thing in the hotel. No screams, nothing."

Johnson pursed his lips. His immediate thought was that it must, somehow, be linked to what Nathaniel had been trying somewhat clumsily to communicate the previous day. "Any theories on who did it?"

"They've no idea."

"Did they get the knife?"

"No. There was no sign of it. Forensics is apparently on it, but first signs aren't promising."

"My God." Johnson hesitated. "It was a bit weird, the meeting with him yesterday at the fund-raiser. I was going to contact him today."

"I know, a strange guy. I had a chat with him after you left. And then, you're not going to believe this, but after I finished work last night, he followed me, at least I think he did, to a restaurant. Came in and sat down. We had quite a conversation. He was obviously trying to get stuff off his chest."

Johnson pulled out to pass a truck. "Followed you to a restaurant?"

"Yes, near my apartment," Fiona said. "He was very off-message, tried hard to paint himself as a kind of black sheep of the family. In the restaurant he came right out with a few comments about the funding for David's campaign coming from illegal sources. Said he'd been in London visiting his uncle and found out a few things. And then he basically said there was some kind of Nazi connection to the money. Then he wouldn't say any more and walked out."

"Really?" Johnson asked. "A *Nazi* connection?"

"Yes, that's what he said," Fiona replied. "I was also going to give him a call to try and have another chat, get a few more details, but then the news came through about the stabbing. I was thinking maybe he's just a bit of a crank, but now I'm wondering whether there's more to it."

Johnson glanced in his rearview mirror. "I also had an odd conversation with him. He talked a bit about it being difficult to raise campaign funds given the economic shitstorm. Then he made some joke about his brother benefiting from a Polish trust fund and a Polish goose laying its golden eggs and drew a kind of swastika symbol in the air. Really bizarre. I thought for a second he was trying to make a joke, then I decided he wasn't."

Johnson came to the end of the bridge and turned right down Cottage Road. "I remember he was having an argument with his brother at that fund-raiser," he continued. "They seemed like they were about to start punching each other at one point."

"Yeah, I saw that."

"Right. So there's a family fight. Then Nathaniel tells you all that stuff, makes a few weird hints to me. Then a few hours later he's found stabbed to death. That seems like more than a bit of a coincidence?" Johnson asked.

"Dunno. But who would do something like that? Surely not anyone in his family. I can't see it. Police seem to be ruling out robbery. His laptop and phone were still in his room; his wallet was still full of cash," Fiona said.

"Hmm. He does seem to have been trying to drop his brother, father, and uncle deep in the crap, that's for sure. And he did seem like a crank, as you say," Johnson said. "But another interesting thing was that his father and uncle were both in the same concentration camp as my mother in Poland, or so he said."

Johnson paused. "I'll have to go, Fiona. I've got a meeting with a client here, starting in a couple of minutes. Are you going to the police, to tell them about your chat with Nathaniel?"

"Dunno," Fiona said. "Not sure what to do. I might, but I'd definitely like to have a look at the story myself. Might do my own bit of investigating, actually. I'm going to think about it. Look, I've got a recording of the conversation I had with Nathaniel in the restaurant, I'll send it to you so you can hear for yourself. Let's keep in touch on this. I'll let you know if there's more developments. Oh, and let me know when you're down in D.C. lecturing again. Perhaps we could catch up."

Johnson drove into the parking lot next to his client's offices, still struggling to digest this new development. "Okay, will do. I need to run, Fiona. Talk to you soon."

CHAPTER FOUR

Thursday, November 10, 2011
  Washington, D.C.

By quarter to eleven, the *Inside Track* newsroom was humming. Journalists were busy on the phones, meeting rooms were filling up, and the noise level was rising.

Fiona walked up to Des, who was sitting hunched in front of his computer screen, surrounded by piles of books, old press releases, and three dirty coffee cups.

Before she could speak, he said, "Can't talk. I've got a news conference in ten minutes. They've brought it forward this morning. Tell me quickly, what have you got for today?"

"Nothing for today, but there is one story I want to chase. David Kudrow—"

"You got a follow-up on his brother's death? The crime desk's all over it. Go and talk to them."

"Well, not on the actual death but on something Nathaniel said to me at that Republican fund-raiser the day before he was stabbed. You know, I mentioned it briefly."

"Yes, yes, get to the point."

"Okay, he spoke to me off the record and gave me a clear steer that there's something weird going on over how his family is funding David's campaign. Maybe there's a link to his death in there. Problem is, it's gonna take some time to investigate and stand it all up. It might involve some work in the U.K. where his uncle lives as well. I think it could be a really great story, though. Is there any chance I could get some time off the diary to have a look at it?"

Des stared at her. "You winding me up? Nice idea, but let's get real, there's no bloody chance, Fiona, I'm sorry. You know how busy we are here. The primaries are going to be kicking off before we know it, and there's a hell of a lot of mainstream stuff going on."

He drummed his fingers on the desk. "We need you to do probably three big political analysis pieces over the next week or so in addition to the daily stuff. If you think it's a runner, why don't you get one of our freelancers to pick it up, someone who's got more time? We have a decent budget left for that sort of thing. Now I've got to get back to this. Conversation over. Okay?"

"I thought you'd say that." She sighed. "Okay, I'll think about it. I don't like the idea of handing over a great story to a freelancer, though."

Fiona ambled to her desk at the far end of the newsroom, past the photocopier and the watercooler, the piles of paper standing next to the shredder, and the bin overflowing with paper and plastic cups.

She sat down at her desk across from Penny Swanson, her assistant, who had moved with her from *The New York Times*.

"Any luck, Fiona?"

"Nah, he's not biting. Didn't think he would with all this going on. He's suggesting using a freelancer, but I don't want to give this one away."

Fiona pursed her lips. "I was thinking, and you'll probably laugh at this one, that I'd like to try and get Joe Johnson to have a look at it."

"Joe, huh? Don't tell me he's back on the scene?"

"Well, no, he's not back on the scene, actually. By coincidence, he was there at the GOP fund-raiser earlier this week when I picked up this story. He got some info too. I spoke to him on the phone this morning. Thing is, it could be just up his alley given this Nazi angle—if it's true, that is. He's an investigator; he tracks people down. That's what he's good at, finding stuff out. Doesn't mind getting his hands dirty either: ex-CIA, then the OSI and all that."

Fiona folded her arms. "I've seen how he operates. He seems to have this knack for digging out information and finding people that others just don't have. Remember when we were both at the *Times,* how he came up with all that fantastic stuff for me on that U.S. Nazi story, that senator, William Marsh? I got three front pages out of that. You know how he got that? He somehow pinpointed exactly who had the right info, arranged some subterfuge to get into that person's office, and raided their filing cabinet. Photographed the lot. Risky, but it paid off. I don't think he ever told his boss how he did it. That was when that SS guy ended up getting life at the International Criminal Court. So what I figure is, he can do the hard work, the legwork. Then I can write the story and take the credit."

Penny chuckled. "Yes, I remember it. You don't change, Fiona. Sounds like a bit of a long shot—great story if it works though."

"Yeah, I bet he'll cooperate. I have a feeling he's at a loose end up there in Portland."

* * *

Portland, Maine

Johnson felt his calves tighten as he neared the end of his three-and-a-half-mile run around Back Cove, an almost square-shaped inlet off Casco Bay, north of Portland's city center.

When the sun shone, it was a pleasant run, but not on a drizzly day like today. He felt better for the exercise, though, which had cleared his head.

As usual when out running, he had been able to do some thinking. Today the bizarre circumstances surrounding Nathaniel Kudrow were on his mind.

But apart from that, he found he was having one of those days when he was missing his wife, Kathy. It had been six years since she had finally surrendered to the cancer that had tortured her body.

In October 2006, a year after her death, he had left his role as a senior investigative historian at the OSI and moved the family from Washington, D.C., to his hometown of Portland so that his sister, Amy Wilde, and her husband, Don, could help with the children; they didn't have any of their own. That had proved a lifesaver, because at the same time he had started his own private investigations business and sometimes needed to be away from home.

But while living in Portland allowed him more flexibility to look after his children, he wrestled with the negative impact it had on his career. The truth was, his work as a freelance investigator in Maine just didn't have the same buzz as his old Nazi-hunting role with the OSI, or as his time at the CIA, for that matter.

Amy, who was two years younger than him, often asked him what was wrong with just having an ordinary, local job. Maybe she was right. What *was* wrong with ordinary, exactly?

He struggled to answer the question. What was it with people, with *him*, that they were so often driven by something, a need to define themselves?

Damn ego, that was the problem.

He stopped running where the trail around Back Cove went past the top of his street, Parsons Road, and walked the remaining distance to his house, a two-story cape with green shutters and a double garage. He took out his key and opened the front door.

Johnson picked up his phone and checked it, relieved there had been no further calls from the assistant principal's wife. However, there was a text message from an old buddy.

Hey Doc, how goes it? I'm in Portland next Wed interviewing someone. Can you meet? Can't stay over, I'm on a flight back to D.C. at 4 p.m. Maybe a beer? I'll bring the smokes. You still allowing yourself the odd one these days?!! Vic

Like many of Johnson's friends, Vic Walter called him by the nickname "Doc," in a reference to his doctorate in history from the Freie Universität Berlin. He had been one of Johnson's closest friends since the two of them worked closely together in Pakistan and Afghanistan for the CIA in the late 1980s.

Vic was still with the Agency, based at the organization's Langley headquarters just outside Washington, D.C., having worked his way up into a senior supervisor's role within the Directorate of Operations. A bigger cog in the management machine than he once was, he often joked.

Johnson texted him back, suggesting they meet at his favorite Portland coffee shop, Crema Coffee, on Commercial Street.

Then he remembered he hadn't checked the mailbox, so he went back outside.

There was a letter from Phillips & Co., one of the main Portland law firms. Strange, he'd had nothing to do with them since his mother had died ten years earlier. *What's this about?*, he wondered.

Johnson took a beer from the fridge, then went to his living room and sat in an armchair that faced the garden. He slit open the envelope.

Inside were two sheets of paper. The first was a typewritten letter from John Phillips, the lead partner at the firm.

Several months prior to the death of your mother, Helena Johnson, in 2001, she issued strict instructions to us to pass on the enclosed letter from her to you on the tenth anniversary of her death, at which point, as I believe you are aware, the outstanding $10,000 cash in her trust fund will be transferred to you. As you know, that date falls on November 10, 2011. Therefore, in accordance with her instructions, I am forwarding it to you. If you have any questions, please do not hesitate to call.

Johnson unfolded the second sheet. This was very weird. Ten years since his mother had passed away, yet now he could almost smell her scent and hear her voice again.

It was her final letter, he realized, which was presumably written when she knew her end was near.

As with most of her notes, it was typewritten on her favorite battered old Remington.

Dear Joe,

So, a decade after my passing, here I am again. As you will know from the attorney, I hope, the final $10,000 I left you in my will is now being transferred from my trust fund specifically for the benefit of my grandchildren. I would like it to be used for an educational purpose. Sorry, you will undoubtedly think a letter from the grave a *little strange, and you're right. But I thought it would be nice to leave a note along with the money.*

I thought I would also give a gentle reminder, if needed, to continue to do what I used to ask you all those years ago. Remember the story I left with my will? If not, please read it again.

Maybe by now the murderers who were in charge at Gross-Rosen have faced trial or are dead. But if not, please either keep pushing for justice yourself or urge on others.

I managed to forgive those men, as you know. Without that, I couldn't have continued. Yet for the thousands they murdered, and I was almost one of them, justice must be done—in court, not by the bullet. I think you'll know exactly what I mean by that.

Don't give up, Joe boy. These people can run and run, but they can't hide forever. Your skill lies in finding them. Remember that suffering produces perseverance; perseverance character; and character hope.

All my love,
Mom

The sentiments were typical of his mother: hard and soft-nosed, all combined in a few paragraphs that somehow encapsulated her character.

Don't give up, Joe boy. How often had he heard her say that when he was growing up?

Johnson's daughter, Carrie, strolled in, threw her school bag on the floor, and sat on the sofa opposite him, still wearing her navy school blazer and beige pants, her long brown hair tied in braids. Cocoa followed her in and jumped onto the sofa next to her, his ears pricked, and licked her on the chin, as usual.

Carrie stared at her father, fifteen but going on nineteen, as he often told his friends. "Dad, are you all right? You look upset." She sounded concerned.

Johnson turned away, trying to shake off the emotion that

had overwhelmed him. It was that line. *Justice must be done—in court, not by the bullet.*

Of course he knew what she meant. *But why did she need to write that?* It felt as if an old wound, dating back to an incident during his time with the CIA in Pakistan and Afghanistan, had suddenly been reopened.

Johnson faced his daughter. "I'm fine," he said. "So, how was school? Anything good happen? Anything bad?"

Carrie laughed. It was a routine exchange between them. "No, not really, just a bit of hassle from my math teacher again. He keeps picking on me. I don't know why; I'm getting good enough grades."

Johnson put the letter down. "Well, I would just concentrate on quietly getting on with your work. If you do that, I don't think he'll keep on having words with you."

She tossed her head and pulled her mouth to one side. "Okay, okay. What about you, anything interesting going on?" she asked.

"Well, I've just had this letter from a law firm. They've sent me a note that your grandma left for me when she died. A bit strange—she told them to give it to me on the tenth anniversary of her death, which is today."

His daughter inclined toward him on the sofa. "A letter? What about?"

"It was mainly about transferring some money from her trust fund, which will benefit you and Peter when you're both older."

Carrie nodded. "It's funny, I was thinking about Grandma the other day when we were talking in school about our earliest memories. I must have been five when she died, but I can remember her somewhat. Little things. Then I thought of her again, because we're learning about the Holocaust. I know she survived that, though you don't talk about it much.

I'd like to read that memoir of hers that you mentioned a while back. Have you got it somewhere?"

"Yes, I do have it," Johnson said. "The problem is, it's extremely upsetting. She was treated very badly in the concentration camp, and she tells exactly what it was like. It was awful. I think it would be better to wait a year or two until you read it, when you're just a little older."

Johnson paused. It was always difficult to get the balance right between educating his children on big issues such as human rights while at the same time shielding them from the worst of the gory details.

He looked at his daughter. "Do you understand what I'm saying?"

"Kind of," Carrie said. "But we are learning about the way the Nazis treated the Jews, anyway. The gas chambers, the tortures, and so on. I do have quite a good idea of what happened. It's all in the history books."

Johnson nodded. "I know. But this is different. Reading something like this really hits you hard, especially when it involves someone in your family. It's not like reading a history book about someone you've never known."

Carrie was definitely maturing by the day. At some stage, probably quite soon, she might be ready to hear the whole of her grandmother's story, and he would give her the manuscript. But not just yet. And Peter would definitely have to wait several years. It was just too raw, too harrowing, too close to home.

Johnson's mother, born Helena Meller, had grown up in a Jewish family in southern Poland before she was imprisoned by the Nazis. Somehow, she had managed to survive for two years in various concentration camps.

Her life had been saved by being transferred in December 1944 from a camp in the Gross-Rosen complex to the Brünnlitz camp, which decades later was featured in the film

Schindler's List. Brünnlitz supplied labor to an ammunition factory set up by Oskar Schindler, an arrangement which meant that some of the inmates, though not all, avoided onward transfer to extermination camps.

Helena had been eventually released when the Red Army arrived in April 1945, just after her twentieth birthday. Although originally a Jew, she later became a Christian, moved to Portland, and married Johnson's father, Bernard, who had died in 1992 from cancer.

When Helena herself died in 2001, she left with her will a manuscript containing a long account of her life in the camps. She had hammered it out on her typewriter during the 1970s and '80s on lined notebook paper that was now yellowing around the edges.

Johnson had been shocked when he read it for the first time. He had never known it had existed until then, and although his mother used to talk a bit about the camps and tell the occasional story about how the Nazis treated the Jews back then, she never did so in graphic detail. He thought that perhaps she couldn't bear to speak to her children about the worst things, so she wrote them down instead. He hadn't read the manuscript since probably 2002.

Carrie leaned back on the sofa. "I know you don't want to tell me the details, but being in the camp must have affected Grandma, right? After she got out, I mean?"

"It did," Johnson said. "She often talked about how hard it was to cope and sometimes cried if she was telling a story, which is probably why she never told us too much. She was a survivor, Carrie, an amazingly strong woman, like I'm sure you'll be someday."

Carrie perked up at the compliment. "Thanks, Dad."

It was true, his mother had been incredibly strong. "She had a few sayings which she said got her through the camps," Johnson said. "The main one was biblical. 'Suffering produces perseverance; perseverance, character; and character, hope.' That's from Paul's letter to the Romans. She used to say it to herself all the time. I could see why, after what she went through."

Carrie smiled. "She was some lady, that's for sure. Anyway, so how was your trip, Dad? You had another lecture, right? What was this one about?"

"It was about the controversy when the CIA employed a lot of ex-Nazis after World War II to spy for them," Johnson said. "Many of the Nazis knew a lot about Russia, which were the new enemy then. Lots of them were given entry into the U.S. as a payback. They were given a safe haven here, no questions asked, a few thousand of them—mass murderers, torturers, sadists, you name it. My talk was partly about how the OSI was set up in 1979 inside the Department of Justice in Washington to track down those Nazis, who were scattered across the country."

"Cool. You had a really badass job, Dad."

"Carrie, language."

Carrie just rolled her eyes at him. "Right, sorry. I'd best get going on my homework."

"Okay, and if you're going upstairs, ask your brother if he needs any help with *his* homework."

Carrie walked out, the sound of her shoes echoing down the hallway. A few seconds later he heard her screaming up the stairs. "Peter, *Peter* . . . Dad wants to know if you need help with your homework."

Johnson turned on the television news and watched for a while. The second to last item was about the killing of Nathaniel Kudrow. Police in Washington were drawing a blank with their inquiries and were appealing to anyone who had seen anything suspicious at the hotel where he was staying to get in touch, the crime reporter said. There was a very short sound bite from an interview with his brother, David, reinforcing the police request.

The reporter said that according to police, Nathaniel had traveled quite extensively over recent months in Europe, South America, and North America, and police and the FBI were looking at whether there might be a link between these trips and his killing.

Once the bulletin had finished, Johnson turned off the TV and sat back in his armchair. He gently banged his head back a couple of times against the headrest. He'd better get his mother's memoir out of the safe and read through it again the following day.

A letter from the grave . . . a bit weird, that. But then again, his mother had been eccentric. He eyed the letter. *Keep pushing for justice.* Johnson snorted to himself. *I wish . . .*

CHAPTER FIVE

Thursday, November 10, 2011
  Buenos Aires

Ignacio Guzmann could feel his blood pressure rising, try as he might to stay calm.

He sat in the driver's seat of his father José's old black Mercedes outside the old man's house in the Recoleta suburb of Buenos Aires.

Guzmann senior would only buy German-made cars and had always refused to travel in his son's fifteen-year-old white Renault Mégane. So Ignacio had driven to Recoleta, parked his own car, then switched vehicles.

An angular, slightly stooping figure emerged from the black front door of the house on the corner of Ombú and Martín Coronado Streets. The two-story property had originally been white, but the paint was peeling, stained green and black in several places. Three of the black shutters were hanging off their hinges at an angle, and the paint on the doors and metal fencing and gates was also patchy.

It stood in contrast to the other, much smarter homes on the street.

Come on, you old bastard, hurry up. Ignacio felt tired after the previous day's long flight back to Buenos Aires.

A group of children ran past, sprinting from one of the many trees lining the street to the next, mock fighting and shouting insults at each other.

Ignacio watched his father limp stiffly from his gate, his right leg dragging a little as always, a silver-topped walking cane in his right hand and a scuffed black leather attaché case in his left.

He appeared younger than he was, Ignacio thought. José's thin, lightly wrinkled face, slim figure, and the sharp parting in his closely cut white hair meant he could pass for someone in his late seventies. But according to his Argentine passport, he was actually ninety-one.

Despite his age, José still kept a firm grip on his family gold and jewelry manufacturing and retail business, SolGold. It had outlets across Argentina and imported gold and other raw materials and products from various countries.

The old man inched his way to the car. "Can't you get out and hold the door open for me?" he said in Spanish. "This arthritis is a killer."

Ignacio hopped out and complied.

José eased himself into the back seat. "So, I see you're back."

"Yes, *padre,* I'm back."

"Where have you been?"

"Oh, just away for a few days. Took a break. Had a few things that needed sorting out."

"Away where?"

Ignacio ignored the question. His father was sometimes like a dog that wouldn't let go of a bone. He got back into the car and drove off through Recoleta, one of the city's most affluent suburbs and part of Barrio Norte, or "north neigh-borhood."

"Where are we going? The usual, Café Nostalgia?" Ignacio asked.

He could see his father nodding in the rearview mirror. "Yes, Nostalgia." Normally José's manservant Juan drove him to the café on a five-way, tree-lined crossroads in Palermo. There he would send Juan to the newsstand to buy him a newspaper, usually *Clarín,* Argentina's biggest-selling daily and then he would sit for an hour or so, catching up on the latest news.

It must have been at least a year since Ignacio had last been out with his father, who he assumed must be desperate for a chat about something.

Ignacio parked outside the ground-floor café.

"*Hola, Señor* Guzmann." The waiter nodded at José as he limped over to his usual square wooden table by the window. "Your usual double espresso, sir?"

"Yes, and make it quick. Bring me a slice of chocolate cake with it."

Ignacio ordered a cappuccino. He decided to make an effort.

"How long have you been coming here now, padre?"

Before his father could reply, a fat black cat jumped onto the seat next to him. José reached for his cane, poked it toward the cat, and hissed loudly, "Get out, go on, move, damned animal."

Ignacio noticed the barista girl working behind the large silver espresso machine at the bar. She kept flicking her head sideways to stop her blond hair from falling into her eyes.

His father spotted him looking at her. "If you hadn't screwed up with that wife of yours you wouldn't need to be eyeing up women like her. Who was it in the end, the jazz bar stripper who finally finished off your marriage?"

Ignacio ignored the well-aimed barb, but his father wasn't going to stop there. "I don't suppose you see much of your kids now, after that?"

That much was true. He hadn't seen his two teenagers in more than nine months. His ex-wife, who had taken over their former home in Palermo, made sure of that.

"Unlikely, when she won't let them near me," Ignacio said. "I'm looking at legal action, but it's just too expensive."

The waitress arrived with their coffees and his father's cake.

"So, padre, you obviously needed to discuss something," Ignacio said. "What's the problem?"

José swapped his regular glasses for a gold-rimmed reading pair and removed some files from his attaché case.

"You won't be aware of this, I don't think, but the business is going downward, quickly," the old man said. "Another thing you probably don't know, as you were away, but I had to sack Pancho last week, and I just thought I'd run a couple of things past you."

Ignacio sat upright. "You sacked Pancho? What happened there then? I thought he was a top guy?"

Pancho wasn't on the official staff of SolGold but had run its finances and accounts for nearly thirty years.

"He used to be, yes. When the country was in the shit in 2001, he sorted us out, got us back on track, when you were in the army. But recently, not so."

Argentina had defaulted on its debt and slashed its budgets for the armed forces in 2006, putting Ignacio out of a job, along with many of his other army colleagues. After that, his only option was his father's gold and jewelry business.

What was it his father had told him? *So the dog returns, tail between his legs, older and probably no wiser.*

Ignacio suddenly felt alarmed. "So, padre, you're not trying to tell me you want me out?"

"No. But we've got to do something. The company's suffering huge losses."

Ignacio sat back. He was well aware of that from the hours he had secretly spent trawling through the company's accounts on his father's computer late at night, not that he was going to reveal that.

"We're *losing* money? I thought we were healthy?" Ignacio said.

"No, we're not," the old man said. "I'm working on a plan. The manufacturing can stay, but the first part is to get rid of some of our shops. Out of the twenty, I think six are a waste of time, so they're going."

José had mainly kept Ignacio away from balance sheets, profit-and-loss accounts, and SolGold's own stores and jewelry production operations. Instead, he had given his son a job as head of sales, looking after third-party jewelers in the tourism market.

As part of that role, Ignacio had taken a trip up to the far north of Argentina six months earlier to visit a few potential clients. He had also made an unscheduled stop for a couple of days at SolGold's jewelry production site in Puerto Iguazú, on the border with Paraguay, where even he—a hardened ex-military guy—had been deeply shocked at what he'd seen. It was something he planned to raise with his father at the right time, not now.

Although Ignacio didn't have a business background, he had learned fast in his new role. His accountancy studies and experience managing large budgets while in the army had helped.

To Ignacio, it had initially seemed odd that his father couldn't make more profit from his sales of mid-market gold necklaces, rings, and other trinkets. There was a boom happening and Argentina's GDP was rising at more than 9 percent a year. So he had made it his business to find out why there were problems—doing so well behind his father's back.

José picked up a file and pointed to a number. "Look, gold prices were $270 an ounce back in 2001. Now, over $1,700. It prices customers out, and worse, it kills profit margins. We're not generating enough cash, and overheads on these shops are high."

He sighed. "I've spent fifty-five years building this business. I'm not going to see it flushed down the toilet." His face colored, and he slammed his cane hard against the leg of the table.

Ignacio involuntarily flinched as his father waved the stick. The sight of it brought back bad memories, even four decades later.

The old man took another sip of coffee. "Twenty, thirty years ago I would have sorted out the problems I've got myself. Now I can't."

Ignacio folded his arms and reclined, looking at his father. He was already quite well ahead with forming his own plans about how to resolve the business's problems and his personal financial situation. Speed was now critical in delivering them; he knew that. And they weren't plans he was going to share with his father.

"Yes, well, you sorted out quite a lot of stuff when you were younger, didn't you? Before you came to Argentina." Ignacio stared his father in the eye.

His long-held suspicions about his father had been confirmed after discovering some private papers in a folder hidden away in his attic two years earlier, the contents of which had stunned him.

But the old man had always avoided any discussion about his roots. In Ignacio's younger years, every time he asked, his father had changed the subject, so he eventually gave up.

This time José's eyes flickered a little before their steely blue facade was restored. "What are you on about? Let's get the bill." José nodded across the room at one of the waiters.

* * *

Portland, Maine

Johnson had intended to delve into his mother's memoir on Thursday afternoon, but had gotten sidetracked by a series of phone calls and e-mails relating to the ongoing search for the assistant principal and his eighteen-year-old girlfriend.

It was therefore well into the evening when he finally managed to sit down in his office and pick up the thin file, entitled "Gross-Rosen: A Survivor's Account."

He flicked through the first few pages, which described his mother's background in Warsaw and her feelings of terror after the SS caught her and her family hiding in the attic of their house.

There was a section on the horrific three-day journey without food spent crushed into a train car with numerous other Jews—several of whom died—en route to the concentration camp. And then he found on page thirty-two the segment he remembered reading previously.

Daily Life in Camp

Every day is a cycle of fear in camp. I was afraid of dying most of all, of course, but apart from that, afraid of being hungry and having no energy and then afraid of not being able to do the work the guards ordered and afraid of the beating that would follow.

Afraid of other prisoners and what they might do, because some lost their sanity and their goodness. It seemed impossible that I could survive, once I was in there. I still can't believe I did.

During those months in 1944, the daily battle for food in Wüstegiersdorf, a subcamp of Gross-Rosen, was a total challenge of strength, cunning, ingenuity, and desperation.

We were given just one slice of bread each, in the morning, and then the decision was whether to eat it immediately, which avoided it being stolen, or to try and save half to eat later in the day with the watery soup they served.

Aggressive prisoners, or those who had gone insane, would just steal food off others, sometimes threatening them. One woman, Elizabeth, took the bread I had saved one day. She came behind me and held a very sharp piece of hard wood to my throat—what could I do?

Some prisoners lost it completely, physically and mentally, and were like walking dead.

They were as thin as it is possible to be and still move, but their muscle control had gone, including their bowels, and they would defecate or piss where they stood. This caused the guards to whip them or hit them with sticks.

They sank into their own oblivion, no longer thinking, just grabbing anything to eat, such as grass or bits of earth or wood. I was really afraid of them and of becoming like them. They were walking skeletons, with no flesh, really, and eyeballs that sunk backward into their sockets and bones that stuck out like the ribs on the meat I used to see in the butchers' shops.

We did anything to get extra food. Rats were a good option, as there were sometimes a lot of them, until the guards caught on to what we were doing and poisoned them. I caught a couple by managing to hit them with a piece of wood, which seemed like a miracle. Cooking them was a challenge, but we did it.

I was put into a work gang loading bags of cement onto railway trucks for twelve hours a day, but we had to walk ten kilometers to get to the loading place, going past fields on the way. Sometimes I managed to run into a field and grab some potatoes and beets without a guard noticing. I had to eat them immediately, raw, so they wouldn't see.

The cement bags were useful too, as insulation for our frozen bodies. I wore them like a jacket, with holes cut out for my head and my arms. They were a temporary perk, until I was moved to a different job. They made the difference between sleeping and not sleeping in the freezing cold wooden bunks inside the huts where we lived.

The bunks were stacked three high and were often covered in fleas, which jumped all over prisoners who already had lice infestations and permanently weeping sores on their bodies.

Johnson tore his eyes away from the page and gazed out the window. He realized he was gripping the file so tightly his knuckles were showing white. It was the kind of tale he had often heard from witnesses he had interviewed while on the trail of any number of sadistic Nazi war criminals.

Indeed, it was exactly what had spurred him on to ensure they went to court to answer for what they had done.

But reading his own mother's account was something quite different. He looked up at the ceiling for a few moments to compose himself, then carried on.

The cruelty of the SS camp commanders was indescribable, unfathomable. I could not work out how such depths of cold hatred and savagery could exist in a person. Any excuse to beat one of us, any reason conjured out of nowhere, any minor fabricated indiscretion—they would grab it, a horrible thin smile on their lips. Inflicting pain, agony, humiliation, and then eventually death, was their daily reason for living.

For them it was the only way to be. To follow orders and to cause pain.

Did they have a choice? Of course they did. And they chose the way of darkness always.

The daily roll calls were a ritual of agony for all of us, of fearful expectation. And it was the time when the SS officers held the stage and could terrorize all of us at once.

The camp commanders Captain Albert Lutkemeyer and his number two, First Lieutenant Erich Brenner, were the ringleaders. They were a double act of utter sadism.

One day, at the end of May that year, the guards were all walking up and down the endless lines of prisoners at roll call in the yard slowly, looking around them, like cold-eyed, emotionless lions prowling, hunting for a victim. I always tried to avoid making eye contact, always stood motionless. But this day, Brenner stopped in front of me, about half a meter away.

He squared his shoulders, his feet apart, and put his hands behind his back, holding his black leather riding crop whip, which he used to lash us with. His words to me were "You—you never look me in the eye, do you?" Then he repeated them, shouting at the top of his voice, screaming. He said it was disrespectful to avoid eye contact and that he was going to teach me some manners.

Then he turned to one of the Jewish kapos, the Jews who had either volunteered or had been told to do certain jobs to help the guards, and told him to fetch the ox whip.

I was shaking with fear because I had previously seen the first lieutenant whipping prisoners with it while they were held motionless on a whipping block.

Now it was my turn. The guards called this torture the fünfundzwanzig, German for "twenty-five," because it involved that number of strokes with the whip across the buttocks. I've never felt such pain, and even now, I can't put into words how it felt.

Then and now, I've no idea how I avoided fainting, but I think this was the only thing that kept me alive, because if I had lost consciousness while the first lieutenant was beating me, I'm certain I would have been shot. That's what happened to others.

Afterward the guards were instructed to leave me standing in the Appell yard, where the daily roll call of prisoners was taken, for a whole day in the sun without food or water, and that no one must speak to me, and I mustn't sit or lie down.

And that's what happened. It was summer, and the sun shone from a cloudless sky for the whole day. I must have been very close to death. I had blood running down my legs from the whip, and I was horribly sunburned on my head and hands and feet, in utter agony.

I was unconscious for quite some time toward the end. I must finally have passed out; I don't know how long for.

Afterward I developed some sort of infection from the whip wounds and even today bear those scars. The camp doctor came to look at me. He could do nothing, or wanted to do nothing.

But I prayed to the Almighty while I was out in that Appell yard, and he spoke back to me and told me I would live. And I did, somehow. He also told me I was loved and had to forgive those SS commanders for what they had done, or I would go mad.

And that was true. I had a sudden realization that inside me, I couldn't choose my circumstances, but I could choose my response.

That is how I survived the whipping and how I survived Wüstegiersdorf.

Yet those who perpetrated these crimes, even if forgiven, must face justice.

Johnson flicked through the rest of the document. It included many more pages detailing camp life and then the utter relief his mother had felt upon unexpectedly being transferred to another camp prior to the end of her ordeal in 1945, when the Russians arrived.

It also described how, by the time she was released, two of her ribs were misaligned, causing her permanent pain, from where she had been knocked over and kicked by guards.

Helena, standing five feet eight inches tall, weighed just

80 pounds when she was finally freed, compared to the 125 pounds she weighed before her long ordeal began.

His mother. What a remarkable, strong woman she had been. Johnson could still hear her voice very precisely in his head.

He turned around to his computer. There were two new e-mails sitting in his inbox: one from the assistant school principal's wife, which he ignored, and one from the Simon Wiesenthal Foundation, set up by the famous Nazi hunter of the same name. It was announcing the organization's 2011 *Annual Status Report on the Worldwide Investigation and Prosecution of Nazi War Criminals*, the latest update of a document first published in 2001.

The report included a list of the most wanted former Nazis. The numbers on the list had dwindled sharply over recent years, due mainly to death from old age, with the odd successful prosecution to celebrate.

Johnson scanned through it, tapping the desk with his fingers.

Yes, the names were still there. Those bastards from Wüstegiersdorf had never been caught.

CHAPTER SIX

Friday, November 11, 2011
Portland, Maine

Johnson was busy typing an update on the missing assistant principal when, not long after his children had headed off to school, an e-mail alert popped up on the top right-hand corner of his computer screen.

He pressed his lips together and opened the message.

Hi Joe,

Just following up on our phone chat, and hope your meeting was ok :)

This Nathaniel Kudrow thing. I have a gut feeling there is a great story in there somewhere. Not just his actual death, and our crime guys are on that one, but how that might be linked to what he said about the campaign funding.

It would fit into the election agenda ahead of 2012. Our editors here are very, very eager to pursue this.

Apart from Nathaniel's info, my sources tell me David Kudrow's got a big campaign fund, but nobody can work out where it's all come from.

I've been speaking to a few people, and they're convinced there's something not right. One said to me that Kudrow's father, Daniel, and his uncle Jacob in London are basically just small businessmen, yet they seem to have enough money to bankroll Kudrow's campaign. So how do they do it? Where's the money coming from?

Given the Nazi angle, would you be interested in chasing it for us? We can pay you out of our freelance budget. Our rates are quite generous, plus very good expenses.

Could start with the company accounts if you can get hold of them. It's a private jewelry business, Kudrow Group. They have a chain of shops, Kudrow & Co., and a factory somewhere.

Fiona

Johnson leaned back in his swivel chair and spun round full circle, whirling past the whiteboard, the maps of the U.S. and the world, and his printer and scanner, then coming to rest in front of his computer again.

What to do? He didn't feel very sure about taking on something that would involve working closely with Fiona. Then again, it had been years. They could keep it professional, couldn't they? He considered the whiteboard, on which he had written his current list of jobs, along with a couple of prospective ones, all in red felt-tip pen.

His typically tech-minded son, Peter, teased him frequently about the whiteboard, calling it "very retro." He had scribbled at the top of it *Dad's iBoard*.

"I just don't see how you can be an Apple guy with a whiteboard on the wall," he'd said over breakfast just that morning. "You're a dinosaur, Dad!"

Johnson often played a game with himself, writing tabloid-style alliterative headlines on the whiteboard for the jobs he was working on, trying to make them sound more interesting. *Teacher trapped in teenage tryst*, was his latest.

But truthfully, no matter how he dressed them up, none of the four he had listed were anything other than small-town stuff.

So what about this one from Fiona? Nazi money? It seemed unlikely. She knew exactly which buttons to press. It would mean time in the U.K. away from the kids, and there wasn't much information to go on. Could Nathaniel even have been put up to it?

But then again . . .

What was it his old OSI boss Mickey Ralph used to say? *Never die wondering, my friend.*

He'd adopted that philosophy during his career at the OSI and beyond, drawing many, many blanks in his investigations but then sometimes coming up with the odd jewel, the occasional high-profile prosecution. The letters of thanks received from former victims of the Nazi perpetrators and their families, all kept in a box in his study, made it worthwhile.

Johnson scrolled through his text messages until he found the one from Vic about their planned meeting for the following Wednesday. He sent a short note back, asking if he was free for a phone chat.

A couple of minutes later the phone rang. It was Vic, using his personal cell phone but over the military-grade encryption system the two of them always used when calling each other. It was an old habit.

"Vic, how you doing buddy?"

"Good, nothing changes here. How's things with you?"

"Okay-ish. Could do with a bit more action work-wise, but generally all right. Thanks for calling back. I'm looking forward to catching up on Wednesday."

"Yeah, likewise, been a while."

"Listen, I'm just after a favor, actually."

Johnson went on to explain what he needed and the urgency of the request. "I'd like to know as much as possible about the Kudrow companies in the U.S., in the U.K., in Argentina. I want turnover and profitability over the past several years, and margins. If possible, I'd like those numbers for the different divisions of these companies, as well as the parent business. I'll need balance-sheet strength, levels of debt, and anything that you can find on their suppliers and their customer base. Also which of the Kudrow family are listed as directors of these companies. And keep a particular eye out for anything that looks out of the ordinary," he said.

"Is that all?" Vic asked.

Johnson ignored the slight note of sarcasm in his friend's voice. "You've always been a wizard when it comes to company accounts, so I thought it might be up your alley. Those private companies can be hard work to research."

"They can be, I mean, they obviously don't file public accounts, but there's ways and means, credit reports and so on. I think I can get something by the time I see you next week. I'll get Neal on the case as well. He's sitting here next to me."

Neal Scales was another of Johnson's former CIA colleagues who worked with him in Pakistan and still worked alongside Vic.

There was a short silence before Vic added, "Just to let you know, Joe, we do have to be careful with this sort of personal information request these days. We're not meant to do them, as you know."

"Yes, appreciate that, Vic. Anything you can do would be very helpful, and I'll see you soon. Thanks again, buddy."

Johnson ended the call and sat, deep in thought.

He, Vic and Neal always reminisced about their time in Pakistan and Afghanistan, as operatives for the Near East Division. But it was often black humor: they all knew it had been a difficult period for Johnson.

The three of them had been based in Pakistan's capital, Islamabad, where the CIA's station was located on the third floor of the embassy building inside a walled complex. But occasionally there was a need for covert trips up to and sometimes over the border into Afghanistan, which was then occupied by Soviet forces.

Johnson, like his mother, was a prolific linguist who had rapidly picked up Pashto and so was a natural choice for such operations. He had become fluent in Russian and German during four years in Berlin in the early '80s to research his Ph.D. on the economics of the Third Reich. That was in addition to the Spanish he had learned at school and at Boston University alongside his history degree courses, and other languages picked up later in life. These included Serbo-Croat, acquired during an OSI investigation in 1999, and Arabic, which he learned with the assistance of a Washington-based friend who formerly worked for the Al Mukhabarat Al A'amah, the Saudi intelligence agency.

One morning in April 1988, only a few months before the U.S. embassy in Kabul was closed, Johnson and Vic were on one such trip to the dusty eastern Afghan city of Jalalabad, a long and dangerous forty-five miles from the Pakistan border. They were returning from a meeting on the eastern edge of the city with a highly placed Afghan mujahideen rebel commander whom Johnson had recruited six months earlier —a prized agent inside the regime who supplied a flow of information that delighted the deputy director at Langley. The object was to try and get from the agent a better idea of what was happening to the huge volume of weapons the

Americans were supplying to the rebels—under a project called Operation Cyclone—to help them in their battles against Soviet forces.

After the meeting, as they walked back to their car, Johnson checked behind them just in time to see his agent being marched from the supposedly safe house in which they had been talking and bundled into a car waiting in the street. The agent had clearly been compromised, and his captors, it emerged afterward, were the KGB, who were everywhere in Afghanistan at that time.

Then, a moment later, Johnson spotted a rooftop gunman and yanked Vic into a doorway just as a hail of bullets crashed into the wall next to them.

It was an extremely close thing. One of the bullets caught the top of Johnson's right ear, leaving him with a nick, a scar for life—a small U-shaped hole with a slightly ragged edge, as if some small animal had bitten a piece out of it.

The two CIA men took cover in a derelict building, where they were pursued by the gunman. In a tense standoff, Johnson, blood still flowing from his ear injury, shot the gunman dead with his 9 mm Beretta from a range of about twenty yards, before the duo escaped down an alley. They eventually made it back to their car and over the border into Pakistan.

All hell broke loose in the days that followed.

Langley went nuts at the loss of one of its top agents.

"Deeply unimpressive. We're meant to be protecting our sources, not throwing them to the Russians for lunch," was the payoff line in one encrypted telegram that came out of the director's office.

Pakistan's Inter-Services Intelligence played hell with Langley, demanding to know why the CIA was recruiting and running its own agents in Afghanistan rather than working through them, as had been agreed.

The U.S. chargé d'affaires, who was running the Kabul embassy because the previous ambassador had been assassinated in 1979, went ballistic because an Afghan—albeit a pro-Soviet one—had been shot dead by an American on home soil, and he was left to clear up the diplomatic mess.

Johnson's reputation, previously rising, was ripped to shreds. He felt terrible at the loss of his agent to an unknown and probably gruesome fate at the hands of some KGB thug executioner.

But what deeply troubled him and Vic was that this had all happened despite their tradecraft being impeccable and that they had been 100 percent certain they were *black*, completely free of surveillance, when they entered the meeting with the agent, who had been similarly certain. Their strong suspicion was that they had been seriously compromised by a mole within the U.S. embassy in Islamabad who had leaked details of the meeting to the KGB.

Interestingly to some of the conspiracy theorists at the Islamabad station, the incident had followed a series of personality clashes between Johnson and his boss in the CIA's Near East Division, Robert Watson, who at that time was chief of station in Islamabad—the role in which Watson had made his name.

However, the identity of the mole was never discovered.

During the course of the internal inquiry that followed—some called it a whitewash—Vic argued strongly for Johnson. But it was in vain: Watson called Johnson in and informed him he was being banned from any further cross-border work: effectively grounded in the embassy. He was the scapegoat.

"I'm not going to support you over this," Watson had told a shell-shocked Johnson, whose ear was still bandaged. "We need people who are disciplined, who will use first-class tradecraft to run their sources and won't risk torpedoing operations for the rest of us by working asshole-fashion in the way you've just done."

Strangely, the fact that the tradecraft had been almost flawless, that Johnson had saved the life of another of his top operatives, and that he had developed other first-class sources among the mujahideen in Afghanistan and had run them effectively and safely didn't appear to have been factored into Watson's decision.

Instead, Watson set Johnson to work on developing sources who could provide information about Pakistan's growing, highly secret nuclear weapons program. Again, Johnson delivered the goods, while Watson took the credit at Langley, thus adding to his burgeoning reputation.

But during 1990, Johnson made a mistake. He became entangled in a brief affair with Jayne Robinson, a U.K. Secret Intelligence Service officer based in Islamabad. Unfortunately, someone mentioned the dalliance to Watson, for whom that was the final straw—or maybe the final opportunity, some people thought. He was heard storming around the station muttering something about what if it had been a Russian honeytrap and how could he ever trust Johnson again.

Another verbal lambasting and a written warning ensued. Once Watson had made up his mind, it was just a matter of time. Johnson was recalled from Islamabad to Langley in the September of that year.

Two days later, just after Johnson celebrated his thirty-second birthday and only six years after he joined the CIA, the game was up. Johnson walked out of headquarters for the final time, carrying his belongings in a black plastic bag.

Johnson shook himself out of his reverie—Pakistan seemed like a lifetime ago in some ways, yesterday in others. He never did find out what had happened to his agent, with whom he had built a good relationship. It seemed unlikely he would have survived, but who knew? Maybe one day he would go back there and try to find out, he mused.

He stared at Fiona's e-mail on his computer screen and hesitated, of two minds.

Finally, he decided to leave it and closed the e-mail. But he very much doubted it was the last he would hear of this particular request, knowing Fiona Heppenstall.

CHAPTER SEVEN

Sunday, November 13, 2011
Buenos Aires

The man sitting on the bare concrete floor aimed his Beretta Bobcat straight at Ignacio Guzmann's chest. "Boom," he said, pulling the trigger.

There was a loud click as the hammer dropped onto the empty chamber. One of the two men on the threadbare green sofa sniggered momentarily.

Ignacio, settled on a matching green armchair covered in oil stains and grease, didn't laugh. "*Idiota*. I hope you've got a snap cap on that, otherwise you're going to damage the firing pin. They're expensive," he said in Spanish.

"Yeah, yeah, of course," his friend Diego Ruiz said as he pointed the gun at the man on the sofa who had sniggered, Alejandro Garcia, and repeated the procedure. "Boom."

This time, the others remained silent.

Diego started to strip the weapon.

Ignacio watched him for a few seconds, then jumped up

and grabbed Diego by the throat, forcing him backward until he toppled over and his head hit the concrete floor with a thump. "When you're in my house, you don't do that. Not ever, you asshole, got it?"

"Okay, boss, okay, sorry. Only joking." Now he wasn't smiling.

The men were in an upstairs room in a small two-story house, no more than a rough shack made from cinder blocks, crudely painted an orange-red and capped with a rusty corrugated iron roof.

The property, near the junction of Carlos H. Perette and Prefectura Naval Argentina, was on the edge of the notorious shantytown Barrio 31, a stone's throw from the busy dockyards and their giant container ships.

It was only three or four kilometers from José's house in Recoleta, but Ignacio always felt as though he were traveling from first to third world every time he made the trip.

The downstairs front door was protected by a full-length padlocked metal grill. There were more grills across all the windows, one of which had been smashed, and a spiderweb of white plumbing pipework spilled out of the upstairs frontage and down to street level.

The house next door, wedged tightly against its neighbor, was made out of two shipping containers perched precariously one atop the other, with a homemade external staircase of planks linking the two.

Ignacio walked to the window and peered outside. An abandoned old Ford stood rusting in the potholed road. Two chickens squawked as a couple of young boys chased them from an alleyway, and a toothless old man perched on a small wooden stool was offering marijuana to passersby. The driver of a yellow and black taxi stopped to buy some, honking his horn repeatedly as he did so.

Ignacio turned and put his coffee cup down on a rectangular table fashioned from a piece of chipboard.

Alejandro and the other man on the sofa, Luis Castano, were both puffing at cigarettes. Diego briefly ceased cleaning the Beretta to light a joint. He rubbed the back of his head where it had made contact with the floor.

Ignacio had thought carefully about what to tell his old army friends. He decided to keep it brief. They didn't need to know all the details about how he'd gotten his information or what problems he'd already had to sort out. But he was going to have to give them some background if he was going to get them on board.

"Look at this," Ignacio said. He spread out a map of London over the table, which was illuminated by a single bare light bulb dangling by a frayed cord from the ceiling, around which swirled a thick fog of tobacco and cannabis smoke.

"I've spent the past few months doing a lot of work to find out why my father's business is such a pile of shit. The biggest problem is that he's been overpaying for his gold."

He locked eyes with Diego, the man who had been his biggest ally in the army and had remained his most trusted friend once they became civilians. He had also worked on army budgets and was the only one among them who had a business brain.

"He's been paying 6 percent above market prices. And guess what his profit margin should be, if it was a properly run business? About 6 percent. That's why he's losing money. He just pays up. If he keeps that up, he's going to go bust," Ignacio said. He put his forefinger to his throat and slashed it across to underline his point, then folded his arms. "Our job is to find out where the gold comes from, how it's being sourced and transported, and exactly which individuals are doing it. And we need to find out fast. I need to put a stop to the overpaying, and if we can screw the supplier, then so much the better. If it's illegal, maybe we can get a slice of it. Blackmail them or something."

He explained that the gold destined for his father's business was sent by a car-parts company in London to a supplier in Argentina called Oro Centro. He pointed to a location on the map to show exactly where.

"And also, I've discovered payments from SolGold to Oro Centro go into a Guatemalan numbered bank account. Looks like dirty money to me."

Diego, puffing away on his joint, cocked his head. "A car-parts business?"

Ignacio nodded. "I've seen invoices." He thought for a moment. "Maybe while we're in London we can put one over on the Brits to make up for what they did to us in the Falklands. Goose Green and Port Stanley." The other three men, all veterans of the 1982 war against the British, gazed at him silently. They had all lost friends in that conflict.

Ignacio said, "You, Diego, need to get yourself and Alejandro over to London straightaway. Do a recce. The next available flight, if possible. You'll need to find someone who you can persuade, by whatever means, to give us the information we need on the gold source."

Diego stood up. "Before we get into that, I think you'd better give us some idea of what's in it for us. And who's paying."

"Yeah, needs to be a good day rate," Alejandro said, leaning back on the sofa. "Sounds risky."

Ignacio pushed his right fist into his left palm. "You'll all get a cut if we can do this right. I'm going to put this business back on track, and you're all going to be the first to get jobs. If we screw some gold out of the supplier, we'll share that too.

"Luis, sorry, you will have to stay here and look after things at this end. We'll need someone on the ground here. Then I'll head to London myself, as soon as I can finish tying up a few loose ends. Shouldn't take more than a couple of days."

Diego took a few more pretend shots with his Beretta, this time without pulling the trigger. "I'm going to need a grand up front, in U.S. dollars, and in cash, okay?"

The other two men nodded.

Ignacio hesitated. "Okay, okay, I'll sort it. I'll buy the tickets and get the cash for you, and then you can go."

Diego said, "You said we'll get jobs. What about your old man, José, if we get what we want? He's the boss."

Ignacio bent forward. "This business is worth shit all the way he's running it. If we can fix it, I'll sort my father out in my own way." He tapped a finger against his temple.

His mind drifted back to his childhood, as it often did when discussing his father. Memories of beatings, hours spent in a darkened cupboard, and crying himself to sleep were the ones that formed the darkest, most vivid images in his mind.

"I've been in this shithole for two years now, since I split up with the wife," Ignacio said. "I went from having two kids, a nice house, four bedrooms, and a decent car to this, a stinking hovel next to a sewer. Haven't seen my kids for months. You guys are the same. We've all got to get out of this piss-flooded fleapit. I'm desperate, guys. What is it now, six years since we all left the army? And how much have we earned between us since?"

He made a circle out of his forefinger and thumb and held it up. "Just about that much. We've got *nothing* to lose and a lot to gain, provided we move fast."

CHAPTER EIGHT

Wednesday, November 16, 2011
Portland, Maine

The wind whistled through the fractionally open car window and blew horizontal the Stars and Stripes in front of Portland Head Light, as if in a salute to the old landmark. Behind it, dark clouds skimmed in from the north and the waters of Casco Bay worked themselves up into a frenzy of whitecaps.

"Why the hell have you brought me here, Doc? It's just a lighthouse, isn't it? And it's freezing." Vic appeared slightly bemused as he stared at the tall white structure towering over the red-tiled former keeper's cottage in front of it.

"It's one of Portland's sights, over two hundred years old."

Johnson had picked up Vic outside the Hilton hotel and had then driven the fifteen minutes across the Casco Bay Bridge to the old lighthouse.

"I sometimes come here to walk and think. It also has the advantage that nobody can hear us," Johnson said.

They sat on a bench along a path left of the lighthouse

overlooking the bay, where ferries were busily transporting their passengers to the nearby islands: Cushing Island, Peaks Island, Little Diamond Island.

As a boy Johnson had spent hours sitting on those ferries with his friends during school holidays, sailing off to imaginary lands far away and doing bold deeds.

Still the same dreams. Nothing's changed, he thought.

"How was the interview this morning?" Johnson asked.

"Fine. Routine—just data collection, really," Vic said. "I'm not sitting here for long, so I'll get to the point." He ran his hand through his receding light brown hair, which was gray around the temples. "I've had some luck with your stuff."

He took a small notebook out of his pocket, adjusted his metal rimmed spectacles, then turned his head to Johnson. "We're not having this conversation at all. We didn't meet up, you didn't ask for anything, and I'm not giving it. Understood?"

Johnson nodded. "Come on, Vic, agreed. Just spit it out."

Vic flicked his notebook open. "Good. Right, first on the financial side: it's interesting. The Kudrow U.S. business all seems aboveboard. They have a jewelry shop chain with fifteen shops, mainly in cities on the West Coast, and then a couple of manufacturing units. However, they also seem to have a sort of one-man subsidiary in Buenos Aires. It doesn't feature on the credit report at all, but we picked it up from banking records. It operates its banking facilities out of Guatemala, and then there are periodic transfers of cash onward to Los Angeles."

"Hang on a minute." Johnson reached into his jacket pocket, took out his own notebook and mechanical pencil, and began to scribble, holding the page down with his free hand to stop it flapping in the wind. "Okay, go on."

"The Buenos Aires arm, called Oro Centro, has an erratic turnover but high profitability when it does business. Maybe its purchasing costs or raw material costs are low or some-thing. I don't know; it's an odd one. It's only got one or two customers, the main one being a gold manufacturing and retailing business in Buenos Aires, SolGold, run by a guy named José Guzmann."

"Guzmann, did you say?" The name sounded vaguely familiar.

"Yeah." Vic turned the page of his notebook. "That's about it in a nutshell. Except that, overall, profit margins are very high, at around 25 percent, because of the Argentine business pulling them up. So the business as a whole made a pretax profit of about $8 million U.S. dollars last year, which in itself was quite high. But some years it's been much higher. For example, in 2005 it was $45 million. Amazing numbers. Then other years, absolute peanuts by comparison, a few hundred thousand and a couple of times making losses." He scratched his head.

"The volatility from year to year is the odd thing. Don't know why that is. The U.S. business trades on margins of around 5 percent, which looks normal enough. The U.K. busi-ness—well, here's the weird thing. There's nothing listed under the Kudrow name, and yet you said David Kudrow's brother operates there, didn't you?"

"Yes, Nathaniel was over in London quite recently, visiting his uncle Jacob," Johnson said. "He said he'd found out a few things while he was there, the implication being that there was something wrong. They definitely have a business there. And given the hint about a Polish trust fund and a Nazi connection to the money, it may mean a trip to the U.K., as a starting point, if it stacks up. Although that is probably a big if."

"Okay, leave it with me," Vic replied. "I'll see if I can find out some more on the U.K. I haven't had enough time to delve into it properly yet."

Vic took a pack of Marlboros out of his pocket. "Want a smoke, for old times' sake?" Years ago they had chain-smoked their way through Pakistan and Afghanistan.

"Kept us sane back then, these smokes, didn't they. Light up and forget the shit and the bullets," Vic said.

Johnson hesitated. "Shouldn't really—trying to keep myself fit. But what the hell." He took one of the last two cigarettes remaining in the pack and the lighter that Vic held out. "Zero chance of being able to light these things in this wind."

He tried five times, hands cupped protectively, before his cigarette eventually lit. "Out of practice. Maybe I should smoke more."

Vic chuckled. "Yeah, well, sounds like you've got plenty on your plate."

"Yes, I've got plenty on my plate, all right. Including a certain Fiona Heppenstall. Remember her? The political journalist? I told you about her a few years back."

Vic gave Johnson a sideways glance. "Ah yes. Can't forget her. What's happening there, then?"

"She's trying to persuade me to look at this Kudrow issue," Johnson said. "We picked it up between us at a Republican fund-raiser in D.C. last week. She wants me to do some investigative work on it, basically. I've been a little dubious, although what you've said is interesting."

Vic nodded. They puffed away in silence for a few minutes.

"So how are the guys back at Langley?" Johnson asked. "Is old Watto still there? Not that I give a rat's ass about him."

"Watson? I can't stand him. He keeps going on. He must be sixty-five now, still irritating the crap out of everyone, smoking even more than I do. His wife left him ten years ago, and his daughter moved to Australia, I've heard: work and money are all he's got. Someone told me he bought a huge house a few years back and just rattles around in it by himself."

Johnson gave Vic a sidelong glance. "Even now I still don't get what his problem was with me in Afghanistan." He took a deep drag on his cigarette, then added, "I still think about what happened in Jalalabad. Do you think he could have been the mole in Islamabad, that he could have tried to pull the trigger on us?"

Vic shrugged and bent his head to keep his cigarette out of the wind. "I doubt that, Doc. Watson is a CIA lifer, not a mole—that's my view. He's an unfair, entitled hard-ass and a pain in the balls to work with, but that's about it, I think. We'll probably never know who *was* the mole now. You screwed up, though, having that fling with the British girl, Jayne. That gave him the excuse he was looking for. Anyway, you shouldn't still be chewing over that twenty years later. You've got another job, another life. Never looked back, I thought?"

"Yes, I know, you're right," Johnson said. "Dented my pride at the time, I guess."

It had been the hypocrisy in Watson's criticisms that had hurt the most. Johnson knew that Watson had run a few operations that had for various reasons resulted in the deaths of innocent Afghan civilians, let alone armed gunmen. And nobody was going to convince Johnson that the drone strikes Watson had run in Pakistan had been as precise as PR statements claimed.

"He's always done what he's wanted, Watto," Vic said. "It's like he runs a CIA within the CIA, his own empire. And nobody does anything about it. All well above my pay grade, but it's strange. The director's office seems to tolerate it. I'd like to know why."

Before Johnson could reply, Vic threw his cigarette butt on the floor and ground it out with his heel. "Okay Doc, we're going to have to scoot. My flight leaves in just over two hours, and I need to get to the airport. Me and my missus are meant to be at my brother's house tonight for a big party. She won't be happy if I'm late back. And with Thanksgiving coming up next week as well, we've got a lot to do."

Johnson said, "I know the feeling. Thanks a bunch, Vic. That's a great help."

As he drove Vic to the airport, Johnson replayed parts of their conversation in his mind. His thoughts kept returning to the business in Buenos Aires the Kudrows were selling to.

The name Guzmann definitely rings a bell.

CHAPTER NINE

Thursday, November 17, 2011
  Portland, Maine

Carrie and Peter were chattering away about Thanksgiving. As always, they were both excited about the prospect of the now-traditional family visit to their Aunt Amy's house for lunch, even though the day itself was still a week away.

But although Johnson listened, his mind was focused on something entirely different.

He left the kitchen and walked back into his office, murmuring to himself. "Guzmann, *Guzmann*, who the hell *were* you?" He knew Guzmann definitely wasn't one of the Nazis on his old target list, but at the same time he was convinced there was some oblique connection.

At just after three o'clock in the afternoon, he wandered into the garage where he kept his old OSI files, stacked in numbered and dated cardboard boxes on four long wooden shelves. Periodically, he'd been tempted to throw them all out but always resisted the urge.

For each of the investigations he had carried out, he had started a new notebook and often collected his own copies of any additional documents in thin cardboard folders—in addition to those kept in OSI offices. They had been culled from archives in various parts of Western, Central and Eastern Europe and, thanks to the fall of communism and the end of the Cold War, in the countries of the former Soviet Union, where files were previously sealed.

There were copies of Nazi Party files from the Bundesarchiv, the German Federal Archives, in Berlin—where Johnson's former German girlfriend from his student days in the city, Clara Lehman, still worked. Alongside them were German army files from the Deutsche Dienststelle, the German Information Office, also in Berlin. There were copies of microfilmed documents from the U.S. National Archives just outside Washington, D.C., selections from the massive holdings of Soviet-era trial and interrogation transcripts held by the U.S. Holocaust Memorial Museum in D.C., and many more. All of them had some significance to the investigations he had carried out over the years.

Maybe the answer was lying in these files somewhere, he thought. But there were hundreds of files stacked up on the shelves. *Where to start?*

He pulled down one of the large cardboard boxes at random, marked 1993, carried it into his office, and started going through it.

In its entirety, his collection represented the work that he had enjoyed—following the paper trail of archived records, documents, and statements, then backing it up by tracing witnesses to secure interviews and testimonies. It was like putting a jigsaw puzzle together, often with many missing pieces.

In doing so, he had felt as if he were one-third historian, one-third investigator, and although he wouldn't admit it openly, one-third spy. There was no doubt his CIA surveillance and relationship-building skills, used in locating suspects, witnesses and holders of information and persuading them to trust him, were a large factor in his success.

His boss at the OSI, one of the attorneys who carried out the prosecutions, sometimes told Johnson he was lucky. But he believed he had made his own luck through sheer persistence and, often, what he called "unorthodox innovation."

Johnson continued to sift through his large, tatty black Moleskine notebooks and to pore over printouts of micro-filmed SS memos, SS transfer orders, concentration camp rosters and incident reports, birth certificates, bank statements, and private letters and statements.

The box was full of memories. But half an hour later, he put it back again. There was nothing relevant to Guzmann. Then he pulled down another box, this time for 1999. Same process. But again, nothing.

He wandered back into the kitchen and made himself coffee.

Johnson was sure that in one of the boxes there was a reference to Guzmann, but he really couldn't recall where, and it wasn't a name he had indexed.

He spent the next few hours going through them one by one, scanning the notebooks and flicking through the accompanying papers, with only a forty-five-minute break to make dinner for himself and the children at seven o'clock and then a fifteen-minute break for a quick cigarette after Carrie and Peter had gone to bed at ten.

Johnson had gone through almost two-thirds of the files when he found it at just after one o'clock in the morning—a dog-eared old red cardboard folder dated September 1996 with a name scribbled on the front in blue felt-tip: Jan Van Stalheim.

Van Stalheim had been an SS captain known to have committed multiple horrific murders of innocent Jews at the Dachau concentration camp in 1943 and 1944. He had been suspected by the OSI to be living under a false name in Denver, of all places, and therefore was high up on its wanted list.

But he had disappeared from Denver by the time investigators got there. The subsequent trail had been a tortuous one but had eventually led Johnson to Buenos Aires, where Van Stalheim was by then known to have fled.

And there the scent went completely cold. There were no more leads and he was never found.

Johnson's handwritten notes in black ink from the time were still there in his file. He felt his adrenaline start to pump as he read it.

> *Van Stalheim believed to be living in Buenos Aires. Local source, a journalist, notes that Van Stalheim was apparently seen six months ago, several times visiting a gold trader, SolGold, run by José Guzmann. Recommend that OSI allocates resources—either myself or someone else—to visit Guzmann undercover and check out.*

He had circled the comment in red ink and underlined it.

"We never did, pity," said Johnson to himself.

Then he laughed to himself. He should have remembered it. September 20, 1996. His birthday. He was turning thirty-eight that day, and he had flown home from Buenos Aires because Kathy, pregnant with Carrie, was past her due date and had called saying she thought her contractions had begun. It had been a false alarm, but Carrie then had arrived on the twenty-third.

A yellow Post-it note stuck to the front of the file, in Johnson's handwriting and also in red ink, stated that nobody in the OSI had ever subsequently visited Guzmann.

Johnson had taken a couple of weeks off after Carrie's birth, and then when he had returned to work, he had been sent down to Florida to help on another case instead. Then his boss at the time had received a phone call from somebody at the CIA saying they were pursuing Van Stalheim, and the OSI should back off.

Looking back, Johnson remembered feeling frustrated and wishing the OSI had a wider reach to investigate former Nazis outside the U.S. He recalled how his investigator's instinct had been piqued by the possibilities.

Johnson continued reading through the file, checking for other relevant details, but then gave up.

The caffeine that had kept him going until the early hours had finally ceased to have an effect; the garage was cold, and he needed his bed.

"Van Stalheim—a shark that got away," Johnson said to himself.

He had a sudden realization. Previously, he had been unsure about taking on the Kudrow story. But now? There was no decision to make.

He flicked his computer on and began to write an e-mail to Fiona. It didn't take long.

Fiona, I've been thinking about the Kudrow job. Okay, I'm going to do it, provided I can do it my way, to my timetable and without any interference from you. My rate for this job is $1,100 per day, in view of the risks and complexity.

Joe

He pressed the send button and then wrote another equally short note to Vic to tell him what he was planning.

Johnson climbed the stairs and sank into his bed. As he drifted off to sleep, he had a surge inside him of, what? Yes, adrenaline, but also something else. *Optimism? Anticipation?*

For certain, it was something that lifted his mood.

The more he thought about it, the more certain he became. Professionally, it felt as though he were back in business. A journey into his future beckoned—or was it his past?

CHAPTER TEN

Friday, November 18, 2011
  CIA headquarters, Langley, Virginia

By twenty past nine, Vic and Neal had already spent three hours revising and tweaking a report compiled by some of their more junior officers about the unexpectedly close cooperation between the Taliban and Al-Qaeda, who were trying to inflict maximum damage on U.S. forces withdrawing from Afghanistan.

Vic stood up. "Right, Neal, ready for a break?"

The two of them made their way to the CIA's Starbucks coffee shop just outside the main cafeteria, known by many of the staff as the Stealthy Starbucks. Unlike at other Starbucks outlets, the baristas here were not allowed to ask for customers' names and write them on their coffee cups; management at Langley deemed it too much of a security risk. The till receipts named it only as Store No.1.

"Look at this line! Ten minutes just to get a drink and a croissant. Ridiculous," Neal said.

Eventually, they were served and went to a free table in the far corner.

Neal, also a supervisor, although one rung below Vic, took a sip from his latte and put his cup down on the table. "So, how was your junket in Portland?"

"Junket? Come off it. Portland is Portland. I just got the interview out of the way as quick as I could, then caught up with Joe for an hour or two. Didn't have much time, actually; I was running late for the airport. Thanks for helping me out with the stuff for him, by the way."

"No problem. Was it okay?" Neal asked.

"I think so. He seemed happy. The financials stuff on the Kudrow business were just about what he wanted, and I talked him through that up-and-down earnings volatility you spotted," Vic said.

He stirred his drink. "One interesting thing was the name of that jeweler guy we unearthed in Buenos Aires, José Guzmann. Joe thought it rang a bell with him, something from one of the Nazi hunts he did at the OSI, so apart from the David Kudrow investigation, I think he's going to check out the Guzmann business, too. He sent me an e-mail this morning saying he was going to do the job."

Vic picked up his coffee and nodded at a svelte middle-aged woman with long red hair who was walking past, a latte in one hand and a muffin in the other. "Hi, Helen," he said, smiling.

She grinned back, winked, and continued on.

"How does Watto manage to get a secretary like that?" Neal asked.

"Doesn't deserve her."

"I know. You should get her a transfer to our section. I've seen her giving you the eye. You be careful. Anyway, what was I going to say?" Neal said, trying to refocus his gaze on Vic. "Ah yes, Guzmann, the customer of the Kudrow business, I remember. Yeah, I hope Joe gets a result. He's definitely felt left out on a limb since leaving D.C."

Vic nodded. "That's the thing with Joe. Up in Portland he feels like he's isolated. That's probably why he's interested in this Kudrow thing. When he picked it up he was in D.C. at a Republican fund-raiser with that political journalist he had a thing with a few years back, after his wife died, remember? Fiona Heppenstall—you must remember."

Neal fell back in his chair, grinning. "Yep, I remember."

"Fiona asked him to help her with the Kudrow story," Vic said. "It's given him something bigger to sink his teeth into. Got his mojo going again. It might mean a trip to the U.K.; one of the Kudrows has a business there."

He drained his coffee. "Actually, I think he misses the Agency still, after all this time. You can take the man out of Langley, but taking Langley out of the man's another thing. That's why the OSI suited him. I think some of our techniques were very useful to him."

Neal stood up. "Yeah. You're right. I wonder how I'd get on outside the Agency. Not well, I suspect. Look, we'd better get back and get stuck into that report. Time's marching on."

Both men had spent their entire careers in the Directorate of Operations, the clandestine service. Together they had built a formidable knowledge of Afghanistan, Pakistan, and the various factions operating in the Near East and Middle East.

As they walked off, Neal glanced briefly at a tall, gray-haired man who seemed to be in his late sixties and was sitting by himself at the table directly behind them. The man put down his coffee and the newspaper in which he had appeared to be engrossed.

* * *

Later that morning, while he was driving from Langley to a meeting on Capitol Hill, the same tall, gray-haired man pulled off the road and dialed a number in Miami from a prepaid burner cell phone.

"Simon, it's GREYHOUND here in Washington. I'm checking in with some information."

"Okay, thanks. Information about whom?" the man who called himself Simon asked.

"Someone on our list of protected people in Buenos Aires, VANDAL," the gray-haired man said. "Somebody on our watch sheet is apparently renewing his interest in VANDAL. A man called Joe Johnson, lives in Portland, Maine. Worked for the Agency in the '80s, Near East division, got fired, and became an OSI investigator, which is why he's on our radar. He's been on our sheet since the early '90s. We need to let VANDAL know. It's a potentially dangerous situation for him."

"Right, got it, that's Joe Johnson. Anything else on him?"

"It's been a while since he was active," GREYHOUND said. "He left the OSI five years ago, but he's obviously still got an interest in our group. Sounds as though he's looking to investigate VANDAL, from what I've heard today."

"And how did you pick this information up, exactly?" Simon asked.

"It was curious. Not my normal channels. A conversation between a couple of operatives, former colleagues of Johnson going years back. It was difficult to get a proper feel for what was going on; it was a short exchange, but there was also something about an investigation into David Kudrow, the Republican running for the nomination. They also mentioned that Johnson was planning a trip to London."

"Interesting. Anything else to add?"

"That's about all I have," GREYHOUND said. "I thought I should pass it on. Perhaps you can add it to the file we have on Johnson." He ended the call, then waited for a moment and dialed the number for another burner phone.

When the line picked up, he identified himself.

"It's GREYHOUND here."

There was a brief silence at the other end of the line. "What have you got for me," asked Robert Watson, chief of the Near East division in the CIA's Directorate of Operations.

"It's about one of your former operatives, Joe Johnson. You may recall him?"

Another silence, followed by a quiet snort. "Yes, what's he up to?" Watson asked.

"I've just had to put a call in to Miami about him. He's active again, chasing one of our old assets in Buenos Aires, VANDAL."

Watson, whose main focus was now on Syria after a spell in the Special Activities Division working on the Pakistan drone strike program, swore quietly. "Okay, thanks for letting me know. Anything else?"

"No, that's it."

"Okay, that's going to complicate things. I'll talk to Miami and Tel Aviv. Don't worry, I'll deal with it," he said. Then he hung up.

* * *

Buenos Aires

"Not bad for ninety-one, although I think your blood pressure needs watching. It's quite high, which at your age we need to be careful with," Dr. Hernanz said in Spanish. "But it's more your state of mind I'm worried about."

José shrugged. For several years he had been visiting his

doctor saying he was feeling depressed, lethargic, and irritable. He had tried various types of antidepressants, but none had any lasting effect. Indeed, some had made him feel worse.

Dr. Hernanz folded his arms and placed them on the desk. "You know, I think it might be worth going to see a psychologist, with a view to some cognitive therapy. With some of my other patients, cognitive therapy has worked quite well, particularly where the psychologist looks at the person's past."

José's eyebrows flicked upward at the suggestion. "I really don't think so. Not at my age."

Dr. Hernanz put up his hand. "Hang on a minute. I was going to say that the psychologist would get the patient to talk a little about the patterns of thinking they are in, why they have occurred, key influences over the years, particularly when young, to see if there is any underlying cause, and then hopefully help with some techniques to get the patient into a different pattern of thought. I think even at your age, you could benefit from this."

Almost imperceptibly, José shook his head. "I doubt that it's something I'd find helpful. Not talking about my past."

"Okay, Señor Guzmann, I still feel you should think it over. Just let me know if you change your mind."

José stood and limped toward the door.

"How's that knee?" Hernanz called after him.

"Still the same. I put up with it," José said without turning. He made his way out of the doctor's clinic, just around the corner from his house in the Recoleta barrio, and blinked in the glare of the sunlight, which reflected off the pavement.

He made his way slowly onto Ombú Street and stopped several times to rest. It was a hot afternoon. Once he was back inside his house, he went into his living room and sat down in his favorite black leather armchair in front of his television. He stared at the blank screen.

At around half past five that afternoon, his cell phone rang. An unidentified number. José shook his head impatiently and awkwardly jabbed with his forefinger at the screen.

"Hello? Guzmann here."

"Señor Guzmann. Hello, it's Simon here in Miami. I have a question for you. Did your dog enjoy his walk this morning?"

José sat motionless and said nothing for several seconds. He hadn't received a call from Miami for probably ten years at least, maybe twelve. It was never good news. He had to stop and think what the correct response to the question was; it had been so long.

What was the reply? He scanned his living room desperately. *Come on, think, think . . .*

Eventually he remembered. "Hello, Simon. Yes, my dog had a good walk, thank you. He's now asleep in the kitchen in front of the fire." José had never owned a dog and didn't have a fireplace in his kitchen.

"That's good to know, Señor Guzmann. Do you still have your encrypted phone? I've tried to call it but it's switched off. I don't want to take any risks."

Guzmann did have one in his bedside drawer but hadn't used it for a long time. "Give me five minutes, then call me on it. I might need to charge it." He cross-checked the number then hung up feeling slightly disoriented. *What the devil's this about?*

A short while later, Guzmann had located the phone and was sitting on his bed. He plugged it into its charger because the battery was indeed flat. When it rang, he clumsily keyed in a code number and answered.

"Señor Guzmann, it's Simon here again. I have some information for you; are you ready?"

"Yes, yes, go ahead, I'm ready," José said, his composure now regained.

"Okay, we've had a tip from Washington. It's concerning an old OSI investigator, a man named Joe Johnson, also former CIA. He now runs his own business; he's an investigator. Mainly domestic cases up in Portland, Maine. You may know it."

"Yes, yes, I know where Portland is. Get to the point."

"Okay. Johnson appears to be carrying out some sort of inquiry, and someone has given him your name, we gather from our sources. The inquiry's into a business run by the Kudrow family, based in Los Angeles. This is the same family to whom David Kudrow belongs; he's trying to get the Republican nomination for the U.S. presidential election next year. Johnson's been told that Kudrow has a link to you. We thought you should know in case Johnson's inquiries take him down avenues that we may not want him to go down. You understand?"

José was holding his cell phone so tightly his hand began to shake. "I understand perfectly."

"Good. The other piece of information is that Johnson's working with a political journalist, Fiona Heppenstall, who writes for a U.S. news and commentary website, *Inside Track*."

The man who called himself Simon paused. "Any questions?"

José scratched his head. "I want to know one thing. Do we need to take any action of any kind at this stage? It sounds like we probably should."

"No, not right now. We don't think so. But we're monitoring things, and we'll let you know if that changes. I'm going to e-mail you a photograph of Johnson, which is a few years old, but you should recognize him if he does happen to pop up. It may be helpful. I will also send you a photograph of the journalist. I suggest you keep your encrypted phone charged and switched on in case I need to contact you. Any further questions?"

"No, I've no questions." José slowly removed the phone from his ear and jabbed once again at the screen.

He sat still for a short while, then said out loud to himself, "No action, that's their view. Well, if they're not going to take any action, I will." He picked up his other cell phone and tapped on the speed-dial number for his son, Ignacio.

CHAPTER ELEVEN

Friday, November 18, 2011
Washington, D.C.

The senior journalist followed Des Cole out of the *Inside Track* afternoon editorial meeting and stood still for a moment as he watched Des return to his desk.

What he'd just heard him say, almost as a throwaway right at the end of the meeting, was stuck in his head.

Zac Butler was the features and entertainment editor at *Inside Track*. He also happened to be heavily involved in fundraising for the Republican Party in the capital.

The longer Zac thought about it, the more it became clear in his own mind that he had no choice.

He walked around the corner and went into a small meeting room where he could make a private call on his cell phone. He dialed a number.

"Hello, Philip Pietersen."

"Philip. It's Zac. Listen, there's something you need to know. It's about David."

"What about him?"

Butler glanced through the glass window of the meeting room and lowered his voice. "I've just picked up that one of the investigative reporters here, Fiona Heppenstall, is having a close look at his campaign funding and where it's coming from. She thinks there's something illegal about it."

"You're joking? As if we haven't got enough problems, what with Nathaniel."

"Sadly not. She's had a tip-off from somewhere. In particular, she's going to have a look at David's father and uncle, you know, their gold and jewelry business. I've just heard her boss talking about it. I mean, nothing's happened yet, but he mentioned it right at the end of the meeting, when we were talking about possible story assignments during the run-up to the primaries."

"Shit, shit, shit. That's all we need at this stage. The campaign's going like a steam train."

"There's more. She's got an investigator to work with her, a guy named Joe Johnson, who apparently used to be some hotshot at the Office of Special Investigations, a Nazi hunter. I thought you should know."

"*Joe Johnson?* Sonofabitch. I just had both him and Fiona at one of our fund-raisers at my house only last week. What the hell's going on?"

"That's a good question. A damned good question."

* * *

Portland, Maine

"Hello, Mrs. Richardson, some good news. I've found out where your husband is," Johnson said, propping his phone between his left ear and his shoulder while simultaneously doing an Internet search on Jacob Kudrow. "He's with the girl at the Eastern Slope Inn over in North Conway. It's definitely him."

There was a minor explosion at the other end of the line as the assistant principal's wife swore violently. "The bastard. How the hell did you find him?"

Johnson said, "I just worked my way through that list of holiday places you sent me. I phoned the Eastern Slope just now, posed as his brother, and found out that he and his, um, daughter, as he's apparently described the girl to hotel staff, are staying in one of the town houses at the back of the hotel."

After Mrs. Richardson decided immediately to take a drive over to New Hampshire and confront her husband herself, rather than involve the police, Johnson put the phone down.

He went over to his whiteboard and, using his red marker pen, crossed through *Teacher trapped in teenage tryst.*

Below it, he started writing. *Johnson launches hunt for . . .*

He broke off mid-sentence and sat down, staring at the whiteboard. After a few minutes, he got up and walked back to the board. He wrote two more words to complete the sentence: *Nazi murderer.*

It wasn't alliterative, but he didn't mean it to be. This was serious.

Johnson sat down again. Where was the best place to start? Maybe Jacob Kudrow would be a good starting point, given Nathaniel's comments, but where to find him? *Wait. Nathaniel's funeral!*

Surely, Nathaniel's uncle would attend to support his twin as well as pay his own respects to his nephew. When Johnson finally found the funeral information online in an obituary— it had been open to the public, probably because of David's campaign—he cursed. He was a day too late.

Johnson sighed. *Back to the drawing board. Where shall I focus first? London or Buenos Aires?*

The trail was stronger in London, given Nathaniel's revelations about his trip there to visit Jacob. And in any case, *Inside Track* would be paying him for the Kudrow story, at least initially. That should be the starting point.

Johnson then wrote an e-mail to Ben Veletta, a former colleague at the Office of Special Investigations, which in 2010 was formed into a new unit known as the Human Rights and Special Prosecutions section, though it remained within the Department of Justice. He asked Ben, who was deputy chief historian in the HRSP, to check the Nazi Party personal files, available at the National Archives in Washington, D.C., to see what he could get on both Van Stalheim and José Guzmann. If anyone could find what he needed, Ben could.

That done, he refocused on Jacob. Normally, finding an address and contact details online for someone posed no problem, even if it was in another country.

But between calls to various hotels seeking the missing assistant principal, he had already spent more than two hours that morning searching for a trace of Jacob. There was nothing on the U.K. electoral roll, and the online telephone directory also turned up a blank result. Similarly with marriages, births, and deaths records: nothing.

It was very odd that U.K. records showed nothing for Jacob, while U.S. federal census records revealed clear details, year after year, for Jacob's twin brother Daniel, living in Anaheim outside Los Angeles, David, also in Anaheim, and Nathaniel, Redondo Beach.

Has the old man moved elsewhere? Fled? Changed his name? And if so, why?

Johnson decided it would be easier to complete his searches once he arrived in London, where he knew there was one person who could help: Jayne Robinson, who still worked at SIS and who, he knew very well, had done a long stint at its Buenos Aires station in the past. She could advise on the Argentine end of the operation, too.

In fact, the last time he had seen her had been over dinner in the Argentine capital in 1996, not long after she had begun her four-year posting there and when he was in pursuit of Van Stalheim.

Johnson began to write an e-mail to Jayne, outlining what he needed. He still thought back with some nostalgia on the fling he had enjoyed with her in '90, despite it having been a factor in him losing his job at the time.

CHAPTER TWELVE

Saturday, November 19, 2011
London

Dark-suited hedge-fund managers clutching takeaway coffee cups picked their way through the puddles on the corner of Berkeley Square, and the flashing orange Belisha beacons guarding the zebra crossing appeared like splashes of color on a monochrome photograph.

It was the grayest of days in London's Mayfair district.

A short distance away, Jacob emerged from the black front door of his three-story terraced house in Hay's Mews, dressed in a black woolen overcoat and a Russian-style fur hat that covered his snow-white hair and wearing gold-rimmed glasses.

He turned around. It was his second day back in London after his nephew Nathaniel's funeral. No more than a few degrees above freezing, and it was raining. Thank the Almighty that Daniel had been able to fly back with him. They needed each other at times like this.

Jacob stepped gingerly onto the pavement. Rainwater dripped from the window boxes hanging above the garage doors to his left.

A few seconds later his identical twin appeared in the doorway, his pink cheeks laced with delicate, tiny red veins. The only noticeable difference in appearance between the twins was that Daniel wore black-rimmed glasses.

The two men, now aged eighty-seven, walked pokily, shoulders hunched against the drizzle, past the Running Footman pub and around the corner to the Lansdowne Club, a private members' club and hotel.

"Good morning, Mr. Kew. Nice to see you again. I was sorry to hear your sad family news from our manager here. I remember your nephew from when he was here not long ago. We've been thinking about you," the doorman said to Jacob, who was flexing his knee with a grimace.

Jacob nodded. "Thank you. It's been a difficult time."

They made their way into the club's Thirties Room, an Art Deco-style sitting room.

"Jacob, why did you ever bother with this Jack Kew business? I can't get used to it. Never could."

Jacob stopped and sighed. "I've told you dozens of times, it made sense to have as much clear blue water between us as possible and still does. And once I got a British passport, a British name made it easier coming in and out — fewer questions from customs."

"Let's sit there," Jacob said, pointing at a pair of antiquated but comfortable-looking red armchairs near the window. He smoothed his hair, lowered himself into his seat, then waved at a waiter and ordered two cappuccinos.

Daniel also sat. "Six years since I was here last. Looks like they've smartened it up since then. So you brought Nathaniel here when he was over a few months ago?"

"Yes, I did. I'll not forget it now. That was the last time I saw him, that trip."

"I think he liked it over here, out of the limelight," Daniel said. "He watched David's career skyrocketing, and I don't know, I think he felt a bit desperate." Daniel inched his chair closer to the table and lowered his voice. "We need to talk. Something else has come up. I had an e-mail last night from David, saying his campaign manager had a call from one of his Republican Party cronies who's an editor at a news website in D.C. Apparently a political journalist at the same website, a woman, is looking into our family finances. Not just David's but all of ours."

"I can't believe it," Jacob said. "You'd have thought they'd leave us alone in our grief—at least for a time."

Daniel sipped his coffee. "You would think so. Trouble is, campaign finance is a bit of a hot potato at the moment for the media. They're starting to show interest in where the money's coming from. Apparently, the woman has some investigator helping her. The word is they think something illegal's going on."

Jacob drummed his fingers on the table. "Can't the party do something to head it off? They must be able to pull some strings, talk to the editor. That's all we need, especially with David at this stage. He's doing well. Gets good write-ups from the British press, even *The Economist*."

He picked up his coffee cup, but then his cell phone rang in his pocket, making him jump and spill the hot liquid on his trouser leg. He swore, then pulled out his phone and answered it.

"Hello, Leopold?" Jacob said.

The caller was Leopold Skorupski, owner of Classic Car Parts, which was located right next to Jacob's own business in East London.

"Jacob, I've been trying to get hold of you at home. I didn't realize you were out. Just a quick call to let you know

I've had some bad news. One of our guys, Keith Bartelski—you know him—he's disappeared. The police are involved."

Jacob sat and listened quietly for several minutes while Leopold described what had happened. Keith was one of Leopold's longest-serving employees. He had been abducted but had somehow managed to send an emergency text message to alert Leopold, who had contacted the police.

Jacob ran his fingers several times quickly backward and forward through his white hair and shut his eyes, the phone to his left ear. "Hell, I don't believe it," he said.

He sank further down into his chair.

"According to the text from Keith, it sounds like a gang of Argentinians," Leopold said.

"*Argentinians?* Do police think he's still alive, or—"

"They don't know," Leopold said. "Sorry Jacob, I've got to go. I've got a detective waiting here. I'll speak later."

"Okay, well give me a call if you hear any more. Speak later." He hung up and looked at Daniel. "You must have caught most of that."

"One of Leopold's guys has gone missing?" Daniel asked.

Jacob nodded. As he did so, his phone pinged. He stabbed at the device with his forefinger and read the screen.

He shook his head and showed the message to his brother. "There, have a look at that. Leopold's forwarded me the message he got from Keith. Looks like Keith sent it from another phone, not his own."

Urgent Leopold, been kidnapped by some gang, I think Argies. Very threatening but don't know what they want. Haven't said. Don't know where I am, an apartment somewhere. Using one of their phones they left in the toilet. Don't reply. Bart

Daniel paused before speaking. "Argentinians? Goddammit. You don't think . . . ?"

Jacob shrugged. "I really don't know. It can't just be a coincidence, can it?"

He waved at the waiter, then lifted two fingers and pointed to his coffee cup. The waiter nodded.

"One thing I do know," Jacob said, "I don't want the police nosing around down at the workshop, and of course neither does Leopold. The other guys must be all worried senseless. They must all think they could be next."

"Hmm, I can imagine," Daniel said. He drained his coffee. "Is the workshop clean at the moment? You know what I mean. If not, get it cleaned up."

"I wouldn't describe it as clean. There's still bits and pieces in there. We'll get it done."

The waiter arrived with the two additional coffees and a plate of cookies. "There you go, Mr. Kew. Compliments of the house."

"Thank you so much," Jacob said.

Daniel took a cookie. "There was another thing I was going to talk to you about. Something Nathaniel mentioned to me a few days before he died. He said he found out when he was here in London that you were writing a memoir. I was a bit surprised."

Jacob's eyes shot up. "He said *what*? How the hell did he know about that? I never mentioned it to him. He must have nosed around among my papers and seen my notebook. That's worrisome. I keep it locked up with all the old invoices and stuff that go back years. It's been in the safe. I *have* been writing something, but I don't know if it'll come to anything. I thought the whole thing would make a good story once we're all gone. It's all part of a plan I've been thinking about. I'll tell you about it sometime. I'd like to tie things up neatly, eventually: the story of what's happened to us."

Daniel raised his eyebrows. "You're telling me you're putting all that down on *paper*? Are you *crazy*?"

PART TWO

CHAPTER THIRTEEN

Monday, November 21, 2011
CIA headquarters, Langley, Virginia

There was a loud beep from the huge monitor screen mounted on the meeting room wall. *Moshe Peretz, Tel Aviv, calling,* said the on-screen message.

Robert Watson ran his fingers through his white hair and checked his notebook on the desk in front of him. *Johnson/VANDAL,* he had written at the top.

"Right, let's do this," he said out loud. He pulled his angular frame up straight, pushed back his shoulders, and tapped his fingers on the table.

A new high-security video conferencing system had been installed in Watson's dedicated meeting room the previous week, and he still hadn't found time to go through the full thirty-minute online training module on how to operate it. He pressed the green button to accept the call as his secretary, Helen, had instructed.

The face of a thick-set man with a clipped gray beard

appeared on the main part of the screen, while a smaller window showing Watson popped up in the bottom right-hand corner.

"Ah, Robert, *shalom*," Peretz said. "It's been quite a while. Good to speak to you."

"Yes, quite a while," Watson replied. "*Shalom* to you, too."

"I saw your e-mail," Peretz said. "So, about our man VANDAL. You think this Joe Johnson guy might threaten the status quo?"

Before Watson could answer, the sound system emitted three beeps and went silent. He could see Peretz speaking on the screen but couldn't hear him.

Irritated, Watson picked up the remote control and tried to regain the sound. But nothing worked.

Watson threw the remote on the table and sighed. "Useless . . . Moshe, I don't know if you can hear me, but the sound's gone at this end. We've got a new system here, and I'm still getting used to it. Give me one minute, I'll just get someone to sort this out." Then he limped over to the door and called out. "Helen, I've lost sound. Can you look at it for me? Sorry, I need to do that training module."

The limp was a legacy of a gun battle in late 2001 at Tora Bora, in the caves of eastern Afghanistan, when Watson had damaged a knee ligament while working as part of a CIA National Clandestine Service team that unsuccessfully hunted for Osama bin Laden.

His secretary turned around, a half smile on her face, and walked across to the meeting room. "Did you lock it? You need to do that on this new system to confirm you recognize the other party and that the call's secure. Otherwise it assumes there's an unrecognized caller at the other end and shuts the mike off after a few seconds."

Watson shook his head. "Okay, thanks. Things used to be so much simpler. What's wrong with a phone call?"

Watson said. "We waste far too much time fiddling with technology."

He didn't add that, in any case, the conversation with Peretz was one he really didn't want to go through with. Not now, after so long.

Helen quickly adjusted the sound settings with the remote and handed it to Watson. "There you go, boss. Yes, you should do the module. It's straightforward enough—you won't need me then. Off you go." She flicked back her long red hair and walked toward the door.

"Are we okay again?" Peretz asked.

"Yes, sorry about that," Watson said.

"Okay, Joe Johnson and VANDAL. So you think Johnson might be a threat, and—"

Watson interrupted. "Stop there, Moshe. Just wait." He watched Helen until the door closed behind her. Now his level of irritation had heightened further—partly because of the technology hiccup but also because the Israeli wasn't sticking to protocol.

"You can continue now. The room is clear," Watson said.

"Sorry. Is Johnson a threat to VANDAL?" the Israeli said.

"Yes, he will be if he makes any headway," Watson said. "It's early. All we know is, he's just started on a trail that might not lead him anywhere."

Peretz paused for a few seconds. "It could be very embarrassing for us if Johnson gets to VANDAL and all the details come out. Personally, for both of us, I mean, as well as organizationally."

Watson knew exactly what he meant. There was no need to verbalize it.

"Let's not jump the gun," Watson said. "If it develops, we can sort it out here, don't worry, but I'm under orders to let you know. My plan is to monitor the situation. If Johnson's inquiry fizzles out, as I expect it might well do, we can let things lie. I do have an agent in Buenos Aires, Agustin Torres, whom I will brief and bring into the picture if required, although I think that unlikely. Agustin would be able to take care of VANDAL—and take care of Johnson, too, in a different sense of the word."

Watson watched Peretz's reaction carefully on the monitor screen, but his face remained inscrutable.

"So, the big question is, how much more is VANDAL still worth to the Mossad?" Peretz asked.

"I don't know. There can't be much left."

"Yes, that's my thought. Thing is, you do realize how big an exception to the rule this situation has been? Normally the Mossad would have finished it a long, long time ago. For us, it's been purely about the money—as we both know very well. If there's no more upside, the bosses upstairs here might want to cut and run. Don't expect any sentiment from them toward VANDAL," Peretz said.

Watson felt his chest tighten. That was the difference between Langley and Tel Aviv.

"You can damn well tell them I've personally gone to a huge amount of trouble to make sure it's been a problem-free arrangement," Watson said. "America's had no benefit from VANDAL at all since the '60s; you've had it all. But maybe stupidly, there's still an obligation felt here, at high levels in the Agency, toward the old bastard. He did a lot to help us back then, with all the Russian intelligence material. So we should be allowed to handle him now. You've got to respect that. Honor among thieves."

Peretz gave a thin smile. The Israeli had clearly caught Watson's ironic humor. They didn't need to make any direct reference to the benefits both of them had personally received over the years from maintaining the status quo, as Peretz termed it.

But for Watson, it wasn't *solely* about the money, and he was certain Peretz knew it.

"All right, calm down. You honor me, I'll honor you," Peretz said. "I'm just warning you about the way it might go. You know what senior management are like here with assets who are no longer of use to them. It's a mercenary approach, unlike with you guys. Okay, let's speak again soon. Keep in touch."

"Right, let's do that. Have a nice day," Watson said as he ended the call. He threw up his hands and slumped back in his chair.

"Damn kikes," he said out loud. He sat there for about ten minutes, thinking through his options and tapping the table with his fingers.

I'd better give Miami a call, he thought.

* * *

Portland, Maine

It was always difficult to explain to Peter and Carrie why he was going away, even now that they were older. Johnson found it was an automatic cue for excessively puzzled looks and dramatic resigned expressions.

He had already told them, but now with only an hour to go before the taxi arrived, he was bracing himself for a repeat performance over breakfast. He thought momentarily about not bothering, of e-mailing Fiona and telling her it was off.

As soon as he had mentioned the trip, Peter had stared at him for several seconds. "You do realize you're gonna miss my basketball game on Thursday?"

Johnson mumbled an apology. Peter had become the starting point guard for his school team six months earlier, after a huge improvement in his ball-handling and passing skills.

Peter ignored his father's attempt to rationalize his absence. "What time's Aunt Amy going to be here?"

"Soon after I'm gone," Johnson said. "I know it's not ideal, but it's going to happen occasionally with the type of work I do, as you know. Look, I'd rather be here with both of you, but I've got to earn some money—and I've got to do something I enjoy doing as well. It's important, as you'll learn when you're older."

"Don't worry, we'll be fine," Peter said, although his frown indicated otherwise.

Carrie, as always, then launched into a barrage of questions. Who, what, how, where, why? *She'll be a journalist or a lawyer someday*, Johnson thought.

Johnson began his well-rehearsed explanation, but then he switched gears.

"Carrie, I'm on a mission. It's important to me," Johnson said, correctly anticipating that was language she would understand.

"Okay, I get it," she said, turning back to her cornflakes.

His phone beeped. The taxi was outside. Johnson picked up his bags and hugged his kids goodbye. "Amy should be here in about twenty minutes," he said. "Just make sure you treat her well, okay?"

In the cab, he checked his e-mails on his phone. There was one from Fiona.

Hi Joe, sorry, I just remembered I didn't send you this. See attached. I recorded the short conversation I had with Nathaniel in the bar in Washington. Am sending you the MP3 voice file. Have a listen. Might help. And yes, my boss has agreed upon your daily rate.

Thanks, F

Just as well the rate was agreed, Johnson thought, given that he was already en route. He tried to download the attachment, but the 3G data connection was too slow, and it wouldn't load.

Johnson shrugged his shoulders and removed his spiral-bound black notebook and a black pen from the small black backpack containing his encrypted laptop and other essential items for the flight.

The good thing was that Jayne had confirmed her willingness to help him out—and was looking forward to seeing him again after so long. Indeed, he had just that morning sent a small package to her in London by secure courier.

Johnson had a novel to read on the flight: Daniel Silva's spy thriller, *The Rembrandt Affair*, which he'd been meaning to start for two months. And what about a film? He picked up his iPad and started flicking through his movies.

He settled on *Tinker, Tailor, Soldier, Spy*. "In the bleak days of the Cold War, espionage veteran George Smiley is forced from semi-retirement to uncover a Soviet agent within MI6." Yes, that was the one—summed it all up. And he had loved the John le Carré spy novels when he read them years ago.

He put the iPad back into his bag as the taxi driver pulled up outside departures.

This was it. Back in action again. Back in from the cold, as Smiley would say.

CHAPTER FOURTEEN

Monday, November 21, 2011
Buenos Aires

"Sorry, baby, I can't take you on an aircraft," Ignacio said quietly, "as much as I'd like to. Might not go down too well with security."

"What's that?" called the woman from his bedroom, where he had left her lying naked on his futon, smoking a joint. "Come back in here. I'm feeling *so* horny. Who are you talking to?"

"No one, Lucia, just talking to myself."

He put the Glock 9 mm semiautomatic pistol carefully back on the rough plywood shelf in his living room, next to a photograph of his two children and another of his mother.

Ignacio, wearing the only smart shirt he owned, walked back into the bedroom and took the joint from his girlfriend, who was trying to do some stretching exercises as she smoked it.

He took a drag and then extinguished it, placing it in an

ashtray on a plastic crate that served as a bedside table. She squealed as he rolled on top of her and grabbed her wrists, pinning her to the futon.

"Sorry, I'd like to, but I'd better go. I've got dinner with the pig, sorry, my father, in half an hour. That'll be a first. Don't think he's ever bought me dinner before," Ignacio said. He stood up. "I'll see you later."

Twenty-five minutes later, Ignacio arrived at the Hotel Panamericano, on 9 de Julio Avenue. It was one of the city's landmark buildings. Ignacio could remember the huge cranes dominating the skyline as it was being built in the early 1980s, when he was in his late teens and went out drinking in the bars and clubs nearby.

Ignacio sat on a sofa in the lobby and stared through the window, which was splattered with raindrops from a summer storm outside.

It would be his second face-to-face encounter with his father in two weeks. What *did* the old bastard want? Clearly he was up to something. Well, he wasn't the only one. Would he apologize? Unlikely. Ignacio laughed to himself.

His feelings for his father were almost always very negative, but somewhere, deep inside . . . well, the guy was still his father. No matter how hard Ignacio tried to wipe away the deep-rooted desire for reconciliation, it occasionally bubbled uncontrollably to the surface, like trapped gases through hot spa waters, leaving him a little confused.

There was emotional difficulty involved in sitting and actually conversing with his father. But the food? That was something altogether less complicated.

Ignacio asked for a copy of the menu, and by the time his father arrived, he had already decided. If his father was paying, he was going to take full advantage.

When the old man did show up a few minutes later, raindrops were splattered over his thin summer coat.

He limped across the white and black patterned marble floor in the lobby and nodded at Ignacio. "You made it. That's a start."

In the hotel's Tomo restaurant, with its luxurious padded walls, drapes, and discreet lighting, a waitress took them to a quiet table for two in a corner.

José ordered a bottle of 2005 Bodega Catena Zapata, a malbec, and then proceeded to make small talk, almost without pausing, about the issues at each of his stores scattered across the city: poor stock records, shoplifting, alcoholic managers, the new IT system.

He therefore made painfully slow progress with his main course and was only halfway through his trout in lemon cream by the time Ignacio finished his Patagonian lamb gigo medallions.

Ignacio put down his knife and fork, folded his arms, and watched his father. He would slowly lift his fork to his mouth, take a bite, and chew. Then he would talk for a couple of minutes before repeating the whole process again and again. Ignacio pressed his lips tightly together.

The restaurant was filling up. Two middle-aged women, one in a black dress, the other in red, both wearing gold necklaces, sat at the table nearest to them. A pair of younger couples, all sophisticated jokes and designer labels, worked their way through French champagne at another table.

Eventually Ignacio said, "So, padre, what are we here for? What do you want to talk about? Is it more of the same?" He picked up a piece of bread and began chewing it.

The old man put his fork down. "Are you going to stick it out—working in the business, I mean?"

Ignacio shrugged. "I've got to do something, though I'm not here for the money, exactly."

"Look, I need to be up front with you. I've got a problem," José said.

Ignacio swallowed the bread and sat back, staring at his father.

The old man flagged down a passing waiter and ordered another bottle of malbec. Then he peered over his glasses across the table. "The thing is, it might put the business at risk. I was told this morning that someone's investigating one of our gold suppliers, Oro Centro. They sell us gold for our factories and have done so for a long time. And Oro Centro gets its gold from a sort of sister company in London."

He took his glasses off. "What I don't want is for this *particular* investigator to probe too much into the supply company, into what they sell us, and then into our business."

Ignacio thought quickly. Should he continue pretending he didn't know much about the inner workings of his father's business? He couldn't admit to secretly trawling through the accounts and reports, so he didn't have much of an option.

"Right, but you're going to have to explain. How does it affect us? And who's behind the London company?" Ignacio asked.

The older Guzmann tapped the table with his fingers and pressed his lips, hesitating. "It's because I don't want this investigator, name of Joe Johnson, finding out about my involvement. It could screw us up. It's about stuff in the past. If it were fifteen or twenty years ago, I would have sorted it out myself, you know what I mean? Now I obviously can't do that."

Ignacio struggled to contain himself. "Stuff from the past?" His father obviously didn't mean the dark cupboards and the beatings.

His father ignored the question and looked down. "I don't exactly know who the people are behind the gold supplier. I've been trying for years, off and on, to find out but never have. But they know things, somehow. If they tell this Johnson guy and he goes public, it would finish me off, destroy my reputation. Our customers would vanish, and that would be the end of the business. That's not in your interests, is it?"

So, it *was* just about the money. He wasn't going to apologize.

"I'm not always sure your interests are the same as mine," Ignacio said, trying to keep the edge out of his voice. He reclined in his chair. "Just tell me, what are you suggesting I do, then?"

"I need you to sort out this investigator before he does any damage."

Ignacio raised his eyebrows. "You *what*?"

His father bent toward him. "Take him out," he hissed. "Is that clear enough? Someone's got to."

Ignacio could see the dark-haired woman in the black dress looking at them out of the corner of her eye.

José lowered his voice to a whisper. "Johnson used to work for the CIA and also investigated former Nazis in the U.S. I've got a photo my contacts e-mailed to me. He apparently lives in Maine, but he's going to London soon as part of his investigation. I've been told he's going to focus on our gold supplier. You need to get over there. I'll give you the details of the London supply business. Johnson's also working with a political journalist in the U.S. named Fiona Heppenstall. I've also got a photo of her, which I'll send to you."

Ignacio sipped his wine. He wasn't going to tell his father he already had his own trip to London planned or that two of his guys were already there. And he definitely wasn't going to tell him about the other damage-limitation measures he had already taken.

"I don't know," Ignacio said. "Don't you think taking someone out, as you put it, especially in London, might carry the odd risk or two? Just saying."

His father's face was taking on a red hue. "That all

depends on whether you think seeing this business disappear into the sewer is more of a risk to you."

A waiter arrived with their desserts.

"Hmm, but the business is losing money. You said so your-self. I'm going to be away for the next few days, just taking a break. I'll think about it. I do have some contacts in London who might help. I'll speak with them and let you know."

Ignacio and his father carried on eating in silence. There seemed little else to talk about. An image of Lucia on the futon flashed through his mind.

So what should he do? Halt the crazy gold-purchasing arrangements his father had in place? Yes. Work out where the gold was coming from? Yes. Was it legal? Could he take advantage if not? Questions, questions.

Ignacio knew the old man was right about some things, even if he hated him.

If this guy Joe Johnson was threatening to destroy his old man's reputation in the short term, that could finally sink the already struggling business. Not what Ignacio wanted right now.

As they stood up to leave the restaurant, Ignacio had a thought and turned toward his father. "Before we go, one other question. This gold supplier, what's their story? Do they buy the gold they sell to us from a private source? Or off the market? Where do they get it from?"

José averted his gaze before replying. "I'm not sure. Perhaps you can find that out, too."

Ignacio looked down at his feet and sighed. Getting a straight answer from his father had always been too much to hope for.

The waitress brought their coats. Ignacio briefly thought about helping the old man with his, but then left him to it.

* * *

Ignacio arrived back at Barrio 31 earlier than he expected. But he found he couldn't get into his shack immediately because police were breaking up a mass gang fight in the road outside, so he waited some distance down the road until it was cleared.

Once inside, he sat down on the wooden chair in his bedroom and relit the remains of the joint that Lucia had been smoking earlier in the day. She had gone off to work at a nearby bar.

The trip to London had taken on another dimension. What to do?

He checked his watch. It was now quarter to eleven. He shrugged, then dialed a number on his phone. It rang for about twenty seconds before Diego answered.

"Hello, Diego, just calling to update you, *amigo*. I'm taking a flight tomorrow night. I'll be there on Thursday."

There was silence at the other end.

"It's the middle of the night here," Diego said eventually. "I was asleep. Look, forget it. We're making progress. We've pulled a guy in who works for the car-parts company."

Ignacio took a deep drag from the joint and rolled his head from side to side. "Go on."

"We caught him after work in a bar. Bought him a few beers, got him hammered, and offered him a lift home. We've had him here for three days."

"Three days? You're joking?" Ignacio put his hand to his forehead. "I told you, there's no rush. The police will be all over it."

"Nah, it's fine. They'll never find us here, and he doesn't know where he is."

Ignacio shook his head. He took another long drag from his joint. "So what *has* he told you, exactly?"

"Not much yet, but we're working on it. Hopefully by tomorrow."

"Okay, but go easy. It's London, remember, not Lima. Any luck with the weapons?"

"No, not yet. I'll tell you when we do." There was a loud beep on the line, followed by a silence and a couple more beeps.

"Diego, you still there?" Ignacio said. "Hello? Hello? There's one really crucial thing I need to . . . " But Diego was gone.

CHAPTER FIFTEEN

Tuesday, November 22, 2011
London

Johnson paced up and down his room at London's Tower Hotel, kicking the carpet as he went. Jacob seemed to have vanished off the planet.

After a lot of digging, he'd managed to turn up traces of the man—up to a point. Johnson found clear references on various databases to a Jacob Kudrow in the United Kingdom from 1948 to 1971 at three different addresses.

In fact, there were either census or electoral roll records for all of those years. It was definitely him, because there was only one Jacob Kudrow, and there was a Daniel Kudrow listed at the same address in Whitechapel, East London, in 1948 and 1952. Perhaps that was when Daniel moved to the United States.

The last address, from 1966 onward, was in Hay's Mews, Mayfair.

"Hmm, Mayfair. Must have been doing all right for

himself by 1966 to buy that," Johnson said to himself. He made a note of the address listed.

But after 1971? Nothing.

He must have moved. But where to?

Marriage records? Nothing.

What if Jacob had changed his name? And if so, why would he belatedly do that in 1971?

Johnson walked over to his laptop on the table and closed it. Then he called room service and ordered a double espresso. The lack of sleep on the overnight flight had left him feeling somewhat foggy, and he needed something stronger than what the capsule coffee machine on the table was going to give him.

Room 532 at the Tower Hotel was a typically smart but bland four-star room in a bland four-star hotel. A businessman's hotel. Neat, symmetrical, modern. Johnson sighed. At least the place was near Jayne's flat.

But if he didn't have a five-star place to stay, at least he had a fifth floor, five-star view overlooking the River Thames and Tower Bridge.

When Johnson had landed at Heathrow Airport earlier that morning, he had been greeted by the sun shining from a sky punctuated with only a few fluffy white clouds.

Now a dense bank of dark gray clouds was rapidly covering the capital from the east. The wind was increasing in velocity by the minute, and a few snowflakes were starting to whistle past the hotel window.

There was a knock at the door. Room service had wasted no time in bringing up the coffee.

Johnson settled at the table next to the window and drank it, then sat thinking and scribbling occasionally in his notebook.

He picked up the complimentary copy of *The Daily Telegraph* that had been left on the table. The main headlines were all about President Obama's imminent visit to the U.K. to see Prime Minister David Cameron, the Queen, and a string of other key people. *That will be a real circus,* Johnson thought.

Then he pulled on his coat and took a few ten- and twenty-pound bills out of his bag and stuffed them into his wallet, removing the dollar bills. He also put his main cell phone and a spare phone in his pocket. The second one was for use with pay-as-you-go SIM cards, for security purposes as needed.

As an afterthought, he also took a scarf and a dark gray wool hat from his suitcase.

By then, the combination of caffeine and a new feeling of intent had left him somewhat perkier. He headed out the door.

* * *

Buenos Aires

Ignacio was in his neighbor's house in Barrio 31, negotiating a protection deal for his own property for the period he expected to be in London, when his phone rang.

"Hey, *jefe*, it's Diego. Some good news. My old Argentine army buddy, who lives south of London, has come up with the goods. He brought in three Browning HPs for us. A good piece of kit. They'll do the job."

"Okay, at least something's going right—more than it is here. I'm just trying to make some arrangements to stop my house from being firebombed while I'm away. It's not going well. Also, we've got another problem. I was about to tell you last night, but then we damn well got cut off. The thing is, there's somebody else on the chase—actually, two people."

Ignacio went on to tell Diego about his conversation with his father and the potential threat that Joe Johnson posed to their plans.

"This guy Johnson's gone to London already. He's staying at the Tower Hotel, near Tower Bridge. I got his number from his website, phoned, and pretended to be a possible client. His daughter told me where he was. Easy, very easy. He also has this woman journalist he's working with, a Fiona Heppenstall. I don't know whether she's in the U.K. or not. But I'm going to e-mail you photos of them. It's Johnson we need to target, mainly."

Ignacio took a breath. "We need to give him an opening shot, a warning, and if that doesn't work, we'll up the ante. Now here's what I want you to do."

He spent several minutes reeling off a series of instructions before ending the call.

CHAPTER SIXTEEN

Tuesday, November 22, 2011
London

By the time Johnson had completed the ten-minute walk to Tower Hill underground station, followed by a short train ride to Blackfriars, the unseasonably early snow had become heavier. As he emerged into the open air again, the wind was whipping it into flurries around his ankles.

He walked across the road, down Tudor Street, and through an ancient archway into the legal quarter—the Inns of Court—marked by a mixture of quaint brick and stone buildings, small courtyards, arches, and gardens.

Not far to go now. He knew it was a slightly circuitous route to his destination, but he liked this particular area of London.

Johnson passed Temple Church on his right and finally emerged at The Strand, a busy artery packed with buses, taxis, and cars, running parallel to the Thames. Snow formed a coating across his shoulders and the top of his hat.

His destination lay right in front of him across the zebra crossing: the tall Gothic stone arches and edifices of the Royal Courts of Justice.

Johnson went through the old lobby area, with its battered, characterful wooden swing doors, and joined a short line to put his coat, jacket, and small backpack through the security machine.

He felt dwarfed inside the cavernous Great Hall, which formed the main common area of the courts, with its decorative patterned stone floor and high vaulted windows.

It was full of people sheltering from the weather, shivering like him as they brushed snow off their bags and coats.

After checking at the information desk, Johnson made his way up a tangle of old stone staircases and through dark corridors that smelled of cleaning fluid and floor polish to Room E15.

A red-haired lady with black-rimmed glasses sat behind a plastic screen. Behind her were dusty bookshelves, a cluster of desks piled high with papers and books, and computers.

Johnson approached the woman and stood before her. She clearly wasn't going to acknowledge him.

He coughed. "Excuse me, I'm trying to find a record of someone's change of name by deed poll, probably in the 1970s."

The woman finally peered over her glasses at him. "Sorry, can't help. We only keep records for the past five years here, and you can't view those; they're confidential. The summary of any name changes is published in *The London Gazette*, You can see them there. We don't have them."

She shifted back to her computer screen, so abrupt in manner that Johnson, disconcerted, turned and made for the doorway.

As he did, he heard her voice again behind him. "If it's an old record, 1970s, you need the National Archives at Kew, down in Richmond. Take the District Line to Kew Gardens. They'll help you look. They have the detail that goes into the *London Gazette*. But you're likely to be wasting your time."

"Why is that?"

"Well, only about 5 percent of those who change their names have the details enrolled. It's not required. Good luck." She turned away once more.

Johnson ambled back to the Great Hall. He felt very tired again.

He realized he hadn't let his sister or children know he had arrived safely in London. He sat down on one of the red padded stone benches lining either side of the imposing hall and took out his cell phone.

His daughter answered.

"Hi, Carrie, it's Dad. I'm safely in London now, so I thought I'd call and let you all know. Why haven't you gone to school yet?"

"I wasn't feeling well this morning, so Aunt Amy said I should stay home. I'll be okay."

"All right. Make sure you have some soup for lunch if you're not feeling well, okay? Just in case," Johnson said.

"Yeah, I've already told Aunt Amy that's what I'd like. So relax, Dad. Oh, and by the way, someone called for you here last night, after you'd gone. He said he might have some work for you. I told him you'd gone to London so you might not be easy to contact, but he said he was also going there and wanted to know which hotel you were staying at. I gave him the details and also your e-mail address and phone number. Is that all right? It was a foreign-sounding guy. He had a Spanish accent."

Johnson snapped upright. "A Spanish accent? Are you sure? Did he leave his name?"

"Yes, definitely Spanish, the same as my teacher at school.

He didn't give his name. I did ask, but he refused to give it. He just said he would contact you."

"Can you check the number he called from? It should be on the phone."

There was a pause as his daughter checked. "Yep, it's international—54 11 5843 1119." Johnson wrote it down.

Fifty-four was the international code for Argentina, Johnson knew. So who could the caller have been?

"Dad, Dad? Are you listening? Earth calling . . . I'm talking to you . . ."

Johnson could hear Cocoa barking somewhere in the background, but he was too preoccupied to ask whether the poor dog was getting enough exercise in his master's absence.

"Sorry, darling. Listen, I've got to go. Remember what I've told you before. If people call asking where I am, it's best just to take their number and tell them I'll call them back. Then send me the number. Don't tell them where I am, okay?"

"Okay, Dad. Sorry, I knew that. I just forgot."

"It's okay. And tell Amy and Peter I called, and I hope you feel better soon. I'll call again tomorrow. Bye then, Carrie. I love you."

"Love you too, Dad."

He ended the call.

As he did, he remembered that today would have been his wife Kathy's fifty-third birthday, had she still been alive. He sat and stared up at the high dusty vaulted windows.

They had met at Boston University, where Kathy had majored in English Literature, and Johnson, two months her senior, had majored in history. But they had only gotten together in their thirties when both ended up working in Washington, D.C.—Johnson with the OSI and Kathy as an editor for a large magazine publisher.

He quickly had a conviction that she was his soul mate and they were married on July 16, 1994. So to lose her in

October 2005, at the age of forty-six, when Carrie was just nine and Peter only seven, had knocked him off his feet.

Johnson stood. He couldn't dwell on all that because he knew if he did, the complex cocktail of chemicals inside him that governed his mood and state of mind, would quickly turn his world black, making it difficult, sometimes impossible, to focus on the task at hand, as it had done in the couple of years following Kathy's death.

He needed to get moving and concentrate on something different, something more positive.

* * *

Exiting the National Archives at Kew, Johnson shook his head. After hours of searching through several large bound books containing a myriad of different deeds covering 1971 to 1980, he had found nothing.

He wandered into a small shop nearby to buy a chocolate bar and three pay-as-you-go SIM cards for his second cell phone. He handed them to the man behind the counter; then as he sometimes did when feeling stressed, he had a sudden urge.

"Anything else?" the shopkeeper asked.

"Uh, yes, twenty Marlboro Reds please, and a lighter."

The National Archives had seemed like a last throw of the dice to Johnson. He unwrapped the pack of cigarettes, lit one, and wandered down the road. He felt as though he badly needed a smoke.

What next? He was starting to feel more like a genealogist than a war crimes investigator.

On the underground train returning to Tower Hill he thought of his conversations with Nathaniel and Fiona. Was there anything else either of them had said that might help?

He was well aware he hadn't yet downloaded the MP3

voice file Fiona had sent him of her conversation with Nathaniel in the Washington bar. That might contain some useful material.

Johnson jumped off the underground at the next stop, South Kensington, and found a coffee shop outside the station entrance.

After ordering a latte and pastry, he slotted the first of the SIM cards into his spare cell phone.

Then he logged his main phone on to the shop's Wi-Fi, plugged in his earphones, and downloaded the file from Fiona's e-mail. He began to listen.

"We're off the record again, right?"
"Yes, absolutely."

Johnson recognized Nathaniel and Fiona's voices immediately. Nathaniel continued.

"Okay, good. There are a few things I didn't mention earlier today. It's regarding the source of much of the funding for David's campaign. I believe it's coming from less than straightforward sources and could even be illegal. You'll probably say I'm not close to the business, and that's true. But I've been to London recently to visit my uncle, and I discovered a few things that I probably wasn't meant to."

"Forgive me for being a little cynical, Nathaniel, but why are you telling me this? It's family, right?"

"Correct. But they don't see it that way. I'm not one of them, those high achievers, movers and shakers. I get marginalized, not favored. David's different; he gets the treatment. An easy life. You go and work it out. Follow the money trail—where it comes from and where it goes—and you'll get to the bottom of it."

"Sorry, you're talking in riddles. The money trail—what do you mean?"

"I mean the Nazi connection."

"Come on, what's this all about? I think it's time for a bit of straight talking . . . Is it Nazi money, then?"

"Nazi money? You could say it's something like that. You're a top journalist. As I said, you'll work it out. I've got to go. Said too much already."

There was silence for a few seconds, then Nathaniel continued.

"By the way, it's all going to be in his book. Jacob's writing a memoir —in his little red book. He wants it to be published when he's dead and buried, although I suspect that's going to be a while yet. Go and find him in London. He'll tell you. He'll be in his dilapidated old workshop or at the synagogue. I've got to go now. I'll speak to you soon."

There was a rustling, and the recording ended.

Johnson took his notebook and pen out of his backpack, pushed the slider back to the start of the recording, and listened again—and then again, writing in his notebook as he did so.

He sighed. *A dilapidated old workshop or a synagogue.* Yes, but where? How many old workshops and synagogues were there in London?

CHAPTER SEVENTEEN

Wednesday, November 23, 2011
London

Jayne Robinson propped her elbows on the table and rested her chin on her palms.

The face was a little more lined but the look was still just as combative, Johnson thought. The whiskey-low voice that used to turn him inside out hadn't changed, either.

After several exchanges of text messages, Johnson had arranged to meet Jayne for breakfast at her favorite haunt—the Dickens Inn, in St. Katharine Docks, near his hotel and only ten minutes' walk from her apartment in Whitechapel. She was so busy at work, she said, that was the only slot left in her schedule.

The Dickens Inn was built around a centuries-old timber frame with balconies overlooking the marina and its array of yachts.

At a wooden table in a discreet corner of the bar, Johnson

outlined between mouthfuls of scrambled eggs why he had come to London.

Jayne nodded. "You've always liked to be a righter of wrongs, haven't you? That's good, I guess. You need a reason to keep going."

"It's something different," Johnson said, "Something that might be big. Unlike my usual workload."

"That's what I'm missing myself right now," Jayne said. "This Nazi thing sounds interesting, if it stacks up. Maybe a big if."

She thought for a moment. "So the guy who was stabbed, Nathaniel—was he kosher, so to speak? Or were you being had?"

"I don't know. I think he was kosher," Johnson said. "That's what I need to check out. And was it a coincidence that he was killed after talking to Fiona and me? Seems unlikely. If the Kudrows are involved with dirty money, then it's a big story. But it's the Guzmann angle that gets me, the Buenos Aires jewelry business. I had a note to investigate there years ago when I was chasing an SS guy, but I never did. Now I'm wondering if he could still lead me somewhere. Problem now is, the twin over here, Jacob Kudrow, seems to have vanished. I've got to find him before I can do anything. I was thinking you might be able to help with that. Maybe in Argentina, too, if needed, as you know it so well."

Jayne's face was doubtful as she spread honey on her toast.

"Maybe." She took a bite. "I'd love to get back to Argentina. But it's a bit tricky for us, getting involved in an off-the-books inquiry as a sideline. It's potentially sackable at SIS. You must know that."

She brushed back her short dark hair from her forehead. "I'll have to go through the correct channels and speak to my boss. He might be sympathetic. He spent a lot of time hunting down war criminals in the Balkans after the war there a few years ago. We both did, after our stint tackling the IRA in Belfast finished. SIS sent us out to the old Yugoslavia, mainly in Croatia and Bosnia, and we worked there together in the early 2000s until both our covers got blown. It was a big job for us back then."

"So you think he might give you some time?" Johnson asked.

"Maybe. If it's just a case of some Polish Jews doing something illegal, well, that's not an SIS job, it's one for police. If it's serious crime, it could be one for MI5. But if it's a Nazi project . . . hmm . . . he might bite as long as it's not too time consuming."

"Okay, thanks. Don't do anything that'll get you in trouble, though. Anyway, how are things? How's life?" Johnson asked.

Jayne sighed. "I've been a bit down in recent months. Don't tell anyone, but I'm seriously thinking of packing it in. I used to enjoy it out in the field when I was more junior. Places like Buenos Aires, Belfast, the old Yugoslavia, and so on. But now I'm nearly fifty, I'm back in the U.K., in management, and I just feel like a cog in a big Vauxhall Cross machine."

She was referring to the MI6 headquarters building at Vauxhall Cross, on the south bank of the River Thames, three quarters of a mile up river from the Houses of Parliament in Westminster.

"We're kowtowing to you Americans half the time rather than doing our own thing," Jayne said. "I tell you, top brass are terrified of the senior guys at Langley. I've got no ties, no kids. I could just take off and do something completely different."

"I thought you were a lifer there?" Johnson said, surprised. Jayne, who had grown up in Nottingham, had joined the Secret Intelligence Service after graduating from Cambridge

University, where she had studied international politics, and had acted in a variety of roles thereafter, both in the U.K. and overseas.

"Not anymore. It's different. All the cost cutting's taking its toll," Jayne said. "But you don't want to hear about that. Back to your problem. I think you might have to do something old-fashioned. Go and wear out some shoe leather. The Kudrows were originally Polish Jewish, right? Why don't you go and try the synagogues. There used to be a huge Polish Jew community in the East End of London, in this area where we are, Whitechapel, and the area around here. There's still a lot of them there. Someone might have heard of him. They're a tight-knit bunch."

Johnson sat upright. She always thought of an angle. "You're right. I'll try that." He made a note of what she'd said in his notebook, then beckoned the waiter and ordered two more cappuccinos.

Jayne reached into her bag and, like a conjurer with a top hat, withdrew a small package which she placed on the table next to Johnson's glass of orange juice.

"There you go," she said. "Your new legend, I assume."

Johnson picked it up. It was the package he had sent by courier to her a few days earlier. "Thanks," he said. "It's not a new one—it's an old, well-trusted legend. I'll need that later this morning."

He sipped his juice. "So are you still shooting? You were sharp," he said.

"Well, you weren't too bad yourself—though I think I took the money off you, usually. Yes, I still do a bit. Usually the rifle range with a friend, but just air pistols." She shrugged. "It's just an excuse for a drink afterward. We grumble about work, put the world to rights."

"Yes, don't go rusty. I might need you. Speaking of which, do you have a gun at home?"

"No, I don't," Jayne said. "And I can't get one, so don't ask. I haven't used one in a work situation since I was in Sarajevo. What about you?"

Johnson took a breath. "You know me, always tended to be more of an intelligence gatherer than an—"

"Action man?"

"Though sometimes needs must when the devil drives," Johnson said. "Difficult to separate the two in this job."

"I seem to remember you swearing you'd never use a gun in anger again after that incident in Jalalabad."

Johnson raised an eyebrow. Nobody was going to let him forget. First his mother, now Jayne.

"Thanks for reminding me," he said. "I haven't—there's been no increase in the body count since, although there's been a few close calls. I do try and keep my hand in, though. I've got a couple of friends who shoot, so we go out and put some targets on trees. I've got a Smith & Wesson revolver at home."

Jayne gestured to his right ear. "You never did get that injury fixed. I thought you were going to have it sorted out?"

"Yes, I was, but I didn't like the idea of admitting I'd had plastic surgery. It's part of me now, a talking point." He smiled. "Anyway, enough of that. There's a few other things I want to run past you."

Johnson checked that his and Jayne's phone encryption software were compatible. They were. He didn't want to take any unnecessary risks.

"And what about if I need some other bits and pieces? Bugs, surveillance gear?" he asked.

"Might be able to do something. I've got a box of toys under the bed at home." She raised her eyebrows and almost smiled.

"I bet you have," he murmured.

* * *

"If you need a bit of poke, you've got it there, sir. This one's got a twin turbo, so you'll be from a standing start to sixty miles an hour in under six seconds, no problem. You're lucky. We've only got one of those and it's always out, normally. It's often Americans who take it, like yourself, and usually financial types: bankers, brokers. You don't look like one of those. So, Mr.—sorry I've forgotten your name. Was it Wilkinson?"

"Yes, correct, Philip Wilkinson. And you're also correct in thinking I'm not a financial type," Johnson replied.

He couldn't decide which car to opt for. The man at the rental company near Aldgate had offered him either a BMW or an Audi.

He went for the BMW in the end, a black 335i three-liter, six-cylinder model with darkened windows.

Johnson fished in the pocket of his blue linen jacket and removed the contents of the package that Jayne had returned to him earlier. Sending it to her by courier had enabled him to avoid carrying it through customs.

There was a good reason for the maneuver. Johnson had never talked about it, not even with his closest friends, but just after leaving the OSI he had quietly acquired two new legends—completely false identities, including U.S. passports, credit cards, bank cards, driver's licenses and birth certificates—through a contact who was a former police officer. It had felt like being back in the CIA again.

One of the legends was in the name of Philip Wilkinson, the other in the name of Don Thiele. Both carried Johnson's photograph and were linked to addresses of two different uninhabited houses somewhere in the middle of rural New Hampshire.

Johnson didn't ask too many questions about where they had come from. As long as he paid off the credit card bills and the bank accounts stayed in the black, he shouldn't encounter a problem.

He normally deployed the Wilkinson legend when required, keeping the other in reserve. After several years, he had become quite comfortable slipping into his alternative identity—a single man with no dependents who was a sales representative for an American industrial pumps business.

Now, he had a gut feeling that for this job, it would be wise to switch to Philip Wilkinson rather than use his real name for the car rental.

Johnson paid for the car with the Wilkinson credit card and pocketed the receipt and documentation to make sure he remembered to include it in the list of expenses he needed to claim back from Fiona.

He left the rental office and climbed into his car, feeling happy with his choice. The BMW definitely had "poke" and would do the job. After driving it back to the hotel, he left it in the parking lot and headed up in the elevator to his room.

Johnson's only worry was that the car wasn't very inconspicuous.

CHAPTER EIGHTEEN

Wednesday, November 23, 2011
London

Lying on the floor just inside his room when he got back to the Tower Hotel that evening was a white envelope, marked with Johnson's name, that someone had pushed under the door.

He ripped it open with his finger. Inside was a single sheet of paper carrying a handwritten message in blue felt-tip:

> *Mr. Johnson*
> *In your interests, stop the operation you work on now.*
> *There is implication that you do not understand.*
> *And there will be consequence you definitely will not like.*
> *You have been warned.*

Johnson reread it, scratching the old nick at the top of his right ear. The writing was large and bold, probably a man's, and was either the work of an ill-educated person or someone not using their native language. Or was the grammar deliberately poor?

He had received such notes and e-mails several times before in his career. They were almost to be expected.

Johnson remembered the conversation with Carrie.

He was also going there and wanted to know which hotel you were staying at . . .

They had moved more quickly than he thought. It was maybe time for him to move as well, then.

Johnson went downstairs to the hotel restaurant and ate a pizza, together with three beers. He felt as though he needed them.

While he was eating, his phone rang. It was an encrypted call from Vic. Johnson keyed in the requisite code.

"Vic, I'm in London, near Tower Bridge, eating a pizza. What have you got?"

"Tower Bridge, eh? Nice. Better than me—I'm still in the office. Listen, I've picked up something from my network here. You might remember Helen, Watto's secretary: long red hair, good-looking for her age. Been here twenty-five years. Useful to keep in touch with as she knows everyone. She remembers you—thought you were badly treated."

"Yes, I remember her. Nice lady."

"Yes," Vic said, "I had a chat with her last night. She's professional, discreet with everyone, but she's got a conscience, and she does tell me the occasional snippet, especially if she thinks someone's been unfairly treated. She let slip that Watto called her in to sort out some problem with the new video conferencing system during a call. He was talking to a certain intelligence agency in Tel Aviv."

"What about?" Johnson asked.

"Well, there's the thing. She just heard one line of the conversation, and it was about you. The Mossad guy, a regional head called Moshe Peretz, named you. He was asking

Watto whether he thought you might be a threat to VANDAL. That's a cryptonym, of course. It took me a while to find out who it was referring to, but I got there eventually."

Johnson guessed what Vic was going to say next. "VANDAL is Guzmann, right?"

"Correct," said Vic. "But how the hell Peretz and Watson knew you might be looking at Guzmann, I have no idea. That's Langley for you."

Johnson exhaled hard. "That's just unbelievable. Tel Aviv? Is she sure about that?"

"Yep, she's sure. Helen's good. She won't have made a mistake."

Johnson's mind was already in overdrive. "Yes, but hang on, just thinking aloud here. If the Mossad is worried about someone being a threat to Guzmann, there's most likely going to be only one reason why."

"Precisely. He's providing them with something valuable, most likely information, access, contacts—I don't know. Could be anything."

"And what's Guzmann got to do with Watto? That raises the stakes," Johnson asked.

"I don't know—yet. I'll find out. Look, I've gotta go now. I'm in a rush. That's all I know so far. Good luck with it, Doc. I think you just need to remember that Watto's tentacles extend a long way, inside the Agency and outside it. Just be careful. You know what I'm saying?"

Johnson shrugged. "Yes, I know what you're saying."

"Okay. Talk to you again soon."

"Yes, thanks for the call, appreciate it." Johnson hung up.

Once he was back in his room, he made an encrypted call to Jayne.

"Jayne, something's come up." He recounted what had happened with the threat letter and then the call from Vic.

"There's something deep going on," Johnson said. "For Guzmann to have a cryptonym at Langley, and with the Mossad, tells me he's been important to them for some time. Maybe Guzmann's been an agent?"

There was silence at the other end of the line as Jayne digested the information. He could almost hear her thinking and shaking her head, probably silently cursing him.

"It's quite possible, definitely," Jayne said. "I know the Agency and the Mossad were very active in Buenos Aires when I was there, and I'm sure they still are. Okay, then. Given the letter, it might be wise to stay in my spare room, if you like. Come over, and we can discuss it."

As Johnson finished repacking his suitcase, he didn't know if he was being unnecessarily paranoid or just sensible in moving to Jayne's place.

Or maybe, he thought, he really wasn't being very sensible at all in staying with an ex-girlfriend in her small apartment, even if it did have a spare bedroom.

Either way, he wasn't staying at the Tower Hotel any longer. He went down to the lobby and paid his bill.

Johnson didn't need telling that if Langley and Tel Aviv both had an interest in Guzmann there was almost certainly something there worth him pursuing. But that worked both ways; it was also now quite likely they would put Johnson under the microscope, too. They wouldn't allow a potential investigation into a key asset to go unchallenged.

And if Watson was the involved party at the CIA that was not just irritating, but alarming.

The question remained, though: why was Guzmann a key asset? Johnson's regret at not pursuing the man back in 1996 now deepened a few more degrees.

Given all that and the warning note, he decided to step up his own countersurveillance routine, which in recent years had been a habit only at a very basic level.

He scanned the area carefully around to make sure he wasn't being watched or followed, then went outside into the parking lot and put his bags next to the BMW.

Then he did a lap of the parking lot, glancing at all the cars, searched underneath his car, and finally checked the wheel wells, just to be sure.

Once he was as satisfied as he could be, he put the bags in the back of the car, got in, and drove off.

* * *

The dark-clothed figure slouched low in the rear seat of the silver Ford Focus, hidden in the shadows at the back of the Tower Hotel's parking lot, was almost invisible behind the car's blacked-out windows.

Alejandro Garcia took a sip from the dregs of the now-cold coffee he had bought a couple of hours earlier and yawned. He was almost at the point of giving up and going back to base for some sleep.

But then he saw a figure emerge from the rear entrance at around quarter to eleven. He grabbed his military binoculars and focused. It was Johnson, clearly recognizable from his photograph, carrying a black backpack and a small suitcase.

Alejandro watched as Johnson, who was wearing a black jacket, jeans, and black leather lace-up shoes, checked around the parking lot.

Then he returned to the BMW, got down on his hands and knees, looked underneath the car, and checked the wheel wells. Alejandro smiled to himself. Johnson finally put his bags in the car, climbed in, and drove out through the barrier.

Alejandro climbed swiftly into the front seat, started his engine, and followed some distance behind. He was only just in time to see Johnson leave the main road and then pull into the twenty-four-hour Minories public parking garage on the corner of Shorter and Mansell Streets.

Alejandro followed into the parking garage and slid his car into a space on Level Two, one level higher than where Johnson had parked his BMW. Then he walked silently to the concrete pedestrian stairwell and waited until he heard Johnson's footsteps below.

Once the footsteps had faded, Alejandro followed down the stairwell. He eventually emerged from the building at ground level and moved straight into a dark alcove. He searched first right, then left.

The only person in view was a man walking away from the parking garage up the road, wearing a pale-yellow baseball cap, a white hoodie, and jeans, with a small backpack on his back.

Cursing, Alejandro scanned the area. There was nobody else in view. He looked again at the man in the baseball cap, then realized. The clothes might have changed, but the black leather shoes and the backpack hadn't.

Okay, Johnson's a pro, but maybe not quite pro enough, Alejandro thought. He had seen all this before. His stint in the Argentine army's intelligence service had left him well practiced.

Johnson went up the road toward Portsoken Street. Alejandro, clinging closely to the shadows of an overhanging building, followed some distance behind. Johnson then proceeded to take a left turn, followed by another. Then he paused, took his phone out and appeared to make a short call.

Alejandro remained motionless in an alcove of an office building. Johnson finished the call and took yet another left, seemingly heading back in the direction of the parking garage where he had started.

But when Alejandro turned the corner back to the parking garage, Johnson had vanished. Cursing, Alejandro walked almost at jogging pace along the road, checking a couple of narrow alleys to both the right and the left as he went. But there was no sign of the American.

After another ten minutes of scouring the area, Alejandro kicked the ground and decided to give up.

At least he knew where Johnson's car was. He returned to the parking garage and took a few photographs of the black BMW on his phone, then he dialed a number.

"*Hola*, Alejandro here. I've got his car, took a few photographs. He's moved from the hotel, but the bastard gave me the slip. He may have spotted me tailing him, not sure. I'm heading back now."

"You need to take a refresher course, I think," Diego said. "Get your ass back here then, quick as you can."

Alejandro shook his head, got in his car, and drove off.

* * *

They sat at Jayne's small circular wooden dining table and pored over the handwritten note together. After the empty hotel room, a day largely by himself, and then the note, the company felt good to Johnson.

"It looks childish at first glance, but it's got a slightly official manner to it," Jayne said. "The word *operation*, and the way it mentions implication and consequence. I may be wrong, but that's my initial impression. It's the sort of terminology someone like a police officer or a soldier would use."

"Maybe," Johnson said. "I also think it's written by a foreigner, rather than someone who's just badly educated. Someone badly educated probably wouldn't use that kind of vocabulary in any language."

"You look as though you need a whiskey," Jayne said.

"Yes, I do," Johnson said. "Apart from the note, someone tailed me when I left the parking garage to walk here a short while ago. I spotted him and shook him off by cutting down an alley. But it's worrisome."

Jayne pursed her lips. "Good to know you've not forgotten your streetcraft," she said as she got up to fetch the whiskey.

Johnson observed Jayne's flat; it was smaller than he expected. A clean, modern apartment within a block that was maybe ten years old, definitely no more than fifteen.

The spare room had a double bed with a sunny yellow bedspread but no other furniture apart from the fitted wardrobe and a bedside table.

A small balcony off the living room looked out toward Tower Bridge, and there was a galley-style kitchen and a small dining area. A black leather sofa and two matching armchairs stood in the living room.

It was really a flat for one person, with room for occasional visitors. A minimalistic, low-maintenance property. At London house prices, she could probably sell it and swap it for his large house in Portland and still have change left over, Johnson calculated.

The bookcase was crammed with the legacy of Jayne's various overseas postings: travel books, political biographies, military histories, and novels from all over the world, a few of them written in foreign languages. Johnson knew that, like him, Jayne was a natural linguist, fluent in French, Spanish and Russian, and spoke excellent German and Serbo-Croat.

Jayne returned with a glass of single malt and put the bottle down on the table next to Johnson.

"Have you had this flat swept recently?" Johnson said. It had crossed his mind that Jayne's paymasters might well be checking her place. He didn't want his discussions fed back to Vauxhall Cross, Langley, Tel Aviv, or anywhere, for that matter.

"Had someone in privately to do it twice in the past year.

Found nothing," Jayne said. "So, what about this Mossad connection?"

She was clearly unconcerned.

"I don't know," Johnson said. "It doesn't add up—"

Jayne interrupted. "No, it doesn't add up. My thoughts exactly. I know a bit about the Mossad, and given their track record, they would have taken this Guzmann guy out years ago, decades ago, if he'd done anything Israel didn't like, for sure. Or alternatively, if he wasn't of any use to them anymore. End of story."

Johnson took out his phone and checked his e-mails. There was, at last, a reply from his former OSI colleague Ben at the HRSP. He opened it swiftly.

Nothing positive for you, Joe, unfortunately. There's no record at all of a José Guzmann in the SS files—no hits. Sorry. Van Stalheim's file is there, but we never traced him, and he vanished after that inquiry you worked on back in '96. He's probably dead. Keep in touch. Happy to help on these things occasionally. Ben.

Johnson closed the e-mail, then collapsed back in the chair and sighed. He could see this one was going to require some persistence.

CHAPTER NINETEEN

Thursday, November 24, 2011
London

"Better look out around here. Keep your wallet hidden and your phone in your pocket. You want to be careful, mate. I grew up in Peckham. Hated it," the taxi driver told Ignacio.

Ignacio would have laughed had he not been so tired after his thirty-hour journey via Houston and Chicago. Just as well the driver didn't live in the crime-ridden hellhole that was Barrio 31, where he had to pay his neighbors protection money to look after his house while he was away on business, he thought.

He paid the driver for the journey from Heathrow Airport and walked up a short gravel driveway to the door of the house, which had probably been a pub in a former lifetime, judging by its design and the fittings outside.

Ignacio was about to knock when he heard a bellowing scream from inside that was instantly muffled. A man's scream of pain.

Momentarily, the prospect of sitting down with his group of hot-headed, cannabis-fueled ex-army friends and working out a viable plan to solve his family business's problems was not an appealing one.

We've had him holed up in the house here for the past three days, trying to pump him for information.

He exhaled hard, then knocked.

A minute later, the front door opened a fraction and a scarred face framed by greasy dark hair peered out. "*Hola, Ignacio . . . at last. Come in. We're busy here,*" Diego said in Spanish. He led the way through a wood-floored living area, with high ceilings and walls stripped back to the brickwork.

"What is this place? It looks like an old bar," Ignacio asked.

"Yeah, used to be a pub called the White Ram, the rental guy said. Good, isn't it?"

Diego continued into a kitchen with a long wooden table in the center.

On the table Ignacio saw a fat gray-haired man strapped down with black bindings that ran underneath the table, holding him tightly in place, pressing down on his fleshy chest and belly. He was naked apart from a pair of dark blue boxer shorts. In his mouth was a bright red plastic ball that was fixed in place with gaffer tape.

His left foot stuck out at a right angle. Neither his big toe nor the one next to it had nails, just a mess of ragged red flesh where they had been. The wounds dripped blood slowly onto the floor. Next to his foot on the table was a pair of pliers covered in blood.

At the bottom of the table, wielding another pair of pliers, stood a grim-looking Alejandro. The two missing nails were lying on a piece of newspaper on the floor, tiny pieces of red flesh still attached.

The man on the table had his eyes closed, but he was still breathing.

"He's finally started talking a little," Diego said.

Alejandro bent down and put a bowl on the floor to catch the dripping blood.

Ignacio stood, both hands on hips, taking in the scene quietly. Then he fixed his gaze on Diego. He distinctly remembered giving instructions to keep the man blindfolded. Now he had seen all of them.

Ignacio sighed heavily and clenched his fists. "Okay. What's his name? And what have you got him to say?"

"Keith Bartelski's his name," Diego said. "First the gold. It's coming from Poland. He's told us that much. The old man who runs the gold business, Jacob Kudrow, although he calls himself another name, Jack Kew, fetches it. He works with another old man who runs the car-parts business next door, Leopold Skorupski."

"Yes, but Poland's huge," Ignacio said. "Where exactly? That's what I want to know."

"He won't tell us exactly where, says he doesn't know. I think that's bullshit. He also said something about a map in a filing cabinet in the office. Another thing, he also said the old man's grandson knows where the gold is. But he wouldn't tell me how they transport it here or how they get it to Argentina."

"A grandson? Who's that?" Ignacio asked.

"His name's Oliver Kew, and he's at Bristol University. That's all he said."

"Interesting. Has he said why they are doing it? And how they've managed to keep forcing my father to buy at such a price?"

"No, nothing. But there's another eight toes to go. And ten fingers and thumbs."

Keith jerked his head upward and groaned. His eyes

flicked open and he stared at Ignacio and Diego. He made a loud moaning noise behind the ball gag, and then the back of his head crashed back onto the table with a loud thud.

Ignacio walked to the window. Raindrops streamed across the glass. Outside, the road was a gray metal river, the silhouettes of cars and trucks duplicated by their reflections beneath them. The only color came from passing red London buses. A morass of black clouds sped from north to south, losing its definition as the rain descended.

He faced Keith. "Hmm, two nails. It is possible, isn't it, there's just a faint possibility, that he doesn't actually frigging know."

Diego shrugged. "It's possible."

Ignacio hesitated. "All right, keep at him for a while. See if we can get any more. But blindfold him and keep him that way. Just don't kill the idiot. Not yet. We also need to sort out this Johnson guy. What have you found out about him? Where's he staying? Has he got a car?"

"Yes, he's got a black BMW. He's got it parked in a public parking garage up near Tower Bridge. We tried to follow him, but he gave us the slip, so we're not sure where he's staying. We're trying to spend as much time as we can watching, but we can't do everything."

Ignacio folded his arms. "All right. What about his car?"

Diego stared at his old army colleague. The flicker of a grin crossed his face. "You mean . . . ?"

Ignacio nodded.

CHAPTER TWENTY

Thursday, November 24, 2011
London

"I'm trying to find a synagogue with a strong Polish community," Johnson said to the administrator at the Central London Synagogue. "I've got an elderly aunt who's recently moved to London and she needs a place to go where she feels at home."

The man tugged at his beard and peered at Johnson over the top of his rimless glasses. "There's still a few, though a lot of the Polish Jews have moved out now," he said. "There were a lot in the East End, but nearly all of the synagogues have long since closed."

However, he listed a few names, which Johnson wrote down.

It wasn't until he had been to a couple that he realized it was Thanksgiving Day. What better way to spend it than trailing around synagogues in London on a seemingly fruitless search for Jacob Kudrow. So far, nobody had heard of him.

The next one on Johnson's list was the Bevis Marks synagogue, next to the odd-looking office building called the
Gherkin at St Mary Axe. It might be traditionally more
Iberian Jewish than Polish, the Central London Synagogue
administrator had said, but it was definitely worth a try.

Bevis Marks, a brick building bearing a plaque that dated
it to 1701, was dwarfed by ugly concrete and glass office
blocks that surrounded it on all sides.

The old and the new. It reminded Johnson why he loved
London.

Inside, two middle-aged ladies in the administrative office
exchanged blank looks after he launched into his inquiry
about Jacob Kudrow.

Well, alternatively, did they know anyone in the jewelry
trade who worshipped there? More blank looks. Well, there
was one old East Ender called Al who knew everyone and was
often around, but he wasn't now. Maybe he should try
Hackney and East London synagogue, one of the ladies
advised. There were a lot of skilled craftsmen in that area.

Johnson walked out and tipped his head up. It was
starting to get dark. Realistically, he could see the chances of
tracking down Jacob Kudrow by traipsing on foot from one
synagogue to another were hovering somewhere between
zero and outer space, as Vic used to put it.

He sat down on one end of a long wooden bench in the
courtyard just outside the synagogue.

The words *needle* and *haystack* danced around inside his
mind, turning themselves into images that grew increasingly
vivid and animated the more he ruminated on them, like
some kind of Disney cartoon film.

The needle and the haystack.

Johnson shook his head. Then he remembered the pack
of Marlboros in his bag, lit one, and took a deep drag. The
sensation of light-headedness felt good.

An old man wearing a cloth cap and a faded three-piece suit wandered in through the gate and sat at the other end of the bench.

Johnson finished his cigarette and stubbed out the butt on the ground. Then he took out of his pocket the bar of chocolate he had bought at Kew Gardens. As he peeled back the wrapping, the man watched him intently.

"You go to this *shul*? I saw you come out." He spoke in a cracked, croaky voice.

Johnson glanced at the man. "I'm sorry?"

"This synagogue—do you go here?"

"Nope, just visiting."

The old man grunted. "You American?"

"Yes, from Portland, in Maine. On the East Coast." Johnson held out his hand. "I'm Joe Johnson." The old man grasped it with a cold hand, which Johnson noticed was mottled with dark veins and purple blotches.

"Al Nicholson. Nice to meet you. I've been here forty years. Used to be a great *shul*, this one. Ain't many people left now, compared with back then. The youngsters, they don't want to know anymore."

Johnson offered him a piece of chocolate. He took it.

"Thanks. So what brings you here?" he rasped.

"I was trying to find someone, but I'm not having any luck."

Al grunted. A minute later he said, "Who is it, the person you're looking for?"

"An elderly man, probably older than you: a jeweler by the name of Jacob Kudrow who runs a gold business. He's a Jew, from Poland originally."

"No, never heard of anyone of that name. I know a few jewelers, though. I worked for one, a long time back, for a few years before I retired, not far from here. They're still there."

He started coughing, a hacking, wheezing cough that, once started, he struggled to stop.

Eventually it subsided, and Al blew his nose loudly. They sat in silence for a few minutes, eating the chocolate.

Johnson said, "So who was the man you worked for? Maybe he would know my guy."

Al started coughing again, apologizing between each croaking bark. "This is going back to the late '80s. The boss there was a guy called Jack Kew."

Johnson sat thinking. "So you don't know if he's still alive? He wasn't from Poland, by any chance?"

"Not sure, but he wasn't English. Definitely not. You could hear his accent. It was a funny business, old-fashioned. It had been there for years. It's still there. There's another business next to it, a car-parts company. Jack was matey with the owner, a guy called Leopold. Can't remember the surname."

This has to be worth a look, Johnson thought. *Maybe I just got lucky for a change.*

"Where is this place?" he asked.

It was a run-down old warehouse down Plumbers Row, a street just off the Whitechapel Road, Al said. "It's only a mile or so from here. It's near where the old Great Synagogue used to be. That got destroyed during the Blitz."

He described the warehouse in some detail. "You can't miss it; it's the only building on that road that looks like that."

Johnson got out his notebook and wrote down Al's address and phone number.

"You can give me a call if you need any more help," he told Johnson. "Just one thing, though, I don't know if Jack will still be alive. He had a bad heart. In and out of the hospital, as I remember. And that was, when, back in '89, I imagine."

* * *

Des Moines, Iowa

David Kudrow was already in full flow when Fiona bustled in, her hair windswept and tangled.

"Sorry I'm late. Flight was delayed," she said as she showed her press identity card to the public relations man who was handling media at the Republican presidential candidate debate. He checked her name off an online list, handed over her press credentials, and allowed her to pass through to the debate floor, where she took a seat among other journalists.

"The U.S. economy is really struggling to recover right now. Nobody here in Des Moines needs to be told that. And I believe there's worse to come. Obama is three years into his presidency and has promised a lot, but he's failed to deliver," Kudrow told the audience gathered at Drake University's Sheslow Auditorium.

Five other candidates for the Republican nomination were sharing the stage with Kudrow, including Mitt Romney and Newt Gingrich. It was a key debate in the race for the nomination.

Kudrow's voice rose as he continued. "As it stands, unemployment is over 9 percent in this country. That's almost double the level of only a few years ago. It's a disgrace. This presidency just isn't working—in all senses of the word."

There was loud applause from the eight-hundred-strong audience packed into rows of red padded seating on the floor in front of him and in the balcony above. TV cameras panned the room, focusing on a number of people who stood to clap.

Fiona surveyed the room. Some journalists were typing

furiously on their laptops and tablets. Others scribbled in their notebooks.

Kudrow jabbed his forefinger at the nearest TV camera. "Obama is not a friend of business—but I am. I would repeal Obama's disastrous Dodd-Frank Act. It has crippled smaller banks across this country by swathing them in red tape.

"In trying to stop the big banks from misbehaving, he's discouraged the rest from lending to small-business owners struggling to get their new ventures off the ground— including many right here in Iowa. Because of him, they're less inclined to lend to homeowners who are desperate to move somewhere they might actually find a job.

"This is having a crippling effect on the housing market and on the wealth and spending power of tens of millions of innocent people.

"Dodd-Frank must go, Obama must go, and I'm the man to replace him."

Kudrow came under fire from some of the other Republican candidates, particularly Romney and Rick Perry, but many of the criticisms the others threw at him over his business record were greeted by boos from the audience.

After the debate had finished, several candidates, including Kudrow, made themselves available for follow-up question-and-answer sessions with journalists in the so-called "spin rooms" located behind the auditorium stage.

Some journalists made a beeline for Romney, but Fiona joined the group of about fifteen who gathered around Kudrow.

She felt herself tense up as the first question came from a journalist from a rival political website.

"Mr. Kudrow, can you tell us about your funding plans, and specifically how your family and their businesses plan to support your campaign if you get the nomination? We've picked up that you have a huge campaign fund already secured, but your family business isn't that large, so how have you managed it?"

Kudrow brushed the questions aside, talking about a broad range of support from a variety of sources, including other businesses across the country. Fiona didn't want to fuel that particular line of inquiry, so as soon as he finished speaking, she quickly asked a pointed question about his economic policies, which changed the angle of attack for the whole group of hacks.

The final question came from a TV journalist. "Mr. Kudrow, is there any progress in the police investigation into your brother's death that you can tell us about?"

"No, the police are continuing to work hard—we're all working hard to try and get to the bottom of it—but there's been no progress so far," Kudrow said. "If there is you'll be the first to know. As you can appreciate, it's been an incredibly difficult time for all of the family."

The session finished and Fiona turned away, almost bumping into Philip Pietersen.

"Hi Philip. Everything going according to plan?"

Philip frowned at her. "Not really. What's this I hear about you investigating David's campaign funding?"

Fiona stepped backward. How the hell did he know that?

"I don't discuss stories I'm working on. You should know that," she said. "If it affects you or your candidate, I'll come and let you know at the right time and ask for a comment."

"Well, there's nothing underhanded going on here, I can assure you of that," Philip said. "I think you should back off. I'd focus on those who really are manipulating the system, not people like David. I hear you've got Joe Johnson helping you as well?"

"I don't know who's told you that, but I'm not going to get into a discussion about stories that we may or may not be looking at and who may or may not be helping us, okay?"

Philip wagged his finger. "You're barking up the wrong tree, Fiona."

She shrugged. "Sure, sure. Like I said, I'll let you know if I need to talk to you. I don't right now."

Fiona squinted at him. "Have there been any developments on the Nathaniel Kudrow killing?"

"No, there's no developments to my knowledge."

"And have they questioned David—officially, I mean? They didn't get on, did they, David and Nathaniel?"

Philip eyed her steadily for a few seconds. "It's not for me to comment on who's been questioned. You'd better talk to the police or the FBI about that one." He turned and walked off.

Fiona checked her watch. Only one hour to deadline. She quickly found a quiet corner at the back of the auditorium and phoned her editor.

"Des, hi, it's Fiona. The debate's finished here, so I'll file a story as quickly as I can bash it out. Kudrow had a good evening, took it by storm, especially on the economy. I get the feeling that if he puts in a few more performances like that, he's going to take out Mitt, for sure. However, I'm worried about the other story we were talking about recently, Kudrow's funding. I've just spoken to his campaign manager, Pietersen. He knows we're investigating and that Joe Johnson's helping us. He was quite aggressive about it—told me to back off. How the hell would he know about what we're doing?"

"No idea," Des said. "He can't do anything about it, in any case. I'd just carry on. I hope you didn't reveal that he was right?"

"Of course not. Didn't give him anything. As you say, doesn't matter. I think this story's gonna be a biggie for us—could be absolutely huge. It's going to stop the campaign train dead in its tracks if we can get it out there before the primaries. And if there's a link to Nathaniel's stabbing, it'll be even bigger."

"I agree," Des said. "You carry on with it. You're doing a great job."

"Another thing," Fiona said. "I asked Pietersen if David had been questioned by the cops or the FBI about his brother's shooting and he just looked at me, told me to talk to the police, and walked off."

"Okay, I'll get the crime reporter here to see if there's any update on all that."

Fiona moved her phone to her other ear. "Thanks. We need to keep moving, because it looks like one or two other journalists are starting to latch on to the funding story. There were questions from at least two other hacks in the spin room afterward. We're on the front foot with that story, and I don't want anybody else getting hold of it. Joe's over in London now and working on it, but I'd like to keep on top of it myself too."

She hesitated. "I was going to suggest something. Obama's due in the U.K. on his visit in a few days. I'd like to join that trip, and then I can check on what's happening with Johnson at the same time."

She waited, picturing Des sitting at his desk in Washington, surrounded by the day's batch of empty coffee cups and the detritus of his lunch and dinner.

"I'll have a think about it," Des said after a moment. "Can't make a decision now, I've got too much to focus on here. Got to go. Speak later."

At least he didn't rule it out, she thought, as she put her phone back into her bag. There's hope yet. She smiled to herself. *Maybe Joe might like a bit of extra help.*

CHAPTER TWENTY-ONE

Friday, November 25, 2011
London

Jayne wasn't quite how Johnson remembered her. She used to be a joker, the first to poke fun at those in authority.

"You've changed," he said. "I remember in Pakistan you had a standard routine. Every time you came off the phone with one of your bosses in London, you'd slam down the receiver and moan about 'jobsworth' civil servant managers or something like that. Then there was that impression you did at the Christmas show, with the bowler hat and cravat. That was hilarious. Must have been in, what, '89, I think."

Johnson sipped his coffee. "Now you're giving me a lecture over breakfast about not breaking the law or invading someone's privacy. You've become one of them."

Jayne put her hands on her hips. "Very funny. Maybe that's why I need to get out. We've all changed. You certainly have. But I'm trying to keep you out of trouble. Here you go. You didn't get this from me. You can link it up to your phone."

She threw a box containing two bugging devices across the dining table at him. He caught it neatly in his right hand. "Thanks."

"What are you planning to use it for?" Jayne asked.

"Not sure exactly. But I'm going to try and find the Kudrow workshop. So we'll see."

"So you're going to break in and plant one of those, are you?" she interpreted, nodding at the box.

Johnson shrugged. "All for the greater good."

"I spoke to my boss," Jayne said. "He was reluctant but did finally agree to let me help you out a bit. He's chased war criminals himself before in Bosnia and Croatia, so he gets what you're doing. He says the only condition is that if there's any criminal activity going on, we have to hand it directly to either the police or MI5, okay?"

Johnson nodded.

"Good. I've managed to pick up some info for you," Jayne said. She sat down. "First, Internet traffic. I got my old friend Alice, who's one of the technical people at GCHQ, to run a survey last night. There's been several hits on your website and several searches for your name, some from an IP address in Buenos Aires. I've still got good contacts at the SIS station in Buenos Aires. They're trying to get details of whose computer it's coming from. Second, you mentioned the gold dealer José Guzmann. I had a check run on him, too. I couldn't find any more than what you had. But there's also an Ignacio Guzmann—that's his son. Now listen to this: the son flew to London yesterday via Houston and Chicago. I got that from a check on customs and flight bookings. We've no idea where he is now, but we're trying to find out."

"His *son?*" Johnson asked, perking up. "Do you know why he's in London?"

"No, not yet. I'll try and help where I can, but you know we've got the Olympics in London next year, and I've got my hands full at work with a security report on that, so crazy busy right now," Jayne said. "I do have a photo of the son for you, though. We got it from his passport records."

She took out her phone and showed Johnson a photograph of a fit-looking, middle-aged man with a deep tan and receding light brown, almost blond, hair.

"That's him. I'll text you the photo." Jayne tapped on her phone for a few seconds, then got up. "I seem to be doing all your donkeywork for you. You'll owe me after this. I've got to go and get a shower, otherwise I'll be late for work."

"Okay, do thank your GCHQ and Buenos Aires contacts. Much appreciated, and I do owe you already," Johnson said.

Like his former colleagues, such as Vic and Jayne, Johnson had always been amazed by the ability of the U.K.'s Government Communications Headquarters and its U.S. equivalent, the National Security Agency, to rapidly cull data from people's digital footprints. Technology had certainly changed the spying game beyond all recognition.

As Jayne put her coffee cup on the tabletop, Johnson noticed her thin blue knitted-cotton pajama top that clung tightly around her and the matching shorts that rode right up her thighs.

She hadn't lost her figure, nor that slow, lithe way of moving. He wasn't surprised: she had always been a regular at the gym and ate healthily, judging by the contents of her fridge. And yet she still liked a drink.

But she definitely had a harder edge about her.

He briefly wondered if he should gently reminisce about the affair they had in '89 in Pakistan but decided against it, at least for the time being. She hadn't mentioned it, and he might embarrass himself. It had been a long time ago.

Instead, Johnson told Jayne about his visits to the National Archive and the encounter with the old man who had given him the lead on the jewelry company off the Whitechapel Road.

"Can we check who owns the property?" he asked.

"Okay, give me the address, and I'll get the listings for it." She loped off into her bedroom. A minute later he heard her shower running.

Johnson took his coffee and sat down in one of the black leather armchairs. He leaned back, rested his head, and closed his eyes.

First, a sketchy lead from oddball Nathaniel, who's now dead. Then a link between the Kudrows and a gold dealer in Buenos Aires from my distant OSI past. Next, a threatening note. Seemingly by coincidence, the son of the Buenos Aires gold dealer is now in London. And old Jacob Kudrow has been living under an alias, probably since the 1970s. What next?

Indeed, what next?

Go and find him . . . He'll be in his dilapidated old workshop or at the synagogue.

Johnson opened his eyes and drained his coffee cup.

Better try the workshop, then.

* * *

Once Jayne had gone, Johnson showered and got dressed.

He had a thought and quickly typed out a text message to Jayne.

Didn't mean to start something. I'll buy you a bowler hat. Thanks for your help. If the workshop draws a blank today I'm back to square one. Wish me luck. x

Johnson stowed the box Jayne had given him in his backpack, along with his notebook and a small camera, and put on his warm black jacket and wool hat.

He decided that if he was going to take proper counter-surveillance precautions, it would be sensible to find an alternative route out of the apartment block other than the front door, so he walked along to the end of the corridor and located the door to the fire escape stairwell at the rear of the building.

After going down to the basement, he walked through a bicycle storage area and past a large air-conditioning unit to a steel emergency exit door.

Johnson pushed the door gently open and emerged into a narrow alleyway next to a small park at the side of the building. Then he vaulted over a wall into the park and mingled with a crowd of office workers and mothers pushing strollers. From there, he walked along Portsoken Street, away from the main entrance to the apartment block.

Though it wasn't raining, the blanket of gray clouds had remained, and the wind had increased during the night, with gusts strong enough to periodically push him slightly off balance.

He also did a proper check for anyone tailing him. There was no sign of any coverage. He made a right, and then it was only a short walk under an old iron railway bridge to the Minories parking garage, next to Tower Gateway station.

Once in the parking garage, he swiftly stepped into a darker area behind the ticket machine on the ground floor, where he had a clear view of the path leading up to the parking garage and back to the railway bridge. Here he waited and checked again for anyone following.

Eventually satisfied, he paid for his parking ticket and climbed up the concrete staircase to the first floor to retrieve his car. Again he checked underneath the car and the wheel wells before leaving.

It was only a mile or so from the parking garage to the address the old man outside Bevis Marks Synagogue had given him. He turned right off the Whitechapel Road, and there it was, on Plumbers Row. There was no mistaking the building, given the description the old man had provided.

Johnson parked on the other side of the road, behind a builder's truck. Then he clamped his phone to his ear, as if he were making a call, and took a good look.

The building, which had the date 1892 carved into a stone plaque built into the wall, was at least forty yards across and three stories high, with brickwork that was grimy and heavily stained black in places with the imprint of London's dust, dirt, and pollution.

It formed a sharp contrast to the smart mini supermarket on Johnson's side of the road and the new red brick apartments next door.

The workshop had a large curved central archway with black gates that formed the main vehicle entrance. A smaller pedestrian gate was inset into the left half of the main gate.

Most of the building's windows were bricked up, and the others were guarded by rusty iron burglar bars.

On the right side of the central entrance archway was a sign that read Classic Car Parts. On the left was another sign that said Kew Jewellery U.K.

A large number of weeds and a couple of small saplings sprouted from the gutter at the top of the building. A long, dark green stain was spreading down the brickwork from a leaking pipe.

Johnson took it all in. So this was it. *Dilapidated* . . . too right it was. He was no property expert, but it crossed his mind that a developer would make millions out of the site.

He took his pack of Marlboros out of his bag and lit one, winding down the car window a few inches, and checked his watch. It was just twenty past nine.

A slow trickle of workers began to arrive at the workshop,

either walking or on bikes, mostly wearing overalls, stained fleece jackets, heavy boots, and woolly hats.

Johnson lit another cigarette and watched.

At around 9:45 a.m., a dark green BMW 5 Series, an older model, drew up outside the gates. The driver jumped out and opened both rear doors. An old white-haired man climbed carefully out onto the pavement.

Daniel Kudrow. Johnson jerked up in his seat. He recognized the old man immediately from the Republican fundraiser in D.C. where he had been remonstrating with his son David. White hair. And the black glasses were quite distinctive. It was definitely him.

Seconds later, another man, who looked virtually identical apart from his gold-rimmed glasses, stepped out of the other side of the car.

That must be Jacob.

The men both wore dark gray coats and black pants and were of very similar height and build. Johnson grabbed his camera and quickly took a picture of them through his car window.

Daniel slapped his twin on the back, said something, and then they both stood back, looking up toward the top of the building. Daniel gestured at the top, and then they both turned and disappeared through the pedestrian gate. The green BMW drove off.

So this business, Kew Jewellery U.K., was run by Jacob Kudrow under the alias Jack Kew.

Finally. Johnson exhaled, feeling suddenly relieved. After days of seemingly banging his head against a brick wall and getting nowhere, this felt like a real breakthrough. He had found the workshop and had even found the Kudrow brothers.

But what now? He sank back in his car seat and tried to think.

He couldn't just walk in there. Or could he?

His phone pinged again as a short e-mail arrived from Fiona.

> *Hope you are making headway. I don't want to run out of time. Any updates?*
>
> *Things heating up here. David Kudrow taking GOP primary by storm, doing much better than Romney. Will make our story even bigger.*
>
> *There's no police or FBI progress on Nathaniel investigation. Weird. Still don't know what police/FBI view is on any possible David involvement.*
>
> *Where you staying in London? I know the East End a bit from when I lived there for six months back in the late 1990s.*
>
> *F.*

Johnson tapped out a quick reply.

> *Staying with an old friend in an apartment near Aldgate. Made a little headway. Old Jacob Kudrow seems to be living under an alias, Jack Kew. I've just found Jacob's workshop. Now working out what to do next.*

The last thing he wanted was for Fiona to know he was staying with another woman, let alone an old girlfriend. No ex ever appreciated those kinds of details. In fact, as soon as he sent it, he regretted even telling her he wasn't at a hotel.

Johnson started the engine of his car. As he did so, the green BMW reappeared around the corner and pulled up outside the workshop. This time another man climbed out. He was taller than the twins, maybe slightly heavier, and bald, with a few wisps of gray straggly hair, and he was dressed in working overalls, not a suit. But he was probably almost as old as the Kudrow twins.

The man bent down and spoke to the driver of the BMW through the open window, giving Johnson time to take a photo of his face when he stood again. Then he too disappeared through the pedestrian entrance. The large gates opened to allow the BMW through, and it disappeared from view when they closed behind it.

Another old guy. Johnson wondered, was this the Leopold Skorupski whom the old man had mentioned?

He let out the clutch and drove back the way he had come earlier that morning.

As he headed back into the Minories parking garage, he passed a silver Ford Focus parked in the first spot after the entrance.

* * *

Diego, in the driver's seat of the Ford Focus, sat up sharply when he spotted Johnson's black BMW go past them. He nudged his accomplice, Alejandro, and pointed.

"Here he is. That's his Beamer. I'll follow him up the ramp. Got the box ready?"

Diego started the engine, pulled out, and followed Johnson's car to the second floor.

There Johnson found an empty space and maneuvered to reverse into it.

Diego drove the Focus past him and swiftly parked in a bay thirty meters away.

As he did so, Alejandro pulled out a small black box from a bag, flicked up an antenna, and pressed a switch on the side. An LCD display lit up on the front of the unit.

They watched as Johnson picked up his backpack from the passenger seat, got out, and closed the door, slinging his bag over his shoulder.

At the same time, Alejandro held up the black box and

aimed the antenna toward Johnson's BMW. He pressed a button on the front, which beeped twice quietly.

Johnson walked away from his car, held out his key fob, and clicked the lock button. Both indicator lights on the BMW flashed.

In the Focus, a green light on the front of Alejandro's black box illuminated briefly, and it beeped again.

As Johnson continued walking toward the stairwell, Alejandro grinned at his companion.

"Got it?" asked Diego.

"Yep. Now we can get to work."

* * *

Keith Bartelski sat slumped and semiconscious in the wooden chair in the middle of the kitchen, his arms behind him and tied to the back of the chair with rope.

Spittle leaked from one corner of his mouth, past the red ball gag meant to muffle his screams. Meanwhile, blood oozed from a kitchen towel that had been taped to his left foot as a makeshift bandage.

Ignacio circled Keith.

The area just below the man's ribs, around his kidneys, reminded Ignacio of the surface of one of the blueberry cheesecakes his mother used to make when he was a kid.

The door opened and in walked Diego and Alejandro. "Johnson's car lock is fixed," Diego said. "As soon as we get the bomb, we can instal it."

"Okay, good," Ignacio said. "I'm expecting our delivery man to arrive here any minute."

He sighed. "I'm looking at this guy Bartelski. You can give him a break now. I really don't think he knows where that gold is coming from. Either that or he's got balls of steel . . . and Brits don't have those. We've proved that."

Diego nodded. "I agree, *jefe*. He told us Poland quite early on, but since then, *nada*. If he told us that, he would have also told us exactly where, too, if he knew. That's my opinion."

Ignacio folded his arms, nodding at his two companions. "I don't think he's any more goddamn use to us. And you idiots screwed up by not keeping him blindfolded." The two men looked a little sheepish.

"I think we move on to our next option. This asshole may not have the information we need, but we know who else does," Ignacio said.

Then the doorbell rang.

Ignacio went to answer it. He put the security chain on before peering out. "Ah, *buenos dias*, Felipe." He looked over his shoulder at Diego and Alejandro, then undid the chain and opened the door.

A thin, dark-skinned man with longish black hair stepped in, gingerly carrying a square cardboard box similar in size to those used for pizza deliveries but deeper. On top of it was another smaller box. He put them down on the kitchen tabletop and took off his brown leather jacket.

"This is Felipe," Ignacio said. "I worked with him in the army ten years ago. He's based over here now, running his own supply business. Best not to ask who for."

Felipe nodded at the other men. "I see you've been busy." He glanced briefly at Keith, who groaned loudly.

"I'm going to explain this once, as I need to go, so listen carefully," Felipe said, speaking in rapid Spanish. "You've probably heard of this device if you're all army guys. It's an FMK-3 anti-tank blast mine. Argentine-made."

He picked up the larger cardboard box and gingerly opened the lid so the device inside was visible. Made of green fiberglass, it was around ten inches across and about three inches deep. Built into a recess in the center was a small round plastic unit with an eight-pointed star molded on the top.

There were two small circular openings on the sides, one with a yellow plug inserted and the other with a domed metal cover.

Felipe pointed to the device. "If you've come across these before, it was probably in the Falklands, where I think you all did time?"

"We've seen them before, but you'd better remind us how to use them," Diego said.

"Okay," Felipe said. "This has got more than six kilos of C-4 explosive inside—it's mainly RDX, and that's easily going to blow a car away. When you want to use it, you have to take out this yellow transit plug on the side and insert this detonator. It's been adapted for use with a separate trigger rather than by pressure on the top from a tank or armored vehicle, which would be the case in normal use." He took out a green plastic detonator plug with a yellow stripe from the box.

"It also has a strong magnetic plate attached to the bottom, so you can attach it to any metal surface in a car," Felipe said. "I've also got a trigger for you, a remote control which you can operate manually." Felipe picked up a black box with a rectangular red button in the center and an antenna. "It's a simple remote. It works via a radio link up to a range of about five hundred meters. That connects to a small receiver next to the bomb, which is this little black box here." Felipe held up a second, smaller black box, the size of a cigarette packet.

"It's connected to the electrical firing circuit so when you press the button on the trigger, it will complete the circuit and detonate the bomb. It's powered by this nine-volt battery."

Then he demonstrated how to connect the receiver, detonator plug, and mine.

"The best place to hide it is in the engine compartment, effectively right in front of the steering wheel," Felipe said. "If you can't access a metal surface, just wedge it in and tape it in place so it can't move. It's unlikely to be spotted there, whereas if you put it underneath the car, who knows . . . someone might see it if they do a check, or it could even fall off. Stick it where I'm telling you. No problem. Boom."

He threw both his hands upward theatrically in illustration, his face deadpan.

CHAPTER TWENTY-TWO

Friday, November 25, 2011
London

Johnson strode up to the reception desk, his backpack slung over his shoulder, but found the area deserted. He pressed a small doorbell on the security window, then put an elbow on the counter and waited.

The small customer waiting room for Classic Car Parts was seriously in need of redecoration, he thought to himself.

It had dark red clay floor tiles and brick walls that had been whitewashed many years earlier, judging by the grime that had collected in the grout. There were six basic metal-framed chairs. Four wall lights, all with dust-covered bare tungsten bulbs, illuminated the room.

Behind the reception desk and security window lay a long counter lit by a fluorescent strip-light. To the right of the reception desk was a connecting door to the staff area, marked Strictly Private.

In the center of the room was a battered old coffee table

with a chipped glass top, on which lay a small pile of magazines: *Practical Classics*, *Classic Cars*, *Classic and Sports Car*, and
the previous day's copy of *The Jewish Chronicle*.

Still no one came.

Johnson pushed the doorbell again and sat down. He had
decided to make his move only an hour or so earlier, after
receiving a text message from Jayne. According to her information, the workshop had originally been purchased in the
name of Jacob Kudrow in 1952, but the deeds showed a
change of name to Jack Kew in 1972.

She had also confirmed that Jacob still lived in the house
in Hay's Mews, the address where he had been listed as an
occupant in the electoral roll records that Johnson had previously found. The records showed Jack Kew as an occupant of
the property since 1972. That explained everything.

Johnson continued to wait. He had already tried reception
at the Kew Jewellery U.K. business next door, but the door
there was locked, and a Closed sign hung in the window.

After a couple more minutes, he heard footsteps
approaching behind the half-open door at the back of the
reception area.

A muscular forearm, tattooed with a black snake,
appeared around the door, followed by a man's head.

Seeing Johnson, the man walked up to the glass security
screen. "What do you want?" he asked.

Johnson stood up and walked to the counter. "Hi, I've got
an old 1961 Beetle I'm trying to restore, and I need a new
steering column, for starters. Is that something you can help
me with?"

The man gave him a puzzled look and pursed his lips.
"Maybe. We might have one, but I'll have to go and look
for it."

"That's fine. Thanks. You're not very busy this afternoon?" Johnson said.

"No, it's dead." He looked inquiringly at Johnson. "We don't see many Americans in here. What's your name?"

"I'm Philip Wilkinson. And you?" Johnson held out his hand.

"Jonah Hennessy." His bearlike handshake squeezed Johnson's hand. Then he disappeared back through the door.

Johnson picked up a copy of *Classic Cars* and sat down again.

There was the sound of footsteps on a creaking staircase, followed by a couple of thuds and a crash. Then, faintly, he heard Jonah swear.

A couple of minutes later, he reappeared. "I can't find it right now. I know we've got one. Thing is, I've got a problem. I have an emergency dentist appointment at the surgery across the road right now, which is going to take about half an hour. I can't miss it. I've had a real problem with a filling that came out. It's been agony. You can wait here, or would you like to come back? There's no one else here."

"It's fine, I'll just wait here and read these magazines. No problem."

"Okay, I do apologize for this. I'll see you shortly." Jonah went out the back door again. There was a distant slam as the exterior door closed.

Johnson waited a couple of minutes, then stood, trying to decide what to do. He moved toward the connecting door, its Strictly Private sign looming large at him. *Sometimes in life, opportunity just knocks*, Johnson thought. Or was it some sort of trap? Did they know? They couldn't, surely.

He pushed at the door, expecting it to be locked. It swung open, its hinges squeaking. He passed through the reception area and pushed at the next door. It too opened.

Then Johnson found himself in a dark passage. Jonah must have turned the lights off. What should he do? He had a mini flashlight attached to his key ring, but using that or the flashlight on his phone would look very strange if someone did return. Then again, he could just say that he couldn't find the light switch, which actually would be true. He flicked on his flashlight.

Now he could see that at the end of the passage, facing him, was a white wooden sliding door, which was closed. On the left was another white door, also closed, and on the right near the sliding door was the entrance to a toilet. It stank.

Next to the toilet, also on the right, was a wooden staircase. Almost without thinking, Johnson moved toward it, his rubber-soled shoes squeaking on the tiled floor.

He took one step up the dark-stained wooden stairs, then another. On the third step, the plank beneath his foot made a sudden loud crack, and Johnson jumped, his heart accelerating.

He stood still, listening. But nothing.

Johnson gingerly climbed up one flight, around the corner, then up another flight to the first-floor landing. In front of him was a glass and wood door, its original green paint badly chipped and worn down to the gray undercoat or even bare wood in some places.

Johnson held the flashlight in his teeth and felt in his pocket for a pair of thin latex rubber gloves, which he put on.

The glass was covered in dust and marks, but in the dim light from an inside window, Johnson could see it was a storeroom, with racks up to the ceiling filled with pieces of equipment.

Outside, a police siren howled, getting louder and more piercing as it drew nearer. Johnson felt himself go taut; he bit his lip. The police car went past the building, and the sound level fell back.

What should he do? If someone came now, Johnson's chances of talking his way out of the situation were slim to none. There was no reason to be upstairs.

Johnson decided to look for the office. He pushed open the storeroom door and moved along the central corridor to the other end, then through a door into another dark passage.

What now, turn on the light? That might be visible from outside. But there were no windows, so *some* light would be okay. He'd keep using his mini flashlight, although this time he moved his thumb partly over it so only a sliver of light emerged. It was enough and less risky.

There were three doors off the passage, the last of which, facing him at the end of the corridor, had a white sign fixed to it, with black lettering: Kew Jewellery Staff Only Unless Authorised.

It must be a connecting door to the Kudrow business, Johnson thought. He remembered the old man at the synagogue telling him that Jacob and the owner of the car-parts business worked closely together.

Johnson moved down the corridor. His eyes were getting used to the darkness now. He nudged the connecting door with his elbow. It moved under the weight of his arm. Should he risk it? What if there was a burglar alarm?

But it was, after all, Jacob's office that he really needed to see.

Johnson stepped through the door, closing it slowly and silently behind him. He found himself on a carpeted floor instead of the bare boards of the car-parts business.

No alarm sounded.

The only audible sound was the faint brushing of Johnson's shoes on the carpet and his breathing.

Still moving by the fragments of light from his mini flashlight, he tried to look around. He had emerged at an upper landing, with stairs going up and down. There were more doors ahead of him along the landing, all white. Facing him at the end of the landing was a much wider door fashioned from unpainted paneled wood and with a brass handle.

At the top of the stairs, Johnson noticed a white electronic security system control box with a keypad and a small LCD display screen was fastened to the wall.

He frowned. It was clearly an electronic burglar alarm that required a code to arm and disarm it. A small green LED light flashed every few seconds next to a label that read Not Armed. He took out his phone and snapped a photo of the unit.

Then he used his flashlight to carefully examine the keypad, up close. After a few seconds, he saw what he was looking for and typed in a note on his phone.

As Johnson crept forward, he could see an old brass plate on the door. Private—Managing Director's Office.

This must be it.

Suddenly, the silence was split by Johnson's phone, which emitted a shrill ring from his pocket. It made him jump almost off the ground.

He swore softly as he scrambled to get it out, his thumb getting stuck in his belt. Once out of his pocket, it fell, hitting the floor with a thud, still ringing loudly. Johnson moved to catch the phone with his right hand but dropped the key ring and flashlight, which lit up the whole landing with its beam.

Johnson grabbed the phone and eventually managed to hit the red button to cancel the incoming call, which he saw was from Fiona, of all people.

Then he fell to his knees and seized the mini flashlight and key ring, which were lying right on the edge of the landing, under the banister and a quarter of an inch from falling to the ground floor. Now his heart really was pounding.

Johnson froze where he was, on his knees, sweat now trickling down his forehead. He cursed himself for his amateurish error in not turning the phone to silent.

Johnson remained still for several minutes, until his

pounding heart rate dropped a little. He wiped his brow with the back of his hand. There was silence.

What to do? Press on or retreat? Johnson turned his phone to silent, then stood up. He edged to Jacob's wooden office door, turned the knob gently, and pushed.

It gave a squeak that seemed to echo across the dark landing.

The office was slightly illuminated by the remnants of late afternoon daylight coming through a window, where the thick maroon curtains had been left open.

Johnson's first thought was that it was like going back in time.

An enormous old oak writing desk, with a red leather pad inset into the middle, stood in front of an ornate brick fireplace, laid ready with wood and coal and surrounded by a large hearth.

The only obvious concession to modernity was a computer and keyboard on the desk. Behind it was a large oak chair with a leather padded seat.

Also on the desk was a large metal statuette made of two flat rectangular plates of steel, with oval holes and patterned indents down each side. The two plates were leaning against each other to form a pyramid, and other triangular pieces of metal filled the gaps at each side.

The walls were half paneled with wood up to head height. A chandelier comprising several small candle light bulbs was suspended on a chain from the ceiling.

Johnson noticed in the far corner there were two metal filing cabinets. After drawing the two heavy curtains across the window, he made his way to them.

Should he risk the mini flashlight again? He switched it on and pulled open the top drawer of the filing cabinet.

It contained around twenty different dividers, each marked with a different company's name. These must be the customers, Johnson surmised. They all appeared to be U.K.-based jewelry shops and retailers. He shut the drawer.

The middle and bottom drawers were locked, as were all the drawers in the second filing cabinet. Where was the key? Johnson stepped to the wooden writing desk and pulled the three drawers open in turn. They were all full of assorted junk —old pens, pencils, erasers, paper clips, a hole punch, and even a jeweler's loupe—but no keys.

Then he noticed a thin sliding wooden panel at the bottom of the desk, the kind that holds paper clips and staples in a compartmentalized tray. It clicked open when he pushed it, and there was a set of six small keys.

Johnson checked his watch. More than fifteen minutes had passed since Jonah had disappeared to the dentist, although it felt like hours.

Using the keys, he opened the other five locked cabinet drawers. Two were empty, and the third contained electricity, gas, and other utility bills. The fourth contained a similar set of dividers, each carrying the names of people, presumably employees, and their contracts of employment. Ah yes, there was Jonah's.

One left to go.

The sixth drawer was also empty, apart from one divider hanging from the rail, labeled Exports. Johnson stared at it, then pulled it out.

The file contained several copies of invoices sent from Classic Car Parts to a company called Oro Centro. There was no address. Most of them were yellowed and fading, the earlier ones were handwritten, the later ones printed, and all of them were on various sizes of paper. Johnson quickly realized that some were for very large amounts, all in U.S. dollars. All were stamped as paid. The dates started at 1959 and ran at regular intervals through to the latest, which was 2004.

Vic had told him the Kudrows' U.S. business had a Buenos

Aires subsidiary called Oro Centro, of which Guzmann was a customer. Johnson had a note of it in his book. *Oro* . . . "gold" in Spanish.

Johnson raised his eyebrows as he read through the invoices. The first he looked at, from August 1970, was for just over $3 million. The next, dated July 1973, was for $4,354,931. Johnson shook his head.

All the invoices had the same two words in the sale details column: *For Services*.

Some services, Johnson thought.

He took out his phone and took photographs of some of the larger invoices, then swiftly put them back, locked the cabinet, and replaced the keys in the writing desk.

Johnson then took out from his backpack one of the small voice-activated listening devices Jayne had given him. He pressed a small button on the base of the unit, which was similar in size to a plastic cigarette lighter, peeled off a plastic protective film from its white adhesive pad, and fastened it firmly to the underside of the desk, behind a wooden strut.

What next? A jewelry business must have a safe some-where, probably a large one. Johnson would bet his life savings on it. But where was it? His eyes searched the area.

Built into the wall, to the right of the fireplace, were two white cupboards. Johnson pulled the first one open to find a selection of single-malt Scotch bottles, a silver tray, and some cut crystal glasses.

Behind the second was an old steel safe, its surface rusting slightly in places, a Whitfield's Safe & Door Company brass plate screwed to the front above a numbered dial and a brass pull handle. Johnson tugged at it, but it was locked.

Old but solid. A real museum piece. There was no way he was going to get into that in a hurry, he thought. But it certainly appeared as though it was frequently used. The brass handle was shiny and dust-free, as was the dial.

Johnson took out his phone and took a couple of photographs of the safe. He consulted his watch again. Twenty minutes gone. The sudden realization that time was running out on him, fast, caused his adrenaline to kick in again.

He shut the door concealing the safe, walked to the curtains and pulled them back, then retraced his steps out of the office, across the landing, through the connecting door, and back through the storeroom.

Moving quickly now, he headed down the stairs. He was intending to take a left back through to the customer reception area when one other thought struck him. He should check what the other two doors were down here. They might provide him with an alternate way in. Maybe he could even bypass the alarms.

He took a right, through the sliding white wooden door next to the toilet.

Johnson found himself in a workshop with tools hanging on the walls, as well as jacks, spare wheels, car parts of various types, drills, and other equipment. The place was black with grime and stank of engine oil.

Parked just in front of a large steel roller door, which presumably led into the yard, were two ancient Volkswagens, one a Beetle and the other a T2 panel van.

Johnson flicked on his mini flashlight again. In one corner there was a small room made of gray cinder blocks with a sign on the door marked Boiler Room—Keep Out. Sliding his thumb over the flashlight, he walked quickly to the door and slipped inside. Time was running out now.

Johnson peered into the gloom. A large, ancient-looking metal boiler with a small hinged fuel door at the front stood in one corner. Johnson touched it with a finger; it was cold and unlit, although next to it was a large pile of coal ready for use in an enclosure also made of cinder blocks.

Coal. Johnson almost chuckled to himself. He hadn't seen a boiler fueled by coal since he was a kid, when his parents had one at their house in Portland. His dad used to bring in large, filthy lumps on a shovel from an outhouse. It was utterly inefficient.

This boiler seemed to be of a similar vintage to his father's old coal model, except much larger.

He leaned over the pile of coal. Behind it was a wooden plywood hatch, about three-and-a-half feet across, hinged on the right-hand side, with three bolts on the left holding it closed. Presumably, when the pile of coal needed to be topped up, more was shoveled in through the door from outside.

Johnson stood, hands on hips, then made a decision.

He bent over the coal until he could just reach the bolts holding the door and slipped all three of them open. The door stayed in place. He grabbed a brass handle screwed to the inside of the door and pushed slightly. It moved, and Johnson felt a blast of icy cold air rush in from outside. That would do.

He pulled the coal store door shut again, leaving the bolts unlocked, replaced the plank against the wall, and went out of the boiler room into the workshop. Then he walked back through the white sliding door into the corridor, quietly closing the door behind him

On the wall in the corridor, Johnson saw another burglar alarm control unit identical to the one he had seen upstairs near Jacob's office. Stepping up to it, he closely examined the keypad, as he had done for the other unit, until he saw what he needed and made another note on his phone.

Abruptly, Johnson stood still.

The staccato sound of hard-soled boots echoing on tiles came from behind the other white door to his right. Thinking quickly, he ducked into the toilet and flicked the light on, then silently shut the door behind him.

He could hear someone emerge into the corridor.

Johnson removed his rubber gloves and stuffed them into his pocket, then flushed the toilet, washed his hands in the basin, and opened the door again.

In the corridor, Jonah stood facing him, a large looming figure, his hands on his hips.

"Sorry, I needed the loo. Hope you don't mind," Johnson said.

Jonah remained momentarily silent. He regarded Johnson, his eyebrows raised, forehead furrowed.

"This is the staff area, you know. It's private. Didn't you see the sign?"

"Yes, I saw the sign. I was just desperate. Sorry again. I didn't realize you were going to be gone so long. Thing is," Johnson said, looking at his watch, "I'm meant to be in a meeting soon, over near St. Katharine Docks, so I'm not going to have time now to sort this out. Is it okay if I come back tomorrow afternoon? I really need that part."

Jonah looked not just disbelieving but quite threatening. Or was Johnson imagining it?

"Right," he said, looking Johnson squarely in the eye and crossing his arms. "That's fine . . . Mr. Wilkinson."

CHAPTER TWENTY-THREE

Friday, November 25, 2011
London

Johnson handed over a five-pound bill at the kiosk outside Aldgate underground station, picked up his chocolate bar, and waited for his change. Then he took an evening newspaper from the man handing them out next to the station entrance.

The front page headline read, "Obama Declares U.S.-U.K. An 'Essential Relationship.'"

He read on.

> *"The U.S. President Barack Obama flew into London's Stansted Airport last night to be greeted by Prince Charles and the Duchess of Cornwall.*
>
> *President Obama, who is traveling with his wife, Michelle, will hold an initial meeting with Prime Minister David Cameron at 10 Downing Street this evening.*

It is only the third state visit to the U.K. by a U.S. President in the past 100 years.

Obama, followed by a large U.S. press entourage . . . "

The report continued across the front page and on to pages three, four, and five, together with a series of large photographs of the U.S. President with Prince Charles.

Johnson opened the chocolate bar and broke off a couple of squares, then sat down on a bench. After finishing the chocolate, he lit a cigarette.

He now felt exhausted and extremely hungry. The chocolate was the only thing he had eaten since breakfast.

Then someone tapped him firmly on the shoulder. He whirled around.

"Dammit, Fiona . . . you made me jump. You keep doing this to me. So where did *you* come from? What are you doing here?"

"Well, thanks, nice to get a welcome. Thought I'd check on how you're doing. I'm over here to cover the Obama visit. It was a last-minute decision by my editor, so I only arrived this morning. I did try to call you earlier, but you cut me off."

Johnson rolled his eyes. He didn't need reminding of the call that had given him a panic attack on the pitch-dark landing at the warehouse.

"How did you know where I was?" Then he remembered the e-mail exchange.

Fiona slid onto the bench next to him. "You said you were staying near Aldgate, so I thought I'd come and find you. I knew you'd be through the station at some point, so I just decided to head over here. I was about to call you again when I just spotted you lighting that cigarette. I've been sitting over there for a while." She gestured toward another bench farther along the path.

Johnson felt quite irritated but, despite himself, couldn't help but smile. She was so persistent, it was almost amusing.

He studied Fiona. Her long dark hair had tangled in the wind and blown over her face like a lace veil, and she had that trademark hint of a smirk around her mouth. He noticed her deep brown eyes, which to him always seemed so . . . well, confident.

"Sorry, Joe, it *is* my story. So I thought I'd better come and see how you're making out with it while I've got the opportunity. Now, tell me. Any headway?"

Johnson hesitated. Should he tell her about that afternoon's events? It was certainly headway. And she was the one paying his wages, or at least her company was.

He started his story, but then hunger overwhelmed him.

"I need some dinner. What about that place over there? I was checking it out earlier." He gestured to an Italian restaurant, La Piazetta.

Over pasta, with which Fiona insisted on ordering an expensive bottle of Barolo, Johnson talked her through the saga thus far. He started with how he trailed around London trying to find out Jacob's alias and ended with the race against the clock in the old warehouse earlier that afternoon.

"So we've got invoices showing these huge sales to Oro Centro," Johnson said. "They don't say what was sold, although I think we know. But assuming it's gold, there's nothing to say where it came from in the first place. Neither was there anything to show onward sales to a customer. That's the key. It's possible the answer could be in the safe. Either way, I'd like to take a look. But I don't have a clue how we get into it."

Fiona said nothing. She sipped her wine, then propped her elbows on the table and put her hands together, fingertips pointing up in a pyramid. "Me neither. But I know a man who might."

Then she took another sip. "Thing is, I don't know how to get hold of him." She said she had a phone number for her contact. The problem was, it was in a notebook in her apartment, in Washington.

Johnson listened as Fiona made a phone call to her sister Margaret, who also lived in Washington, and persuaded her to drive to her apartment and find the notebook.

While they were waiting, he and Fiona opened another bottle of Barolo.

Finally, Margaret found it.

"Sis, I owe you one, you're the best," Fiona said as she ended the call.

"So, success?"

"Yep!"

"Okay, now tell me about this guy you're trying to locate," he said.

"Let me give you the background."

In February 1997, Fiona—then a crime reporter—had worked on a story about a robbery on a bank vault in Charlotte, North Carolina, in which more than $5 million in jewelry and cash had been stolen.

Nobody was ever convicted for the crime, but Fiona managed to get a scoop on the unusual techniques used by the burglars in getting into the vault.

"I got it through this underworld contact, a shady guy to say the least, who put me on to this British safe-cracking expert he knew, called Bomber Tim."

Johnson started laughing.

"I know, I know, don't ask," she said. "We just called him Bomber. I didn't ask any questions. He was living in New York, and it turned out he had given a load of advice and equipment to one of the gang members, though he wasn't part of the gang himself."

To secure the interview, she had agreed to be blindfolded

and driven to a nondescript third-floor apartment in Brooklyn at three o'clock in the morning.

"It was nerve-racking, I tell you," Fiona said. "I didn't know what I was getting into."

Once the story was published, quoting unnamed sources, Fiona had been hauled in by detectives and by the FBI, who wanted to know who those sources were.

"Thing was, up until then, they'd told nobody how the job had been done, and they thought one of their own officers had leaked the damn thing," Fiona said.

She came under heavy pressure but refused to divulge anything, citing her constitutional rights as a journalist. The case had further fueled the ongoing battle between the media and the state, about reporters protecting their sources and whether the state had the right to force them to disclose sensitive information under certain circumstances.

"They locked me up for a day and a half in a cell in this Brooklyn police station, which of course triggered wall-to-wall media coverage," Fiona said. "I told them nothing, and eventually they had to let me go when the ACLU turned up the heat. I spent the next two days doing interviews all over town—you know, *Meet the Press*, the *New York Post*, several radio stations. Got my fifteen minutes, if you know what I mean. I flew the flag for civil liberties and reporters' rights and had a pretty good time with it."

It had been the story that made her name as a tough reporter.

Afterward, Bomber Tim decamped back to his home city in the U.K., Liverpool, where he subsequently bought himself a nice ten-bedroom manor house in the countryside with about twenty acres of land, stables, and an indoor swimming pool.

Two years later, Fiona received a handwritten note, including a phone number, thanking her for her silence and telling her she should get in touch if she ever needed help in the future. She had scribbled the man's phone number in her notebook.

Johnson nodded. "He sounds like a character, as well as a useful contact. The thing is, it isn't just the safe in that warehouse. There's also a couple of burglar alarms, you know, the type where you have to input a code on a keypad to disarm them."

"I doubt that'll be a problem for him," Fiona said. "But let me ask him."

She stood up and put her coat on. "Wait here, Joe. I'm going outside to give him a call. The bastard had better still be alive, though I wouldn't put money on it. He drank like a trout and smoked like a Rastafarian at New Year."

He watched as she walked slightly unsteadily toward the door.

* * *

Johnson sipped his wine and took in the restaurant. It wasn't the best Italian place he'd ever been to. Near the window was a long table full of scruffy, drunken traders who were downing shots of tequila in turns.

On the other side of the room was a table of six Japanese tourists showing each other their cameras, all of them deep in discussion about the merits of each. Johnson had to smile.

The waiters all looked bored and disinterested, to the growing annoyance of a couple in the corner who seemed to be having trouble getting their attention.

Outside, Johnson could see Fiona sitting in a bus shelter next to the restaurant, phone to her ear, presumably trying to get the goods from a locksmith in Liverpool.

Twenty minutes later, she strolled back into the restaurant and pumped her fist in the air.

"He's coming on the train in the morning. Great guy. He remembered me very well. Said he hasn't done a job at all for the past four years, and he sounded quite excited. He said he still owes me one so doesn't need to be paid a lot. We're going to meet him off the train at Euston."

Johnson gazed at Fiona. His mind flashed back to how she had looked back in 2003, when he had first worked with her on the California senator story. Absolutely stunning then and still pretty gorgeous now—especially when she was all lit up like this. However much he thought they weren't suited, he still admitted an attraction.

Johnson had initially felt resentful that she had turned up out of the blue and effectively gate-crashed a job he had specifically told her he wanted to handle his way, with no interference. But she'd just saved his ass.

"I have to admit Fiona, you sometimes do have a few tricks up your sleeve," he said.

"I'm always full of surprises. You should know that," she replied, winking.

They ordered two Scotches on ice to celebrate and asked for the bill, which by then stood at more than £200. Johnson let her pay with her company American Express card.

"So, there's still no progress on the Nathaniel Kudrow investigation, then?" Johnson asked.

"No, it's strange. Police have gotten nowhere with it and neither have the FBI. They have some CCTV film of a dark-haired guy leaving the hotel about the time they think the stabbing took place, but the pictures weren't great. They've also had appeals for witnesses running on national and local media. They seem to have a ton of people working on it, but no result so far. I've asked the crime guys at work to keep me updated if they pick up any developments."

Fiona stood. "We'd better go. I'm at the Crowne Plaza hotel next to Blackfriars. I need to get some sleep. Got to write a piece in the morning before we go to meet Bomber. Are you going back to your friend's place? What's his name again?"

"Robinson," Johnson replied, a little relieved she wasn't suggesting a nightcap.

They walked to the door, said goodbye to the waiter, and moved outside. Johnson paused in the entrance long enough to check the road in both directions. There was nobody obviously watching or loitering.

The drizzle had started again, making the pavement slippery underfoot, and the temperature had dropped further. Back in Portland, he would have expected snow. Here he wasn't so sure.

Feeling guilty, although he didn't know why, Johnson told her that his friend Robinson had a first name—Jayne. He had expected some sort of reaction in return.

But Fiona just folded her arms in mock annoyance and cocked her right eyebrow. "Really? Okay, well, at least you'll get your shorts washed after you've removed them, then."

She headed toward the underground station with a wave.

Johnson watched her head down the stairs and out of sight, realizing two things: one, he'd had a fun evening after a stressful day; and two, Fiona didn't seem to be holding a torch for him after all. He'd worried about it for no reason. It had been a little arrogant of him, really.

Johnson chuckled to himself and lit a cigarette as he walked to Jayne's apartment.

CHAPTER TWENTY-FOUR

Friday, November 25, 2011
London

Alejandro reversed the Ford carefully into a vacant spot in a side street about a quarter of a mile from the Minories parking garage.

He turned off the CD player, which had been blasting out Coldplay's album *Viva la Vida*, a favorite since they had seen the band at River Plate Stadium in Buenos Aires the previous year.

Diego, sitting next to him, pulled on his wool hat. "I think the parking garage will be quiet enough now. Let's get this job done."

"Yeah. I'd rather be back home, though," Alejandro said. "It's not good—freezing our balls off here. Back home it'll be baking hot. Nice evening beer, cool chick. Dinner to follow. Taxi home. That's what we should be doing."

Both men got out of the car, and Diego removed a large backpack from the trunk, in which he had stowed the anti tank mine, the detonator, and the other equipment from Felipe. Then they set off on foot to the parking garage.

A careful survey of the garage over the previous two nights had told them there was always one security guard on duty, who sat in a small office on the ground floor.

Every hour on the half hour, the guard patrolled the building on foot, starting at the top and working downward, which took twenty minutes.

When he got back to his office, the guard very often spent ten minutes making a cup of tea or another drink in a small kitchen before resettling in his seat in front of a bank of ten black and white security video screens. Diego had noticed the guard paid scant attention to the screens and instead spent most of his time reading a paperback novel.

Although there were video cameras mounted on walls on each floor, the ones on the second floor were some distance away from Johnson's car. There seemed little chance of their faces being discernible on video.

Diego's plan was to wait until the guard was on his patrol and passed down from the second floor to the first. Then they could make their move. That should give them fifteen to twenty minutes before the guard was back in front of his video screens.

When they arrived at the parking garage, Diego checked his watch. It was now 11:35 p.m.

"The guard should be up on the third floor," Diego said. "Let's wait on the first until he comes to the second."

The two men waited silently in the deserted stairwell until they heard footsteps echoing from above, as the guard made his way down the stairs and onto the second floor. The door clanged shut behind him.

Diego and Alejandro pulled their wool hats down over their foreheads, slipped on latex rubber gloves, and made their way up the stairwell to the third-floor landing. There they waited until they heard the guard move to the first floor, and then they quietly descended to the second.

Johnson's black BMW was parked where he left it. The only other remaining cars on the floor were a gray Range Rover, an Aston Martin that Diego assumed must belong to some late-working banker, a battered old Vauxhall, and a Mercedes so dusty it must have been standing there for weeks.

If the security guard did return, Alejandro and Diego had agreed to say the BMW had battery problems and they were waiting for the Automobile Association to turn up with a replacement.

Diego approached the BMW, removed his backpack, opened the car door, and released the hood, which clicked open. He removed the mine and other equipment from his backpack, went to the front of the BMW, and lifted the hood fully. He had difficulty finding space for the antitank mine in the engine compartment, but eventually managed to wedge it in and secured it with duct tape before installing the detonator.

He then taped the remote control receiver next to it and met Alejandro's eyes, seeking approval.

Alejandro assessed the arrangement with a doubtful expression, then whispered in Diego's ear. "Is that secure enough? It doesn't look like it'll hold in place. You don't want it to move around. It's damn heavy."

Diego nodded and cut off another strip of tape, which he fixed in place. "That should be fine," he murmured. "It can't move around too much in there."

Diego pulled the hood down and clicked it shut, then checked his watch. It was now three minutes to midnight. He inclined his head to Alejandro, indicating that they should go. Alejandro nodded.

The two men made their way silently back down the stairwell and out of the entrance. As they left, Diego caught a glimpse of the security man sitting in his office, drinking a cup of tea and reading his book.

The two Argentinians made their way back to their car.

"Hopefully, Johnson doesn't decide to check his oil and spot it—unlikely if it's a hired car," Diego said. "We'll need to keep a check on his movements so we can set off the firework show at the right time. We might need some way of luring him into using the car."

His phone beeped loudly twice in his pocket. He took it out and read the messages. He turned to Alejandro.

"They're from Ignacio," Diego said. "It's not good. It looks like the guy we've had tied up tried to escape from that back bedroom. Worked his ropes loose and was halfway down the fire escape. Shit, I'm surprised he could walk in that state. Good job Ignacio managed to catch him—but he's pissed. He wants us back there fast."

The phone beeped again and then again. Diego looked again at the messages.

"He's asking if we had checked the guy's ropes. Did you? He's obviously trying to blame us for it, as usual."

Alejandro frowned. "Don't think it's going to matter much now. Wouldn't like to see what Ignacio does to him."

* * *

When Johnson got back to Jayne's flat, it was almost half past eleven at night. She was lounging on her sofa sipping a glass of white wine, her back to him.

Standing behind the sofa, he said, "Glad to see somebody's feeling relaxed."

She turned around. "Hardly. I've been manic, actually. This Olympic security report is tough going. I only got home half an hour ago. You made any progress?"

Johnson realized his comment had been crass given the number of hours Jayne was spending at Vauxhall Cross. "Sorry, I know what it's like. Yes, I've made some headway." He recounted the day's events and then told her about Fiona's arrival.

"So, this Heppenstall woman. What's the story? Are you two an item?"

I knew she was going to ask, he thought. *She's curious about everything.* He liked that about her.

Johnson held her gaze. "No, definitely not, although I did make a mistake there, about five years ago. Thing is, work puts us on the same flight path sometimes. She tried to rekindle it once but seems content just to be friendly at the moment."

Jayne pursed her lips. "Sounds like a slightly tricky situation. Yet she's giving you work. I'd keep her onside but not too onside. There's your challenge."

She reclined in her chair. Was she looking relieved?

"So why do you need to work with her on this job?" Jayne asked. "If it's that much of a problem, why not walk away and leave her to it?"

Johnson walked around and sat in the armchair next to the sofa, sinking into the black leather.

"Yes, that's the trick, isn't it? This is a big job for me, though. I need to do something more meaningful than what I've been doing, something worthwhile. And so it's worth any lingering awkwardness, really. And she's got her uses, good contacts and so on, although I still don't actually know where this job is going. It could still turn out to be a dud."

Jayne ran her hand through her hair. "I'd have joined up with you on this one if I had more time and if I wasn't tied in at SIS . . . and if you didn't have the journalist tagging along."

He grimaced. "Yes, well, maybe we could another time.

Anyway, what about you? Still single, still wedded to your work—what's that all about?"

Jayne shrugged. "I like my independence too much. Relationships are good in small doses. Can't even be bothered to flirt much these days. It's either a yes or a no." She glanced sideways at Johnson, in the same way he remembered.

"You're as bad as she was," he groaned.

"Bad? It's yes or no. There's no bad involved."

Johnson got up and poured himself a glass of wine. "Yes feels bad. No feels bad. But changing the subject, I have a favor to ask. You said you couldn't get me a gun, but I have a feeling that one might be useful. I just need something unobtrusive, but it should do the job if necessary. Any chance?"

Jayne pursed her lips. "You don't know what you're asking. Although that could be my exit route sorted out, given that they'd probably fire me."

She sipped her wine and considered. "There might be a way, someone I've just thought of. A friend of mine has a well-connected boyfriend. Let me check with her."

CHAPTER TWENTY-FIVE

Saturday, November 26, 2011
London

Surely this must be an aging jockey or a bookie, not an international criminal, Johnson thought as the man walked toward him, limping slightly, on the platform at Euston Station the following afternoon.

Thin and wiry, appearing to be in his fifties, Bomber Tim was no more than five feet five inches tall and had a virtually bald head, apart from some wispy gray hair at the sides. A pair of thick black-rimmed spectacles completed the look.

He was carrying a battered old briefcase, although Johnson doubted very much there were any documents in it.

Fiona dwarfed Bomber, who was a good six inches shorter, but that didn't stop him from giving her a lengthy hug. Johnson snorted.

Bomber disentangled himself and warily acknowledged Johnson, who offered his hand. "I've heard a bit about you from Fiona," Bomber said in a broad Lancastrian accent as he shook.

"Likewise," Johnson said. "Good to meet you. You're probably ready for a coffee after traveling all this way. I saw you were limping a little."

"I twisted my ankle a couple of weeks ago. It's a little sore," Bomber said. "Shall we go and find a place where we can have a chat?"

Johnson led the way down the platform and out of the busy station, which was full of Saturday shoppers carrying bags, students with backpacks, and families out on day trips.

They found a quiet pub around the corner, The Rocket, sat in a corner well away from other customers, and ordered coffees. Johnson's first priority was to reassure Bomber of his credentials and that he wasn't leading him into some kind of setup.

He briefly ran through his background and gave Bomber his card, and then Fiona outlined their mission in London, without going into too much unnecessary detail about the Nazi elements of the story.

"Okay," Bomber said. "It'll be a change to work with justice in mind, rather than escaping from it, so to speak." He narrowed his eyes at Johnson, his forehead permanently creased.

After half an hour, they ordered another round of coffees, and Bomber finally seemed to relax. "Okay, we'd better talk business. Do you know what this safe is like? I might need to get some other tools, depending."

Johnson showed him the photo he had taken on his phone. Bomber studied it closely.

"That should be easy enough. A very old one, probably from before the war, I think. Whitfields . . . you don't see many of those anymore, apart from in old family-owned businesses or in rich people's houses. That's a combination lock safe. They used to advertise them as impenetrable. What a joke. It's a bit different to that one we did over in Charlotte, you know, Fiona?"

Bomber smiled for the first time, the right corner of his mouth pulling to the side, creasing his right cheek and pulling his left taut. It made him look as though he had some sort of nervous tic. "It's still going to take some time to pick that lock, though. We could need a couple of hours if we're unlucky."

"There is one other thing," Johnson said. "There's also two burglar alarms in there, the kind with keypads where you put a code in. Here, I've got a photo of one of them. They're both the same."

He showed Bomber the picture of the unit.

Bomber scratched his chin and hesitated. "Hmm, I think I can do that. I've got a piece of kit I can use . . . " His voice trailed off and he looked at Johnson.

"You sure?" Johnson asked. "I had a close look at the keypads, and I've got the numbers. They had grease marks on them and were worn a little, unlike the others, which were clean."

Bomber eyed Johnson. "You've done this before?"

"Not exactly, but I know a bit."

"You do, yes," Bomber said, with a new tone of respect in his voice. "That makes it a hell of a lot easier." He seemed somewhat relieved.

"Yes, but how do we know what order the numbers come in? That's the hard part, isn't it?" Johnson said.

"It's hard if you don't have the tools. But fortunately, I've got a device that gets around that. You connect it and it works out the order, goes through all the possible combinations in a flash. If you know the numbers, that dramatically reduces the number of permutations. So it works a hell of a lot faster."

Johnson smiled. "I see." He turned to Fiona. "Just one thing, Fiona. I think three of us going into this workshop is just too many. It would be better, less risky, if I just go with Bomber. I don't want to put you at risk unnecessarily or get you into trouble if it all goes wrong."

Fiona seemed surprised. "No, Joe, it's my story, and I need to go in there. It's the most exciting job I've had for a long time. Remember, we're paying you."

Johnson shrugged, but Bomber tapped his fingers on the table. "I agree with Joe. It needs to be a silent, professional job with as few people as possible. We can give you all the detail you need afterward. Just me and Joe here on this one."

Before Fiona could speak, Johnson's phone beeped. It was a message from Jayne.

I've got the goodies you asked for last night. Meet me at Embankment tube station at 3pm. Don't ask. xx

Fiona seemed to have given up on arguing her case for going to the workshop. Instead, she decided to go back to her hotel and write a commentary article on Obama for her website. She would take Bomber with her and leave him to wander around by himself while she was working.

Later, Bomber would meet Johnson near Jayne's neighborhood. Then, later that evening, probably after eleven o'clock, Johnson and Bomber would walk together to the warehouse. There was no point in taking the car, which might draw attention. Fiona would remain at her hotel.

It was a plan, of sorts. Johnson left them at Euston and lit a cigarette before catching the tube.

He sat on a bench outside the station, smoking it. One of

his main concerns was getting into the warehouse yard, but they would sort that out at the time.

The other was working with an eccentric criminal with a sore ankle whom he didn't know on a job involving an illegal break-in for which silence and speed were essential. But Bomber was a pro, he told himself. What could possibly go wrong?

CHAPTER TWENTY-SIX

Saturday, November 26, 2011
London

The temperature was hovering around the freezing point when Johnson eased himself off the top of the wall and landed softly on the concrete floor of the warehouse yard.

He was followed a few seconds later by Bomber Tim, who seemed to have shrugged off his sore ankle. Or maybe adrenaline had dulled the pain.

Johnson took a pair of thin rubber gloves from his pocket and put them on. Bomber was already wearing his own set of gloves.

Most of the heavy clouds that were hanging over London had rolled away during the evening, leaving the sky clear, with some of the brighter stars visible even through the capital's permanent mask of orange and white light.

Then the dogs started barking. There were two of them, their deep-bass barks interspersed with low-pitched, insistent, growling and snarling.

Big bastards, Johnson thought. But then he realized the dogs weren't in the yard, but behind a fence belonging to a neighboring business a little farther up the narrow alleyway.

Johnson led the way silently to the section of the warehouse wall where he guessed the entrance to the coal bunker was.

He was wrong, though. And after another few minutes of searching, the dogs were still barking. Bomber tapped Johnson on the shoulder and pointed to the high wall of the warehouse, which was being periodically lit up by flashlights. The guards in the neighboring premises were checking what was disturbing the dogs.

Every sound seemed magnified. The traffic noise had faded almost to nothing, so there was no background noise. Then a nearby church clock struck midnight: twelve deep, sonorous tones.

Then at last, Johnson found the exterior entrance to the coal hatch, hidden in a brick enclosure where the warehouse's trash was stored. He had to carefully move two of the bins to one side to get to it.

Then he gave the hatch door a small pull. It was still unlocked, and Johnson felt a wave of relief.

The two men had had a long discussion before approaching the warehouse about how to handle the burglar alarm. Johnson knew they had around thirty seconds, maybe a minute, to act before the alarm went off, all hell broke loose, and the police came running.

Bomber's earlier words floated into his mind. *We'll have to be ready to exit quickly if it goes wrong—or if you've screwed up the numbers you gave me.*

Johnson opened the door fully and crawled through on all fours. Bomber was close behind, a leather tool bag strapped to his back.

They stood up inside. There was silence. No beeping alarm.

Johnson moved quickly across the boiler room, brushing past large cobwebs. A rat scuttled across the floor in front of him. Johnson imagined Fiona squeaking in surprise if she'd been there.

He opened the boiler room door, and that was when the loud, intermittent beeping began, coming from the direction of the corridor, behind the white sliding door.

He stepped past the two old VW vehicles, across the filthy workshop, and through the door to the burglar alarm unit, which continued to squawk loudly. Bomber followed.

Johnson flicked on his mini flashlight and held his thumb partially across the beam to limit the amount of light being emitted.

On the display screen of the alarm unit, a counter was going down with every second that passed. A red light flashed on the unit next to a label that read Armed.

Twenty-one, twenty, nineteen, eighteen . . .

Bomber whipped a small screwdriver out of one pocket and from another pocket took a small black box the size of a cigarette packet, from which two wires protruded with small alligator clips on the end.

In a flash, he unscrewed a panel at the base of the unit and took it off. Then he connected the clips to two nodules, pressed a button, and held the box in front of him, waiting. Johnson watched, mesmerized, as the numbers on the unit continued to descend.

Eleven, ten, nine, eight, seven . . .

Then five digits appeared on the screen of Bomber's little box. He rapidly tapped the numbers into the wall unit, his fingers moving in a blur.

He let out an audible sigh of relief as the beeping stopped.

Johnson glanced at the readout on the front of the unit. *Two*, it said.

The red LED light went out, and instead, a small green LED began to flash next to the label that read Not Armed.

The two men stood motionless for several seconds, although to Johnson it seemed like an eternity. He could feel his heart pounding.

Bomber removed the wires and replaced the panel he had unscrewed from the alarm unit. Then Johnson pointed up the staircase.

Their footsteps as they ascended the wooden stairs sounded to Johnson like a herd of cattle in the darkness, and he winced with every step. The plank that had made a cracking sound like a rifle shot on his last visit did the same again, this time under Bomber's foot.

They arrived at the connecting door between the car-parts business and Kew Jewellery U.K., and Johnson pushed gently at it with his fingertips. It didn't move.

The door was locked.

He turned and shrugged at Bomber, who gestured to the lock, then to his bag. Johnson gave him a thumbs-up sign.

Bomber took a canvas roll-up tool holder from his bag and revealed a variety of picks: mainly long, thin metal tools with differently shaped hooks on the end. A separate set of pouches contained a few L-shaped tension wrenches.

He also took out a tiny LED flashlight and an eyepiece shaped like a mini telescope, no more than an inch or two long. He removed his glasses and instead attached the eyepiece to his right eye with an elastic headband.

Bomber then turned on the flashlight, peered into the lock through the eyepiece, and selected one of the hooked tools, which he inserted into the keyhole, followed by one of the smaller L-shaped tools. From there, he spent a few seconds minutely adjusting the position of the tools, occasionally pushing one downward and twisting with the other.

The door swung open, and the second alarm system began to beep. Johnson realized he had been holding his breath. Now he let it go with an audible sigh. Bomber had opened the door surprisingly quickly.

Johnson and Bomber half ran across to the other alarm, where Bomber repeated his performance with the small black box. This time, he managed it with seven seconds to spare. He gave a self-satisfied smile.

They continued across the pitch-black landing. Johnson opened the door to the managing director's office, which squeaked for an alarmingly long time as it opened. Nothing seemed to have been moved since Johnson's previous visit.

He pulled the curtains and shut the door, and using his mini flashlight for illumination, he opened the cupboard hiding the safe and indicated to Bomber that he could start work.

Bomber said nothing. He studied the safe for several seconds. Then he reached into his bag and pulled out a doctor's stethoscope, which he attached to the front of the safe, right next to the round combination dial, using a rubber suction cup.

Johnson knew a little about safecracking. Years before, at the OSI, he had spent a week in San Diego hunting down a brutal Latvian SS commander who had a holiday home near the beach. Johnson had gone to the empty property with an OSI colleague and a locksmith who had been hired to open the man's safe. They had found nothing, but he had picked up a few pointers from the locksmith.

Bomber took the wooden chair from behind the writing desk and sat down in front of the safe.

With the stethoscope earpieces in position, he spent a long time turning, extremely slowly, the numbered dial of the safe first clockwise, then counterclockwise. At regular intervals he changed the direction of the dial.

From what Johnson recalled of the San Diego locksmith's on-the-job tutorial, Bomber was trying to work out exactly where on the dial a lever inside the lock was making contact with notches cut into the rotating wheels. Tiny clicks and vibrations would give him the clues he needed.

There was silence in the room, apart from the occasional rustle of Bomber's clothing as he changed position and one unconsciously whispered expletive. Outside, there was a distant hum of the occasional vehicle passing up and down the Whitechapel Road.

Johnson checked his watch: 1:15 a.m.

While Bomber worked away, Johnson turned his attention to a fresh search of the room. He started with the floorboards and worked his way around, looking for loose or freshly screwed boards that might indicate a hiding place. There were none. The skirting boards and bookcases also yielded nothing, and neither did the rear and side panels of the drinks cupboard. With a built-in safe, Jacob Kudrow probably felt in no need of secondary secret storage places in his office.

It was 1:55 a.m. when Bomber turned around and spoke for the first time. "Three wheels. Makes it easier. Pen?"

Johnson pulled a pen from his jacket pocket, somehow knocking his pocket notebook on the floor with a small thud as he did so, triggering an irritated look from Bomber.

Bomber took two sheets of graph paper from his bag, on which he drew a rough table with numbers up one axis and across the other. He went back to the dial and every so often marked a point on the graph.

Johnson surveyed the room. It was sparsely furnished, and minimally decorated. A real old man's office, he thought. On the wall behind the writing desk were two large, faded color photographs, both taken in bright sunshine following heavy snowfalls.

The first was of a castle with a large copper-topped bell tower, the metal bright green after years of oxidation, that was partly covered in snow. It stood high on a rocky outcrop, dominating the surrounding white-forested landscape and town.

Underneath the photo, a small label read Książ Castle. Johnson had no idea where that was but assumed it was somewhere in Poland.

The second photograph showed an elegant church in a village set against a backdrop of snow-covered wooded hills, its tower consisting of three tiers of decreasing size. In the foreground to the right was a road sign: Gluszyca.

Johnson again noticed the strange sculpture standing on the desk. It reminded him of one of the odd postmodernist artworks made from pieces of industrial metal that were sometimes in town centers in the former manufacturing heartlands of the United States' Rust Belt, like *The Workers* statue in Pittsburgh. On one side was a small engraving of an old Roman chariot pulled by horses.

Then at around quarter to three, Johnson's attention was diverted when Bomber put the pen down. He had written three numbers on the sheet.

Bomber concentrated on the dial again. Not long afterward, there was a click, and Bomber turned, a broad, lopsided smile on his lips. Behind him, the safe door hung open.

Johnson stood and silently shook the diminutive safe-cracker's hand. He read his watch: 3:13 a.m. He moved to the safe. Inside was a bundle of papers in a clear plastic folder, a black jewelry box, and an old red notebook.

He picked up the papers and quickly sifted through them: receipts, order forms, and some photocopies of invoices. He read a couple. They included some sales dockets from Oro

Centro to SolGold for similar amounts to the ones he had photographed previously between Classic Car Parts and Oro Centro.

The sales dockets again only specified the sale as "services." There were too many to look at in detail now.

He opened the black jewelry box. Inside were two gold rings, both of them very worn, with scratches and tiny dings. Possibly wedding rings, Johnson mused.

And the red notebook. Then, Johnson remembered.

It's all going to be in his book. Jacob's writing a memoir—in his little red book.

He flicked open the notebook. It had a bent and slightly rusted black wire spiral binding. The cover was battered and worn, as if it had been carried in many briefcases and written in on many desks.

The first page carried a title at the top in large letters: *Survival and Redemption—My Memoirs.* It had a date at the top, *21 September 1994,* which was underlined.

Inside, the lined paper was covered with dense, somewhat shaky handwriting in a variety of colored ballpoint pens: black, blue, green.

The entries were all dated, starting in 1994; the most recent was only a fortnight earlier. It clearly wasn't a diary but rather some sort of narrative.

No time to read it now, though, Johnson thought. He quickly checked inside the safe again. That was it. Nothing else. He had to decide what to do with these items. *Quickly, quickly, make up your mind . . .*

He replaced the jewelry box in the safe and put the bundle of papers and the red notebook in his backpack. There were too many papers here to photograph them one by one, and time was running out.

Johnson closed the safe and nodded to Bomber.

A minute later, they were back out on the landing,

treading softly over the carpeted floor and toward the connecting door to the car-parts business.

Johnson immediately felt quite relieved.

He'd had visions of being trapped in the building when the first employee, or security or someone, arrived in the morning. In fact, he was surprised there were no overnight interior security patrols in a business like this. Obviously, Jacob and Leopold assumed the electronic security system, with its link to the police, was sufficient.

Johnson opened the connecting door and turned toward Bomber, who signaled his intention to switch the alarm system back on. But before Bomber could move, a loud metallic crash echoed from somewhere in the Classic Car Parts section of the building, followed by a muffled but unmistakable yelp of pain that sounded like a dog that had been kicked.

The two men froze.

Then they heard the faint sound of two men speaking to each other.

Johnson reached into his jacket pocket and took out the small Walther pistol Jayne had given him earlier. He looked at Bomber, then pointed at the connecting door and shook his head.

Johnson quietly closed the connecting door again and looked around. There were three other white painted doors off the landing, which he hadn't had time to explore on his previous visit. He opened the nearest and put his head around the door. It was some kind of workshop. Beckoning Bomber, he walked in, then closed the door behind them.

Whatever the noise was downstairs, it wasn't good news. The first thought Johnson had was that CIA operatives were on his tail—Watto's stooges. He discounted that idea because of the noise and the talking; it seemed unprofessional.

Johnson indicated with his forefinger that they should

stay put until whoever was downstairs had gone. Bomber nodded, visibly chewing the inside of his cheek.

The workshop was L-shaped: a section disappeared around a corner out of sight at the window end. At least that would give some cover if needed. A workbench on the left-hand side of the room was lined with tools, and there was a computer, its plug hanging loose, at one end.

Next to the workbench stood a large black cabinet with two large tubular steel vessels in the center, one on top of the other, with other strangely shaped steel and glass vessels positioned around them. From them a tangle of pipes emerged.

On the front were a number of colored operating switches and a timer dial, together with a digital screen. The machine was turned off.

Against the other wall stood a large metal unit with a circular opening in the middle, inside which another metal vessel sat.

"Gold-refining unit. A friend has one," whispered Bomber.

One yellow sign with red writing on the wall stated Warning—Extremely High Temperatures 1093°C. There was a skull and crossbones symbol next to the lettering. Another sign read Personal Protective Equipment Compulsory.

The unit appeared as though it had not been used for a long time. He ran a finger along the top. It was covered in a fine film of dust.

On another unit against the window lay a series of shallow bowls, large ladles, and molds, also covered in a layer of grime.

It was the molds that caught Johnson's attention. He quietly picked up one of them and examined it more closely.

Then there was the sound of two gunshots from downstairs.

* * *

After the gunshots, Johnson and Bomber sat silently in the workshop for another three quarters of an hour. Johnson instructed Bomber to sit out of sight of the door, around the corner of the L-shaped room. Johnson held the Walther in his right hand and rested on the edge of his seat, covering the entrance.

There were a few distant sounds and the occasional muffled voice. Then there was the sound of a door slamming from right outside in the corridor, followed by at least two sets of footsteps and men's voices whispering.

Spanish. Johnson realized these men were the Argentinians —not the CIA or the Mossad.

There was no mistaking where they were heading. The direction of their footsteps followed by the long squeak of a door told him they had entered the managing director's office where Johnson and Bomber had been just a short time before.

There was more conversation, with the occasional raised voice, and then a few thuds and a crash, which sounded like a filing cabinet drawer being banged shut.

The Argentinians, assuming it was them, were being a lot less careful than Johnson and Bomber had been. The risk was that they would attract attention from security or someone else outside, with potentially dire consequences for Johnson and Bomber, as well as for themselves.

One thing Johnson was almost certain of: they wouldn't have an expert safecracker with them. He was also quite sure they wouldn't have found anything particularly useful, unless they had somehow come across something he had missed. That seemed unlikely.

Johnson thought about the bug he had planted underneath the writing desk in Jacob's office. Since placing it there on his previous visit, he had checked it a few times using an app on his phone, but the device, which operated using a 3G data service, had not registered any activity.

He fleetingly thought he might give it another try. It might be useful to listen in to the other intruders' conversation. But that would create noise, and he didn't have any headphones, so he immediately discarded the idea. His second thought was that the Argentinians might find the bug and remove it.

Ten minutes later, there was another loud squeak from the managing director's office door and another trample of footsteps heading in the other direction.

A door banged shut. Presumably the connecting door.

Then silence again.

Johnson felt as taut as he ever had.

It was 5:30 a.m. by the time Johnson dared to think of leaving the workshop. "Think they've gone," he whispered.

Bomber nodded vigorously.

They inched out of the workshop door. It was dark and silent on the landing.

This time, after they passed through the connecting door to the car-parts business, Bomber left it unlocked and also didn't bother resetting the burglar alarm.

"We might need an escape route," he whispered.

Johnson took baby steps as they moved down the corridor and through the storeroom, remaining right next to the wall to minimize the risk of creaks from loose floorboards. Every few seconds, he paused and listened.

Silence.

The stairs remained ahead of them. Johnson knew it was going to be impossible to descend to the ground floor quietly.

If there were people down there, they would have plenty of warning of the two men approaching, simply from the unavoidable creaking of wooden planks.

He just had to hope that whoever had been there really had gone.

It took them until 5:50 a.m. to make it to the bottom corridor near the bathroom. Still silence.

Johnson pushed back the sliding door to the car workshop an inch at a time, until the gap was large enough for them to squeeze through.

They had just entered the workshop when, in the gray gloom, Johnson saw Bomber step sharply to one side and hold out his hand, palm up. He pointed upward with his forefinger and looked up.

"Wet," he whispered.

Johnson held out his hand and also felt a drop of something fall onto his palm. *Weird,* he thought. It now seemed certain the other intruders had gone, so he decided to risk flicking on his mini flashlight.

Immediately, he saw a pool of red liquid on the floor, at least two feet wide.

And only then did he shine the flashlight upward.

A man's body, naked apart from a pair of blood-soaked underpants, was hanging ten feet above their heads, suspended from the high workshop ceiling by a rope attached to his wrists.

Blood dripped from his bare feet, and wounds were visible on the man's torso, from which blood was still oozing.

His head was slumped forward, his chin resting on his chest, his eyes wide open, his stare frozen forever. There were two holes in the man's forehead, also oozing blood.

Johnson momentarily felt bile rising in his throat but managed to quell the reflex. Instead, he indicated with a movement of his forefinger that they should get out quickly and walked toward the boiler room door. After a second, Bomber followed.

Behind them, blood continued to drip to the floor.

CHAPTER TWENTY-SEVEN

Sunday, November 27, 2011
London

Bomber pocketed the envelope full of twenty-pound bills that Fiona had instructed Johnson to hand over upon completion of a successful mission.

"Thanks, you did a great job," Johnson said. "Now let's get out of here." He peered around the corner of the alley in which they were standing. "We need to move quickly now before police or someone else turn up here."

They moved out into the Whitechapel Road, where every other car seemed to be a taxi. Bomber hailed one and turned to shake Johnson's hand.

"You're a pro," Bomber said. "Let me know if you ever need another job done."

He climbed into the cab, and then he was gone.

Johnson pulled a wool hat down over his ears and forehead, then turned around. Down Plumbers Row, a couple of hundred yards behind him, two men were arriving on bicycles at the main gate of the jewelry workshop. They unlocked it and let themselves in.

The day shift obviously started early. They had gotten out just in time, he thought.

He realized he felt completely drained. It was almost six o'clock in the morning, and he hadn't slept for twenty-four hours.

Johnson set off at a brisk walk toward Jayne's flat. A few minutes later, two police cars hammered past him in the opposite direction, sirens blaring and flashing lights strobing the whole of Whitechapel Road alternately blue and red as they went.

He watched as they screeched onto Plumbers Row, then disappeared from view in the direction of the workshop.

Johnson took out his pack of cigarettes and lit one. In the freezing cold December air, the smoke mingled with the vapor from his breath to form a foggy jet in front of him as he exhaled.

He couldn't get the picture of the bloody body out of his mind.

The unanswered question remained: who was it?

Johnson turned his phone back on. He had kept it switched off during the workshop break-in, partly because he didn't want a repeat of his scare on his previous solo visit, partly because he wanted to reduce the chances of anyone tracking him using GPS or triangulation.

Two minutes later, the phone rang. It was Fiona.

"Hi, Joe, how did it go?"

"Call me back on Skype," Johnson said. "It's more secure." He didn't want to discuss details of a burglary over an open cell phone connection. Fiona didn't have encryption on her *Inside Track* cell phone.

Fiona duly called back, and Johnson spent the next few minutes giving her a summary of events at the workshop, including a no-holds-barred description of the body hanging from the beam, which triggered a series of questions he was unable to answer.

"Put it this way," Johnson said, "Your friend Bomber definitely earned that envelope."

"Three grand," Fiona said. "Better be worthwhile. Let me know when you've read the notebook. I'd like to get a feel for what's in it. I think it's going to be the centerpiece of any story I write."

He promised to call her back later when he'd had some sleep and read through it, then ended the call.

Johnson tried to think through his next steps but couldn't get his brain to function.

Jayne had already left for work when he walked in. Or maybe she hadn't even come home.

Johnson didn't care.

Sleep came as soon as his head made contact with the pillow.

* * *

Ignacio normally had no problem sleeping. Apart from the odd stressful period when fighting in the Falklands and the Gulf during his Argentine army days, he had always been able to catnap at will.

But now he found himself unable to drift off after he and his men had returned from the Kudrows' workshop, despite his exhaustion. Things weren't at all going according to plan.

The first problem was Johnson, the man who appeared to be threatening to sink his father's business and, with it, Ignacio's financial future.

The scheme to remove Johnson using an explosive device in his car was fine in theory. But Johnson hadn't used the

BMW since the bomb had been placed, and who knew when he might do so again.

Ignacio got out of his narrow single bed, lit a cigarette, and paced up and down the bedroom at the back of the converted pub, replaying the events of the last day or so over and over in his mind.

He hadn't originally intended to dispose of Keith, knowing it would inevitably bring police swarming all over both the car-parts business and the neighboring jewelry outfit. A typical half-hearted police search for a missing person would become a full-blown murder inquiry.

And that at a time when Ignacio still didn't have the location of the gold being supplied to his father's business nor any clarity on exactly how Jacob Kudrow was getting away with overpricing it.

He knocked half an inch of ash into an empty flower vase.

Why did I kill him? He kicked the carpet, asking himself the question.

But then, he told himself, he had no choice. Diego and Alejandro had not stuck to his instructions to keep Keith blindfolded at all times. *Idiots, both of them.*

After Keith's near-escape, Ignacio had driven the man to the Kudrow workshop in the middle of the night in a rage. It infuriated him that the man had come so close to escaping. It infuriated him that he didn't know where the gold was. And fury tended to blind Ignacio to reason.

As his old colonel in the Argentine army had told him, *Ignacio, you're hard enough, but the red mist gets you.*

In his rage, he had ordered Diego to put two bullets into Keith's forehead and they had strung his body up on a beam with some rope.

Now, only hours later, he was berating himself. *You always have to make the big statement . . .*

He picked up an empty plastic water bottle and threw it

hard against the wall, then lit another cigarette and continued pacing up and down.

Stopping again, he remembered that although he had failed to find any useful maps or documents at the workshop, he had noticed something in Jacob Kudrow's office—something he felt sure was a point in the right direction. He just needed to check it out.

As Ignacio calmed down, he recalled another thing: although Keith had been largely useless, the man had let slip one piece of information before he died.

And Ignacio intended to make full use of it.

He gave up on the idea of sleeping and went into the kitchen, where he found Diego.

"*Jefe*, I'm just thinking about Johnson," Diego said. He extinguished his cigarette in a dirty coffee cup.

"Don't want to hear it. I need coffee." Ignacio sat down and propped his elbows on the table and his chin in his cupped hands. "All right, what are you thinking?"

Diego explained what he had in mind.

Ignacio shrugged. "Yep, try it then. Sure."

CHAPTER TWENTY-EIGHT

Sunday, November 27, 2011
London

Johnson didn't wake until almost two o'clock in the afternoon.

By that time, the low-lying late November sunshine poured almost horizontally from a cloudless sky straight into Jayne's south-facing flat.

Johnson made himself a coffee and two slices of toast and picked up his backpack, which he had slung on the floor near the door.

He parked himself in one of the black leather armchairs and took Jacob's red notebook out of his bag. The warmth and the creeping sensation of the caffeine that flowed through his system was already making him feel much better.

In the daylight, the notebook appeared even more battered and dog-eared than it had in the faint light of his flashlight the previous night.

The text inside seemed largely intact, as far as Johnson

could make out, but the twisted, rusted wire binding made it difficult to turn the pages. It looked as though water had been spilled on the cardboard cover at some point, making it swell and split at the edge, and there was a large ink stain on the front.

A white six-pointed Star of David had been roughly painted on the cover, probably with correction fluid or something similar. The white paint had become grimy and worn away in places but was still very clear.

It was a familiar symbol to Johnson. His mother had often worn a silver version of it on a chain around her neck, despite converting to Christianity in her forties.

Johnson opened the balcony door off Jayne's living room, went outside, and smoked a cigarette. He then returned to the kitchen, poured another large mug of coffee, and settled back down on the sofa to read Jacob's memoir.

Monday, 18 December 1944

Wüstegiersdorf Camp, Lower Silesia, Poland

That morning, at the snow-covered Wüstegiersdorf subcamp of the Gross-Rosen complex, in the village of Gluszyca, I and the other 2,000 or so inmates were woken up at 5:30 a.m. by the usual deafening blasts on a horn. As was the case every morning, a significant number did not wake—and never would again.

As always, I gazed at Daniel, my twin, and gave thanks that he was still alive. I reached out and touched his hand.

Eight months earlier, in April 1944, we had both been moved from the Pawiak jail in Warsaw to the camp twelve kilometres southeast of Walbryzch in the Owl Mountains.

It was a miracle that we had been able to remain together. Otherwise, neither of us would ever have recognized the other. I weighed around seventy-two kilos when I arrived at Wüstegiersdorf and around fifty-five kilos when I finally got out.

Sometimes I caught a glimpse of my face in a pane of glass. It was shrunken to my cheekbones. My ribs protruded like rails through my skin, and large sores oozed pus and blood.

Daniel was down to fifty-one kilograms when we got out. His eyes, bloodshot and yellow, stuck out slightly from sunken sockets as if they had been inflated with a pump.

We were both twenty years old, but with our shaven heads and gaunt appearance, we could probably have passed for men in their fifties.

I told Daniel to use the toilet quickly before Appell—the roll call. Otherwise we would risk instant execution by having to pee somewhere unauthorized.

The three-story former factory building that comprised the camp, which now had coiled barbed wire surrounding it, contained around one hundred rough wooden toilets: circular holes in a board with no privacy.

Then came the Appell. There were around eighty guards at the camp, and they used Appell as a kind of torture game.

All prisoners had to line up in the yard, including those who had died during the night. This meant bodies had to be dragged outside by the survivors.

The prisoners then had to remain motionless while they were counted, and often recounted, and probably recounted again. It normally took over an hour and a half. Only then were the bodies dragged off to the camp crematorium to be burned.

Sometimes prisoners died during the roll call itself.

Just a few days before, the camp commanders had forced a woman in her fifties to run around the freezing compound for almost an hour until she dropped dead, simply for being ten seconds late to the roll call.

Daniel struggled even more than me in that camp. Often he would dream in the night that I had been hauled off to the camp's crematorium to be burned alive, only to wake up in a sweat.

Then there had been the time at the end of May, not long after Daniel and I arrived at the camp, when a young woman was given the fünfundzwanzig, as they called it: twenty-five strokes with an ox whip. She was then left in the Appell yard for a whole day with no food or water, despite a hot sun.

Her offense? She had apparently failed to make eye contact with the SS first lieutenant when he spoke to her. That's what he accused her of.

Toward the end, she lost consciousness. We saw her lying there and fully expected the guards to shoot her for that, but they didn't.

They eventually let the woman go. In the following days, I saw her a few times. Her cuts from the whip were infected and oozing blood and pus, and she still seemed only semiconscious.

Johnson read those last few paragraphs over and over again. Then, unexpectedly, he felt a tear trickling down his right cheek.

Surely this isn't a coincidence? It must have been her . . . my mother . . .

He walked up and down Jayne's living room several times, trying to compose himself, then went into the bathroom and washed his face.

Eventually, Johnson sat down on the sofa again and continued reading.

Then there were the shootings. Daniel and I saw so many murders committed by camp guards using their prized Lugers, usually on the slightest whim.

I personally saw the camp commanders Captain Albert Lutkemeyer and his deputy, First Lieutenant Erich Brenner, shoot at least sixty in cold blood. There were obviously many more I didn't see.

Across the camp as a whole, I completely lost count. Hundreds. And that doesn't include all the other methods of killing—the gassings, the hangings, the beatings, the furnaces.

This particular day, the commanders were in too much of a rush

for their usual early morning sadism, much to the relief of we
walking skeletons who were parading in front of them.

We were all given the usual breakfast of one piece of hard, dry
bread and a mug full of dirty brown liquid.

Johnson read on. There was a lot more detail about daily life in Wüstegiersdorf, the beatings, and the murders. Following on from that was another section in which Jacob had written about the work the prisoners were forced to do and why.

All the commanders were terrified of Lutkemeyer's boss, the top man,
Captain Karl Beblo, who was a fearsome character with the
brightest blue eyes I had ever seen. Beblo was the local commandant
of the Third Reich's civil and military engineering group, the
Organisation Todt.

The Todt, together with the Minister of Armaments and War
Production Albert Speer, had decided that Książ Castle in
Walbrzych (or Waldenburg, as the Germans called it) should be
turned into a headquarters for Hitler.

I and other Poles hated the way the Germans had many decades
earlier taken over the whole Lower Silesia region, originally part of
the Kingdom of Poland. By the time Hitler invaded Poland in
September 1939, they saw it as their own.

Speer and his team planned to build a complex of tunnels under
the beautiful old castle: a bolt-hole where the Führer could flee if the
war went against Germany. A place beyond the range of British and
American bombers.

They also planned to build more tunnels under the hills on which
the castle stood, as well as under the Owl Mountains, which ran for
twenty-six kilometres southeast from Walbrzych.

The idea was to use them as underground factories to produce
sensitive and highly secret new weapons and other military
technology.

The code name for this scheme was Project Riese—German for "giant."

To build the tunnels, the Nazis brought in a small army of mining engineers.

But the actual digging, the dangerous bit, was carried out by concentration camp prisoners like Daniel and me.

Most of us were Jews, but there were also a few Slavs and other minorities. We were all kept at Gross-Rosen, the network of camps that included Wüstegiersdorf.

The SS cut corners and had no regard for safety. Thousands of the prisoners died, both in the camps and while digging the tunnels. Concrete supports weren't put in place, and tunnel roofs were often unstable. We all knew there were many fatal accidents, all involving Jews. Even the SS guards and commanders were worried, because they had to supervise us.

Lutkemeyer said it was important the work that was to be done that day at the Sokolec tunnels be completed quickly, otherwise the Führer would be angry. This made me take notice.

I heard Lutkemeyer say there was a special delivery of boxes coming, which had to be stowed in Sub-Tunnel A, running off Tunnel Three.

That was bad news because although there was a narrow-gauge railway that ran up to the entrance to Tunnel Three, if anything needed to be transported farther, we had to carry it by hand.

Tunnel Three was a disaster waiting to happen. They had built it into soft sandstone, and it wasn't as stable as some of the other tunnels across the mountain range. The SS were so concerned, they had a couple of small escape tunnels built, one of which I worked on.

There were six guards that day, which surprised me. Normally, there were just two or three. They loaded twenty-two of us onto a truck, then drove us to the railway station, herded us into two cattle trucks pulled by an old shunting engine, and then took us the thirteen kilometres down the valley to the village of Ludwikowice Klodzkie.

Brenner, to his obvious distaste, had been forced to travel with us.

From there, a smaller train took us on the narrow-gauge railway a couple of kilometres up to the tunnel complex in the hills near the village of Sokolec.

A little later, at just before ten o'clock, another Nazi train, pulling five trucks loaded with wooden boxes, chugged up to the Sokolec tunnel entrance, accompanied by heavily armed SS guards.

Our job was to unload the train and carry the heavy boxes far into the tunnels complex, where we had to stack them on pallets.

Johnson went outside onto Jayne's balcony for another cigarette.

He tried to imagine himself in the position of the Kudrow twins and his mother. How would he respond?

Suffering produces perseverance; perseverance character; and character hope . . .

But I would lose my mind completely, he thought. Intelligent men and women were being treated worse than vermin by their fellow human beings.

Then he realized consciously why tracking down the perpetrators was so important to him, why projects such as this current one made him feel he was doing something meaningful with his life. He took a long drag on his cigarette, then stubbed it out and went back inside.

When he resumed reading, the memoir went on to describe how Jacob, Daniel, and the others were forced to spend all morning carrying the boxes from the train, along Tunnel Three, and into the smaller Sub-Tunnel A.

By two o'clock that afternoon, we were all near to collapsing. We had spent four hours carrying the heavy wooden boxes on our shoulders from the train, one box at a time.

It was slow work. We had to walk in single file in the dimmest of light along the rough tunnel littered with pieces of rock that had fallen from the roof.

I had earlier overheard the first lieutenant telling the guards the boxes contained dynamite, but that didn't make sense.

I had seen boxes of dynamite when we were working at the tunnels under Książ Castle during the summer, and they were very different, always with the Dynamit Nobel AG label on. These boxes had no label and were much smaller and heavier.

Given that dynamite is so unstable and dangerous to handle and store, why would they keep it in the tunnels?

Daniel was too tired to care. He kept telling me he couldn't go on much longer.

I remember telling him that he could and must carry on, that we would have another life one day.

Soon afterward, another prisoner, Konstanty, tripped over a rock on the floor and fell to the ground near me.

His box landed on its corner, and one of the slats of wood partially splintered and came away, so I was able to see what was inside. I peered down at it, and I can remember now the shock I felt.

Inside, clearly visible, were gold bars marked with the Nazi swastika, tightly packed with cotton cloth.

There were two rows of bars, ten on each side. Both Daniel and I had trained as jewelers in our father's business in Warsaw, so I knew genuine gold when I saw it.

Fortunately, the nearest guard, about fifty metres away, was engrossed in abusing another prisoner and failed to hear the crash as the box hit the ground.

But I knew instantly they would shoot us both dead if they saw us and realized we knew what was in the boxes. So I helped Konstanty push the slat of wood back into place, and we banged the nails back in with a rock.

Yet, with the splinters sticking out and the broken wooden crosspiece, it was still obvious the box had been damaged.

I told Konstanty to turn the box over so the splintered section was at the bottom, and then told him to make sure that when he lowered it onto the pallet, it stayed that way up, so they wouldn't see it.

He trembled and didn't speak, but his eyes thanked me.

The guard turned around just as Konstanty picked the box up and yelled at him.

As Konstanty walked on, the guard smashed him on the back of his puny calves with his truncheon. But he failed to spot the splintered base of the wooden box.

Johnson checked his watch. It was half past three. He had completely lost track of time while immersed in the memoir. The account was interesting not just because of his mother. There were also strong links to the research work he did for his Ph.D. in Berlin in the early '80s, on the economics of the Third Reich.

His thesis, which he still had at home in Portland, included details of how, for most of the war, Hitler's regime had bolstered its thin foreign-exchange reserves, vital to purchasing equipment, machinery, and engineering products, by plundering the gold reserves of the various countries it had marched into. In all, an estimated $600 million of gold at 1945 prices had been looted from the central banks in Belgium, the Netherlands, Czechoslovakia, Austria, and others. Most of it was melted down and reformed by the Reichsbank into new one-kilogram gold bars.

Johnson turned on his phone calculator app and punched in a few numbers. That was something like $30 billion at 2011 prices, he thought.

He had also done research into how, in late 1944 and early 1945, when the Russians were advancing rapidly west and the Americans and British moving east, the crumbling Third Reich scrambled to hide the treasure it had plundered.

Much of it was stored in disused mines. Some was

dropped to the bottom of lakes.

But now it seemed that from what Jacob had written, some of it was also hidden in the tunnels of the Riese complex.

Johnson was enthused. It had been his love of history, international relations, politics, and diving into the minutiae of investigation that had driven him to join the CIA and then the OSI—the latter, especially, being a place where passion counted for more than money and power. Now he felt as if he was somehow back on home territory. He made himself another coffee and continued reading.

> *By three o'clock, there were only twelve wooden boxes left on the Nazi gold train out of the 200 delivered that morning.*
>
> *By then, of the twenty-two prisoners who had started the day, one had died, Ben Stronski.*
>
> *Ben was nineteen and so frail he was in a zombie-like state, the "walking dead," as those who had given up all hope were called.*
>
> *There was a delay while Ben's body was carried out. So the human chain of prisoners bunched up, and we walked closely together as we carried the last few boxes into Sub-Tunnel A.*
>
> *Then it happened.*
>
> *Behind us, there was a sudden explosion as a large chunk of rock fell from the roof to the ground. Then came another, far louder boom, and the entire tunnel roof fell down.*

Johnson put down the notebook and took a deep breath. Jacob's description of the chaos in the tunnel almost seventy years earlier caused him to have a visceral reaction. He felt grateful just to have air to breathe at this point. He picked up the notebook again and read how Jacob had felt suffocated but had survived, and then he reached the point where Jacob saw some guards with flashlights headed toward him and the other prisoners.

One guard ordered us to pick up our boxes and take them to the pallet where Brenner stood. Then I realized four of the six guards were missing, presumably buried or left on the other side of the rockfall, where the Nazi gold train stood.

Brenner started to rant and complain about the engineers taking too many risks, too many shortcuts. He told the two guards to take us out via the emergency escape tunnel, the one I had helped to dig during a hellish eight weeks earlier in the year. I'd almost forgotten about it—tried to black out the memory.

Our group followed the guards, with Brenner limping along at the back. The only light in the emergency tunnel, cut roughly out of the soft sandstone, came from the flashlights. The passage was only a metre wide and barely high enough to stand in, with a rough roof, walls, and floor.

It cut directly through 150 metres of sandstone. The final stretch was too low to stand in, so we crawled.

At the end, we emerged through a small square opening into a dry, thankfully unused sewer tunnel. Then we proceeded through a metal grate into some woodland near a lake.

From there, the guards marched us through the snow back down the valley to the Ludwikowice Kłodzkie train station. There, the guards pushed us onto the same two filthy metal railway cars that we had arrived in.

Daniel and I were among eleven in the rear car, where a guard began to tie our wrists to a steel bar running the full length of the wall.

I quickly realized the guard was ill with a high temperature. He sweated profusely, despite the freezing weather, and his face was gray.

The guard had tied eight of us, with me next, when his colleague in the front car called to ask for another piece of rope. He jumped out of the car, handed it to his colleague, and then returned.

I had placed my hands behind me, holding the steel bar, but the guard had forgotten me and moved straight to Daniel.

Then he sat on a low stool at the rear of the truck. I just left my wrists behind me, holding the bar, as if they had been tied.

The train moved slowly out of the station along the winding line that led back up the valley to Gluszyca.

After a few minutes, the guard fell asleep.

Unlike Daniel, I had often thought about escaping. I was always working out guards' procedures and delivery truck arrivals and departures, checking which guards might be bribable, and practicing my German.

But the opportunity had never arisen, and the risks were high.

It was now or never. I wasn't sure I still had enough reserves of will power and strength. But I had to try.

Jacob then went on to detail how he untied Daniel and attacked the guard with a wooden plank from the floor. When the guard was unconscious, he and Daniel jumped from the train and waded along a nearby river to throw off any scent, should the Nazis bring dogs to find them. But when they heard nineteen shots, they knew Brenner had killed them all—something that was confirmed much later. After that, there was only one line left in the narrative, a couple of pages from the end of the notebook.

I knew then he would have to pay the price, that there would have to be justice.

Johnson put the notebook down and rested in his chair, staring at the ceiling.

A Nazi gold train.

It was the kind of thing he'd read speculation about many times in newspaper stories over the years. He recalled that some similar treasure had in fact been found by American troops, stashed away in a mine in Germany just after the war had ended.

Johnson gave a suppressed laugh and mentally tried to work out what it would have been worth.

If there were two hundred boxes, each with twenty gold bars, and assuming they were Third Reich bars of a standard one kilogram each, that amounted to four thousand kilograms.

He checked the price of gold on a financial website. It stood at more than $1,800 per troy ounce, of which there were thirty-two to the kilogram. So safe to say, the haul would be worth about $230 million at 2011 prices.

Unbelievable. Had they removed all of it since the war? What had they done with it?

Two hundred thirty million dollars.

Johnson shook his head, almost unconsciously, then picked up the notebook. They must have laundered the gold somehow, reformed it, sold it on, maybe as jewelry. He recalled the array of gold-refining equipment he had seen during his nocturnal visit to the Kudrows' workshop.

He sat thinking for a while. The odd thing was, if they had procured that amount of gold, it wasn't reflected in their lifestyles.

Okay, they were obviously well heeled. Old Jacob had a house in Mayfair, although he'd bought it a long time ago. But the workshop was very run-down. And both Jacob and Daniel still seemed to be working hard even in their late eighties. *Weird.*

He opened the notebook at the back. Then he noticed there was also some writing on the last page, in green ink and underlined twice.

Endgame: A Masterplan.

Next to it was a date, written very recently: *October 10, 2011.*

Underneath: nothing. The page was otherwise blank.

PART THREE

CHAPTER TWENTY-NINE

Sunday, November 27, 2011
London

Jacob walked to the safe and fiddled with the combination dial on the front. The door swung open.

A few seconds later, he lost his balance and grabbed the side of the wooden writing desk with his left hand to steady himself.

"Are you all right?" Daniel asked him.

"No. They've taken it. My notebook. It's gone. Papers, all gone."

"What notebook and papers?" Daniel asked. He stood and went over to his brother.

"My memoirs, in my red notebook. I told you about them. All my invoices and receipts, the gold sales. How could they have gotten in there? Nobody else knows the combination."

Jacob put both of his wrinkled hands inside the safe, running them over the felt lining, not believing what his own eyes were telling him.

"I can't tell the police," Jacob said. "What are we going to do? Daniel, get me a whiskey, quickly, I'm not feeling very good." Jacob sat down.

Daniel opened the drinks cupboard and poured some Scotch into a cut-glass tumbler.

Jacob took it and drank. "All the first part of our story was in that notebook. The camp, how the gold got into the tunnels, our escape, all that. I had a plan to expose him." He put his head in his hands. "It's all falling apart. More than fifty-five years and nothing happens. Now, all of a sudden, it's gone crazy. Nathaniel's dead. Keith's dead. Burglaries, kidnappings, police everywhere."

Daniel nodded. "We need to think this through and make a plan," he said, staring straight ahead.

They had gone straight from Jacob's house to the workshop after a phone call from Leopold, who sounded so faltering and shocked that Jacob initially thought one of his children must have died.

Now police had already sealed off the workshop in the car-parts business next door where Keith's body had been found. Red and white striped tape covered the exterior and interior doors and the windows.

Detectives were hard at work carrying out forensic tests, interviews, questions, measurements, and fingerprint searches.

* * *

Johnson was intrigued by the contents of Jacob's red notebook. But at the same time, he felt a little uneasy.

The revelation that the Kudrow twins had apparently witnessed his mother's torture by a sadistic SS officer changed everything.

It seemed such a massive coincidence that the fate of these three people, among millions of Jews who were incarcerated in thousands of concentration camps across Europe, should have been so closely intertwined.

Was it *too much* of a coincidence? It crossed his mind that someone might somehow be playing games with him. But the detail was too convincing, the emotions too raw, the dates too specific.

He opened his encrypted laptop and worked his way through the three screens of security passwords he had installed. Then he wrote short e-mails to Amy and both his children, giving them a highly edited version of what had been happening and promising to give them all a call the following day.

As he wrote, two new e-mails popped into his inbox.

One was from Vic, asking about progress. The other was from someone called Nat Goodman, with one word in the subject line: Kudrow.

Johnson opened it.

Dear Mr. Johnson,

I understand your investigating the Kudrow jewelry business. I am having busines arangements with the Kudrows before and have something that is interesting for you. A map and some documents. It is possible to collect it from me at car park 4 at the O2 Arena at 11 a.m. tomorrow, Monday. It is next the river. I am waiting in a green Honda Civic.

I can't give any more details.
Please do not reply to this email.
Thank you
Nat Goodman

Johnson snorted. *Amateurish.* Or was it deliberately

designed that way? His mind went back to the threatening note he had found under his door at the Tower Hotel, with its spelling and grammar errors. It was clearly the Argentinians again. The e-mail was from a Hotmail account.

Why would anyone wanting to pass documents to him choose a parking lot at a landmark place like the O2 Arena rather than a quiet pub somewhere? Johnson knew the O2, one of the U.K.'s largest live-music concert venues, which was on the tip of a U-shaped peninsula sticking out into the River Thames a few miles east from where he sat.

Indeed, he had visited the site in 2000 when he was briefly in London as part of an OSI investigation. At that time, it was called the Millennium Dome.

Johnson went outside to Jayne's balcony, lit a cigarette, and tried to think. Jayne had told him that José Guzmann's son, Ignacio, was in London. It had to be him. Johnson also assumed that he was responsible for the dead body in the workshop.

But wait. What if there was something in this e-mail? What if it was someone who genuinely wanted to pass on some information?

Too many questions. Johnson was tempted to forward the e-mail on to Jayne and ask her to get her team at GCHQ to do their forensics on it, but then he decided to sleep on it and discuss it with her first, if she ever came home from MI6, where she currently seemed to be working around the clock.

He sat in a chair on Jayne's balcony and reflected on his progress so far.

When Johnson had started, he had seen the Kudrows as perpetrators of something possibly shady that was funding political activity at the highest level in the United States.

While that was likely to be true, now it felt quite different. *Are the Kudrows the perpetrators, or are they the victims?* What they had done, exactly, wasn't yet fully clear.

He really needed to read the whole document carefully, in detail, and then find a way to talk to Jacob.

One thing he knew: he felt more alive, more vibrant, and more motivated now, doing this, than he had in years.

He reread the e-mail from Nat Goodman and lit another cigarette.

* * *

Washington, D.C.

"I'm really worried about that journalist and the investigator getting into your campaign finances," Philip Pietersen said.

David Kudrow raised his eyebrows. It was something he'd been trying to put out of his mind in order to concentrate on his political messaging.

"It'll be fine," David said. "Don't think there's much to hide—nothing that's going to cause a big issue. My father and uncle have got a long track record."

The two men, accompanied by a security guard, had just a few minutes earlier left David's campaign headquarters, a three-story office block on Maryland Avenue Northeast, after a hard Sunday afternoon of work with the full campaign team. Thirty-five people had given up their planned weekend family activities to come into the office for various sessions to plan strategy, logistics, public relations and media messaging, and finances. Nobody had complained—the steamroller was gathering speed.

David already had two staff members working almost full-time to find a much larger headquarters for the campaign proper, on the assumption that he was going to get the nomination. In that event, the team would mushroom in size many times over.

"I need a drink," David said. He also wanted an hour or two of what felt like a normal life.

They walked into the Argonaut bar and ordered beers. Knowing there was a risk of being spotted and hassled by people wanting selfies and handshakes, Philip had phoned ahead and persuaded the manager, whom he knew well, to let them use the private room upstairs.

They climbed the stairs with the drinks, leaving the security man out on the landing, shut the door, and sat down at a table that overlooked the street.

"To be honest, it's the police and FBI investigation into Nathaniel I'm more worried about than the journalist and the campaign finances," David said, lowering his voice. "They're going through all his bank accounts, phone records, e-mails, everything. I mean, we obviously want them to track down his killer, but who knows what they're going to unearth while they're doing that. He's had a few odd dealings in his time. We all know that. Hopefully there's nothing that reflects badly on me."

"Well, it's inevitable that they'll go through everything and do a thorough job," Philip said. "We'll just have to hope for the best, especially at this stage of the campaign. Things are going so well. So there's nothing to be worried about, you don't think, from your uncle or father's side?"

"No. Not as far as I know. I don't know much about my uncle's business. I've been too busy focusing on my own these past few years and on politics here. I mean, I know he pulled off a few very good gold deals in the U.K. many years back, but nothing untoward, I don't think."

"Okay, fine," Philip said. With everything that had been going on, it was the first chance he'd had to properly brief his boss on his conversation with Zac Butler, the friendly editor at *Inside Track* who had tipped him off about Fiona's assignment. He quickly talked him through what Butler had said.

"Has either Heppenstall or Johnson tried to contact you, by any chance? E-mails, phone calls?" Philip asked.

"No, nothing at all," David said.

"Okay, well, don't respond if they do. I just thought they might have tried. I know they were chatting to Nathaniel at that fund-raiser we had at my house recently, so I thought they might try contacting you directly as well," Philip said.

David scratched his chin and sipped his beer. "Heppenstall and Johnson," he said. "Someone was telling me they were the two who brought down that California senator who had to quit a few years back. They discovered he was sheltering some fugitive Nazi. The guy who mentioned it said Heppenstall wrote several stories about it for *The New York Times*."

"Yeah, it was her. That's what I mean. We should be worried," Philip said. He took a long draft from his glass, then changed the subject and launched into a monologue on his campaign strategy.

"I'm telling you David, you'll take Obama out next year," Philip said. "You'll see. You'll get the nomination. All our hard work's going to pay off, and you'll clean up come the election. People are sick of promises about the economy, about jobs, about improving flows of capital to small businesses and nothing actually happening. All it's going to take is for you to keep up your momentum on all that stuff, and you'll sweep it. Remember Clinton's catchphrase from '92: it's the economy, stupid. Well, it's the same this time around."

David nodded. He sipped his beer and gazed through the bay window at the gentrified H Street Northeast and the Delta Towers hotel opposite. A red and gray Washington Metrobus bound for Union Station hummed past the bar, its passengers peering out the windows.

"Yes, you're right. I don't think there's much that can go wrong," David said eventually. "I'm going to do it for

Nathaniel. In fact, I bet I'm going to get the sympathy vote. Might be the only good thing to come out of what's happened to him."

CHAPTER THIRTY

Monday, November 28, 2011
London

Jayne came into the kitchen area, rubbing her shower-wet hair with a towel, a bath robe wrapped around her.

"Joe, have a look at this. Last night's evening paper. They didn't waste any time."

She threw a copy onto the table.

Johnson hadn't seen the paper, although he had already told Jayne what had happened during the nocturnal visit to the workshop with Bomber Tim and had then shown her the e-mail from Nat Goodman.

The lead story on page three carried a large headline that shouted, "Murder Hunt As Mutilated Body Found in Workshop."

Below it was a large picture of the Classic Car Parts workshop facade.

A Metropolitan Police detective chief inspector was quoted in the story as saying there appeared to be no obvious motive for the killing of Keith Bartelski. The culprits appeared to have entered the building via an unbolted coal hatch door, but there were no other leads so far and no arrests. Police were working around the clock on the inquiry.

Johnson snorted into his coffee.

The report went on to state that the dead man had no immediate family and that his work colleagues, including the business owner, a Leopold Skorupski, had been unavailable for comment.

When Johnson had finished reading, Jayne sat down. "So what are you going to do next?"

"I'm thinking about what to do with this e-mail. It obviously reeks of a setup. A very amateurish one."

"I agree. But on the other hand it might just be—"

"I know," Johnson said. "It might be a lead." He was also thinking it might give him a way of derailing the Argentinians.

"Well, follow it up, but do it your way." She stood and headed toward the door. "You don't need me to tell you what to do. Take the usual precautions. Check it out from a distance. You've got a gun—the one I never gave to you. Get there early. I've got some binoculars in the cupboard over there."

She was right, and that was the way Johnson was leaning. He didn't like leaving stones unturned.

Jayne added, "By the way, one thing you need to know: the police apparently picked up an Argentinian yesterday at lunchtime in south London somewhere. He was in a pub. The police had a tip and found a stash of antitank mines, rocket launchers, and ammunition in his car boot. Name of Felipe—didn't get his surname. I don't know if it's got any connection with your Argentine mob, probably not, but I've asked one of my team to check it out for me. MI5 will be onto it, and I need to log it for our Olympics work. I'll let you know if we hear anything."

"Antitank mines? Do they know what he was planning to do with them?" Johnson asked.

"No, no idea, not yet. Got to go and get dressed and head to work."

With that, Jayne disappeared into her room. She emerged fifteen minutes later to give him a quick goodbye over her shoulder as she headed for the door.

By the time Fiona called him at quarter past eight, Johnson had mapped out a plan in his mind and had a bag packed.

He told Fiona to arrive at the Starbucks café near Jayne's place at ten o'clock. He would meet her, and then his plan would be put into action.

* * *

Diego had just opened a second pack of Camels. *This is getting tedious. Three hours and nothing,* he thought, as he pulled his twelfth cigarette of the morning out from the pack.

He and Alejandro had arrived at the Minories parking garage at just after seven o'clock. They had parked ten spaces away from Johnson's BMW and settled down to wait.

"Did you hear what Ignacio said last night about Felipe, you know, the guy who brought the antitank mine around?" Diego asked.

"No, what was that?"

"Felipe got pulled in by police yesterday. Ignacio's worried he's going to rat on us," Diego said.

"Doubt he'd rat on us," Alejandro said. "He must have much bigger customers than us. I mean, one antitank mine is—"

Alejandro abruptly went quiet and trained his gaze across the garage.

Diego looked up to see the blue painted doors to the stairwell swinging open.

"Here he is," Alejandro said. "Wait . . . there's two of them. There's a woman with him."

Diego snapped upright, emerging from his semi-stupor.

Johnson and Fiona were striding across the concrete walkway toward the black BMW.

"A *woman*? Crap. Ah, don't you remember, Ignacio told us about the American journalist he was working with," Diego said. "I think he e-mailed us a photo of her as well as him. Get it on your phone. Quick, let me see. I'm not sure if the boss wants her taken out as well, but we're not going to have a choice here."

Alejandro pulled out his phone and scrolled through his e-mails. "Here it is. Yes, that's the woman Ignacio mentioned . . . long dark hair. Definitely. Not bad, is she? Nice legs, good looker. It's gonna be a pity."

They watched as Johnson put his black backpack on the ground and checked all around the car. He got on his hands and knees and looked underneath.

"Shit, he's doing a proper check. Just hope he doesn't realize the doors aren't locked when he presses the key fob. That's the critical moment. The lights will flash, but it'll most likely make a different noise," said Diego.

Johnson went around the car again, this time examining the wheel wells.

He stood with his hands on his hips for a few seconds, looking at the BMW, then eventually pressed his key fob. The indicator lights flashed and Johnson opened the driver's door. He climbed into the driver's seat, and Fiona got into the passenger seat.

Diego glanced over at Alejandro. "We got away with it," he said.

Johnson started the engine; a low guttural roar came from the twin exhausts at the rear of the car.

In the Ford Focus, Diego fastened his seat belt and felt the familiar kick of adrenaline and the knot in his stomach that he always got when he was about to go into action.

"He's careful but not careful enough. Okay, *mi amigo*. Let's go." He turned the key, and the Focus's engine sparked into life.

* * *

Johnson steered the BMW out of its parking space, down four sets of ramps to the ground floor, and nosed out into the busy traffic outside the parking garage.

He had set up his cell phone as a satellite navigation device, placing it in a holder with a rubber suction cup that was attached to the windshield.

Fiona fastened her seat belt. "Joe, are you okay? You look a little tense."

"I'm fine."

As Johnson exited the parking garage, he checked his mirror for cars emerging behind him. There was a blue Ford, followed by a dark gray Renault, and behind that, a silver Ford Focus. Johnson couldn't see back any farther than that.

Almost as soon as Johnson left the parking garage, he ran into a line of traffic waiting at temporary traffic lights next to some roadwork. Two police cars waited next to the lights. Officers stood nearby and scrutinized cars as they moved past. It was a common sight around East London.

Once he was past the jam, Johnson drove along Royal Mint Street, a narrow one-way road running parallel to the Docklands Light Railway. One of its electric trains glided past them in the opposite direction, heading into Tower Gateway station.

Johnson saw in his mirror that one of the police cars had pulled out and was following close behind.

It was a bright, clear day, and the sun glared at a low angle through the windshield from the south, dazzling Johnson. He pulled down the sun visor.

Then they were onto the A13, running east parallel to the River Thames.

Johnson glanced to the right and left as he drove. This part of East London was full of old warehouse buildings, many of them becoming increasingly run down and earmarked for demolition. In their place, new steel and glass constructions were going up, and cranes were busy lifting large steel girders into place.

He glanced in his mirror. The police car was still there but slightly farther back, and the silver Ford Focus that had come out of the parking garage was following behind the police car. Johnson looked first at his sat nav, then at the redevelopment projects on either side of the road.

He accelerated hard along the divided highway, which was extremely busy with a mixture of commuter traffic, heavy construction trucks delivering to building sites, and the ubiquitous large commercial white vans ferrying parcels and goods around.

As they turned sharply right around a bend, there was a faint but distinct scraping noise from the engine compartment in front of them, then a slight thud.

"Hear that?" Johnson asked. "Didn't sound too good."

"I heard something, but it was faint." Fiona said. She listened carefully for several seconds, but there were no further noises.

She relaxed and asked, "So have you read all of Kudrow's notebook now? What did you make of it?"

Johnson didn't answer immediately. He again checked his mirror. The silver Ford Focus had overtaken the police car and was now behind him.

"Pretty awful actually. Graphic, gory in places, and the camp they were in was shocking. Brave guys. I find it hard to know how to view the Kudrows, given all that. Victims back then, definitely. But we need to get to the bottom of these gold transactions," he said eventually.

He ran through the contents of the memoir as they drove. "You can read it yourself when we get back," he said.

Johnson braked hard as a white van cut out in front of him from a pharmacy entrance. He checked the mirror again. The silver car had also braked and was hanging back behind him, despite an obvious opportunity to pass.

He continued, "There's still a lot of unanswered questions. I need to talk to Jacob, the old guy, somehow. I'm thinking how to go about doing that."

Fiona nodded.

"And don't worry about this meeting. I'm not intending to make us martyrs for the cause. I just need to know. I think we'll check out the site from a distance before we make any move. I've got binoculars. Any sign of something odd, we're out of there, okay?"

He accelerated hard to pass a truck, then cut back into the inside lane, passed a van, and moved sharply back into the outside lane again.

As the car changed direction, there was another scraping noise, louder this time, and the same thud he'd heard before from the engine compartment. "There it goes again," Johnson said. "Don't like the sound of that. There's something loose, sliding around."

He glanced in his mirror and unconsciously patted the Walther, which he had placed in a holster under his left armpit, beneath his jacket.

"I heard it that time, didn't sound too good. Is everything all right? You keep checking the mirror," Fiona said.

"There's a silver car, a Ford, just behind us. It's tracking everything I do," he said. "I've done a few sharp maneuvers, and it's still right there. It left the parking garage behind us."

"You think so?" Fiona asked.

Johnson was pleased to see she had enough presence of mind not to turn around and look.

"Yes," Johnson said. "Some asshole is following us, definitely."

He put his foot down hard and slammed the BMW down into third gear, and the engine whined at a high pitch as he accelerated into a gap between an ambulance and a school minibus.

The Focus followed.

* * *

Diego was feeling increasingly anxious.

"I can't keep up with the American," he said. "This traffic's ridiculous. Trucks cutting in and out and blocking me. We should have had two cars for this job. Trying to tail an ex-CIA guy with one is just asking for trouble."

Diego accelerated through a gap as a large truck changed lanes, braked to avoid a black taxi, and then put his foot down again to get through a set of traffic lights before they changed to red.

"There he is. I can see him again. I'm going to get a little closer. I don't want to lose him, otherwise we're done," Diego said.

He eased back on the accelerator once he had closed the gap between him and the BMW to around forty meters.

Alejandro held tightly to the black remote-control trigger box on his lap. "Just be careful, Diego. If he spots us following, we've had it. I was gonna blow him up as soon as we were out of that parking garage, but with all those police around, I didn't want to risk it."

Alejandro bit his fingernails. "I think he's already spotted us, the way he's driving. I'm thinking as soon as we get to a clear section of road where there's no shops, we should blow him. Can't do it here though. It's too busy. We can't risk getting stuck and not being able to get away. Let's get farther out of the center. Hopefully the traffic will ease off a bit."

Out in front, Johnson's BMW overtook two large blue delivery vans, but then before Diego could follow, one of the vans pulled out alongside the other, blocking the road. The Argentinian moved into the van's slipstream, his car bumper dangerously close to the rear of the van, then he honked his horn hard.

No response. The two vans continued side by side. Diego slammed his hand down on the dashboard in front of him. "Come on, move, move, move."

Eventually the second van pulled into the inside lane to let him pass. Diego downshifted into third gear, pushed his foot on the accelerator, and powered past, honking as he went. He quickly took his speed up to more than seventy miles per hour, in a zone with a forty mph limit.

After a minute, he could see the black BMW ahead of him.

Alejandro's knuckles had gone white where he was holding tightly to the armrest. "Slow it down, Diego. We're gonna get stopped by the police. You're way over the limit."

But Diego shook his head. "Just shut it. We can't lose him. Ignacio will kill us."

Diego had regained ground to within around fifty meters of the BMW when a large truck in front of him in the outside lane and a taxi in the inside lane both braked to a halt as the traffic lights at the crossroads ahead turned red. He was blocked.

Johnson's BMW shot through the crossroads a couple of seconds before the lights changed.

* * *

Even before the lights turned green again, Diego knew he was in trouble.

The driver of the truck in front had started easing forward and was indicating to turn left at the crossroads. Diego could see it would mean a slow maneuver across two lanes, thus holding up the rest of the traffic.

Diego muttered, "*Bastardo, no es posible.*" He swore again, then banged his fists down on the top of the steering wheel.

The taxi remained stationary so the truck could turn in front of it. After what seemed to Diego like an eternity, the truck completed its turn, and his path was finally clear.

He rammed down the accelerator, and with a squeal of tires, the Focus took off. A few seconds later, the car shot past Limehouse station on the right.

It was Alejandro who spotted the BMW first.

"He's up ahead, turning left. He's trying to run. Quick, go, before this next set of lights changes."

But it was too late.

The traffic lights in front turned red. Diego slammed on the brakes, and the Focus slid to a halt with a screech, just inches from plowing into the back of a taxi.

Alejandro's voice rose. "We're gonna lose him. He's turned left and out of sight. Go around this taxi and through the lights."

"I can't. They're red. There's no way through there. You'll have to blow him now. Otherwise he's gone. Quick, press it."

"What, now?"

"*Si, amigo* . . . now. Go on, press it . . . yes."

Alejandro pushed the red button on the trigger unit.

Diego could see little of what was going on farther ahead, his view blocked by the taxi and other cars and trucks beyond the junction.

But he certainly didn't miss hearing the boom that echoed and rumbled down the road as the six-kilogram FMK-3 anti-tank mine detonated under the BMW's hood.

"*Madre* . . . it's blown," Alejandro said.

The traffic lights changed to green, and Diego, almost hypnotically, let the clutch out and followed the taxi slowly past a Tesco store toward the junction where he had seen Johnson's BMW turn left.

A large cloud of black smoke rose from just around the corner, mushrooming outward.

Diego could now see that a red and white railway bridge, which passed over the junction between the main road and the side road, had partially collapsed.

Large chunks of brickwork and debris lay in the middle of the road, some of it on top of a white van, which was partly crushed, and a steel girder was bent at an angle, also on top of the van. A logo on the back of the van read Dave's Flowers.

Through the wreckage of the bridge, a few yards along the side road, the tangled and bent remains of the black BMW were just visible, its doors blown off.

People ran out of houses and shops, some toward the explosion, others away from it. A small group of young schoolchildren on the opposite side of the road cried and screamed, and Diego could see that the windows and door of a house next to the junction were blown inward. A set of traffic lights next to the bridge had been reduced to a scrambled mess of metal.

A few seconds later, there was another loud bang, and flames erupted from the back of the wrecked BMW. The schoolchildren screamed even more loudly and ran back along the pavement.

Alejandro yelled, "We gotta get out of here, Diego. Move . . . *now*."

Diego felt stunned. He glanced in the mirror to find his ashen face gazing back at him. Then he obediently did a U-turn in the middle of the road and headed back the way they had come.

A minute later, three police cars pounded past them in the other direction, sirens blaring. Diego looked in his mirror and saw them fly past the Tesco store and screech to a halt near the collapsed road bridge.

"I'll let Ignacio know it's job done. Johnson's a goner. And the journalist." Alejandro's voice sounded unusually shaky as he typed a text message into his phone.

CHAPTER THIRTY-ONE

Monday, November 28, 2011
London

"London 2012 is going to be a critical security challenge for both police and security agencies this coming year," Jayne told the meeting of three SIS officers and two technical experts from GCHQ.

It was her second major briefing of the morning, both on the subject of security preparations for the following year's Olympic Games.

She passed around two documents that outlined MI6's strategy. Taking a sip of her cappuccino, she continued. "As you may know, the Games have been the main focus of our planning for a long time. We've recruited more intelligence officers, and we've moved people from other areas on to countering the risk of a terror attack."

She held up the first document. "If you look at this, you'll see there are basically three potential threats. First, Al-Qaeda and its affiliates planning an attack with a resulting mass-casualty scenario. Second, Irish Republican dissident terrorist groups, either through an attack or a hoax, and third, clashes between rival groups or ethnic groups."

Jayne surveyed the others in the room, then continued. "At the same time, we're having to deal with other issues pre-Games, like accreditation. We're going to have 540,000 applications for accreditation from people working at the venues. We'll need to check them all to try and identify anyone who may be a threat to national security."

She outlined how the SIS had reduced its work on other lower-priority areas in order to focus on potential threats and had been "clearing the decks" so that could happen.

She went on, "The problem is that the home secretary's made it very clear to our director general that the other work can't be ignored. It's a difficult one. Our resources are limited."

There was a knock, and an administrative assistant put her head around the door.

"Jayne, the boss wants a quick word in his office, please. It's very urgent. I'm sorry."

Jayne apologized to the others, went out the door, and walked to the office of Mark Nicklin-Donovan, chief of the U.K. Controllerate, her boss. His door was open, and he lifted his head as Jayne knocked.

"Ah, Jayne, just a quick one, for information. There's been what police think could possibly have been a terrorist explosion over in East London, on the A13. A car bomb. There's a black BMW blown up and school kids possibly injured. A disused rail bridge over the A13 has been brought down, so the road's blocked, and a van driver's been killed. Police don't know who the car driver was; it's such a mess they're struggling to find body parts. They're also trying to identify the vehicle and the owner. But given your meetings this morning, you need to know. There may be questions.

You can carry on, and I'll send through any updates as I get them. Okay?"

He looked back down at the papers on his desk and carried on reading.

"Okay, thanks for letting me know, Mark."

Jayne walked slowly out of the office and over to an alcove where there were drinks and snack machines. She took a plastic cup and filled it with water from a cooler.

A black BMW, in East London? That sounded ominous. Wasn't Joe's rented car a black BMW 3 Series? And he was heading that way to the O2 this morning . . .

Rather than go back to her meeting, Jayne diverted to her office, picked up the desk phone, and punched in a number.

Straight to voice mail. *This is Joe Johnson, please leave a message after the tone, and I'll give you a call back. Thanks.*

Jayne hesitated, and her finger hovered over the call-end button. Then she changed her mind.

"Joe, it's Jayne here," she said. "I gather there's been a car bomb explosion in East London. I'm assuming you're not involved and you're okay. If you get this message, I'll be back in my flat at four this afternoon. I'm finishing early after all these late nights. So I'll see you after that. Bye."

* * *

Jayne arrived back at her flat having still heard nothing from Joe since leaving the voice mail on his phone several hours earlier. He also hadn't responded to two text messages.

She walked in, dumped her bags on the table, and sighed. Police had not yet provided her office with the names of those injured in the bomb blast, which meant she would have to make her own inquiries.

Jayne glanced toward the window, then jumped slightly. Through the window blind, the silhouettes of two figures were clearly visible on the balcony. One was fiddling with the handle of the door to her living room.

A jolt of adrenaline shot through her. Her first thought was that she had burglars. Then it crossed her mind that the Argentinians were back, trying to get to Joe.

Jayne grabbed a wooden baseball bat that she kept in her kitchen and took three steps toward the door, holding the bat in readiness. Then the door handle was pushed down, and the door opened a fraction.

"You can stop right there. Come out and show yourself," she shouted.

A figure emerged from behind the door.

"Joe! What the hell!" Jayne exhaled in relief.

Johnson was wearing a coat and a wool hat, smoking a cigarette. With him was a striking woman with long dark hair.

"I was about to call the police in," Jayne said. "You nearly gave me a heart attack out there. I heard about that blast in East London. So it had nothing to do with you—or did it? Did you get my messages? You never replied."

Johnson grimaced. "Sorry. It's a bit of a long story." He turned and stubbed out his cigarette on the patio, then came back indoors.

"I do apologize. I've been so sidetracked, I didn't get to reply to you," Johnson said. "By the way, this is Fiona."

Fiona nodded and stepped forward, rather awkwardly offering her hand. "Nice to meet you. I've heard a lot about you," she said.

"You too. Have a seat. You'd both better tell me what the hell's been going on." Jayne put the baseball bat down and sat on one of the wooden chairs surrounding the dining table, folded her arms, and planted them on the table in front of her. She faced first Johnson, then Fiona.

Johnson coughed, then took out a handkerchief and blew

his nose. "Well, what happened was this . . . " He quickly summed up the car journey to the point where he had become certain they were being followed by the Ford Focus and they had noticed the odd scraping noises coming from the engine compartment.

"My brain went into overdrive at that point. I mean, I realized the silver car had followed us from the parking garage. I was driving like a madman, and he was taking a hell of a lot of risks to keep up with me, so it was obvious what he was doing. And then remember the threats I've had and the dead body in the workshop."

He continued, "To cap it all off you'd told me about that Argentinian who was pulled in for having antitank mines in his car boot. I knew at that stage we had to get out of the car. I just had a gut feeling."

Fiona took up the story. "Yeah, he was saying, 'We've gotta ditch the car, it's dangerous. There's something not right here.' So he swings this sharp left into a side road, screeches to a halt, and screams at me to get out and get behind a wall at the side of the road. So I did that, hiding behind this big thick stone wall in the driveway of a house. Next thing I know, he's joined me. He shoves me to the ground and tells me to flatten myself, and he's got his gun out and is covering the entrance to the driveway. We're on the ground right up against the wall next to some bushes."

She took a breath. "About five seconds later there's this massive bang, and the windows of the house behind us get blown in. It's carnage. The top part of the stone wall behind us has collapsed, there's bits of car flying through the air, and the bridge has fallen down. Unbelievable."

"Bloody hell," Jayne said. "Remote trigger. Probably when you drove down the side road and they lost sight of you?"

"I think that's probably right," Johnson said. "My thought was if they were really chasing us, they'd follow us, and I could take them out with the handgun if they came into the driveway. We didn't get into that situation, obviously. Anyway, we were damned lucky. That stone wall saved us. It was a big bomb. Another few seconds, and we'd have been crow's meat."

"Lucky? Sounds like you made some bloody good calls," Jayne said.

Johnson blew his nose again. "Gut feeling."

Fiona nodded. "Gut feeling that saved my bacon."

"So what happened after that?" Jayne asked.

"Well, I'm screaming by this stage," Fiona said. "Other people are shouting, and all hell's breaking loose. Then you've got a huge black cloud of smoke and dust rising where the car was. People start pouring out of the houses. School kids screaming. Folks yelling into their phones, calling for police, fire, ambulances. It was crazy. Joe was the only calm one."

Johnson smiled. "I knew we had to get out of there. I didn't want to get caught up in some police inquiry, and I'm carrying a gun, remember. So I get Fiona to her feet—we're covered in shit and dust and stuff—and we start walking along the road back the way we've just driven. The traffic starts backing up. People are doing U-turns. I hail the nearest cab, and we make a sharp exit before anyone can stop us."

Johnson caught Jayne's eye. "I'm a bit rusty with this kind of thing."

Jayne pulled up one corner of her mouth wryly. "Doesn't sound like it. They must have a lot at stake here, and you're a threat, obviously. Exactly how is another question. If you're going to get to the bottom of it, you're going to have to move fast, because they're ahead of you right now."

Johnson sighed. "Yes, right. Tell me something I don't know, Jayne. I need the pieces that are missing from the jigsaw, not the ones I've got."

Fiona's phone beeped, and she checked the incoming

message. "It's the office. They want a story on the car bomb blast since Obama's over here. Dammit. I've nearly been blown up and—"

"They don't relent, do they?" Jayne said.

"I can't go out covered in shit like this." Fiona tried to brush off some of the dirt on her coat and jacket. She looked at Jayne. "I don't suppose there's any chance I could borrow a few things, is there?"

Jayne pursed her lips. "Guess so, sure."

Fiona appeared relieved. "Thanks. To be honest, work's the last thing I feel like doing, but I've got a commentary on his visit to write up as well."

Jayne stood and steered Fiona toward the bedroom to find some clothes.

Johnson smirked at her as she went past. "The bomb story? That should be interesting reading. Got any eyewitnesses you can quote?"

Fiona turned and gave him a look.

After she had disappeared, Johnson picked up Jacob's notebook.

It contained answers to a lot of the questions he had. But there was one detail missing. *Why?*

Why have the Kudrows been selling gold to Guzmann? And why's he been buying it in such large quantities?

* * *

Ignacio picked up his copy of the evening newspaper, screwed it up into a ball, and threw it at Diego.

"Que imbecil eres," he shouted. "You fucking dickhead. Read that. You blew it. Johnson's still walking around London. He's alive."

Diego picked up the newspaper.

It was blanket coverage. They had cleared the first five

pages to cover the car bomb story. A huge headline was splattered over the front page, "Two Men Killed As Car Bomb Wrecks Bridge."

There was another strap headline above it, "London on Olympics Terror Alert After Mystery Attack."

Below the headlines was a large photograph of the collapsed bridge, with another smaller picture inset showing the crushed florist's van, complete with firemen trying to extract the dead driver's body from the wreckage. The story told how a passerby had also been killed by the blast as he waited to cross the road near the bridge.

But the front-page story also highlighted that no bodies had been found inside the black BMW.

Another police source indicated the BMW had been rented a few days earlier by an American man calling himself Philip Wilkinson. Checks were being carried out on his background.

Inside the paper, there were various eyewitness accounts, including one from a schoolteacher who was quoted saying he saw a man and a woman jump out of the black BMW seconds before it exploded and run into a nearby driveway. But nothing was seen of them afterward.

There were other quotes from shoppers who had come out of a nearby Tesco store and a man who had been knocked off his bicycle by the blast.

The Metropolitan Police commissioner, head of London's police force, was quoted saying, "We are determined to get to the bottom of who planted this bomb and why. Our officers are working round the clock on this inquiry. Nobody has claimed responsibility so far, and we have no leads on the man and the woman seen running away from the BMW or what happened to those people."

Diego stared at Ignacio from the other side of the kitchen table, not comprehending. "He can't be alive. We blew that

BMW to pieces. He was in it with the woman journalist. We watched both of them get into it at the parking garage and followed them."

Ignacio jerked forward. "I know you blew it to pieces, *idiota*. You blew half of East London to pieces. Except Johnson wasn't in it at the time. He obviously got out before it exploded." He glared at Diego, belatedly registering what he had said, and then asked, "The woman journalist was in the car as well? The American? How come?"

"I don't know why," Diego said. "She got into it with Johnson."

Ignacio kicked a wooden chair, which went flying across the kitchen floor straight into the side of the fridge. He strode into the living room of the converted pub and flicked a button on the television remote control. A BBC news bulletin was already running, and a reporter was speaking to the camera next to the collapsed rail bridge on the A13 road, which remained blocked.

"We've had an update from police in the last twenty minutes," the reporter said. "Forensic tests have shown that the explosive device that destroyed the black BMW was an Argentinian antitank blast mine, they think an FMK-3, of the type that was used against British forces during the Falklands War in 1982. It was detonated using a remote control of some kind. Police have already begun a major search for those responsible and are also investigating how the device could have been brought into the U.K."

Ignacio watched in silence as the reporter continued talking. Then he turned to Diego. "Time's running out. The cops have identified the mine, and they've got Felipe in a cell somewhere. It'll take them about two minutes to realize he's supplied the bomb, and then how long will Felipe last under questioning before he names us? He's bound to rat on us to try to cut some deal with the cops."

Ignacio paced back and forth, tugging at his chin. "They'll be on to us soon, the police. Three Argentinians in London kind of stand out. We need to get moving. We need to figure out precisely where that gold is, then we get out of the U.K. . . . *rapidamente*."

Ignacio scratched his head. "We'll work out another way of getting Johnson further down the line. He can go on the back burner now. We've wasted enough time on him. The priority is that map. I've got a plan B. Is that Ford Focus full of gas? Because we're gonna need it."

* * *

Johnson sat alone on the bed in Jayne's spare bedroom and untangled a pair of headphones that were plugged into his phone.

After pushing the earpieces into his ears, he tapped on an app and keyed in a password, then listened with the volume turned up to maximum.

When Johnson had planted the listening device underneath Jacob's office desk, he had put it into voice-activation mode, which meant it should have called his cell phone if it detected sound. But there had been no such alert —until now.

Why it hadn't activated previously, Johnson had no idea. Perhaps there had been a problem with the 3G signal. Perhaps Jacob simply hadn't used the office, although that seemed unlikely.

Whatever the reason previously, the voice-activation function was now working, because he could hear a conversation. The sound was quite faint, as if the voices were some distance away from the microphone, but he could make out what was being said.

One man was talking about doing another trip east and

there being more stock left. Then he mentioned a master plan.

His master plan . . . that must be Jacob speaking. It was the same phrase he'd written in his red notebook.

Then came another voice, very similar in tone but with a slight American accent. Jacob's twin, Daniel, whom he had seen with Jacob outside the workshop a few days earlier? It must be him. Johnson listened more intently.

"Don't talk to me about master plans. Was Keith part of your master plan? Jacob, let's be honest, we don't need the money anymore. There's not much left, in any case. We should get out of this game now. We're too old. We've been in it too long, and now people are getting hurt, killed. We should have gotten out long ago. That's the truth. It's too close. We've got David's nomination to think about. If this lot gets into the U.S. media and they draw a link, he's finished."

Jacob's voice came again. "No, we don't need the money. But after coming this far, I'd like to finally finish Guzmann off. I'm telling you, Daniel, he's behind all this, though it'll be his cronies or his son doing the dirty work. I saw that text Keith sent to Leopold, saying he'd been kidnapped by Argentinians. It's obvious. They've broken into my safe and taken my notebook. They must want to get to Sokolec next. So I'd like to do one last trip, one last delivery, and do it at a high price. And it's got to be soon."

There was silence for a few moments. Then came a third voice, also that of an old man, with an Eastern European twinge to his accent. Johnson assumed it was Leopold Skorupski.

"The van's still in good condition. We could get Jonah to drive. It's what, nine hundred miles via Leipzig? We could get there in two days. That's doable."

Leopold's voice lifted, now more upbeat and enthusiastic.

"It'd be like the old days. Jonah could do the hard graft, the carrying, and the belly pans. We could give him a big bonus. The customs guys still never check."

Jacob spoke again. He also sounded more energetic.

"There's four boxes left in there, that's all. So that's eighty kilos. We could just about get it all in one go. The refining kit here's still okay. What do you think, Daniel?"

Silence. Johnson's earpiece was working loose, so he pushed it back in again. There was a crackle. Then Daniel finally replied.

"No, it's crazy. We just don't need it. I don't want to risk everything, all David's hard work, just for one last sentimental trip. Apart from these Argentinians, we've got a journalist and an investigator on our tail. If they discovered we were lifting four-and-a-half million dollars' worth of gold out just as the primaries are about to kick off, well, you can imagine what they'd do with that story. David and I would be straight in front of a grand jury."

Johnson couldn't resist a wry smile.

Then Jacob spoke again.

"That's not going to happen. I think we leave this for now. We can talk to Jonah tomorrow. If he's not up for it, then it's not a goer. Come on, let's get back to the house. I'm exhausted."

There was the sound of footsteps, then the loud squeak of the office door. Then silence.

Now Johnson's focus was not so much on the fine detail of how the Kudrow brothers and Leopold had extracted gold from Poland, fascinating though it was. It was on something entirely different that had cropped up during their conversation.

At the back of his mind, a theory was evolving.

CHAPTER THIRTY-TWO

Tuesday, November 29, 2011
Bristol

Oliver Kew was having a good Tuesday night. A very good night indeed.

At around eight o'clock, after several beers in different bars, Oliver and four of his fellow history students walked into the Highbury Vaults, a pub on St. Michael's Hill, not far from the university.

The place was buzzing, and Adele's hit "Rolling in the Deep" was blasting over the sound system.

The five friends were on a pub crawl that had started at quarter to six on the city's historic Corn Street.

The Highbury Vaults looked rather run-down from the outside, with a weatherworn, chipped green front. Inside, though, despite the plain wooden seating and tables, it had a cozy, intimate atmosphere, making it a real student favorite. Oliver, who was nicknamed "Godders" by his friends, particularly liked the selection of Young's ales.

He went to the bar to order a round.

And then he saw her.

Oliver, who was in the second year of a three-year degree course at Bristol University, had first noticed the blond girl in October, a couple of weeks after the autumn term began.

First, he had accidentally collided with her when they both came out of the gym. Then, after apologizing for his clumsiness, he struck up a short conversation, during which he realized she lived in the hall of residence next to his.

Since then, he had bumped into her on a few other occasions, less literally and also, he had to admit, less accidentally.

Now the girl, named Susannah, was sitting in a corner of the pub with three other girls. There was one empty bottle of chardonnay on her table and a second that was only a quarter full. They were all laughing.

After half an hour, he managed to contrive a long conversation with her at the busy bar when she went up to order another bottle. They sat down at an adjacent table when two drinkers got up to leave, and then she unexpectedly slid onto his lap, her long legs hanging over his and her short skirt riding up.

Oliver was slurring his words by now. "You're smart, and you're beautiful, you know. We're going on to a club later. Would you all like to come with us?"

He began to feel a little dizzy as the heady cocktail of alcohol, adrenaline and hormones rushed through his system.

"I'd like to, but I can't tonight. I'm on a special girls' night out," she said. "We've planned it all out. I've got a friend visiting from home." Then she turned her head and kissed him, one hand ruffling his short dark hair, the other resting on his chest.

Then she pulled away and smiled. "I'll give you my phone number. Maybe next Friday night?"

Oliver nodded and pulled out his phone to take her number. "I'd like that. Friday would be great. I'll text you."

He remembered he was meant to go home that weekend to see his mother in Radlett, just north of London, and his beloved grandfather and confidant, Jack Kew, who was meant to come for Sunday lunch. But he could cancel that and go the following weekend instead.

Susannah kissed him again, then jumped off his lap and wandered over to her friends, where she pulled on her coat. A minute later, the four girls had gone.

As soon as they had disappeared, Oliver's friends, sitting ten yards away near the pool table, burst into a round of applause. "Pulled, pulled, pulled . . . " they chanted.

Oliver did a mock bow in their direction, a smirk on his face. Now on a high after his brief encounter with Susannah, Oliver walked back over to his friends. "What about a club? Raquel's is a guaranteed chick fest. It's Tuesday night, student night down there. Come on, guys, I'm on a roll."

He mimed along to Katy Perry's "Firework," now blaring from the pub's speakers, as he pretended to sing into a microphone.

When the song finished, he took another mock bow. More applause.

His friends took little persuading. They staggered down St. Michael's Hill and the steep Christmas Steps toward the city center, with its array of bars and clubs.

They passed along Quay Street, around the bend, and onto the much seedier Nelson Street, with its heavily graffitied concrete walls and stark high-rise buildings standing in contrast to much of Bristol's elegant city center.

Raquel's was on the left, its entrance down a dark passage. It cost ten pounds to get in, and drinks were on the pricey side, but it had dance music they liked and a good ratio of girls to guys. It was one of their favorite destinations for a night out.

Oliver was first to the bar and bought five bottles of Stella Artois and tequila chasers to go with them. "Here's to next Friday and to Susannah," he shouted as they sat down, sinking the tequilas in one go.

An hour and two more Stellas later, Oliver was well and truly drunk. He got to his feet and staggered to the stairs that descended into a basement where the toilets were located.

The bottom passageway was painted entirely black, with large mirrors positioned at intervals on either side. He knew the toilet door was somewhere down at the end of the corridor. But the blackness and the array of mirrors, combined with the volume of alcohol he had drunk, made Oliver feel disoriented and dizzy.

Now where are those toilets? Come on, concentrate . . . Ah yes, there they are . . .

As Oliver neared the toilet door, he became aware of two men approaching fast, very near behind him.

As he turned around, one grabbed him around the waist and the other clamped a gloved hand over his mouth. Between them, they pushed him toward the black fire-escape double doors at the end of the corridor. One kicked open the doors, and the next thing Oliver knew, he was out in the cold night air on the pavement.

Another hand pressed a damp cloth over his nose, and he felt himself being pushed into the back of a car waiting right outside the fire doors.

As the car drove away, the last thing he saw was the flashing neon sign above the club door. Raquel's—A Night to Remember.

A few seconds later, Oliver was unconscious.

* * *

Wednesday, November 30, 2011
  London

"So what will the Argentinians do next? They've failed once. So now what?" Jayne asked.

Johnson yawned. He felt unsure. It was the same question he had been asking himself.

He rubbed his head and walked to the kitchen counter. "I don't know what they'll do next. I doubt they know where the gold is, otherwise they wouldn't be in London. I need to find that out before they do, which means talking to the Kudrow brothers somehow."

Jayne nodded. "Listen, I need to talk to you. That car bomb has set the cat among the pigeons. My bosses are getting very nervous now about the whole security situation for next year's Olympics. The director general has had requests from the secretary of state for more detail on our plans, so that means more reports for me to write."

Jayne's voice rose in tone. "It's all putting me in a difficult position. I mean, if my boss found out you were staying at my place and knew that car bomb was aimed at you, I'd be in trouble. I want to leave at some point in the future, but not right now, and on my terms, not theirs."

Johnson nodded. "Understood. So you want me to find somewhere else to stay?"

Jayne stood and leaned against the kitchen counter, her arms firmly folded in front of her chest, staring at him. "Thing is, I'm worried those Argentinians will find out you're here."

Johnson poured some coffee into a mug and sat down, putting his phone on the table. "Yes, you're right. I need to get out. It's not fair on you."

"You can do one more night, okay? Then you'll have to go,

unfortunately. Sorry, Joe. You can keep the Walther . . . for now."

Jayne picked up her bag. "I've got to go to work now, I'll see you later." She made toward the door.

A few minutes after Jayne had gone, a beep came from Johnson's phone. He picked it up and looked at it. *Kudrow's office, the bug.*

He punched a button on the screen, adjusted the volume control up, and turned on the speaker function.

All Johnson could hear was the sound of a telephone ringing, a digital sound.

Was it Jacob's desk phone, or was it a cell phone?

Probably the latter. Johnson remembered Jacob's desk phone being very old-fashioned.

Then came the sound of a few slow-moving footsteps. And a voice.

"Hello, is that Jack Kew? Or should I say, Jacob Kudrow?"

The caller's Hispanic-accented voice sounded quite synthesized and tinny. Johnson surmised that Jacob must have his speakerphone switched on. This time, Johnson remembered the recording function and hit another button on the screen.

"Who is this?" he heard Jacob say.

Then came the caller's voice again. "You don't need to know who it is. But you do need to know this: we have your grandson, Oliver Kew. I think he knows the exact location of your gold source in Poland. It's near Gluszyca, isn't it? I will be persuading him to give me those details over the next few hours. I need you to remain calm and not to call the police. If they contact you with a report of him missing, I need you to tell them you've heard from him, that he is safe and on his way to your house. Just put them off. Then there will be no problem for either your grandson or yourself. Do you understand?"

Johnson felt his scalp prickle. *My God.* He clasped his forehead with his hands and heard Jacob breathing heavily.

"Yes, I understand," Jacob said. "Please don't hurt him. But I really need to know who you are. Can you tell—"

"Shut up. All you need to know is this: if you make any attempt to locate us or if you inform the police, your grandson will meet the same end as Keith Bartelski. Is that understood?"

Again the sound of Jacob breathing—this time quick, staccato breaths, as if he were hyperventilating. Then a reply.

"Yes, I understand. Please look after my grandson, he's only—"

But Jacob was cut short. The caller must have hung up. Then silence.

After a few moments, Johnson heard a second man's voice, which he recognized as Daniel's.

"Jacob, what the hell. This is unbelievable. I don't understand. Oliver doesn't even have those details, does he?"

When Jacob finally answered, it came out in a croaky whisper. "Unfortunately, he does. The map, the coordinates, the written description. They're in Oliver's Google Drive folder."

Daniel's voice rose. "Can we get into it? Delete them?"

"I'd have to get the password. We just did it for safekeeping. It was Nathaniel's idea, when he was over here not long ago. He suggested that a copy of the map be put into a secure Google Drive folder with a password, that it was safer than a filing cabinet in the office. And he said that because we are getting older, Oliver was the best person to keep it."

"Come on," Jacob said, "we have to go downstairs and speak to Leopold."

There was the muffled sound of receding footsteps, then silence again.

Johnson stood and slammed his fist on the table.

"Shit!"

* * *

Johnson went out onto Jayne's balcony and lit a cigarette. Outside, the temperature had dropped, and there was a hint of drizzle in the air.

He tried to weigh the risks attached to the plan taking shape in his mind. There seemed to be many.

But the more he ran over his options, the more he could see he had little choice if he wanted to confirm the theory that, increasingly, he thought was behind events at Jacob's workshop.

Johnson pulled on his brown leather jacket and his scarf and was about to head out when he had an afterthought. He went back to his bag, took out the Walther in its holster, and strapped it under his left arm, beneath his sweatshirt.

Within ten minutes, he was at the junction of Plumbers Row, just a few yards from the entrance to the workshop. He now knew exactly how he would play this.

The pedestrian gate into the courtyard was open, so Johnson passed through and then knocked on a locked black door on the left marked Customer Entrance.

From behind him came a gruff voice. "Can I help you?"

Johnson turned. Standing framed in the doorway of the car-parts business entrance opposite was Jonah.

"Hello, I was looking for Jack Kew. Is he around this morning?"

"Don't I recognize you? You were in here asking about Beetle parts the other day, weren't you?"

Johnson nodded. "Yes, I was, but that was a separate inquiry for my own car. This is a business query, jewelry-related."

"What's your name? Philip something, wasn't it?"

Johnson thought swiftly. He couldn't use his alias anymore after the rented car-blast incident. "No, not Philip. It's Joe Johnson."

Jonah folded his tattooed arms. "Joe Johnson? Uh-huh. Okay. Give me a few minutes. Just wait here. I'll need to go upstairs." He walked toward Johnson, brushed past him, unlocked the door, and disappeared.

It was drizzling harder now and the dogs at the site next door—presumably the same ones who had been barking during Johnson's nighttime visit with Bomber Tim—suddenly started howling.

Five minutes later Jonah reappeared. "Come this way. Follow me."

He led Johnson across a carpeted reception area, down a short corridor, and then up some stairs. Halfway up, Johnson recognized the first-floor landing. This was his third glimpse of it.

Johnson followed Jonah to the left at the top of the stairs and back around to the large wooden managing director's office door, which was open.

"Mr. Kew, I've got Joe Johnson here to see you."

Johnson walked into the room. The two old white-haired men were sitting behind the desk, Daniel with his black-rimmed glasses on the left, Jacob on the right. Both were dressed in jackets, no ties. Both held whiskey glasses, and a bottle of single malt stood on the wooden desk in front of them. The Kudrow twins.

The door behind Johnson squeaked and then clicked shut. Johnson half turned his head to the left and saw Jonah standing on the inside, arms folded. He watched Johnson while leaning with his back against the door, his lips pressed tightly together.

"So, Joe Johnson," said Jacob, adjusting his gold-rimmed glasses. "I know who you are. Ex-CIA, Nazi hunter, and now you're working with a Washington political journalist. An unexpected visit. How can we help you?"

There was no handshake. Daniel indicated with his hand that Johnson should sit in the chair in front of the desk.

Johnson sat and instantly heard a noise behind him as Jonah moved in close. He felt cold steel on the back of his neck.

"Mr. Johnson, if you have a weapon, take it out and place it on the table," Jonah said.

Johnson first put his hands in the air, then slowly reached under his armpit, removed the Walther, and gently placed it on the desk. Jonah picked it up and moved back to the door.

Here we go.

Johnson shifted forward, anxiously fingering the nick at the top of his right ear. "Mr. Kudrow, I can help you in several ways. Most urgently, your grandson."

It was as if he had touched Jacob with an electric cattle prod. The old man physically jumped in his chair, and his rheumy eyes blinked several times.

"How do you know about Oliver?" Jacob asked. "Who told you? I've only found out this morning myself. Nobody knows."

Now Johnson felt as though he'd gained the initiative.

"I've got my sources, but I'd like to help you get him back. You can't go to the police, not given what you've been up to these past, what, fifty years? Maybe sixty."

There's no going back now.

Johnson continued. "Your grandson's at risk. So is your reputation and your wealth." Johnson turned toward Daniel. "And also, your son David's political career's at risk. Frankly, you're not going to salvage all of them; you've done well to get this far. I know enough to put you both behind bars. But that's not my job."

Johnson started when he heard Jonah moving behind him,

but Jacob flapped the palm of his hand downward in a calming action, shaking his head at his huge bodyguard.

"I wouldn't try anything," Johnson said. He turned to see that Jonah was back leaning against the door. "If anything happens to me, all the evidence I've got will go straight to police and prosecutors. I've arranged it." It was untrue, but it was a tactic he had used before, and it usually worked.

There was silence.

Johnson said, "I'm going to suggest something. I can help find your grandson and get him back. I think the gang that has him is Argentine. It's the same people who killed your man Keith, and the gang is led by the son of the man you sell gold to in Argentina."

The twins shared a look. Jacob's eyes narrowed. "What are you talking about?" he asked.

"I've got very reliable sources," Johnson said. "The point is, I believe that same gang is trying to get to your gold source in Poland. I can also help you with that. We can stop them. In return, I need to know the full story: who exactly you're selling this gold to, how you got it, and how the money's being channeled and used. I don't think you've got any other options right now. I suggest you start talking—and quickly."

Johnson reclined in his chair.

CHAPTER THIRTY-THREE

Wednesday, November 30, 2011
London

Johnson now felt confident he was in control of the proceedings. He pretended to check his phone for text messages but at the same time surreptitiously switched on his voice recorder.

Jacob took a sip from his whiskey glass. Johnson noticed his hand shook, while Daniel just sat silently and watched almost unblinkingly.

It was Jacob who spoke first. His voice trembled a little as he put his glass back down on the desk.

Although Johnson had read much of the detail in Jacob's red notebook, he sat patiently and let him talk. Jacob spent some time describing the horrific conditions at Gross-Rosen and the background to the Riese complex.

Then Jacob moved on to the tunnel collapse and the gold.

"After the tunnel roof collapsed, we were all thrown to the floor, and then there was total silence. I'd gone completely deaf," Jacob said. "There was dirt and dust, and the lights had gone out. It was completely *black* in there. It felt like I was drowning, as though my head was going to cave in. The only way to get air was by covering my nose in my shirt and using it as a filter."

Jacob told how they got out through the emergency tunnel and then recounted the dramatic escape from the train. Then there was the suspenseful wait as the brothers lay in the snow, followed by the series of gunshots as their fellow prisoners were shot.

"I knew then there had to be justice. Daniel and I took our trousers off and started wading up the river, fast as we could, even though we were half dead. We knew we had to move quickly before they came after us with the dogs."

Jacob took another sip of whiskey. He seemed a little overcome. "Bizarre times, back then. I've never . . . " His voice trailed away. Then he gathered himself and resumed the story.

"It was a miracle we got out of the Nazi zone. We had to wade up the river, a stream really, for quite a distance until we reached a few houses. By then it was dark. We thought we'd been quiet, but a Pole from one of the houses must have spotted us in our striped clothing and ran over. We had to trust him. We were just lucky, incredibly lucky. He realized straightaway what had happened and quickly found us different clothes, some bread and milk, and took us on foot through some woods and over a few hills, sticking mainly to shepherd's pathways. We heard dogs barking in the distance behind us, which made us think the SS were on our tail. They'd wasted no time. But it was the river that saved us. We'd left no scent.

"That man saved our life and must have put his own at risk. I wish I knew what happened to him. After a while, we went over the Czech border and came to another few houses on the other side of the hills. We went to one of them, where a man took us into his attic. By that stage, we just couldn't go any farther—Daniel especially. He was totally done in.

"We were shocked to find two British guys there in the attic as well, both of them airmen. They were escaped prisoners of war, dressed in German clothing and with proper German ID documents. They told us they'd escaped from Stalag 344, a prisoner of war camp about a hundred kilometers northeast, and that they were planning to head south through Czechoslovakia and Germany to Switzerland. We waited a few days until we felt a little stronger, and the Poles found us some better clothing, money for the trains, and fake documents stating we were Belgian laborers. Then we just went with the two British. We followed them at a distance so if we got caught, they wouldn't be pulled in as well.

"It took us six days to get to the Swiss border. We took trains through Bayreuth and Nuremberg, using the fake papers, and also traveled at night by foot, going cross-country and hiding in woods and barns during the day. It was nervewracking, I can tell you.

"We got to Singen, near the German-Swiss border, and then just walked about thirty kilometers, following the railway line to Schaffhausen, ducking through the woods and getting over the border near Ramsen."

From Switzerland, the twins had passed into southern France, where the French Resistance helped them pass through Toulouse and Perpignan, then over the Pyrenees and into Spain, where they parted company with the two British airmen.

From there, Spain, which in practice remained neutral during the war, allowed them to cross into Portugal, another neutral country. They eventually got onto a ship from Lisbon to London in February 1945.

Johnson sat, engrossed in the story, images flashing across

his mind like a movie of these two men on their epic journey across Europe, outwitting and outrunning the Nazis who must have been so desperate to recapture them.

But he needed to get the brothers to trust him and get to the point.

He interrupted Jacob's flow. "I've got a question for you both. Do you recall an incident from your time at Wüste-giersdorf when a woman in the camp was ox-whipped and left out in the sun all day?"

Jacob took a deep breath. "Yes, I do. What about her?"

"She was my mother, Helena," Johnson said.

Jacob's eyebrows flicked sharply upward. He took another sip of his whiskey and looked at Daniel, who fell back in his chair and pursed his lips.

There was silence for a few seconds.

Then Daniel spoke first. "Is that why you're here? To tell us that? I'm sorry, but how do we know that's the truth?"

Johnson cursed inwardly. It was a fair enough question. He wished he had brought copies of some of his mother's documents with him. Then he recalled he had scanned the pages of her memoir a few years back. He'd wanted to have a digital copy in case anything happened to the originals. He was fairly positive he'd e-mailed the files to himself. Hadn't he?

"I was hoping that would prove that you could trust me," Johnson said. "I have proof back home in the States: her yellow concentration camp identification badge, a photograph of the scars she was left with after her ox-whipping from the very incident you described. I also have a detailed account of her time in Wüstegiersdorf, which she wrote as part of her will. She died in 2001. Give me a moment, I think I can find the pages from her memoirs for you."

Johnson took out his phone and quickly searched through his archived e-mails. The Kudrow brothers' impatience was almost tangible in the air. Eventually, to his relief, he found the ones he needed and flicked through them for the page that detailed the whipping.

He enlarged it and silently passed it to Jacob to read. Daniel leaned over his shoulder to view the image.

After several moments, Daniel looked up again. "All right, carry on," he said.

Johnson felt unsure how to proceed. He now needed to try and confirm the theory he had formed.

"I guess my mother is one reason I'm here," Johnson said. "For a long time I was a Nazi hunter in the U.S., as you said. That was partly because of my mother's experience in Wüstegiersdorf, which you both seem to have shared.

"But there's something else. In 1996, I was searching for an SS captain, Jan Van Stalheim, whom I tracked to Buenos Aires, where the trail went cold. He'd vanished. But I had a tip that he visited a jeweler in Buenos Aires a few times, someone I meant to go and check out but never did—a man called José Guzmann."

Johnson studied the brothers' faces. "Does that name mean anything to you?"

He felt as though it was the second grenade he had thrown into the conversation in the space of two minutes. It was a gamble. Would it pay off?

Johnson leaned back in his chair and waited. He could feel his chest tensing up a little as he waited for a response.

Eventually, Daniel folded his arms and rested them on the desk. His words were so soft that Johnson had to strain to hear properly. "After we arrived in London, we stayed here for four years. There was the Polish Resettlement Act in 1947, which allowed us to stay. We started to set up a small jewelry business right here, in this building. We'd both trained in our father's jewelry workshop in Warsaw, so it made sense."

He paused, visibly breathing in and out a few times, his

chest rising and falling. "But I'd met an American woman. She was something else, she really was. We just fell in love almost straightaway. She wanted to move back to Los Angeles, so I went with her, and we got married. She died long ago, but that's another story. Over there, I set up my own jewelry business, and it went really well. I was acting as a gold trader, supplying other makers with metal that I bought either off the market or as scrap, which I then melted down and reformed into bars."

Daniel sipped his whiskey, then continued. "Then one day, in '54 I think it must have been, I was at a three-day gold industry conference in Los Angeles. There were hundreds of people there from North and South America. It was basically to bring buyers and sellers together, to talk shop, have a few drinks, you know. On the first evening, I saw this guy who was with an Argentine contingent. I sort of recognized him but couldn't place who it was, and I didn't get the chance to go and speak to him. A thin-faced man with slicked-back hair. I asked someone for his name and was told it was José Guzmann, from Buenos Aires. I spent the whole evening trying to work out where I'd seen him before."

Daniel continued, "It was on the second day that the penny dropped. There were two things. The first was when he smiled. I'll never forget that smile: lips tight together, dead eyes. His hairstyle was different, and he'd grown a moustache. And though the name was obviously different, I realized who he was. The second was when I saw him walk. He had a limp. He must have had an injured right leg, and I remembered that limp, too."

Daniel gazed steadily at Johnson. "His real name wasn't José Guzmann at all. It was actually a man called Erich Brenner—the former commander at Wüstegiersdorf."

* * *

"*What?*" Johnson said.

He knew from his Van Stalheim inquiries that Guzmann had a Nazi connection. But *this*?

Daniel's revelation left Johnson feeling electrified, although he now fought hard not to transmit that to the Kudrows. He wanted to keep the atmosphere as calm as he could so they would remain in the frame of mind that had led them to make these disclosures.

Johnson consciously leveled his voice. "Brenner? So Guzmann is Brenner?"

That would also account for why Ben Valetta could find no trace of a Guzmann in the SS personal files.

"Yes. The smile and the limp," Daniel said. "I knew then. Brenner had limped around in the camp. We all assumed he'd been hurt fighting somewhere. There was one hundred percent no mistake."

Johnson tugged at his chin.

"So what's the significance to you, then?" Daniel asked.

Erich Brenner, the man who tortured my mother, the man who's been on my wanted list for so long. How many dozens of dead ends and false trails have I explored over the years in search of that man?

Daniel looked at him and paused. "You look surprised. You know of this man?"

Johnson nodded. "Brenner was the SS officer, the bastard who ox-whipped my mother and left her out in the sun all day at Wüstegiersdorf. But you must know that."

Daniel silently opened his mouth and tilted his head back a little as he made the connection. "Ah yes, it was him who did it. Of course."

"He was brutal. He killed many prisoners, according to her account," Johnson said. "She very occasionally spoke about him and wrote about him in her memoir. I've spent years wondering where he is, dreaming of bringing him to trial. I've searched for him across four continents. Are you sure it's the same man?"

Jacob gave a short, ironic laugh. "We're absolutely sure. We've been playing him for the past fifty years, screwed him good and proper, and there's been nothing he's been able to do about it. He's the animal who supervised the tunneling work we did at Wüstegiersdorf and the stashing of the gold in the tunnel. He's also the murdering rat who shot the other Jewish prisoners we left behind on the train when we escaped. All nineteen of them."

"And you're certain he's still alive, still in Buenos Aires?" Johnson asked.

"Yes, absolutely, definitely. He must be older than us, though not by much. So he's probably in his early nineties."

Johnson was still struggling to regain his composure. "I screwed up with him. I was within reach of him back in '96. So why didn't you expose him and turn him in? He's been a wanted war criminal for decades."

Daniel grinned. "We've been punishing him for decades. In our own way. Financial punishment. We've been selling him the same gold he forced us to stash in those tunnels. Jacob here has been taking it out of the tunnel, and we've been dispatching it, bit by bit. I think he may have worked out who we are, but he can't do anything—he's a captive buyer. It's been like he's been working all this time for *nothing* —just like we had to do back then. The difference is he's properly fed and has a bed to sleep in at night. We charge him exactly the same prices he can sell it for, and there's been nothing he can do about it."

Daniel shifted in his chair. "He makes zero profit, at least on the gold we sell him. He's no doubt got other sources of gold, so he makes something on those. But he's had to keep on buying, indefinitely."

Jacob said, "We think of it as a kind of redemption—a reverse redemption."

A reverse redemption. That's a new one, Johnson thought.

"Right, I see. But how do you force him to do that?"

Jacob picked up the story. "Simple. We set up a couple of blind companies so he couldn't see who was behind them, then got an intermediary to approach his jewelry business as a supplier of gold and arrange a contract. We channeled the gold and the payments through Guatemala, then supplied him for a year or two quite normally. He didn't know who we were. We kept it all at arm's length. He probably wouldn't have recognized us or known us, even if we hadn't done that. We'd just be another pair of scumbag Jew boys to him."

He sipped his whiskey. "Then, we submitted our trading terms. Either he continued to buy from us at a certain price, or we would expose him, turn him over to—let's say the Israeli authorities. We also set up a scheme so if anything happened to either of us, the Israelis would get all the details. He's not had a choice, not unless he wanted to do another disappearing act and change his identity yet again. It seems he's not had the appetite to do that. Hardly surprisingly, given what would happen to him if he tried it."

"Blackmail, then," Johnson said.

Jacob and Daniel exchanged glances, then Jacob continued. "We also put certain safeguards in place so we could track him if he tried anything like that. And he knew it."

Johnson nodded. "Clever. Very clever. So it all went smoothly until very recently. Now Oliver's been kidnapped, one of your employees has been killed, and I guess the others are pretty terrified to say the least, not to mention yourselves?" Johnson asked. He decided not to mention the car bomb.

"It could be Guzmann's son," Jacob said. "If it is him, he may be trying to find out where our gold is hidden. There's not a vast amount left there, relatively speaking, but enough to give him a very nice early retirement."

I bet there is, Johnson thought. "So how much gold have you removed altogether? And what I don't understand is how you managed to ship it to Buenos Aires. And then how was Brenner able to finance such large purchases? And what have you done with all the money?"

The two old twins exchanged looks again.

"The amount," said Jacob finally, "is something we would never tell. It's enough. The method? Well, that's an interesting one. I've always been a car enthusiast. My friend Leopold, who was also in Gross-Rosen but a different subcamp, runs the business next door, Classic Car Parts, which already had an Argentine link.

"There was a British car company, BMC, which had started in the late '50s to sell its Austins in Argentina. I think they badged it as something else, the Siam di Tella or something like that. Spare parts were needed for local taxi drivers. So Leopold started to make parts and export there. A nice business, good margins. But from there, it was a simple matter to mold the gold into BMC car part shapes, which we painted to look like the real thing. It was almost impossible to tell the difference. Nobody was going to think to check every one. Once they arrived in Buenos Aires, we had them melted down and reformed into ingots and gold bars that we then sold to Brenner."

There was silence in the room for a few moments. Johnson sat back, the sheer magnitude and the audacity of the whole thing starting to sink in. He repeated the number yet again, silently to himself.

Two hundred thirty million dollars.

"You didn't answer my question about how Brenner financed these huge purchases and what you've done with all the money that's come in from the sales to him," Johnson said.

The two twins looked at each other yet again, as if they were communicating telepathically, Johnson thought.

"We only took payment once he'd made the sales, but again, we had what you might call a mechanism in place with the Israelis to make sure that happened. He wouldn't have dared to step out of line. And what happens to the proceeds? Well, that is also something we can't discuss here. All you need to know is, we've not been lining our own pockets with it," Jacob said.

He spoke again, now in a firmer tone. "Mr. Johnson, we'd like to propose a deal. You want to bring Brenner to trial, no doubt. A noble objective. And I want my grandson back, quickly. We also both want to stop Brenner's son getting to what's left of our gold. You know a lot about us now. And Daniel and I need all that to stay a secret."

Stay a secret? Some hope, Johnson thought.

"Of course we want Oliver back," Johnson said, "But after that, the most important thing for me—as it should be for you—is to have Brenner extradited to Germany and prosecuted. For that to happen, I'd need you both to be prepared to identify him and testify against him. You are eyewitnesses, and possibly the only living eyewitnesses for all I know, to what he did in that camp and the minute-by-minute background to the murder of your nineteen fellow prisoners that day."

Now Jacob clasped his hands together.

"You need to find him first. What I'm suggesting is, as you're former CIA, an investigator, you go get Oliver back. In return, I'll help you with Brenner. But you need to bear one thing in mind. You'll need to tread very carefully with us. Understand? You can chase Brenner, fine. But as far as Daniel and I are concerned, just make sure you don't do anything you're going to regret."

"What do you mean?" Johnson asked.

Jacob stared at him. "If you try anything, you'll find out. There are bigger games being played out here. With high stakes." He hesitated. "If I were you, I'd go after Brenner, not after us. He's the mass killer, not us. You need to remember that. Got it?"

"I understand where you're coming from," Johnson said carefully. *Bigger games.* What did Jacob mean? It crossed his mind that there might be some kind of government or intelligence operation going on, in which the Kudrows might be participants.

"And there's another thing," Jacob said. "If you want your pistol back, you can swap it for my red notebook and papers. I have no idea how you got into my safe, but I'd like them back, straightaway."

He's playing poker with me, Johnson thought. *He can't know.*

CHAPTER THIRTY-FOUR

Wednesday, November 30, 2011
  Bristol

Oliver opened his eyes a fraction. The combined effects of alcohol and chloroform, coupled with the shock of the abduction, had left the young student dazed and disoriented.

He wanted to scratch his nose but couldn't move his hand. It was then he realized his wrists were tied with thin red climbing rope to the metal bed frame on which he lay, as were his feet.

He still had on all his clothes from the previous night, minus his black donkey jacket, which had been left behind in the nightclub's cloakroom, and his brown leather shoes.

A piece of rag was stuffed into his mouth, and some sort of tape was wrapped around his head to hold it in place.

What the hell . . . Is this my friends? One of their pranks?

Then in the gloom, he gradually made out a dark-haired man in a black sweater and black jeans standing at the foot of the bed.

It started to come back to him. Oliver had a vague recollection of being pushed out of the fire escape doors in Raquel's and into the back of a car, but after that, nothing.

His head felt as if it were being smothered in a fog, obliterating his senses, removing all feeling, and eradicating his thoughts. He fell back into unconsciousness.

A short time later, he woke up again and saw a different man with black hair, this time wearing a white top, next to him with a gun in his hand.

Oliver jumped. He felt more sober now and extremely thirsty.

The next thing he knew, he heard a hissing noise and an utterly agonizing pain sliced into his right big toe, searing his nerve endings and instantly making him want to throw up. An unbearable heat engulfed his foot, and his entire body tried to buck upward but was held firmly by the ropes binding him. It bucked again, then jerked down. And again.

Oliver screamed into the gag filling his mouth.

The pain diminished a little, but still drilled into the nerves at the end of his toe. Through the mist that fogged his vision, he saw the first man, with the black sweater, stand up at the end of the bed. He was holding a blowtorch with a nozzle at the top, from which a long, narrow blue flame spurted. Oliver had seen these devices at his grandfather's workshop.

He felt the bile move up his throat.

The man with the blowtorch turned a knob, and the long blue flame went out.

Then the other man, next to the bed, spoke. "Okay, *mi amigo*, I want information. And quickly—then we'll let you go. I'm going to remove that gag. If you shout or scream, it goes back in, and we'll do something that will cause you a lot more pain. If you don't answer my questions, there will be much pain. Just nod if you understand?"

Oliver had started out with no intention of telling this guy anything if he could help it. But he now needed the gag out so he could be sick. He tilted his head forward and back. The man removed the tape and the ball of rag.

Oliver turned his head sideways and spewed a stream of vomit over the duvet on which he lay.

"What I want is a map and some detailed directions," the man in the white top said. "They belong to your grandfather . . . but I know *you* have them. The map is of part of Poland. You know what I mean."

Oliver felt as though his head were going to explode. He just croaked, almost inaudibly. "Water, I need water."

The man retrieved a bottle of mineral water from the wooden table under the bedroom window and tipped some into Oliver's open mouth.

Oliver had been well known for being something of a bully at his private boys' school, Harrow. Indeed, some of his young victims would doubtless very much have enjoyed seeing his plight right now.

But like most bullies, he wasn't cut out to be a hero.

The large and extremely painful red burn, which now enveloped much of his right big toe and part of the one next to it, had persuaded him very quickly of that, as had the stream of vomit on the bedspread next to him.

The man in the white top pulled out his phone from his pocket, jabbed at the screen, and held it in front of Oliver.

"Do you see that? Do you recognize that man?" he asked.

Oliver peered at the screen, the intense pain in his foot blurring his vision. It was a photo taken with flash, slightly out of focus, of a man, his back to the camera, arms high above his head and feet stretched beneath him. He seemed to be hanging in midair.

The youngster thought he vaguely recognized the background, which was underexposed, while the figure in the foreground was bright and overexposed. Wasn't that Leopold Skorupski's place?

Then the man flicked to the next picture, showing the man from the front this time, chin slumped on his chest. Right away, Oliver recognized the face of the man he knew well from Leopold's workshop. He felt the vomit rising in his throat yet again and turned as it cascaded over the bedspread next to him.

"That will be you if you don't cooperate," the man said.

After that, Oliver gabbled like one of his mother's backgarden chickens.

The documents were locked inside a Google Drive folder he and his uncle Nathaniel had set up six months earlier when Nathaniel was in London on a visit—which was the last time Oliver had seen him before his death.

Oliver gave the man the e-mail address for the account.

The problem was, he couldn't remember the password.

Stress, pain, alcohol, and the effects of chloroform weren't exactly helping his powers of recall. Back in the summer, he thought he had memorized it well and truly, but now it was gone.

The man sat on a chair next to the bed, pinched his nose with one hand to ward off the smell, and held a laptop with the other.

"You'd better get that little head of yours whirring a little faster, amigo, because the clock's ticking, and when the clock ticks, the blowtorch burns. Come on, hurry. Otherwise the gag goes back in and we start on your toe again." He grinned, the remnants of the previous night's pizza clinging to the gums around his crooked teeth. The other man in the black sweater, who sat in the corner, laughed and waved the blowtorch in the air.

Oliver groaned. The ropes tightly holding his arms and

ankles chafed painfully. "Give me a minute, I'll remember it . .
. Try *Radlett* with a capital *R*."

The man punched it in. "Nope, not that. Next one?"

"What about *Harrow1991*?" He'd definitely used his school
and birth year for a password somewhere before.

"Not that either. I'm going to fetch my coffee, so think
while I'm gone."

It took what seemed an interminably long time before
Oliver finally remembered. He and Nathaniel had made jokes
about it. How could he have forgotten?

"I've got it. Try *Goldenballs2* with a capital *G*." That was
the joke, that the two old twins had first been lucky to live,
then lucky with money.

"Right, finally . . . well done. You've just saved yourself a
lot more pain, son."

The man checked the contents of the Google Drive
folder, then yelled out the door. "Ignacio, we've got it."

Oliver could hear someone running up the stairs.

A third man with light brown hair came in, took one look
at the detailed PDF document on the laptop screen, and then
punched the air. "Well done, Diego—good job."

The newcomer noticed the cell phone and wallet sitting
on the table next to the window. "Is that the boy's phone? I
hope the damn thing's been turned off. We don't want them
tracing it to here."

"Good point, boss." The man called Diego walked over to
the phone and switched it off.

* * *

Wednesday, November 30, 2011
  London

After Johnson had arrived back at Jayne's flat, he castigated himself as he realized, on second reading, that there were enough hints in Jacob's red notebook to have indicated the true identity of José Guzmann, had he spent enough time thinking about it.

He flicked through the pages again. The references there to revenge on Guzmann and making him pay the price should have told him. *Come on, Joe boy, sharpen up.*

He fired off an encrypted text message to Vic in Washington.

A development this end. Guzmann is actually Erich Brenner, SS. Can you check his file and report back pls.

After that, he photographed all the pages of the notebook and uploaded the pictures to his laptop. Then he removed the memory card from his camera, hid it in the lining of his suitcase, and loaded the camera with a fresh one.

Johnson decided not to go into detail with Jacob about how he obtained the red notebook. He would just hand it over and concentrate on finding young Oliver.

As he was about to leave Jayne's flat for the workshop, he had a call from Fiona, asking about progress.

Johnson told her briefly about the latest development with Oliver, then instantly regretted it.

"Joe, Obama's heading back to the U.S. in the morning, and I've now got a few days free before I need to start work again in Washington," Fiona said. "I didn't expect that, but the primaries don't get rolling again until after the New Year, and my boss has told me I don't need to begin on the curtain-raising stuff until next week. I might as well come and join you and help find Oliver. Don't argue—I'm coming. Sorry, I've got to go, there's another call coming in. Speak soon."

She hung up.

As Johnson walked back to the Plumbers Row workshop, he lit a cigarette, taking deep drags on it as he went.

He knew he could probably persuade Jayne to get involved in tracking down Oliver. She could doubtless call in a few favors from her contacts at GCHQ, who would be able to pinpoint the whereabouts of his phone using triangulation or GPS technology. But if at all possible, he would prefer to avoid involving her any further than he had to. He didn't want to get her into trouble at the SIS, and he felt he had pushed the boundaries already.

Back in Jacob's office, Johnson sheepishly handed over the notebook to the old man. He didn't try to apologize. The old man didn't say a word but turned and nodded to a scowling Jonah, who returned the Walther.

"Let's hope you don't need that," Jacob said.

"Let's hope not," Johnson said. "But this Argentinian, Brenner's son, Ignacio, seems to be continually one step ahead. He's smart . . . might be a complete thug, but he's a smart thug." He decided not to add that having seen what Ignacio was capable of, he didn't hold any hope that Oliver was going to remain silent for long.

Johnson looked up. "Does your grandson have an iPhone?" he asked Jacob.

"He's like all youngsters. He's glued to it."

"Okay, can we get his Apple ID? We can use the Find My iPhone tracking tool. If the phone's switched on, we can log on to his account and see where it is on a map. Let's hope the Argentinians haven't disabled the phone."

"I'll phone his mother and check," Jacob said.

"And the father?"

There was a pause. Jacob looked down at the floor. "His father was my son, Adam. He was only forty-two. He passed away ten years ago with liver cancer."

The old man shuffled his feet as he looked back at Johnson. "That was harder than Gross-Rosen. It still is."

It was difficult to know what to say. His son gone and now his grandson in serious danger. Johnson nodded. "I'm sorry. I'll do my best with Oliver."

"Thanks," the old man said.

"But just one thing. Do you have a detailed map of where the tunnels are and exactly how we get to the gold?" Johnson asked. "I'll need to make sure I get there before Brenner's son does."

Jacob hesitated. "You get my grandson back first, then I'll sort that out for you. He's more important." He picked up his cell phone and walked toward the door.

A little while later, Jacob came back with his grandson's account details. Johnson logged on to his account on the computer on Jacob's desk. A map appeared on the screen, with a small green dot in the center.

"It's there. The phone's still switched on. A house in Downend, north of Bristol. Woodhall Close, the top end of the road. It's a cul-de-sac."

He turned around, grabbed a pen, and wrote the address on a piece of paper.

Johnson looked back at the computer screen. As he watched, the green dot abruptly disappeared.

CHAPTER THIRTY-FIVE

Wednesday, November 30, 2011
  Bristol

It was almost dark by the time Johnson steered the rented Volkswagen Golf into Downend, a northeastern suburb of Bristol.

There was just enough light to see a tiny picturesque cricket ground next to a church surrounded by stone walls, the Horseshoe pub and a small shopping center, all surrounded by houses built largely from gray stone.

"Brenner's going to be almost a unique capture, if we reach him," Johnson said to Fiona. "He's been on everyone's lists for such a long time, from the Simon Wiesenthal Center downward. Okay, it's a personal one for me, but it's much more than that. He's just about the only major SS mass murderer still alive for whom there are also eyewitnesses still alive and able to give good evidence against him."

"Yes, the last Nazi," Fiona said. "That's going to be some

story. Just make damn sure I'm around when you finally track him down."

Johnson followed his GPS down Westerleigh Road past a primary school on the right and a cemetery on the left.

Sprawling suburbia. Densely populated and nowhere to hide.

Why would the Argentinians bring Oliver here? Have they moved him?

Johnson spotted Woodhall Close on the right, just past the school. He drove past and pulled to the side of the road. Then he pulled out his laptop, typed in his three passwords, then connected it to the 3G broadband network via his cell phone. He tried again to see if he could get a response from Oliver's phone using Find My iPhone.

Nothing.

He had seen the green dot on his screen earlier that day for all of ten seconds before it disappeared. Now it seemed to be gone for good.

"We'll wait until it's properly dark, then drive up there and back down and have a quick recce," Johnson said.

Fiona's phone rang, and she climbed out of the car and walked back along the road to take the call.

A few minutes later she returned. "Well, now we know. That was Des, my boss back in D.C. Police and FBI have ruled out David from the Nathaniel investigation. He's got a firm alibi that checks out. Hardly surprising really—I couldn't see him doing it."

"No. But they took their time announcing it. So who then?" Johnson asked.

"They don't know. Useless."

The pair of them sat in the car listening to the radio for three quarters of an hour.

Then Johnson restarted the car, did a U-turn, and took a left onto Woodhall Close. It ran straight for fifty yards or so before forking into an oval loop at the top end, with a few small trees and grass in the middle. Semidetached houses lined both sides.

There seemed to be lights on in every house. Cars were in driveways, children were running in and out of their homes, riding their bikes around the oval. They all looked like typical family houses in a quiet cul-de-sac.

Johnson took the left fork and looped around the oval and down the other side. "Can't see anything unusual here."

Fiona suddenly pointed. "That house over there. It's the only one with upstairs lights on but nothing downstairs. All the others are lit up downstairs. It's a bit odd at this time of the evening. No car in the driveway, either."

Johnson braked and parked on the opposite side of the oval to the house Fiona had pointed at. Two of the small trees in the center gave him a little cover.

The property was a typical three-bedroom semidetached house, with a pale-brown pebble-dash frontage, a brown wooden-framed front door, a red-tiled roof, a small front garden, and a three-foot-high brick wall separating the property from the pavement. There was an empty concrete driveway that ran down the side of the house to a garage at the rear.

Lying horizontally on the pavement, up against the garden wall, was an estate agent's To Let sign.

Fiona was right. In contrast to the other properties, there was a light that came from the largest upstairs bedroom window, but it was dim and indirect, as if from a bedside or desk lamp, not a main ceiling light. The white lace curtains behind the window made it impossible to see any more.

A light went on in a bathroom window next to the bedroom, and there was the clear dark outline of somebody moving inside behind the frosted glass. Two minutes later, it went out again.

There remained no sign of life downstairs.

"I wish Jayne were here," Johnson said. "I mean, she's trained in all this. I don't like the idea of putting you in yet another potentially dangerous situation, not after the car bomb."

"I can handle it. I've been in many difficult situations before," Fiona said, looking somewhat offended. "Don't worry."

Johnson shrugged, opened the car door, and picked up his backpack from the back seat. "We need to check out the back of the house. Let's see if we can walk around somehow."

There was no way to get to the rear of the property unseen from the front. Johnson led the way back down to the main road, turned left, then halted in front of the school. "This must join on to the back gardens of those houses. Let's see if we can get to it this way."

The pair walked down a passageway at the side of the school, through an open gate, and found themselves in a playground, beyond which was a playing field. The rear gardens of the houses on Woodhall Close were now on the left, behind wooden fencing.

Fiona nudged Johnson on the arm. "That's the one. No lights downstairs, even from the back, and one on upstairs. Garden looks a real mess."

The rear garden was totally overgrown, with the dead remains of the previous summer's nettles, huge spear thistles, and ground elder forming a dense barrier between the fence and the back door.

Johnson scratched his ear. "We still don't know for sure whether it's actually that house or not. It could be any of them, lights on or not. We're going to look stupid if we end up in a cell because we disturbed an old granny who's just ill in bed or something. But we'll have to do something. Let's take a look. There's a few loose planks in the fence there. We can get close to the house behind the garage without anyone seeing and then up to that window there on the right. It looks like a utility room."

Fiona nodded.

The planks were loose at the bottom but nailed to a cross rail at the top, and Johnson was able to push them to one side almost like a curtain, creating enough space for them both to squeeze through the resultant gap.

They worked their way flush up against the boundary fence on the right until they were behind the garage. Johnson peered cautiously around the corner and, seeing no movement, beckoned Fiona to follow.

Hunching low, he moved quickly across a decrepit concrete patio area and crouched beneath the window at the right-hand side of the house. He carefully poked his head up above the windowsill. The house seemed unmodernized, with old-fashioned single-glazed windows.

The room was indeed a utility space but partly unfinished, with an untiled rough concrete floor, makeshift plumbing for a washing machine that stood in a corner, and wall tiles fixed without grouting in between. The interior door to the room, which Johnson assumed led to the kitchen, was closed.

What a dump. Who would rent this place?

Fiona tapped Johnson on the shoulder and put her cupped hand to her ear, indicating for him to listen, then pointed upward.

He cocked his ear. On the night air, there was a muffled moaning sound, very faint but just audible, which seemed to be coming from the house.

Silence again. *That has to be Oliver.*

A few seconds later, they both instinctively ducked down when a light went on downstairs for the first time, shining through from the other side of the kitchen and partly illuminating it. Then Johnson and Fiona heard the back door of the house open, just around the corner from their position under the utility window.

Then came the staccato tapping of hard shoe soles on concrete.

The footsteps ceased. A double clicking noise followed, and within seconds they could smell cigarette smoke wafting on the cold night air.

Whoever it is must be very close. Around the corner.

Johnson's hand went underneath his jacket: he grasped the Walther in its holster below his left armpit and slowly withdrew the gun. He could feel his chest tightening.

He eased his way on to his knees, got as low as he could, and peered around the corner, looking through the crack between a drainpipe and the wall.

A dark-haired, Latin-American–looking, man wearing a black leather jacket and jeans stood there, no more than five yards away, smoking a cigarette.

Johnson pulled back.

After a few minutes, there were more footsteps and the sound of the back door closing. Then the downstairs light went off again.

Johnson moved his head near to Fiona's left ear. "Latin-American guy, so it's probably them. I'll try the back door. We've got to give it a go. If it's not them, I'll talk my way out of it. Wait here. If anything happens, call the police."

Fiona pressed her lips together tightly but had no option but to nod in agreement.

Johnson, still crouching, inched around the corner and underneath the kitchen window until he was next to the white PVC door, which had a glazed upper half.

He reached out and pulled the handle softly downward. It was unlocked. Using his fingertip, he eased the door open and peeked around the side.

The kitchen was small and almost dark, apart from the

faint light coming from the open door of a microwave oven on the countertop and additional dim light coming from the hallway.

Lying on the small circular kitchen table was a pack of cigarettes, a lighter, and a folded newspaper. Johnson peered over at the paper through the gloom. The masthead was just about visible. *El Mundo*, the Spanish-language daily.

Then Johnson heard footsteps moving rapidly, coming down the stairs.

He didn't hesitate: he took three steps and hid behind the open door that led to the hallway, gripping his gun tightly in his right hand.

Within seconds, the man with the black hair and black leather jacket appeared in front of him, no more than a yard away, standing with his legs apart and facing the other way as he surveyed the kitchen.

Johnson made an instant decision: he twisted the gun in his hand, grasping it by the barrel, and brought the butt down hard toward the man's head. But the man must have sensed the movement. He spun sharply to his right and lifted his right arm in self-defense, deflecting Johnson's blow.

Johnson grasped the man's right arm hard with his left hand.

They grappled with each other, arms aloft, breathing heavily. The man seized Johnson's right wrist with his left hand and squeezed, his long fingernails digging into the tendons at the base of Johnson's palm.

The sudden piercing pain forced him to drop the Walther, which clattered on the hard-tiled floor and spun away to the right.

Johnson shoved the man back, the momentum forcing him into the fridge door, both of his arms still locked with Johnson's above their heads.

But then the man swung his trunk sharply sideways,

throwing Johnson off balance and swinging his body into the door jamb, where the back of Johnson's head crunched hard into the wooden frame. He was now pinned to the door frame leading into the hallway, his opponent's back facing the open outside kitchen door.

Johnson freed his right hand and jabbed the flat of his palm up into the man's jaw, pushing it upward and sideways. Then out of the gloom, a shadow appeared behind the man, and Johnson glimpsed a brick swinging around from the left.

CHAPTER THIRTY-SIX

Wednesday, November 30, 2011
Bristol

The back of Johnson's head throbbed like a lawnmower engine, and he had a headache that had already spread its tentacles to his forehead.

"It's a mess," Fiona said, her face red, her mouth set in a thin line. She sat on a chair next to him with a jug of cold water in her left hand. In her right was a wad of wet paper towel, which she used to dab the back of his head and his forehead. Every few seconds she examined the paper towel for signs that the blood flow was diminishing. So far, it wasn't.

A dark-haired man lay on the floor a couple of yards away next to the fridge. Clothesline bound his ankles together. His arms were tied behind his back, and a piece of rag was stuffed in his mouth. He was conscious and eyeing Johnson with a look of utter fury, but he wasn't making a sound.

There was a small pool of blood next to the man's head,

which had dripped from a nasty gash above his right ear. A brick stood on the floor near the door.

"Come on, Joe, we'd better get the boy from upstairs. We need to get going before this guy's buddies come back," Fiona said. Her voice sounded reedy and stressed.

She handed Johnson the wad of paper towel, which was now more red than white. He applied it to the back of his head.

He felt slightly embarrassed that Fiona had rescued him from a fight which, he had to admit, he was far from certain to have won. But he was also grateful that she had done so with such efficiency.

Johnson decided that a touch of humility would do him no harm at this juncture. "Thanks Fiona. You hit him just right. I didn't know that was in your skill set. I owe you," Johnson said. The man had gone down like a puppet whose strings had been cut.

"Yeah, like I keep telling you, I've got a few tricks up my sleeve." She smiled. "But this asshole must have banged you against the door post just before that. I'm going to untie Oliver upstairs now. Come up if you can walk."

Johnson stood and found the room remained horizontal, so he replaced the Walther in the holster under his arm and followed Fiona into the hallway and up the stairs, clutching his head as he went.

In the first room to the left at the top of the stairs, a bedside light was switched on. There, lying spread-eagle on the bed, hands tied to the metal headboard with red rope and feet similarly secured at the bottom, was a young man with a sock taped in his mouth.

Johnson walked to the bed and took a few seconds to remove the sock and tape from the man's mouth. "Are you Oliver?"

"Yes," Oliver croaked.

Johnson loosened the bindings holding his hands. "I'm working with your grandfather Jacob," Johnson explained, wincing at the pain in the back of his head.

"I'm Joe Johnson and this is Fiona Heppenstall. We managed to track your phone. The gang that took you was looking for some of your grandfather's documents, as you've doubtless worked out."

"Thank you . . . and I'm sorry," Oliver began. "I think I've given them away. My grandfather's documents, I mean. These guys are animals. Look at my toe, it's killing me." He groaned as Fiona carefully untied his badly burned right foot.

Johnson finished removing the rest of his bonds. "Don't worry, you didn't have any choice. Now, listen. How many men were there, and do you know where they went?"

"There were three, but I think two have gone," Oliver said. "They left a few hours ago. They had my grandfather's map and other stuff on their laptop. I had to give them the password. They were using a blowtorch on my foot." He winced at the pain, then gestured toward the device, which was on a table near the door. "I thought they were going to burn me alive or something."

"And how did they get this house? Did they just break in, do you know?" Johnson asked.

"I think I heard one of them say they'd got it on a short lease from an agent," Oliver said.

Johnson supported the boy as he hopped on one foot toward the door and then held him as he worked his way down the stairs, one step at a time. The man in the kitchen was moving; Johnson could hear him bumping around on the floor below. He took out his gun.

The man had rolled halfway across the kitchen and was trying to rub his bindings on the metal crossbar of a kitchen stool in an effort to free himself.

"No, you don't. Stop right there." Johnson aimed the gun at him. "Lie still."

The man ceased wriggling and stared at Johnson, the anger in his eyes being rapidly replaced by fear. Johnson told Fiona to remove the man's gag, which she did.

"I've got some questions, and I need answers. Now. Otherwise we'll give you some of the same treatment you gave to this young man here—with the blowtorch. Do you understand?"

The man nodded.

"What's your name? And don't try giving anything false because I'm going to check it before I let you go."

There was a long pause. Then the man muttered, "Alejandro Garcia."

"Okay, and who are the other two guys in your gang?"

Another long pause. Johnson inched closer and raised the pistol. Alejandro's eyes opened wide.

"It's Diego Ruiz and . . . Ignacio Guzmann."

Johnson gave Fiona a told-you-so look. "Guzmann. Right, and where are they now?"

"They've gone." Alejandro grimaced at him from his position, still curled on the kitchen floor.

"I'm not blind. Gone where?"

Another long pause. Johnson jabbed the barrel of the Walther into his ribs.

"Poland," Alejandro said.

"What time did they go?"

"Six hours ago."

Johnson pressed his lips together. "Six hours. Shit." So they were quite possibly on a ferry or taking Le Shuttle, the car transporter train, through the Channel Tunnel, or were maybe on the Continent already. And they had a copy of the detailed map, which he still hadn't even seen.

He turned back to Alejandro. "Tell me one other thing.

Your friend, Ignacio Guzmann—do you know where I can find his father?"

Alejandro stared at him and said nothing.

"It's the father I'm interested in, not you or Ignacio. The father's a Nazi war criminal whom I intend to take to court. He'll likely be charged with multiple murders dating back to the 1940s," Johnson said.

The news was met with a few seconds of silence. "These are things I didn't know," Alejandro said. "And I don't know exactly where he is, but I think at home in Buenos Aires. I'm not sure where. I've never been to his house."

"You really don't know?" Surely he had to be lying.

"No. He won't be around much longer, in any case."

"What's that supposed to mean? He's ill?"

Alejandro laughed. "No, not ill. Not physically. Maybe mentally. He'll be worse than ill when Ignacio gets back to him, though. It'll be *retribución*, *venganza,* he calls it. I don't know what the right word is in English."

Johnson didn't need the right word in English. The implications of Alejandro's words quickly sank in.

"Why don't they get on, Ignacio and his father?"

"They never have," Alejandro said. "He hates his father because of the way he was treated as a child. Now are you going to let me go or leave me here?" He had obviously decided that Johnson wasn't planning to take his life.

Johnson took a moment to think through his options and made a quick decision.

He replaced the rag in Alejandro's mouth and taped it back in position, then dragged him into the living room, where there was nothing he could use to try and work through his bindings.

Johnson rifled through the Argentinian's pockets and removed his phone, which he checked and pocketed. To his astonishment, there was no password on the device, let alone any encryption. He would sift through the information on it later. He guessed there would be a wealth of useful e-mails, contacts, phone numbers and other saved documents.

"You can stay here," Johnson said. "We'll send the police around to deal with you. That should be an interesting conversation."

* * *

Johnson was feeling more than a little anxious.

Was Alejandro exaggerating Ignacio's intentions towards his father, and deliberately winding Johnson up? Or was he telling the truth when he talked about Ignacio planning revenge against the old man?

Johnson had no way of knowing, although he suspected the latter. Either way, he had plenty of time to mull over the implications while waiting for a nurse at Bristol's Frenchay Hospital to finish patching up Oliver.

While they sat in the waiting room, Johnson sent a text message to Jayne.

Will be en route back from Bristol soon. Oliver Kew safe and with us. URGENT need to check if Ignacio Guzmann and Diego Ruiz are still in U.K. May have left for Poland by air, ferry. Can you check and put block on if possible? They have map taken from Oliver.

Meanwhile, Fiona used a pay phone in the hospital reception area to call the police and anonymously report a burglary on Woodhall Close, saying a gang had left the tenant tied up in the living room.

"Alejandro will have fun explaining that one when officers turn up," she said as they helped Oliver into the car.

After drinking a black coffee bought from a nearby gas station, where he also bought a pack of painkillers for Oliver to supplement those given to him by the nurse, Johnson took off down the M4 highway at such a speed that Fiona had to tell him several times to slow down.

He brushed her off. "We haven't got time to lose. Guzmann will be in Poland well before us, and now I'm worried about what he's going to do to his father. I don't want to take a dead body to a war crimes trial."

Johnson glanced at Fiona. "My gut tells me the best option is to head straight to Buenos Aires and track down Brenner before either his son gets to him, or alternatively, he gets wind of what's going on and flees the country."

Fiona wrinkled her nose. "No, I really don't think that's sensible, Joe. If we're going to make this story believable, we really need to get to Poland and collect the evidence. We need photos of the gold and to actually see the tunnels. If we go to Argentina first, there's a good chance that Brenner's son is going to escape with a multimillion-dollar windfall in Third Reich gold bars. I can't take the risk of all that evidence simply being spirited away."

She was doing it again, thinking headlines and photos, Johnson snorted to himself.

"I don't know, Fiona. I'll think about it."

"Yes, but while you're thinking, just remember *Inside Track* is paying you over a grand a day for this job," Fiona said.

That much was unarguable. But Johnson also doubted that *Inside Track*'s senior editors would want to stand accused of losing Brenner, a Nazi mass murderer. *Fiona must realize that*.

Johnson looked into the back seat of the Golf, where

Oliver was trying to get into his Google Drive account using his phone.

Johnson had a sudden thought. "Oliver, you haven't called your mother and your grandfather, have you? You'd better ring and tell them you're safe. Also your friends in Bristol before you're reported missing, if they haven't done that already. And I don't like to keep pushing you, but any luck with those Google Drive files?"

"Don't worry about my friends. They'll probably just think I got lucky in the nightclub or something. But yes, I'll give them a call," Oliver said. "And no, I can't get into Google Drive. I've tried several times. Those guys must have changed the password on the folder."

"In that case, can you also remind your grandfather that we need a copy of the map of the gold tunnels and the instructions that were in the folder? Tell him it's extremely urgent. I asked him once before but he said he'd sort it after I rescued you," Johnson said.

He could hear the beeping as Oliver started dialing, using the phone that had been vital in tracking him to the house in Bristol.

"Hello, Mum, it's Oliver. I'm safe . . . "

Johnson could clearly hear the loud shriek coming down the line from the boy's mother.

"Yes, I got rescued. Two Americans found me in a house in north Bristol . . . "

Oliver continued to explain briefly what had happened, although to Johnson's relief, he bravely played down his foot injuries.

Johnson could hear his mother speaking for a short time, then Oliver exclaimed, "No way! When did that happen? Hell, poor Grandad. Which hospital is he in?"

After Oliver hung up, Johnson glanced at Oliver in the rearview mirror. The youngster was almost in tears.

"I got the gist of that Oliver. Your grandfather's in the hospital?"

"Yes, he's had a heart attack. An ambulance took him to St. Thomas' Hospital down near Westminster a couple of hours ago."

Johnson grimaced. *This can't be happening.*

CHAPTER THIRTY-SEVEN

Wednesday, November 30, 2011
London

Johnson drove into the small rectangular parking lot at London's St. Thomas' Hospital at just before midnight, feeling light-headed with tiredness.

He had heard of St. Thomas', which had one of the largest heart surgery units in the country. At least Jacob would be in good hands, he assumed.

The view from the parking lot across the River Thames to the illuminated Palace of Westminster opposite, with Big Ben towering above it, was one that tourists swooned over daily. But Johnson was in no mood to appreciate it.

Oliver, whom Johnson had spotted several times in his mirror swallowing more painkillers, was horizontal on the rear seat. There had been no reply from Jayne to his earlier text message. He now sent her another.

We're at St. Thomas' Hospital. Old man Jacob had a heart attack.
All going to shit. Call me in morning ASAP.

Fiona tapped Oliver on the shoulder. "Come on, we need
to go and find your grandfather, quickly. You'll need to do the
talking—he's your relative. Do you have some ID?"

The youngster, still woozy from the tablets, lifted himself
up to a vertical position and winced as the movement triggered the pain in his big toe again. All he had were scans of
his passport and driver's license stored on his phone.

"Should be okay," Johnson said. "Quick, let's move."

The receptionist called for a porter to bring a wheelchair
after Johnson explained that the youngster had a large burn
on his foot and that they had driven from Bristol. Then he
asked where to find Jacob.

"You need the Evans-Watson ward, up on the third floor
of the East Wing. The coronary care unit is down at the end
of that ward on the right," she said.

She looked at Oliver doubtfully. "I don't know if they'll let
you see your grandfather now. It's the middle of the night,
and they have strict visiting hours."

But after looking around to check nobody was listening,
she winked at Johnson and murmured, "The matron's a bit of
a toughie, so if I were you, I would play the sympathy card."

The Evans-Watson ward and coronary care unit was down
a short corridor with a blue vinyl floor and was largely in
darkness apart from a few dim night-lights and a pool of
yellow underneath a desk lamp at the reception desk.

The receptionist downstairs had been correct. The
matron on duty was a stern-looking woman, probably in her
forties, wearing a purple uniform. She approached them
straightaway, hands on hips. Her name badge read Angela
Ballantyne.

Before she even said a word, Johnson lengthened the odds of making any progress.

He began whispering quietly to her in an effort to explain their situation, sympathizing with the number of patients she was managing and apologizing profusely for the unearthly hour, but she quickly interrupted.

"There's no way you can go in," she said. "It's the middle of the night. I can tell you that Mr. Kew is stable, but he can hardly speak. He's very weak. Two of you are not even relatives."

Ballantyne was clearly not a woman to be crossed. She stood, arms folded, her stocky muscular legs slightly apart, blocking their way.

Johnson thought for a second about taking a few twenty-pound bills out of his wallet and trying to bribe her but quickly dismissed the idea. She definitely wasn't the sort.

He took a step forward. "We completely understand, but we've brought Mr. Kew's grandson here all the way from Bristol to see his grandfather. Oliver was injured yesterday, so this family's been having a bad time of it, and Oliver could use a break. The lady and I don't need to go in, but could Oliver just go and see him for five minutes? It might even cheer the old man up."

Oliver sniffled in his wheelchair. Johnson glanced down. He actually had a tear rolling down his right cheek.

The matron hesitated. A ward sister, a younger blond woman dressed in a dark blue uniform, came over and stood beside her. "What do you think, Marcie? Could you go with this young man if we give him five minutes with his grandfather?"

The blond sister looked exasperated. "I dunno. He's a bit frail in there. The consultant's coming around first thing in the morning to see whether he needs surgery or not."

Oliver sniffled again from his wheelchair, then pulled out his handkerchief and blew his nose.

The sister looked down at him. "Okay, then, just five minutes, then you must let him rest." She pushed Oliver's wheelchair to the end of the ward and behind a full-length blue curtain.

Meanwhile, the matron took Johnson and Fiona to a small waiting area behind the reception desk, lit by just one small night-light.

"You two will have to wait here," she said. Then she disappeared through some double swing doors.

Johnson sat down and clasped his hands in front of him, his back hunched. He didn't rate Oliver's chances very high.

The only sounds were of a man coughing loudly farther down the ward and of a woman snoring. A toilet flushed somewhere nearby.

Then came the squeaking of rubber on the vinyl floor and soft footsteps. The blond ward sister reappeared, pushing Oliver in his wheelchair.

She beckoned Johnson and Fiona over and whispered, a little softer in tone this time. "That was okay. It seemed to perk the grandfather up a little. You'll need to go now, though."

Johnson took the wheelchair handles, thanked the woman, and pushed Oliver toward the elevator.

When they were away from the ward and out of earshot of the sister, Johnson asked, "Well, did he say anything? How did he look?"

"He was conscious," Oliver said, "but he looked quite weak, like she said. Very gray. He said virtually nothing. I had about thirty seconds when the nurse went off somewhere. I asked him whether there was another map somewhere. It was strange. He just croaked a couple of words, something like 'hell loss' and then 'pans.' That was it. He said nothing more, just closed his eyes."

"Hell loss and pans?" Johnson felt bewildered. "Did you say it was urgent? What can that mean?"

"Of course I said it was urgent. It was definitely 'hell loss' and 'pans.' I've absolutely no idea what he meant."

Johnson tilted his head back, looked up to the ceiling and exhaled long and hard.

Hell loss and pans. How so very helpful.

CHAPTER THIRTY-EIGHT

Wednesday, November 30, 2011
Buenos Aires

Yet again, Erich Brenner's finger hovered over the encrypted phone he had taken from the top drawer in his bedside table.

He had walked up the stairs from the black leather chair in his living room and had sat on the wooden wicker-seat chair next to his bed on at least five occasions already that evening.

Brenner began to dial: 00 1 305 358 343 . . . Then he stopped before pressing the final digit and instead held the receiver in midair, looking at it.

I don't know. Should I or not?

His survival instinct told him he should do it. He had been keeping the number on a piece of card in the safe in his bedroom in case it was needed.

But instead, Brenner pressed the call-end button.

Then he sat, his spindly legs crossed, a bony elbow

propped on his right thigh and his chin resting on the palm of his right hand.

He felt that somehow, he had let the genie out of the bottle by confiding, at least partially, in his son. At the time, it seemed as though he had no other option. Now, though, he wondered whether it might have been better to wait.

Trying to second-guess what his son might do, let alone control him, was a fool's errand. Brenner had realized that years ago. He had tried a regime of rigid control and punishment when the boy was young, thinking that was the way to bring about the control he craved—the control he had loved in the SS. It was the only method he knew; it was all he had been taught.

But it hadn't worked, just as it hadn't worked in the old days, at least not for long. Instead, the youngster had gone off to join the army.

Brenner stood up and wandered back to his living room, where he sat again in the black leather armchair.

A life spent exiled under a false name with a false passport, in a country he hated, a wife who had left him at the same time as his only son, a business that was going down the tubes, no real friends, and the constant fear of discovery. Overhanging it all was the sense, not of guilt—there was none of that—but of *failure* that had spread through him like a vicious cancer, seemingly untreatable.

He thought back to his struggles as a member of the *Hitler-Jugend*, the Hitler Youth, in his home city of Munich during the economic crash of the 1930s; the never-ending battles to prove he was a better man than the one next to him in the SS. Then came his acceptance into the *Waffen-SS*, the armed division of the organization, and real action, at last. He fought in tanks against the Russians on the Eastern Front and the French in the west with the 3rd SS Panzer Division

Totenkopf, the Death's Head Division. That was when he really made a difference.

Even now, Brenner felt his greatest achievement was his promotion to *Obersturmführer*, first lieutenant, for his role in the advance on Leningrad in 1942 as part of Operation Barbarossa: Germany's invasion of the Soviet Union. He still had the promotion notice hidden in his attic.

But in March of the following year had come the knee injury caused by a small piece of Red Army mortar shrapnel during the Third Battle of Kharkov. It had sliced through a ligament, forcing him to spend six weeks in the hospital, and he was told he wouldn't be able to return to *Frontdienst*, front-line service. In comparison, helping to run concentration camps, first at Auschwitz toward the end of 1943 and then Gross-Rosen the following year, left him frustrated and bored. He had taken it all out on the Jewish prisoners.

But the worst was to come. In fact, nothing much had gone right since that day in December 1944, when he had still been proud to be SS First Lieutenant Erich Brenner.

He had been summoned to the bleak yet beautiful Książ Castle, with its vertiginous walls and domed green copper bell tower, late in the afternoon.

Brenner's thoughts drifted back as he closed his eyes and relived that evening yet again, as if he were watching a movie starring somebody else.

It had been a bitterly cold night in Lower Silesia and a blanket of snow had covered the small elevated city of Walbrzych.

The car that had been sent to collect Brenner had wound its way up a steep road to the castle on top of a rock cliff, north of the city.

As he had climbed to the fourth floor of the castle, Brenner had felt a deep sense of imminent catastrophe.

There, in a small, high-ceilinged private dining room, *Hauptsturmführer* Karl Beblo had been waiting for him.

The memory was still vivid and present and even now gave Brenner nightmares.

The voice had been as cold and slow as the icicles hanging from the castle walls. "You damn fool," Beblo snarled, his pale blue eyes staring across the room from beneath his peaked cap. "So I hear that despite only having twenty-one exhausted prisoners to transport back to camp, you managed to lose two of them on a simple train journey of just thirteen kilometers."

Brenner shuffled his feet, his normally confident, rasping voice quavering a fraction. This was serious. "I, um, we are dealing with the situation, sir, but yes, unfortunately a couple of them did escape. As soon as I realized this, I made the decision to eliminate the other prisoners. I have also begun disciplinary proceedings against the idiot corporal who was meant to be guarding them who fell asleep on the job, together with his assistant, sir."

Despite the air-conditioning in his living room, Brenner began to sweat as he recalled the conversation, as clear and loud as if it had been recorded on one of his many DVDs, which he had racked on a nearby shelf.

Beblo had been one of the senior officers in the *Schutzstaffel*, more commonly known by its short form, the SS, which was Hitler's paramilitary, terror, and surveillance organization.

"So you shot them," Beblo said. "Prisoners whom we need to dig those tunnels. All to make up for your error. Fantastic. Just tell me, *Obersturmführer*, how that was going to help the situation?"

Brenner gazed absently across from his armchair at the empty fireplace, mentally replaying his words as he had tried to reassure his boss.

"Once again, sir, I can only apologize. I, we, have a team

out looking for them now, with dogs, and I believe they will be found within twenty-four hours. It will be a long way below freezing tonight and probably the same tomorrow. The prisoners have minimal clothing, no food, and no proper shoes. The whole region is crawling with SS and Wehrmacht soldiers, sir. They have no chance. In any case, they have no idea what was being stored in those tunnels."

Beblo interrupted him. "That's enough. I've heard enough. Of all the prisoners to lose, it had to be part of this group. You know the sensitivity. You were given clear orders only last week to step up security."

Brenner left the castle with his head down and his reputation ruined. He'd never lost the shame of that moment. It had tainted the remainder of his proud SS career. He still had the official disciplinary notice, also up in the attic with his other papers. Why he had kept it, he could never explain, even to himself, because it was something he had never talked about with anyone, ever.

Brenner opened his eyes with a start, now feeling quite stressed from the memory.

The problem was, back then he had been certain he was correct in all of his assumptions: that the escapees would be found, that his standing with Beblo would be restored.

He checked his watch: 6:45 p.m. He was fifteen minutes late. He reached for a small brown bottle on the table next to him and took out two pills, which he swallowed with some water from a glass that was also standing on the table.

Still, he was lucky to have gotten out of Nazi Germany, he thought. The narrow window of opportunity to escape to Spain, the help he'd received from Otto Skorzeny's organization *Die Spinne*—The Spider—the new passport, the crash course in Spanish, the flight to Argentina.

It could have been worse back then, and the biggest mercy of all was that he'd been able to work with the CIA, trading his knowledge of Russia and his wide range of contacts in the German army intelligence organizations—the Fremde Heere Ost, the Foreign Armies East, and the Abwehr, the German military intelligence organization—for his freedom.

But the subsequent blackmail threats over gold purchases and the gradual dawning over the years that the two escaped prisoners were behind them—plus the paralyzing anxiety about what would happen if he tried to take action against the two Jews, which had been his initial instinct—had left him feeling shackled, as if he were in some kind of open prison.

Brenner's cell phone rang. He picked up the phone and jumped when he saw the caller's name on its screen. Then he pressed the green button to take the call.

"Hello, Ignacio, where are you now? What's happening?"

"Padre, I can't talk for long. I'm in the U.K. at Dover, about to get on a night car ferry to France. We're heading to Poland now. It's a long story, but the bottom line is that your gold supplier, Oro Centro, gets its bullion from another company in London. You know all that, though, don't you? Those are the people who've been screwing you over with the pricing. What you don't know, perhaps, is the owners are two old Polish guys, twin brothers, Jacob and Daniel Kudrow. Do those names ring any bells?"

Should he admit now that he knew? Brenner hesitated.

"No, I can't think of anyone."

"Okay, well try this one. I got into their office in London. On the wall were two large photographs: one of a castle, Książ Castle, and the other of a village called Gluszyca. Does that mean anything to you?"

Brenner, sitting in his armchair, felt his entire body tense up at the mention of the two place-names. "No, it doesn't."

"The other thing is, padre, the Kudrows are both Jewish.

Do you understand what I'm saying? And the gold being supplied to you is coming from near to Gluszyca. I'm not telling you anything you don't know, am I?"

Brenner felt a little dizzy. Should he have been upfront with his son? Now he would be furious.

He tried to think. But he hadn't asked his son to look into all that. How had he learned all that information? Brenner tried to pull his thoughts together. "I don't know about all that. What about the investigator, Johnson. The one thing I did ask you to take care of. Have you done that?"

"Yes, he's been in London too, as you thought," Ignacio said. "I've tried, believe me. I've had a couple of guys here chasing him. We tried to eliminate him, but it didn't work. Not enough time and too many other things to do. I can't do any more with Johnson. We're out of London now."

Brenner felt his mouth dry up, and he reached for his glass of water.

"Well, is there another way to take care of him? Has he talked to the Polish brothers?" Brenner asked. There was no point continuing the pretense any longer.

Ignacio didn't answer right away. Then his son's voice took on a tougher, more abrupt tone. "I don't know. I'm sure he'll probably try and talk to them. It's your problem now, though. I've tried."

"Well, why are you going to Poland? What's the point of that?"

Brenner blanched as Ignacio half laughed into the phone. "Why do you think? There's gold left there, which I want. Then I'll head back to Buenos Aires to take care of a few things there . . . And I'll come around to see you, too." He casually added, "Will you be around?"

It was his tone of voice that did it. Brenner remained silent for a few moments, thinking. Then he replied slowly, "I'm not sure where I'll be." He let the phone fall into his lap.

"Hola? . . . Hola, padre? . . . Hola?"

Brenner was breathing heavily. Eventually, his son hung up.

He sat in his armchair for an hour after the brief conversation with his son had ended.

By then it was past midnight. The moon was high in the sky, and most house lights in neighboring properties had gone out.

The muffled sound of a car passing along Ombú drifted through the house. Somewhere, a dog barked.

Eventually, Brenner stood up, limped upstairs to his bedroom once again, and pulled his encrypted phone out of the locked top drawer of his bedside table.

He felt utterly dismayed that Ignacio had failed to dispose of Johnson. He had screwed that up badly. And there was definitely something sinister about his son's tone.

Brenner felt as though he had managed to keep all the plates spinning for a long time. As long as he'd been able to keep the money flowing back to his tormentors, everything was under control, just.

But there had been no gold and therefore no payments for a long time. And here, unexpectedly, were two threats that money couldn't take care of.

He dialed the number he had almost completed earlier. This time, he pressed the final digit to make the call he had always hoped would never be necessary.

The phone at the other end of the line rang several times before eventually being answered.

"This is Simon. Who is it?" The voice was muffled and tired.

"It's Guzmann in Buenos Aires. I apologize for calling at this hour. I have a question for you. Did your dog enjoy his walk this morning?"

There was a short pause. "Yes, my dog had a good walk,

thank you. He's now asleep in the kitchen in front of the fire. Has something come up?"

"Listen to me, Simon. I've got a major problem. Someone's on my tail: the American investigator you warned me about, Johnson. Now this is what I'd like you to do for me, urgently. First, my passport . . . "

Brenner started to run through the list of requests he had been formulating in his mind for the previous four hours.

CHAPTER THIRTY-NINE

Thursday, December 1, 2011
London

It was quarter past ten in the morning when Johnson was woken by a beep on his phone as a text message arrived. He lay fully clothed on one of the two double beds in Fiona's room at the Crowne Plaza hotel near Blackfriars Bridge.

Sunlight streamed through the window, which looked out over New Bridge Street and the Thames a couple hundred yards away.

Johnson turned over and saw Fiona, still asleep on the other bed, her back to him, wearing a skimpy pink nightshirt.

They had taken Oliver home to his mother's house in Radlett, twenty miles north of London, after leaving the hospital. It had been half past four in the morning by the time they had finally returned and made their way to the hotel.

Johnson picked up his phone. The short message was from Jayne, encrypted as usual.

I've had checks run. Guzmann and Ruiz left Dover by car ferry, P&O, last night for Calais, 11:45 p.m. sailing, last boat of the night. Sorry, too late.

He sat bolt upright. Time was running out.

Johnson still believed that, from his point of view, going to Poland rather than Buenos Aires was a mistake. But he felt hamstrung by his paymaster and struggled to see a way around it.

How long would it take them to get to Gluszyca? He recalled the conversation he'd heard between Jacob, Daniel, and Leopold when they said they could drive there in two days.

But presumably that was by taking it easy. If it was urgent, foot to the floor, Johnson had no idea.

He opened up Google Maps on his phone. Calais to Gluszyca showed 780 miles and twelve hours driving time, traveling via Cologne and Dresden in Germany.

Johnson did a quick calculation. If the ferry crossing took an hour and a half, the Argentinians would have arrived in Calais at about 12:45 a.m., say 1:15 a.m. by the time they got off the boat.

Then twelve hours from there, if they drove nonstop between them, which was a big if, would put them in Gluszyca by around one o'clock in the afternoon, or say two or three o'clock, allowing for stops and delays.

That was roughly four hours from now. And Johnson still had no map. What had the old man meant last night at the hospital? It was beyond cryptic.

Either Jacob hadn't understood his grandson's question about the location of the spare map at all and was just speaking random words, or he had tried to tell him and just hadn't been able to articulate the message.

"Hell loss" and "pans." The words couldn't just be random.

Johnson's instinct told him they had a meaning. But who would know? Daniel, perhaps?

Johnson climbed off the bed and shook Fiona.

A quarter of an hour later, they climbed into the Golf, which he had parked around the corner from the hotel.

"Let's try the workshop first to see if Daniel is there. I'm hoping he's not gone to the hospital. I can't face that matron again," Johnson said.

Fiona nodded. "You drive. I'll check flight times to Poland." A few minutes later, she spoke again. "I've had a quick look. The bad news is there's no major airport at Walbrzych, so we'll need to fly to Wroclaw, which is over thirty miles away, and then hire another car. The flight is over two hours, and that's not including the waiting time at the airport."

"Dammit, Fiona, we'll never make it. I'm still thinking we should go to Buenos Aires. If we can't get a copy of the map, that's what we'll do, okay?"

Fiona reluctantly agreed.

By the time Johnson braked to a halt outside the two workshops, the veins on the back of his hands and on his temple were standing out like lengths of cord.

The small pedestrian gate into the Kew Jewellery U.K. yard was slightly ajar. Somebody was in there. Johnson parked and they walked through. The door into the offices was locked, but the opposite one, for Classic Car Parts, was wide open.

A familiar burly, tattooed figure was sitting behind the glass screen in the reception area, his huge forearms folded, chewing gum. A pack of Rothmans cigarettes and a green plastic lighter were on the desk next to him.

Jonah furrowed his brow. "You again? What do you want? I presume you haven't brought that gun this time."

Johnson shook his head. He wasn't going to admit the Walther was still in its holster under his coat.

"We were wondering if you had seen Daniel around. The jewelry workshop seems closed. Or if not, perhaps Mr. Skorupski?"

"You've heard about old Jacob, I presume?" Jonah said. "He's had a heart attack. Hardly surprising with you and others causing him so much hassle. So obviously his brother won't be coming here. He'll be at the hospital." He looked at Johnson as if the blame for the old man's coronary should be entirely laid at his door. "I'll see if Mr. Skorupski is free."

"Thank you very much. I'd appreciate it."

Jonah swiped up his cigarettes, as if he half suspected Johnson would pocket them, then glared at him and disappeared through the door at the back of the reception area.

Johnson and Fiona sat in the metal chairs, ignoring the magazines on the table in front of them.

Ten minutes went by. Then, eventually, footsteps echoed down the corridor. The door behind the reception desk opened, and a tall, slightly overweight man emerged. Johnson had last seen him several days earlier outside the warehouse, climbing out of the green BMW.

Leopold brushed back the remains of his gray hair with his hand, then wiped it on his dark blue overalls. Then he stooped and planted two large hands on the desk, peering from beneath white eyebrows through the glass screen at Johnson. A brown stain showed in the creases lining his left cheek.

"So, you're the American Nazi hunter." He turned to Fiona. "And you must be the journalist? We meet at last. Mr. Kudrow has told me a lot about you in the past few days. What can I do for you?"

Johnson stood up and went to the counter. "Yes, well I've heard quite a lot about you too. You know we have been working with Mr. Kudrow and we rescued his grandson yesterday from an Argentine gang led by the son of the Nazi."

"Yes, I'm aware of that. I spoke to young Oliver's mother this morning."

"Well, I took Oliver to see his grandfather at St. Thomas' last night. We need a copy of the map showing how to access the tunnels in Gluszyca. The Argentinians have it, and they're heading there right now. Oliver asked about a spare copy of the map, and Jacob said something about 'hell loss' and 'pans.' Does that mean anything to you?"

Leopold limped through the connecting door to the waiting area. Up close to him, Johnson could smell his odor of sweat and oil and got a strong whiff of alcohol on his breath. It wasn't pleasant. His chin and upper lip had a few tiny patches of stubble, which he must have missed when shaving.

"You do know, Mr. Johnson, why we have been doing what we've been doing with Brenner and the gold?" Leopold said.

Johnson nodded. "I get it completely."

"We could have had him killed, you know. But it's not our belief as Jews, to take an eye for an eye, even if he does deserve it. It's true that if you go and read Exodus chapter twenty-one, it does say how the Lord told Moses that anyone who kills another should be put to death, a life for a life, an eye for an eye, a tooth for a tooth. However, we Jews don't believe that should be taken literally, and our Talmud, our Jewish law, doesn't interpret it that way. Nevertheless, we do believe damages should be paid in full. That's what we have been doing: extracting compensation. Jacob calls it redemption. Reverse redemption."

Johnson just nodded impatiently. "Yes, yes, I've heard him say that. Interesting stuff. But what about these things he said last night? If we don't hurry, the rest of your bullion will be gone."

No time for a debate now, Johnson thought. *Never mind that such reasoning has also, conveniently, enabled these guys to sell a huge amount of gold to a forced buyer who should be in prison, no questions asked.*

Leopold paused. "I don't know what he was trying to say. 'Hell loss'? That's an odd one." He screwed up his face and shook his head. "And what else did he mention?"

"Pans."

After a few seconds, Leopold's face lit up. He laughed. "Hell loss and pans. Ah yes, I think I know what he's talking about. Come with me."

* * *

Washington, D.C.

David Kudrow sipped from a bottle of water as his driver swung the maroon Lexus onto Benton Place for a scheduled breakfast update meeting at the home of his campaign manager, Philip.

His push to secure the Republican nomination was going well, despite the stress of a demanding round of meetings, speeches, and interviews, not to mention the demands for a slice of his time from the growing entourage of support staff surrounding him.

And as he expected, he was benefiting from the sympathy vote following Nathaniel's stabbing. But the huge volume of supportive messages posted on his campaign Facebook account and on Twitter had outstripped expectations, and he had received several new requests for interviews from journalists who wanted to write profiles, using Nathaniel's death as a hook.

Funds were being committed at a steady rate by a growing

band of supporters, and David knew that Philip had been very happy with the way his plan was being implemented.

It hadn't surprised David. After all, Philip had proved himself a ruthless businessman; he had clambered up a very greasy pole on his way to the top, and he had proved a similarly ruthless campaign manager by applying the same kind of principles. Plan, plan, plan, then plan some more, was his creed. That was why David had appointed him.

He'll milk it like crazy and take all the kudos if I'm in the White House next November, David thought.

Then David's cell phone rang. He told his driver to pull over and to step outside the car while he took this particular call in private; it was his father, Daniel, calling from London.

David had been trying to get hold of his father for the past three days, but with the constant demands of his business, his campaign, and his family, he missed his father every time Daniel returned his calls.

Half an hour later, David hung up in a state of mild panic.

He sank back into the rear seat of the Lexus.

What should he do next?

His elderly father, normally so clear-voiced and confident despite his age, had sounded hesitant and quavering.

There was some bad news about his uncle Jacob. Yes, he was right now in a hospital in London following a mild heart attack. No, thankfully there was no need for surgery, the consultant had said. *Thank goodness for that.*

But he was ill and would be in there for a little while. Yes, they needed to do further tests.

Then came the real bombshell.

David knew from the tip Philip had received that the political journalist, Fiona Heppenstall, was looking at his family finances and that an investigator, Joe Johnson, was working with her.

But he had continued to put it to the back of his mind. There had been too many other things to worry about.

However, the journalist and the investigator had shown up in London, his father said. And as hard as it was to believe, they had broken into Jacob's workshop at night, hacked into his safe, and found various documents.

No, there was no possibility of reporting it to the police: that would have been suicidal. Why? Well, Daniel had said, he would explain.

And he would have to apologize, but some of it may come as a shock. Yes, he knew David wasn't aware of all the details, mostly, and David was correct, he should probably have told him, but it all happened a very long time ago.

Indeed, it was a shock. As far as David had known, his uncle in London had in the distant past simply done well out of a few very good deals with a gold supplier in Poland that had sold to him on favorable terms. Jacob had made some money. He'd never thought twice about it. Well done, Jacob— a good piece of business.

But no.

Instead, the family wealth was founded on a stash of Nazi gold hidden nearly seventy years ago in secret tunnels in the hills of Lower Silesia. Which David's uncle and father had sold to a man in Buenos Aires. Who happened to be a former SS officer in charge of the concentration camp in which they were incarcerated during the Second World War.

Unbelievable, he thought to himself. Why the *hell* hadn't they told him before?

Then, on top of it all, Jacob's grandson, Oliver, had been kidnapped and tortured by a gang of Argentinians thought to be led by the SS man's son, who was trying to locate the gold. And Oliver had been found, not by the police, but by the investigator Johnson.

It was a difficult situation, his father had said.

He wasn't joking.

Why hadn't he been informed about the status of the Heppenstall-Johnson inquiry and the kidnapping, David had demanded. Surely he had a right to know, as a family member. His father's response, that he didn't want to distract David from the campaign, sounded hollow.

Daniel's attempt at reassurance didn't hold much water; he said that Jacob had persuaded Johnson to focus on the aged SS man in Argentina rather than the Kudrow family. But David knew it was potentially too big a political story to ignore, especially if a top journalist like Fiona Heppenstall was on the case.

David pulled out a fresh pack of cigarettes from his glove box, opened it, and lit one. He sucked in hard. This was all hard to comprehend; there was too much coming out of the blue at just the wrong time.

He sat, immobilized by the impact of what he just heard, smoking almost on autopilot.

When he had finished the cigarette, David opened the window, beckoned his driver back in, and completed his journey up the street to Philip's property.

Philip answered the door with a look of slight concern on his face. "Hi, David, I was expecting you half an hour ago. Everything all right? You're not looking great."

"No, not really, Philip. We've got a bit of a problem. Correction. A huge problem."

Philip studied his face. "You'd better come in. What's been going on?"

Philip led the way through to a large sitting room over-looking a large expanse of landscaped garden at the rear of the house, at the center of which was a putting green. He pressed the button on a wall-mounted intercom and requested coffee.

They sat down on a long beige leather sofa. David spoke

at length, explaining what he had heard from his father, breaking off only when a middle-aged woman wearing an apron came in with two cappuccinos on a tray.

Philip listened quietly until his boss had finished.

Then he began tapping his fingers on the coffee table. "David, you've screwed up badly here. How can you not have known all that when it's so close to home? You told me clearly there was nothing to worry about. It's my reputation on the line here, not just yours, dammit. And how the hell did Heppenstall and Johnson get to know about what's been going on in the first place? Somebody must have leaked it to them."

Philip shook his head. "We can't let this happen, David."

CHAPTER FORTY

Thursday, December 1, 2011
London

Leopold limped his way up the stairs toward Jacob's office, with Johnson and Fiona close behind. "In Greek mythology there's a legend of a god that was the personification of the sun. He was meant to have driven a horse-drawn chariot made of solid gold across the sky each day," Leopold said as they walked.

"Helios?" Johnson interrupted. "I know that legend. You think that's what he was saying?"

"Yes, it must be," Leopold said. "That's the nickname we gave to the old Volkswagen, the T2 panel van we used to ferry the gold back here from Poland. We thought it was really funny. And pans, well, I think he meant the belly pans of the Volkswagen. We stashed the gold bars in the belly pans—you know, the steel plates bolted underneath the engine and the underside of the vehicle to protect it from damage and water and so on."

Johnson said, "Interesting. So are you saying the spare map might be in the belly pan of the Volkswagen? Is the T2 he's talking about the one standing in your workshop here?"

"No," Leopold said. "The T2 in the workshop is a customer's, in for repair. The one we used is in Jacob's garage in Mayfair, still in good working order. But I don't think he's put the map in the belly pans. No, I was thinking of something else. Just follow me and I'll show you."

He walked into Jacob's office and pointed at something on the desk. It was the strange-looking sculpture Johnson had noticed before.

"Ah, I get it," Johnson said. "Two miniature panels shaped like the belly pans, leaning against each other. And there's an engraving of a chariot pulled by horses on one of the panels."

Leopold turned around. "You're quick, aren't you. Yes, I had that specially made for him for his fiftieth birthday in '74. It unscrews and—"

"You mean the map's inside it?" Johnson interrupted. He swore inwardly. The sculpture had been virtually the only possible hiding place in Jacob's office he hadn't examined while waiting for Bomber Tim to open the safe. How had he overlooked it?

Leopold took a Swiss army knife from his pocket and folded out the screwdriver attachment. "I got one of my engineers to make this for Jacob—a great little present, don't you think? We just need to take out this screw here and then that one. They're a bit rusty."

He worked for a minute, then with a squeal of metal on metal, pulled off one of the side pieces of metal.

"And inside, yes, it's here, look!" Leopold pulled out a piece of paper and unfolded it. It was a detailed map diagram drawn neatly in black ink, complete with measurements and a scale.

"Yes, this is it. It shows you where you need to go to find

the entrance to the sewer. I remember. It's hidden, up here near these trees." He indicated with his finger.

The place he was pointing to was near the tiny village of Sokolec, just off a road that led north from a larger village, Ludwikowice Klodzkie.

"The sewer was still dry the last time we went there, though that was a long time ago now. It was meant to serve the Sokolec tunnels complex but was never used. And then you go along until you find the entrance to the tunnel proper here." Leopold pointed to another spot on the map.

"I want to make a copy of it before I give it to you, though." Leopold took the map over to a scanner in the corner of the room and started it up.

"Fiona," Johnson said, "Can you see if you can get us on a flight this afternoon or first thing tomorrow."

She nodded and walked out of the room, tapping a number into her cell phone.

When Leopold had finished, he walked over to Johnson and placed the map in his hand. "Right, all yours. Good luck then. Just one thing. The tunnel is booby-trapped. We put trip wires in there years ago. They're marked on the map, so be careful."

Johnson grimaced and shook his head. "Explosive? Are the trip wires marked on the map that Ignacio Guzmann stole from Oliver?"

Leopold nodded. "Yes, explosive—quite a lot of it. It's the only way we could defend it. We couldn't exactly arrange for regular security patrols. So be careful. And unfortunately, yes, the map he's got will be an exact duplicate of this one."

"Oh, great. Thanks for telling me," Johnson said. Then he checked that Fiona had left before turning to Leopold once again.

"There's one other thing," Johnson said. "Jacob threatened me yesterday morning, before we left for Bristol. He said I shouldn't do anything that might put him and Daniel in danger because I'd regret it, and there were bigger games being played out. He also refused to tell me what the money from the gold sales was being used for. Do you know what that's all about? I'm asking while she's out of the room—just being careful because she's a journalist," Johnson said, indicating with his thumb in the direction Fiona had taken.

Leopold stood still for a moment, looking carefully at Johnson. Then he sat down behind the wooden desk and indicated to Johnson to sit in the other chair.

Johnson complied. Leopold folded his arms on the desktop. "Have you heard of Operation Moses, Operation Solomon, Operation Wrath of God, and Operation Damocles?" he asked.

Johnson consciously tried to remain expressionless. "They're all Mossad," he said. "Operations Solomon and Moses—they were the airlifts of Jews out of Ethiopia and Sudan. And Wrath of God . . . well, that was the Munich Olympics massacre retaliation. And I know Damocles, too, the assassination of German rocket scientists, the Egyptian thing, to stop them from building missiles aimed at Israel. What's that all about?"

Leopold narrowed his eyes a little. "And do you know of Friends of the Israel Defense Forces, the Jewish National Fund, Itamar, and the Hebron Fund?"

Johnson nodded. "I've heard of them. West Bank settlement support funds, aren't they?"

Leopold nodded and cleared his throat. "It's what you might call protection money."

Instantly, it made sense.

"Of course," Johnson said. "The Kudrows have helped fund these projects in return for protection? They've helped fund operations by Kidon?" Johnson asked.

Kidon was the secretive special forces assassination unit

within the Mossad, responsible for notorious operations including Wrath of God, which involved the revenge killing of the Palestinian militants behind the 1972 massacre of eleven Israeli Olympic team members in Munich.

"Correct," Leopold said. "As you can see, they've not spent it all on themselves. Look at this place, it's a dump." He waved a hand around the old office. "Okay, they've done all right out of it, you know, houses in Mayfair and so on, and they've made sure I've been well looked after, too, up to a point, but the vast majority . . . " His voice trailed off.

Johnson tipped his head back and gazed at the ceiling. "So did the Mossad insist on the payments, or did the Kudrows volunteer?" he asked.

"Bit of both," Leopold said. "Call it a compromise."

What was it Nathaniel had said on the recording Fiona sent, Johnson asked himself.

Follow the money trail—where it comes from and where it goes.

"Okay, and in return?" Johnson said.

"In return? The twins have been left alone—by everyone. And the Mossad looks after their own, which is why Jacob told you to tread carefully. He meant it, and you should be careful. Brenner's been given enough hints. He knows if he stopped buying the gold, the Kudrows would automatically inform the Mossad—because obviously Israel's share of the gold sales would also then stop—and the Mossad would strike. That's been the beauty of it. He's had to keep buying," Leopold said.

Johnson fiddled with the old wound in his right ear. "But it doesn't seem to quite fit with the way the Mossad have worked over the years. I mean, ever since the war ended, if they've had a sniff of a Nazi on the loose they've taken him out or had him prosecuted, from Adolf Eichmann on down."

"Money talks," Leopold said. "Israel's been getting a large number of shekels—not massive in the global sense, but enough—made possible by Brenner buying the gold. But now the flow of money's at an end. So I wouldn't like to predict what the Mossad will do next—what they might get Kidon to do."

An alarm bell went off in Johnson's head. "If Brenner went to court and started talking, it could be very embarrassing for them. So, instead you think they might—"

Leopold nodded. "Yes, I think they might."

* * *

London Stansted Airport

The announcement over the public-address speakers at London's Stansted Airport blared across the concourse. "This is a final boarding call for Ryanair flight 8407 to Wroclaw. Will all remaining passengers please make their way to the gate as quickly as possible."

Johnson and Fiona had only just cleared the security check and were repacking their bags. Johnson tried to run through a mental checklist to avoid losing items as he quickly stuffed his belongings back into his bag and pockets.

Laptop, two phones, keys, coins, wristwatch, wallet. Jacket back on. Now belt back on as well . . .

Just at that moment, Johnson's phone rang. It was Vic. He cursed but answered the call.

"Vic, I'm about to get on a plane," Johnson said, tersely. "What have you got?"

"Listen, Doc, I've got some info. I managed to find an old file on Brenner in our archives here. There wasn't much, but it looks like Brenner was on our payroll for a long time in the '50s and '60s, even running into the '70s. He provided contacts among the SS's old spy network in Russia, where he seems to have been well connected, and passed on information from these contacts about Russia's military capabilities: details about the so-called missile gap between Russia and the U.S. It went on for a long time and must have been enough to build a lot of credit with the CIA. Explains a lot. My gut instinct is there's been some sort of unofficial long-running agreement, a stand-off, between us and the Mossad. It wouldn't be the first time, although there's nothing written down as far as I've seen."

Johnson swore. "Well done, the Agency. What a pile of shit. Is that it?"

"I've also got an address for Brenner in Buenos Aires," Vic said. "He lives on a street called Ombú. I'm texting it to you. And that's all for now."

"Okay," Johnson said. "Did you make a copy of the file? It would be useful to have if I need it for evidence, although we might have to make an official request for the original if it went to court."

"No, but I'll scan a copy, on the quiet, if it would help," Vic said. "I'll go and pull the file out again."

"Okay, thanks, if you don't mind, that would be useful. Keep in touch." Johnson ended the call.

They had to sprint virtually all the way from the security hall to the gate, and even then they were the last two passengers to board the packed 8:40 p.m. flight.

Their seats were right at the back, row thirty-three, next to the toilets. It meant battling through a motley collection of businessmen dressed in suits and carrying laptops and people who Johnson guessed were expatriate Polish bricklayers, plumbers, and car mechanics going home for a few days, all jostling to secure space for their bags in the overhead compartments.

Johnson sat down, sweat pouring off his forehead, in the

middle seat of the three to the right of the plane, just as the cabin crew began their safety briefing.

Fiona took the aisle seat to his left, and to his right was an obese man dressed in blue dungarees reading a Polish newspaper, his legs so fat that his knees were encroaching into Johnson's space. He groaned inwardly.

The e-mail from Ignacio arrived just after that. He felt his phone vibrate in his pocket and fished it out.

Hello Johnson. I know what you're doing and why. I know what my father did, his evil. Read the attachments. There's something else, too, which will emerge in time, a real bombshell. He killed a lot of people, and he also killed my childhood. You would be shocked. So I'm going to sort him out in my own way. I don't want any interference from you. Justice will be done. You and the American journalist don't need to get involved. Back off, otherwise I'll take action. And I mean that. Read the attached documents, and you'll see why I'm doing what I'm doing. Then leave me alone.

Johnson reread it several times. There were four attachments, all of them jpeg photo files. He tapped on the first.

It was a photograph of a typewritten memo, written in German on yellowed paper. To Johnson's satisfaction, he was able to easily translate without having to resort to the dictionary app on his phone.

Dated the sixth of October 1942, the memo was congratulatory in tone and came from the *SS Personalhauptamt*, which Johnson knew was the SS Personnel Main Office. It informed Brenner that he was being promoted to the rank of *Obersturmführer*. It stated this was for Brenner's role with the 3rd SS Panzer Division *Totenkopf*, the Death's Head Division, during the invasion of the Soviet Union. It referenced the part played by the *Totenkopf*, a tank unit, during the advance on Leningrad during 1942. There were several official stamps on the memo, one of which showed the SS eagle above a swastika—the official SS symbol.

The second letter, also typewritten and dated the second of November 1943, was again from the *Personalhauptamt*, detailing Brenner's appointment as deputy commander of the Auschwitz concentration camp following an injury sustained at Kharkhov in March 1943. It didn't specify the injury, but Daniel had mentioned Brenner having a limp.

Interesting. Johnson knew that for Brenner to have been posted to a concentration camp, he must have been unfit for *Frontdienst*, service at the front line, and this document confirmed that. He wondered what type of injury it had been and whether it had left any permanent identifying marks that might now be useful, if he was able to track him down. Perhaps that detail might be in Brenner's *Krankenbuchlage*, his military medical treatment records, which would be stored at the *Deutsche Dienststelle*, the German National Information Office, in Berlin.

Johnson clicked on the third attachment.

Betrifft: Versetzung der Obersturmführer Erich Brenner, SS-Nr. 183 656, read the subject line at the top. The transfer of First Lieutenant Erich Brenner, SS number 183 656.

He took a sharp intake of breath when he realized this one was from January 1944, appointing Brenner as deputy commander at the Wüstegiersdorf subcamp of Gross-Rosen. A fateful day—both for his mother and for the Kudrow twins.

The fourth letter had two joint signatories: first the *Personalhauptamt*, and second *Hauptsturmführer* Karl Beblo. But this letter, dated December 21, 1944, had a very different tone.

It was clearly a severe reprimand issued to Brenner and outlined details of an escape three days earlier, the eighteenth of December, by two Jews from a railway car en route from Ludwikowice Klodzkie to Gluszyca. It also accused Brenner of shooting dead—without authorization—nineteen Jewish prisoners who were fit for work. The memo noted the two escaped Jews had not been found.

Johnson fell back in his aircraft seat and breathed out slowly. *Why would Brenner keep these documents? It doesn't make sense.* The other question was, were they genuine?

In the absence of the originals, which presumably Ignacio had somehow obtained from his father—presumably not voluntarily—there was one foolproof way to check their authenticity. If they were genuine, then hopefully copies would be in Brenner's personal SS file, which should be available.

Thank God for Hans Huber, Johnson thought, for the umpteenth time in his career. Huber was the manager of the Wirth paper mill at Freimann, near Munich, where in April 1945, the Nazi leadership sent the entire collection of ten million membership card files for the worldwide Nazi Party to be pulped, just as the Second World War came toward a close.

But Huber defied the Nazi leadership and managed to hide the documents under waste paper until U.S. Army archival experts were able to secure them in October of that year. They were subsequently transferred by the Americans to a Berlin document center, and microfilmed copies were made for use at the National Archives in Washington, D.C. These documents had been the bedrock on which many interviews and prosecutions of Nazi war criminals were founded, including at the Nuremberg trials, and had been a goldmine of evidence for the OSI in its work.

Johnson quickly composed an e-mail to Ben at HRSP.

Hi Ben, could you please check SS files for Erich Brenner and confirm if they include a reprimand for the shooting of nineteen Jews

on December 18, 1944, and confirmation of his postings at
Auschwitz and Wüstegiersdorf camps. Many thanks, Joe.

He pressed the send button.

Then he wrote another to his onetime girlfriend Clara
Lehman in Berlin, whom he kept in touch with periodically,
asking her if she might possibly be able to check Brenner's
Krankenbuchlage at the *Deutsche Dienststelle* to see if there was a
mention in the medical records of an injury, probably to
his leg.

Fiona had finished fixing her seatbelt and pulling some
notes and magazines out of her bag. She leaned into Johnson
and peered over his shoulder at the phone. "What's that?
Anything interesting? You're looking a bit stunned."

She was right. He was.

"It's an e-mail from Ignacio," Johnson said. "He wants to
take things into his own hands with his father. Threatening
me, wants me to back off—as if I would. And you as well. He
must have gotten my e-mail address from my website."

The Boeing 737 was roaring down the runway and then
became airborne, the ground fading away beneath them, but
he hardly noticed, he was so absorbed in the files from
Ignacio.

"But that's not all," Johnson said. "There's four attachments showing proof that Brenner was a deputy commander
at Auschwitz and Wüstegiersdorf, and there's actually a
memo reprimanding him over the Kudrow twins' escape from
the train that also details the unauthorized shooting dead of
nineteen Jews who were fit for work. The SS weren't techni-
cally allowed to kill Jews who were capable of working, as
they were seen as war assets. It was only when they became
too weak or ill that they disposed of them. When I was
working at the OSI, this was the type of documentary

evidence I always looked for, that I'd crawl across burning coals to get hold of. I used to call it the 'proof of the truth.'"

Johnson leaned back in his seat and exhaled. "It's a smoking gun."

Fiona looked over his shoulder at the screen again and wrinkled her nose in disgust. "I mean, just holding those roles is proof enough of what he must have done. Killing went with the territory. But the reprimand—well, I agree, it's a smoking gun. And his son wants you to ignore this and let him deal with it? No. We can't. He's got to face justice. You can make sure of that, and I'll make sure the world knows what he's done and that he's being dealt with. It's inhuman."

She paused. "What I don't get is why he's sent it to you."

Johnson shrugged. "I don't know. Probably just trying to justify what he's planning to do—to us and to himself. In fact, I'm certain that's why. But I don't get why the old man would have kept the documents or even how he was able to do so for so long without detection by someone. Why would he even have brought them out of Germany? But anyway, whatever the reasons, it underlines my point that we need to stop Ignacio before he gets to his father. That's my concern. He obviously thinks a bullet in his old man's head will suffice. And for me, that's why Brenner is the focus right now. Jacob's right. Brenner's the killer. The Kudrows aren't."

Fiona hesitated. "Yes, but the Kudrows are also a massive story. They're funding an election campaign by selling a stash of hidden Nazi gold—to the same Nazi who forced them to hide it during the war. That forces David Kudrow to step down from his campaign for the Republican nomination, and we get all the credit. We need to do that soon—the primaries are due to gear up after the New Year."

In her excitement, she spoke more loudly than she realized.

The woman who was sitting in front of Fiona turned around.

Johnson heard a young boy sitting nearby ask his mother what a Nazi was.

Johnson hissed at her, "Shush, keep your voice down. The whole plane can hear you."

He lowered his voice. "You just need to hang on a minute. The whole objective here is to get the guy to court. If you start running stories before he's been arrested he'll go underground like a rat down a sewer pipe. He'll get a new passport, a change of identity and just disappear. That's what these guys have always done. They're survivors. There are still networks in place to protect his sort, you know, even now, almost seventy years later. They'll just whisk him away."

A sudden suspicion crossed his mind. "You haven't mentioned any of this to your editor, have you? About Brenner?"

Fiona hesitated again. "Well, I mean, I obviously had to tell my boss that I was going to Poland because he was expecting me back in Washington soon. So I just gave him a quick idea of what it was about. But only for information. He won't do anything with it."

She raised her eyebrows at Johnson. "Don't worry, it'll be fine."

"Yes, well, what I'm worried about is that it *won't* be fine if you start talking to editors about it at this stage."

"Okay, point taken," Fiona said, to Johnson's relief. "You're enjoying all this, aren't you? Like the old CIA and OSI days?"

Johnson nodded. He *was* enjoying it, he told her. It reminded him of why he'd enjoyed his OSI role so much. At the OSI, unlike the CIA, he had no longer felt as though the whole objective was to deceive, lie, pretend, and cheat—and not just to the opposition but to one's colleagues and superiors—in order to wriggle up the greasy career pole.

He didn't mind using smoke and mirrors, but at least at the OSI he had felt there was a human justification for the occasional piece of subterfuge.

Maybe Robert Watson *had* done him a favor by firing him, he said to Fiona.

The drinks trolley appeared next to Johnson's right elbow.

He felt badly in need of a stiff Scotch but with difficulty, managed to resist, wanting a clear head to think about the task ahead. Instead, he took a tonic water, no gin.

Fiona declined a drink. Instead, she picked up her notes.

As she buried herself in those, scribbling occasionally, Johnson pulled from his pocket a couple of printouts from a website he had found that had some details of the Sokolec complex. It included a couple of poor photographs of the entrance and the interior of one of the tunnels.

> *The Sokolec tunnels complex is inside the Gontowa Mountain and comprises four tunnels built by slave labor, mainly Jews who were imprisoned in the nearby Gross-Rosen concentration camp.*
>
> *Tunnels One and Two are built into soft sandstone and have collapsed in several places.*
>
> *Tunnel Three is half a kilometer away from the others but has been inaccessible since the end of World War II because of a collapsed tunnel roof.*
>
> *The Sokolec complex is not accessible to tourists, who are advised to visit the nearby Underground City of Osówka to experience the Riese tunnels in safety.*

Brief, and nothing about emergency exit tunnels, Johnson noted. His thoughts drifted back to the e-mail from Ignacio.

There's something else too which will emerge in time—a real bombshell. What could that be? More documents? More evidence about his father?

I don't want any interference. Justice will be done. But if

Ignacio wanted to deal with his father himself, why not just get on with it? Why the need to tell Johnson?

And if he wanted Johnson to back off, why send him a copy of exactly the type of document, containing clearly incriminating evidence, that would only encourage him?

Maybe I'm overthinking it. Maybe Ignacio just wants the world to know what his father's done.

Johnson had a sudden craving for a cigarette.

The whole thing just didn't add up.

CHAPTER FORTY-ONE

Friday, December 2, 2011
Wroclaw, Poland

It was just after five o'clock the following morning when Johnson and Fiona drove out of their hotel near to Wroclaw's Copernicus Airport, just west of the city, in a rented green Škoda Octavia.

Since he had less than four hours sleep, the last thing Johnson wanted for a long drive through the darkness was snow. But the flakes, tiny at first, grew larger and were driven east to west by a brisk wind as Johnson navigated down the A8 highway.

By the time they swung onto the more rural DK35 heading southwest, the now fast-moving flakes had turned into white streaks across the blackness, like a television picture with no signal.

A road sign read Gluszyca 65km. Johnson knew the hotel Fiona had earmarked as their base, the Sowa, was another fifteen kilometers beyond that at Sokolec, in the valley north of the village of Ludwikowice Klodzkie, very near to the tunnels complex.

Another hour and a half, Johnson estimated.

Fiona shifted in her seat and turned toward him. "What I don't get is the CIA connection. What's that about?" she asked.

Johnson put his foot down and changed up a gear. "It's more complicated than I imagined. You're not going to believe half of it."

He ran Fiona through what he had learned about the Mossad connection to the Kudrows and the Israeli projects they had supported, the Brenner background, and the apparently tacit agreement between the Mossad and the CIA to leave Brenner alone, for different reasons on both sides.

"The question is, do I keep pursuing Brenner? And if I do, is it going to piss off the Israelis, and then what might the consequences be? Or do I just let the Mossad take care of Brenner? I don't know what's best," Johnson said.

Fiona lurched forward in her seat, her voice rising. "You're joking, right? You've got to keep going. This could make your career. And if you let the Mossad take care of Brenner, you'll get the same outcome as if Ignacio takes care of him."

"Yes, but you don't know who you're messing with here. You really don't," Johnson said.

"Don't lose your nerve now, Joe. Let's take it one step at a time."

"Easy for you to say. I'd like to get to Brenner as quickly as possible," Johnson said. "But you've insisted we go to Poland so you can get your evidence and we stop Brenner's son walking off with a fortune in gold. So therefore, we've got to find a way to stop him somehow—and fast."

Johnson did his best to calm himself. He didn't want to

start an argument, but Fiona clearly had no real idea how dangerous the waters in which they were now sailing were. Unlike her, he had seen what the Mossad's Kidon unit was capable of.

"Okay, here's an idea," Fiona said. "We let the Polish police do our work for us. If we see the Argentinians go into the tunnel, we call the police and have them arrested, and then that cuts the chances of the old man being alerted and disappearing."

Johnson inclined his head. "Yes, that's one option. We definitely need to prevent Ignacio getting to his father before we do."

He braked hard as a truck in front of them came to an abrupt halt at a set of traffic lights in a village.

The volume of traffic increased as they went farther south. There were few opportunities to pass, and Johnson could average no more than forty kilometers per hour. At least the snow had stopped.

"What do you think about your old boss Watson's involvement with Brenner?" Fiona asked.

Johnson sighed. "He's lost his moral compass, if he ever had one. He's obviously been supporting the idea of using evil to fight evil, Nazis versus the Russians. I never agreed with that. So he's spent decades protecting someone who committed multiple murders of defenseless Jews. Although, frankly, it's probably coming from the top of the Agency."

They were into the Owl Mountains now, running west of Walbryzch, and Johnson noted the occasional brown tourist sign flashing up in his headlights, pointing to some of the Nazi tunnel complexes open to the public. *Podziemne Miasto Osówka,* read one. Underground City of Osówka.

Tours of the old tunnels. The locals were still trying to capitalize on the Nazi occupation seven decades earlier. Who could blame them? It was probably the closest they would get to compensation from the Third Reich for the virtual destruction of their country during the war and then the grim, gray repression of the Soviet era that followed, Johnson mused. It would take a lot of tours to offset that damage.

Not far to go now.

It was nearly half past six by the time Johnson and Fiona reached Ludwikowice Klodzkie. From there they took a left onto a narrow tarmac road signposted Sokolec, then went through a tiny single-track tunnel underneath the railway line and up the valley. Dark trees flashed past in the headlights.

The railway line up which Jacob, Daniel, and nineteen other Jews passed, crammed into a filthy railway cattle car, exhausted, frail, and starving under the malevolent eye of Erich Brenner, almost seventy years ago.

After a mile and a half, on the left, they found Hotel Sowa, "Owl Hotel," next to a lake.

Johnson pulled into the loose gravel parking lot, which was empty apart from three other Polish-registered cars. He turned the ignition off and leaned back in his seat.

His phone beeped. It was a message from Vic.

Joe. Went back to pull out Brenner's file to copy it for you. It had disappeared. Archive staff don't know what happened to it. It was only three hours after I took it out the first time. God knows what's going on. Will make further inquiries and let you know. Vic

Johnson banged his hand down on the car steering wheel. *What the hell?* Now he was completely dependent on Ben and Clara digging out the files he needed in D.C. and Berlin.

He and Fiona climbed out of the car. Hotel Sowa was a basic, low-slung single-story structure with overhanging eaves that reminded Johnson of the roadside motels on the routes in and out of Portland.

They were about to walk through a heavy, half-glazed

wooden door into the central reception area when Johnson glanced to his right.

That was when he saw it, tucked away behind some bushes in another small parking area. A silver Ford Focus with British plates.

CHAPTER FORTY-TWO

Friday, December 2, 2011
Sokolec, Poland

Johnson pushed open the door into the reception area and made his way across the red carpet to an old-fashioned dark wooden desk, behind which stood a grim-looking blond woman in her thirties, wearing steel-rimmed glasses.

She obviously had a well-practiced eye for the nationalities of her guests and offered a half-hearted greeting in passable English.

Johnson did his best to conjure a smile. "Hello, we are staying here tonight, but first we have a meeting with two Argentine men whom we are trying to find. Have you seen them here? One blond, one dark-haired."

The woman, whose garlic-laden breath caused Johnson to recoil slightly, nodded. "Yes, they're staying here. They arrived late last night, but they went out very early this morning, about an hour ago. They didn't say where they were going."

"Ah. But that's their car parked over there, is it?" Johnson nodded his head in the direction of the small parking area where the Ford Focus stood.

"I believe that is theirs, yes," the woman said.

"So they were walking when they left this morning, I assume?"

"I don't know."

Johnson guessed the two Argentinians had arrived late and had bedded down for a few hours sleep. They were probably right now somewhere in the tunnels complex searching for the boxes of Third Reich gold bars.

He thanked the receptionist, then turned to Fiona and jerked his thumb in the direction of the parking lot. "Let's go." He began to walk toward the main door.

Outside in the parking lot, the only sounds were those of the water in the lake lapping against a pebbly beach in front of the hotel and the *twit-twoo* of owls in the trees to their left.

Across the other side of the lake rose the looming silhouette of Gontowa Mountain. It was more a large hill than a mountain, its outline clearly visible against the sky.

What would my mother think now? She who spent months in a concentration camp only a few miles up the valley.

Johnson took out his phone, switched on his maps app, and consulted the printed paper map from Jacob Kudrow's office. He studied it for a moment, then punched in some coordinates: *50°38'33.4" N 16°28'02.6" E*

Earlier, a short distance before they had reached the hotel, Johnson had noticed in his car headlights a rough gravel track to the left that appeared to lead in the approximate direction of the mountain and the tunnels.

He pointed out the detail on the map to Fiona. "I'm certain they will have gone that way. It's the only obvious route to the tunnel entrance. If it gets messy, you'll have to leave things to me. You just get out of there and make sure you look after yourself. You okay with that?"

She nodded.

"Right, let's go," Johnson said. "We're already an hour behind them."

The first pale blue light of dawn crept over the horizon to the east as Johnson, followed by Fiona, walked out of the parking lot. After they passed a house on their right, Johnson veered up the farm track he had noticed earlier. It consisted of two parallel tractor tracks paved with crushed stone, a strip of grass between them.

The track led northwest, past the other side of the house, through some trees, and over a field toward a denser copse of trees on the other side.

Johnson rechecked the maps app on his phone before continuing out of the copse, left across the grass and inside the line of the trees, mostly pines. They climbed cautiously and silently up the hillside and into denser woodland consisting of pines, rhododendron bushes, and some brambles.

Johnson finally saw what he was looking for. Around twenty yards ahead of him was a small square concrete structure, so heavily laden with moss and ivy that it was scarcely visible amid the trees and bushes grown up around it. It had a deeply rusted metal grill, around three-and-a-half feet square, which was hinged on the right-hand side. The grill was open at a right angle.

Then, through the trees, came voices.

Johnson pulled Fiona down behind a rhododendron bush, its thick dark leaves providing good cover.

One man emerged backward from the grill, bent double and crouching to avoid banging his head, around which was strapped a bright headlamp. He was carrying one end of a wooden box. Johnson recognized the man from the photograph that Jayne had sent him. His receding light brown hair and deep tan was unmistakable.

Ignacio Guzmann.

As he continued backward, another man, dark-haired this time, came into view, holding the other end of the box. He too wore a headlamp that shone brightly into the predawn gloom. *That must be Diego Ruiz.*

As soon as they were clear of the grill, they lowered the box gently to the ground and stood out of breath, hands on hips, their black jackets, pants, and wool hats covered in dust, sand, and grime.

* * *

Ignacio felt no dissipation of the tension that had held him in an iron grip for the previous several days. His objective was so close, he could almost touch it. And yet . . .

One box of gold was out of the tunnel, only three more to go, and then half of his task would be done. After that, there was just one remaining objective left to be completed in Argentina.

His big concern, however, was the two Americans, Johnson and Heppenstall, and whether they were on his tail. But all he and Diego could do now was to work as fast as possible before time ran out.

The map he had obtained from young Oliver Kew's laptop had been incredibly accurate, providing measurements and coordinates that had taken him to the entrance of the emergency tunnel.

And the narrow tunnel itself, despite being flooded in places and, due to a few partial roof collapses, occasionally difficult to navigate, was in better condition than he had expected.

The only notable obstacle had been the three trip wires,

which were marked on the map but were nevertheless extremely difficult to spot in the darkness of the tunnel, even with the help of powerful headlamps.

Ignacio couldn't see what the trip wires were attached to, as they disappeared into a tangle of tree roots and sand. Neither could he tell whether they were active or not. He had to assume they were linked to some kind of explosive.

He stood in the cold dawn until he'd gotten his breath back. It had taken more than twenty minutes for him and Diego to carry the twenty-kilogram box out of the tunnel.

It was heavy and quite bulky, and given the trip wires, Ignacio had thought it safer for them both to carry the box.

Now he changed his mind. Speed was important. Three more individual trips would take more than an hour and twenty minutes, not including the return journeys. That was too long.

"*Bien,* Diego, let's get the next couple of boxes out. I think this time we just take one each. It will be quicker. We don't know if anyone is going to come."

Diego nodded. "Yep, they're not as heavy as I expected."

Ignacio stood thinking for a few more moments.

"Come on, *jefe*, we need to move," Diego said.

"Give me a second. I'm just thinking. I can imagine my father working here, sixty-seven years ago. Probably tall, arrogant, wearing an SS uniform, and terrifying the hell out of a bunch of half-dead Jews."

The documents he had found, including the disciplinary letter about the killings, had told him all he needed to know. He was certain there must have been many more murders, too. He shook his head at the image.

How did my father and a whole generation of Germans fall in behind Hitler's bullshit, turning some of them into mindless killers who would follow instructions without question?

Then he checked himself. *Who am I to judge? Me, a killer myself.*

"What's up, *jefe?*"

Ignacio turned around. "Nothing. *Vale, vamos,* let's go. I'll go first." He led the way back into the sewer, dropping to his knees and crawling through a mess of mud, old leaves, and animal droppings.

After a short distance, he saw the square opening above him that led into the escape tunnel. Without the map, he would almost certainly never have seen it.

He hoisted himself up and climbed into the gap. Then he crawled until the roof became high enough for him to stand up and walk.

Beyond that, the tunnel was like something out of the goblin stories his mother had sometimes read to him as a child: protruding tree roots, rocks sticking out at odd angles, water dripping from the roof, piles of sandy soil on the floor where the tunnel ceiling had collapsed, and green slime everywhere.

Ignacio made his way slowly forward, searching for the first trip wire. There it was, at shin height, pulled taut and difficult to spot with its rust coating against the dirty, sandy floor.

He stepped carefully over it.

Ignacio turned and watched as Diego also slowly navigated the trip wire.

The going was a little easier now.

It was another fifty or so meters to the next trip wire. Ignacio was forced to take extreme care on the wet, slimy rock surface just before it. He eased himself over the wire to safety.

Ignacio looked back again. Diego was now out of sight and some distance behind him, although he could see the faint glow from his headlamp around a corner.

He walked a little farther, where he had to squeeze past a large pile of rock and soil that was almost blocking the passage; it had fallen a long time ago, judging by the amount of green algae covering it.

Once past that, he decided to wait for his colleague and sat down on a rock in the nook between the tunnel wall and the pile of debris, leaving him with a glimpse of the approaching Diego.

The barrel of his Browning, in a small holster at his side, dug into his hip, so he took it out and placed it on a smaller rock to his left.

Finally, Diego arrived at the second trip wire. His right foot landed on the same piece of slime-covered rock that Ignacio had negotiated a few moments before.

Diego's boot slipped and slid sharply backward, throwing his weight forward. He tried to correct himself by pushing his left leg in front of him, but he stumbled and lost his balance.

In order to avoid falling facedown on a stone surface, Diego instinctively threw his right arm out in front of him. As it came down, his forearm crashed hard into the taut trip wire.

The last thing Ignacio saw was a massive white flash and he heard a deafening bang. He felt a searing heat, and a tsunami of dust and soil hit him in the face.

Just before he passed out, Ignacio sensed a second explosion coming from the opposite direction.

CHAPTER FORTY-THREE

Friday, December 2, 2011
Sokolec, Poland

Johnson and Fiona sat behind the rhododendron bush for at least ten minutes after the two Argentinians had disappeared into the tunnel.

By then it was light enough to see back down the hill to the lake below them and the hotel beyond that.

Then, finally confident that Ignacio and Diego weren't going to reemerge for a while, Johnson walked to the entrance to the sewer. He peered into the void, as if examining a display in a museum.

Fiona joined him, then took her camera from her bag and took a few photographs of the entrance.

"I don't think we should go in there now," Fiona said. "What we could do instead is just jam this grill shut so those two are locked in. Then we leave and call the police from a distance."

Johnson considered the idea. "Yes, not bad, I like that."

He walked around the entrance to the sewer and climbed on top of the mound of earth into which it was set. From there he could see farther up the hill through a clear channel between the trees.

Just as he stepped up, there was a muffled roar from the direction in which he was looking. A plume of dust and smoke rose into the air a hundred yards away, just in front of the trees. Seconds later, there was another smaller boom, with more smoke, from inside the trees.

From his vantage point, Johnson could see the explosion had created a large crater in the ground.

"Shit!" Johnson said. "What was *that*? I think they've triggered the damned booby trap down there. Leopold warned me about it."

The sound of the explosion echoed around the valley, a low-pitched rumble that reverberated from one side to the other.

Then, silence. Even the birds had stopped singing.

Johnson stepped forward. "We'd better go take a look."

They walked cautiously toward the crater, skirting around large bushes and pine trees as they went, until they arrived at the sink hole.

Across a rectangular area around twenty-five yards long by around three yards wide, the surface of the forest, thousands of tons of earth and rock, had sunk downward by about ten feet.

A couple of large pine trees growing on the fringe of the sunken area had fallen over completely, and another tree was now lurching at a dangerous forty-five-degree angle.

Smoke seeped up through crevices in the sandy soil.

Johnson and Fiona looked at each other.

Fiona shook her head in disbelief. "Holy shit snacks. That's the gold gone, and those two guys gone with it." She reached for her camera.

* * *

Ignacio opened his eyes, then panicked. He was sure his head was about to split open from the inside out. Pressure built in his skull, and he couldn't hear a thing.

Where am I?

It was dark, apart from a strange light that shone from above his eyes sideways across the floor. He lay on a pile of earth, his head resting painfully on a piece of wood, and then he coughed as he breathed in dust.

Slowly his consciousness returned. The bang, then the flash, came back to him.

The trip wire . . . Diego fell on it.

He put his hand to his head, which throbbed, and felt the grittiness of stone and soil in his hair; then he found the headlamp, still switched on and functioning.

The ringing sound coming from somewhere deep within his ears was unnerving. He scraped his hand along the floor, then banged it harder. He could see his hand move, could feel the slight vibration as it hit the floor, but could only hear the ringing.

Ignacio sat up. By the light of his headlamp, he could see to his left an impenetrable mass of rock and soil but no sign of his friend Diego. To his right the tunnel was still intact.

There's only one way to go now.

He tried to stand and instantly felt dizzy. His vision blurred, and white specks flicked in front of his eyes. He collapsed back down. After a few moments, he tried again and felt better.

Ignacio wended his way through the tunnel. He spoke out loud. "*Hola.*" Now he could hear his own voice just a little.

He vaguely remembered hearing and feeling the force of a second explosion from this direction.

The tunnel curved at forty-five degrees around a large

rock. Around the corner, he could feel cool air gently streaming against his face, and up ahead . . . *Is that a chink of light?*

That hadn't been there on his previous trip through this tunnel half an hour earlier. He walked closer.

A huge mound of earth and rock blocked the tunnel in front of him where the second explosion must have caused it to cave in.

But here, at the point where the pile of debris climbed to meet the roof of the tunnel, was a gaping hole about three yards wide. Ignacio peered up and could clearly see a clump of pines and rhododendron bushes.

He scrambled up the pile of earth and rock, sliding back down as the debris gave way beneath his feet, but he managed to reach the top. Levering himself on his elbows, he climbed out and stood up.

There was no way to get back to the three other boxes of gold that remained underground. He and Diego had found the boxes in a much larger tunnel connected to the narrow emergency passageway, still on the decrepit wooden pallet on which they had been placed in December 1944.

But they had at least managed to get one box out.

Ignacio turned with the thought of returning to the box. Then he saw something that caused him to drop to the ground

Less than fifty yards away, on the other side of a rhododendron bush, stood the two Americans, Johnson and Heppenstall. They were looking into a massive crater. *Shit, shit, shit,* Ignacio said to himself.

The pair were talking to each other and gesticulating. Then Johnson turned his head and pointed in Ignacio's direction a couple of times. He was clearly telling the woman they should go that way.

Where's my gun? With a sudden surge of panic, Ignacio realized he had left his weapon in the tunnel.

Too late to go back.

He stood and, crouching low, walked away from Johnson toward the trees. What to do? He had to get to his car and then leave as quickly as possible.

And what of Diego? He must surely be a goner.

At the thought of his partner, Ignacio hesitated only for a second. As soon as he was sure he was completely out of view of the Americans, he broke into a steady, military-paced run. He clutched his inside jacket pocket, where something heavy banged against his ribs.

Every step jarred his throbbing head, which felt ready to explode, but he didn't stop. He knew what he needed to do next.

Ignacio pulled his phone from his pocket as he ran and called a cell phone number in the Czech Republic. The conversation was an extremely brief one.

Fifteen minutes later, Ignacio was in his silver Ford and accelerating hard down the narrow valley road away from Sokolec and through the tiny single-lane tunnel under the railway line.

He narrowly missed a baker's delivery van as he emerged at the other end and screeched to a halt at the junction with the main road in Ludwikowice Klodzkie. Ignacio picked up his phone and quickly checked his maps app.

The signpost at the T-intersection pointed right to Walbrzych and Wroclaw, and a smaller sign below it, also pointing right, read Wroclaw Airport 81km.

* * *

"There was another explosion inside the trees, which went off just after the first one," Johnson said. He turned away from the huge crater in front of them and pointed toward the pines to their right.

"It was over there. We'd best take a look at that, too."

In the trees, around a large rhododendron bush, there was another hole, smaller than the first but similar.

Fiona gaped at it. "There must have been two booby traps down there then. Well protected for sure. It's like Fort Knox." Then she realized what she had said and added, "No pun intended."

She focused her camera on the crater in the ground and took two photographs. "That's all I'm gonna get, dammit—no pictures of the gold and the tunnels now. My boss will have me for breakfast after trekking all the way out here."

Johnson went over to the edge of the crater and peered down. "Come here. There's an opening into the tunnel here, where the roof fell down. You can get in."

Then he saw them.

"Quick, Fiona, look, there's a set of footprints here. Someone's climbed up and out. One of them must have gotten out. You can see the prints clearly on the soil where they've clambered up."

Johnson stood and walked around near the hole. "More footprints heading that way." He walked farther into the trees. "They're going in this direction. Dammit, I bet Ignacio got out. I can just feel it." He swore loudly.

"If there's only one set of prints, that means there's still one of them down there," Fiona said. "Either alive or dead."

"Most likely dead, then. One wouldn't just leave the other." Although he wouldn't put anything past Ignacio. Like father, like son.

He pulled out a pack of cigarettes and a lighter and, as an afterthought, held the pack out to Fiona, who took one. Johnson flicked the spark wheel on the lighter, cupped his hands, and lit first her cigarette, then his own.

He inhaled deeply. "Right, we need to get back to the hotel, quickly. If it's Ignacio who escaped, then he won't come back here. He'll head for his car. The tunnel is dead. So there's only one thing left for him to do, and that's in Buenos Aires, not here. We've got to try and stop him. If it's Diego who escaped, he'll also try and head home, for sure."

"So we just leave whoever's buried down there?" Fiona asked.

Johnson grimaced. "We just haven't got the time or tools to start digging, Fiona. The hotel and the authorities will have to sort it out."

He straightened and started walking back the way they had come, puffing at his cigarette as he went.

Then he remembered the box of bullion, threw his cigarette on the ground, and broke into a run. "Come on, quick, let's move. We'd best hide that box of gold back there first."

The box of bullion was still where the Argentinians had left it near the sewer entrance. Johnson put it well out of sight under a rhododendron bush and threw some dirt and leaves on top and around it for good measure. Hopefully nobody would see it. In any case, he didn't really have a choice. They needed to run.

By then, the sun was glinting off the icicles, and frost hung from the tree branches out in the valley.

When they arrived back at the hotel, the silver Ford Focus had already disappeared. Johnson picked up a stone from the ground and flung it into the lake.

The hotel receptionist came out to the parking lot when she saw them. "You've missed one of the Argentine men. He left in his car, maybe five or ten minutes ago. Covered in mud and dirt. I don't know where he had been."

"Which man was it?" Johnson asked. "The blond one or the dark-haired one?"

"The blond," she said.

Johnson nodded. That figured. He made toward the green Škoda Octavia, then had a thought. Turning back to the receptionist, Johnson said, "Call the police and tell them there's a man stuck on the hillside over there in a collapsed tunnel. They'll find him. Say it's urgent."

Two minutes later, Johnson and Fiona accelerated out of the parking lot. "That's it," he said. "I'm not letting that Argie thug get away with this. We're going to find the old man."

CHAPTER FORTY-FOUR

Friday, December 2, 2011
Ludwikowice Klodzkie

Fiona hung on to the passenger door handle as Johnson turned right at the T-intersection and floored the accelerator into the bend, causing the back of the car to swing out slightly.

The green Škoda sped away from Ludwikowice Klodzkie in the direction of Wroclaw. Johnson somehow kept both hands on the wheel while gripping his phone between his hunched shoulder and his left ear, listening to the ring tone.

Eventually Jayne answered.

"Joe, where the hell are you? What's happening?"

"Jayne, it's not going well. To cut a long story short, Ignacio or his friend Diego blew up the tunnel, so Ignacio didn't get what he was after, but he's disappeared. We need to know where he is and if he's on a flight back to Buenos Aires. Probably from Wroclaw Airport, then via some other hub, maybe London or Madrid or whatever. Can you get someone to run checks on passengers?"

Jayne sighed. "Look, Joe, it's difficult. I've been told I need to back off . . . " Her voice trailed off.

"What do you mean, back off? This is urgent."

"Never mind, don't worry. There's stuff going on here at work. I can't talk now."

The phone went dead.

I need to back off. What was she talking about?

Half a minute later his phone beeped as a text message arrived from Jayne.

> *I'll try. There is someone I know in France, a woman I used to work with who is now at Interpol down in Lyon. I can't guarantee anything. Difficult here. Frankly, I'm pissed off with it all. Can't wait to leave.*

Johnson groaned. It crossed his mind that someone at Langley might have spoken to Jayne and her boss. That would be typical. *Robert Watson?*

They were only a couple of miles away from Wroclaw Airport when Johnson's phone rang. It was from a U.K. cell phone number, although not one Johnson recognized.

This time, Fiona held the phone while Johnson spoke.

"Hello?"

"Joe, it's Jayne. I'm ringing from a private cell phone number. Daren't use my work phone. Sorry about the cloak and dagger, but I need to tell you, there are strings being pulled. Unbelievable, really, but my boss called me in. He said he'd taken a call from your favorite man at Langley, Robert Watson."

Johnson felt his body stiffen. *I knew it. Watto, still playing his games.*

"Screw him," Johnson said.

"Yeah, I know," Jayne said. "Watson has requested that we do nothing to assist you and that we ensure no other British authorities do, either."

"Does he know you've been helping me already?"

"No idea. It's quite possible. But he's apparently also contacting Berlin with a similar request. I mean, it's not official or anything. It was an under-the-table ask, a quid pro quo for some help on another job, actually, but I thought you should know what's going on and why I'm a bit limited."

But the good news was, Jayne continued, it hadn't stopped her speaking privately to her Interpol contact in Lyon, who had worked quickly and had checked flight departures from Wroclaw.

There was an Ignacio Guzmann booked on a Lufthansa flight leaving Wroclaw Airport in just under two hours' time, at 11:30 a.m., for Frankfurt, with an onward booking on the long-haul flight from Frankfurt to São Paulo.

"*São Paulo?*" Johnson asked. "Are you sure? That's odd. Why the hell would he be going to Brazil?"

"No idea, but it's definitely São Paulo."

Johnson calculated quickly. It would probably take them an hour and a quarter to get to Wroclaw Airport, and assuming Ignacio remained ten minutes ahead of them he would get there maybe forty or forty-five minutes before the flight departed. That was cutting it a little fine, but it was a small airport, so he would probably have enough time to navigate through security and passport control before the gates closed.

"Okay. Looks like this is our chance to trap the bastard, then," Johnson said. "He won't be able to take a weapon into the airport, even if he's got one, and he'll be boxed in once he's in the terminal. So if we can get airport police or security to detain him until we can arrive, we can apprehend him then. Once we've done that, the Polish police can take over."

Jayne agreed that was the best option. "I'll talk to someone I know at the British Embassy in Warsaw and get them to liaise with the airport authorities and police at Wroclaw. They'll have all the contacts needed."

"But you're not supposed to be helping me, are you?"

"Screw them," Jayne said. "That's a problem for another day. I'm going to call Warsaw now, and I'll give you an update once I've got the wheels moving." She ended the call.

Johnson accelerated through some traffic lights, which had just turned red, and passed a truck, cutting back in just in time to avoid a refuse truck coming the other way.

"Let's see if we can catch up with Ignacio," he said.

"Give it a go," Fiona said. "He's only in a small Ford, so we've got a chance of overhauling him."

Although Johnson, at times, hammered the Škoda at speeds of up to 140 kilometers per hour on a series of winding country roads, they were also held up for what felt like an interminable seven or eight minutes behind a slow-moving tractor, with no opportunity to pass.

There was a further delay at a set of temporary lights, set up to manage traffic flows around some roadwork.

Johnson doubted that, overall, they had made up any ground on the Argentinian, and depending on his timing with the tractor and the lights, it was quite possible he had extended his lead.

By the time Jayne called back forty-five minutes later, there was still no sight of Ignacio.

"My Warsaw contact has the airport police on standby," Jayne said, her voice squawking in a tinny, distorted manner from Johnson's phone, which Fiona had switched to loud-speaker mode. "They've been briefed, as have the chief executive and head of security at the airport."

"So what's the plan?" Fiona asked.

"Okay, this is what will happen," Jayne said. "When

Ignacio checks in at the Lufthansa desk for the flight, the desk person will take his passport for checking and then hold him up. There'll be a mysterious computer glitch or something. There'll be two armed police loitering nearby, just in case. As soon as you get there the check-in people will take Ignacio off to a side room, telling him they need to resolve something before they can confirm his seat. If he resists, the police will assist. Once he's in the side room, that's when you'll be able to do your bit. The chief executive will meet you at the information point, near the check-in desks. Then I'm hoping we can make an arrangement for police to help you further after that."

"Okay, great," Johnson said. "Sounds perfect. You're a star, Jayne. I assume Polish police will have grounds to hold him anyway, given that he's attempted to remove and steal gold that doesn't belong to him. We can sort the rest out once we're there."

At just after 11:05 a.m., somewhat later than he had hoped, Johnson braked to a halt in the drop-off zone in front of the terminal. He flicked on the Škoda's hazard lights, and he and Fiona ran through the glass doors.

In front of them was the information point, next to which a silver-haired man in a dark suit and a red tie was standing, looking a little agitated. He was flanked by two armed policemen. This, clearly, was the chief executive and the posse of officers who had been delegated to detain Ignacio.

Johnson walked up to them and introduced himself and Fiona.

The silver-haired man nodded in recognition. "I'm Wojtek Geremek," he said, in accented English. "I've been briefed on what's happening. Good to meet you."

Johnson had no time for pleasantries.

"Where's our man Guzmann?" Johnson asked, staring toward the check-in desk, where there was a short queue comprising a few businessmen in suits, two elderly couples with large suitcases, and a young man with a guitar case.

"He's not arrived yet," Wojtek said. "He's booked on the Lufthansa flight to Frankfurt, there's no doubt about that, but he's certainly not tried to check in." He glanced at his watch, then at the check-in desk to his left.

"He's not checked in? But he was well ahead of us. Probably ten minutes ahead, and he must have made up more time on the road, because we were held up a couple of times," Johnson said.

"Yes, but he's not here," Geremek said. "The gate will be closing in five minutes. He's definitely not going to make the flight."

"So where the hell is he?" Johnson said, his voice rising.

Geremek shrugged and put his hands in his pockets. "I don't know. We've had our security team looking out for his car, which I understand is a silver Ford with British plates, but there's been no sign of it coming into either the drop-off zone or any of the car parks."

"Well, could he have got in another way?" Fiona asked.

"Not possible," Geremek said. "In any case, we have a photograph of him, which was supplied through the British Embassy in Warsaw, and there's been nobody matching the description either in the terminal or on the airport site. We've been watching the closed circuit television monitors like hawks."

CHAPTER FORTY-FIVE

Friday, December 2, 2011
Ludwikowice Klodzkie

When Ignacio had finished checking his map at the T-inter-section in Ludwikowice Klodzkie, he had ignored the signs pointing right to Wroclaw Airport.

Instead, he yanked his steering wheel hard left and, with a squeal of tires, let out the clutch and accelerated away from the T-intersection.

His destination lay only twenty-five kilometers in the opposite direction.

Soon he was traveling southeast past schools, run-down houses, and shops at speeds almost double the legal limit.

Ignacio swung a hard right, heading south toward Nowa Ruda, then on to Sarny and past the old border customs building at Tlumaczow before a blue sign flashed past: Česká Republika.

Even now, having crossed the border into the Czech Republic, Ignacio didn't allow himself a smile. In the village of Otovice, he pulled over next to a pebble-dashed gray church with a red brick bell tower and a memorial to the dead of 1939–1945.

He dialed the same number he had called earlier, when running away from the collapsed tunnel. He exhaled with relief when the call was answered almost instantly.

"*Hola,* Ignacio?"

"*Si,* Alfonso, *que tal?* I'll be there in five minutes, okay?"

"Okay, I'm circling the airstrip, landing in two minutes. It'll be a fast turnaround, so make sure you're ready. *Hasta pronto.*"

Ignacio slammed the Focus back into gear and sped off, leaving a hail of gravel splattering into the war memorial behind him.

As he drew near his destination, he could see a small twin-engine turboprop aircraft flying above him. It banked sharply to the right and then descended rapidly, disappearing behind some buildings.

Ignacio drove into the village of Martínkovice, then swung right at a crossroads, next to a handsome white school building behind a decorative metal fence.

He rushed along a country lane lined with leafless trees until he saw what he was looking for.

There were a couple of frayed wind socks billowing in the wind, a corrugated steel hangar, a few old buildings behind a rusty pink wrought-iron gate and a link fence, a two-story control tower with a few radio masts, and a small radar scanner on the roof.

Beyond the buildings was a grass airstrip. A faded sign on one of the buildings, partly obscured by a tree, read Airport Broumov.

Airport? It was more like an abandoned industrial unit in Barrio 31.

On the grass, the aircraft was already taxiing toward the

control tower. Its wings bobbed slightly as it bounced over the field.

Ignacio turned into the gate and sped straight to the front of the small tarmac parking lot to the left of the control tower.

Then he jumped out of the Ford, grabbed his backpack, and sprinted over the grass toward the plane, a Cessna 340.

As he did so, two men emerged from the tower and ran toward him, shouting and waving their arms in a clear indication to stop.

The pilot already had the rear door of the six-seater open, and Ignacio climbed swiftly into the aircraft. As soon as the door closed, Alfonso hit the throttle. The Cessna accelerated quickly in the direction of the grass runway. The two men were still in pursuit, shaking their fists. Then they gave up. Ignacio saw one of them throw his hands up in frustration.

Ignacio climbed through to the copilot's seat, where he strapped himself in. Within a minute, the plane was airborne again, flying low over Martínkovice, where it banked right and headed west at an altitude of no more than five hundred feet.

"*Todo bien?*" the pilot, Alfonso, finally said.

"*Si, no hay problema*. At least, not now. Thanks for getting here on time, *amigo*. So, is our route clear?"

"Yes, it's clear. We're going probably about 650 kilometers, so roughly two-and-a-half hours in this baby. She moves. We can cruise at three hundred an hour. I just need to keep her fairly low—helps avoid the radar, mostly."

"*Perfecto.*"

Ignacio was confident there was little chance of Johnson being able to track him on his current journey. Indeed, he hoped the investigator had been diverted onto the false trail he had left by booking a flight from Wroclaw via Frankfurt to São Paulo under his real name.

He was also glad the pilot's plan was to fly low. That way, his cell phone would continue to operate, which was important, as he had a call to make.

Ignacio dialed a number in Buenos Aires.

"Luis? *Hola*. Yes, it's Ignacio here. Listen, the tunnel was a disaster. That idiot Diego set off a booby trap that blew the whole tunnel up and himself with it. We got nothing, no gold."

Ignacio listened as Luis tried to commiserate with him, then he interrupted.

"I'm on my way back now. I need you to do something for me. You need to put a track on my old man. I want to know all his movements. Don't let him out of your sight. But be subtle, got it? *Vale, muchas gracias* . . . "

When he ended the call, Ignacio reached into his inside jacket pocket and removed a single rectangular object, almost four inches long and an inch and three quarters across, yellow-brown in color, with an eagle and swastika marking on the front and the words *Deutsche Reichsbank*.

Underneath there were other markings: *1 kilo Feingold, 999.9*, followed by a six-digit number prefaced by the letters *DR*.

Ignacio kissed it.

A single, gleaming, solid one-kilogram gold bar, worth, he calculated, about $50,000.

Not quite what he had hoped for but a long way better than nothing.

He placed it carefully in his backpack and took out a small brown paper package.

Unwrapping it, he removed a small red booklet.

The front cover was resplendent. On it were printed several words in gold lettering:

Europäische Union

Bundesrepublik Deutschland
Reisepass

He opened the passport and managed a thin smile.

Inside was a photograph of himself, and next to it the name of the holder: Franzes Konigen.

PART FOUR

CHAPTER FORTY-SIX

Friday, December 2, 2011
Wroclaw Airport

It was only when the pushback tractor began to propel the Lufthansa Boeing 737 away from the terminal gate and onto the taxiway that Johnson finally gave up.

He turned to Fiona. "Look's like the bastard's given us the slip. Neat trick. You've almost got to admire him."

"Can you get Jayne to check at other airports?" Fiona asked.

Johnson shrugged but placed an encrypted call to Jayne's cell phone and explained what had happened.

"Maybe it was a decoy booking," Johnson said. "He must have known we'd check. Can your Interpol friend down in Lyon do another scan for Guzmann at other airports and airlines within range of here? Maybe he's taken a different route. Try airports within, say, a hundred fifty kilometers of Ludwikowice Kłodzkie to start with."

"You're sounding completely deflated," Jayne said.

"Too damn right," Johnson said. "I think the asshole's slipped through our fingers. We've wasted a huge amount of our valuable time coming here when we should have gone straight to Buenos Aires."

He glanced at Fiona, who turned away in embarrassment, then went on. "We've missed grabbing Ignacio and it's given Brenner time to get out and away. We've probably lost both of them."

Twenty minutes later, Jayne called back.

She had requested a check for Guzmann's name, and also for any anomalies, such as passport details that didn't tally with passenger names, involving anyone booked to fly from airports within a hundred-and-fifty kilometer radius. There was nothing so far.

"My friend at Interpol is now widening the search to look at flights from all European hub airports to Buenos Aires, and she'll report back within an hour or so," Jayne said. "The thing is, it's not an official investigation, just a friend doing me a favor, so she has to keep it low-key."

Johnson gently chewed the inside of his cheek. "Hmm, well, Ignacio won't have gotten further than a hundred fifty kilometers by now, for sure. He's driving a Ford, not a Ferrari. Sounds like he must have another plan. Maybe he's traveling under another passport, a different name."

He thanked Jayne and ended the call.

Johnson gazed around the Wroclaw departures terminal. "Fiona, perhaps you could try and get us on the next available flight to Buenos Aires, while I just work out what we do next."

He tried to think through the issues he was facing.

Apart from Brenner, there was Watson. If the CIA veteran was taking remote measures such as asking other intelligence agencies across Europe to ensure he received no assistance, then it seemed logical to assume he would probably also deploy one of his own CIA assets in Argentina to try and exfiltrate Brenner to safety.

While Fiona wandered off toward the Lufthansa ticket office, he tapped out a text message.

> *Jayne, we still need to get to Argentina, and I'm going to need help there. I need someone who knows the region well, speaks Spanish, and can help me out. I'm guessing you've finished that Olympics report by now. If you're so pissed there you'd like a new challenge, get yourself on the next flight. If not, do you know any other assets there who might be able to help? Let me know what you think. Joe.*

Johnson sent the message to Jayne's cell number, then looked across the concourse at Fiona, who was standing at the back of a long line at the Lufthansa desk. He doubted she would be happy given how possessive she felt about this story, but backup was backup.

* * *

Great Falls Park, Washington, D.C.

Robert Watson had driven from the CIA offices at Langley to Great Falls Park, next to the Potomac River. It was one of several places he occasionally visited when he needed some thinking time or to make calls without the threat of surveillance by anyone at Langley.

As he limped to a bench at the side of a hiking path, well away from any bushes where eavesdroppers might be concealed, he clamped his phone to his ear, using a pretend call as cover to gradually turn a full circle as he carefully scanned the area. He had no reason to think he was being tailed, but one could never be too careful.

Watson dropped his bag, containing VANDAL's CIA file, on the bench and sat down. He wasn't going to take the risk of leaving the file in his car, particularly after having discovered that someone else at the Agency had been reading it just a few hours before he had retrieved it.

He hunched his already-tense shoulders, took his encrypted phone from his pocket, and dialed a number. The plan Watson was about to suggest was a gamble, but he felt he had no other option.

"Moshe, it's Robert here," he said when the call was answered.

There was a two-second silence at the other end of the line before Moshe Peretz, sitting 5,900 miles away in Tel Aviv, replied.

"Shalom, Robert. Do you have an update?" the Mossad intelligence chief asked. "And what's that noise in the background?"

"It's water. A river. It's where I come when I need to think. We need to decide what to do. There have been developments here."

"Go on, what?" Peretz asked.

"Apart from Joe Johnson, there's someone else out to get VANDAL."

"Tell me," Peretz said.

"It's his son. The only difference is, he wants the old man disposed of, not put in court, my sources tell me. He could do it, too; he's an army thug and has a long record. He's been out of his father's business until recently—didn't know what was going on. But now he's found out and has gone looking for the gold, my guys in London tell me. He drove from London to Poland yesterday with another one of his gang."

Watson swept his hand through his white hair and looked down at the smooth river waters upstream to his left and then the white foaming maelstrom of a waterfall just below his vantage point.

"So what next?" Peretz asked.

"Well, I've been doing a bit of thinking since we spoke last. We both have a lot to lose if the old man ends up being dragged to court by Johnson and starts squealing under pressure. A huge amount. We've got to protect ourselves."

Watson placed his hand on the bag containing VANDAL's CIA file.

Peretz snorted. "If that happened, the press would have a ball, whether from the CIA or the Mossad angles. But, like I told you before, the people upstairs here might take the view that if the funding has dried up, they'll take alternative action on Brenner. But what's your solution? Do you want me to talk to the director here and get Kidon involved?"

"No, no, not yet," Watson said. Calling in the Mossad's murky assassination unit at this stage would be unnecessarily messy.

"I think we should let the son and Johnson fight it out over the old man," Watson said. "That's the lowest-risk, cleanest option for us both. My money would be on the son doing VANDAL over before Johnson gets there. And then I'd put more money on him disposing of Johnson, too. As I've told you, I know Johnson from way back. He's ex-CIA; I fired him. He doesn't have what it takes: I doubt he's going to do much when it comes down to it, but I don't want to risk it unnecessarily."

"So we let the son do the wet work for us, instead?" Peretz asked.

Watson switched his phone to his other ear, checked around him, then continued,

"Exactly. And if he can also see off Johnson, that's the other problem solved."

Watson looked up to the sky and waited.

There was silence at the other end of the line.

"Okay," Peretz said eventually. "Let's go down that route, at least for starters. There's obviously a risk attached, though. If the son doesn't do what you expect, we'll have to act swiftly ourselves on Johnson. I can issue instructions at this end if you can't handle it. I very, very definitely don't want this going to court."

"Okay, agreed." said Watson. "Me neither."

"So how are you going to make sure the son gets there first?"

"I'm getting surveillance put on VANDAL," Watson said. "I've got an asset in Buenos Aires. He'll make sure."

He hung up, then straightaway dialed another number in Miami.

"Simon, it's Robert," he said, when the call was answered. "Some good news. I've made progress regarding VANDAL. Tel Aviv is going to do nothing for the time being, which gives us some breathing space to get him out of harm's way."

He paused. "Activate that new passport request for VANDAL as soon as possible and get it to him. We also need to put travel delays in place for Johnson en route to Buenos Aires, which is where he's inevitably heading now. Get your team to have him blocked from using direct flights—force him to use a circuitous route or something. And once he does get there, make sure he's held up at the airport. Get it done. Thanks."

"I'll make sure that happens. Keep in touch," Simon replied.

Watson hung up, sat back on the bench and cursed. He really should have planned further in advance for this type of eventuality. Such a long time period with no visible threat to VANDAL had bred complacency. It was very unprofessional.

Still, with luck, he should be able to get VANDAL out of

Argentina safely without anyone doing him over. That would be a win-win.

* * *

London

Jayne sat and stared at the text message from Johnson for several minutes.

> *I need someone who knows the region well, speaks Spanish, and can help me out . . . If you're so pissed there you'd like a new challenge, get yourself on the next flight.*

She certainly felt pissed—and she definitely needed a new challenge.

Johnson was also correct in that the Olympics security report was complete and sitting in her boss's inbox.

After almost three decades in the SIS machine, her plans to head for the exit in the coming months were now quite advanced. That said, she didn't want to leave under a cloud, and taking part in some off-the-books operation in Argentina would almost certainly cause blowback of epic proportions if details found their way back to Vauxhall Cross.

Jayne weighed her options.

She could certainly be of help to Johnson—of that there was no doubt. She still had several highly placed contacts in Argentina with whom she had maintained relationships of sorts since her posting to the Buenos Aires station from 1996 to 2000. They included a couple of the agents she had run in the police and military machines, who had provided her with a steady flow of information about everything from naval mines and internal security to the fledgling Argentine nuclear weapons capability. The posting had been a good period for her, professionally.

Clearly, if Joe's plan to capture Brenner came to fruition, then that would be extremely high-profile and would trigger widespread media coverage across the globe.

But would it be possible to keep her role under the radar? If it were simply a question of giving him some support and hopefully helping deliver a successful conclusion, she could melt into the background immediately afterward and leave Joe to deal with the aftermath.

The problem would be if it all went tits up. That would be another story.

Jayne stood in her office in SIS's Vauxhall Cross headquarters and looked out the rain-spattered window across the gray expanse of the River Thames. A line of red London buses were queuing on the steel and granite structure of Vauxhall Bridge.

There were just over three weeks until Christmas, but she knew there would be no one to prepare with, wrap presents with, or celebrate with. So why not head off and instead do something different, stimulating, and interesting? And do it with someone for whom she still had a lot of affection and respect.

That decided it.

She walked out of her office and along the corridor until she reached Mark Nicklin-Donovan's office, then knocked quietly on the door, which was half open.

The head of the U.K. Controllerate looked up from his desk, which was covered in papers and reports. The cover of the one in front of him looked familiar to Jayne—it was her tome on Olympic security. Mark had a red pen in his hand and smiled as she entered. Always a good sign.

"Jayne, just making a start on your report. Looks good at first glance. Nice job. What can I do for you?"

"Mark, sorry this is short notice," Jayne said, "but I'm still owed two weeks' leave this year, and to be honest, I'm feeling exhausted after ploughing through that report. It hit me this morning. Would you mind if I take ten days off, starting tomorrow? I might head off for a few days of sunshine somewhere."

Mark raised his eyebrows, as Jayne had expected he would. Normally she booked her leave months in advance.

He paused, then shrugged. "Okay. As long as you're back by the fifteenth, as we'll need to start revising this report then. Thinking of anywhere special?"

"Not sure. I'm going to look at what's available."

He nodded. "Fine."

Jayne thanked him and headed back to her office, feeling light-footed.

She put on her coat, threw a few belongings into her bag, and walked to the lifts, while developing mental plans. It would probably make sense to travel under a legend, one of which she had carefully compiled prior to her stint in Argentina and which she still used on occasion.

Twenty minutes after she arrived back at her apartment, Carolina Blanco, a British national born in Buenos Aires of British parents on January 10, 1962, was booked on a direct British Airways flight to the Argentine capital, leaving at 10:25 p.m. that same evening.

Then Jayne began to make a mental list of what else she and Johnson would need. A car she could hire at the airport. Most other things she already had, apart from a gun and ammunition. But who was she going to call to procure those?

Her only likely candidate in Buenos Aires—and she grinned at the thought—was a police officer, now very senior, although when she had recruited him as an agent in her second year in Argentina, he had been further down the career ladder. Carlos Campos, currently chief of the Federal

Police, was someone for whom she had a soft spot, although not in a romantic way. She kept in touch via the occasional e-mail, as she tried to do with several of her former agents. She never knew when she might need them.

Carlos always used to joke with her about the number of firearms—illegal, confiscated, lost, and otherwise procured—that he had stashed in a secure cupboard in his office.

Jayne never asked too many questions about where they came from or what Carlos did with them or, for that matter, about anything to do with his obviously well-padded bank account. Likewise, Carlos never asked too many questions about what Jayne was planning to do with the information he passed to her, particularly about the corrupt activities of many of Argentina's senior politicians and military leaders.

It was a neatly symbiotic relationship. Jayne assumed that Carlos had other similar relationships with all kinds of people scattered across the country—probably from both sides of the legal divide.

She picked up her phone and dialed Carlos's number.

"Carlos. *Que tal?*"

"Jayne! Good to hear from you. *Como estas?*"

He was astonished to hear she would be back in Buenos Aires the following morning and seemed to understand when Jayne was unable to explain exactly why. She went through the usual ritual of inquiring after Carlos's family, then explained she was in the city for a short time on a private job and that she needed a favor.

"Your firearms cabinet. Does it need a clear-out?" she asked.

She was unsurprised to hear Carlos had a variety of weapons that he could offer. They settled on two Berettas.

"Anything else?" Carlos asked.

Jayne listed a handful of other items, including binoculars and a small camera with a zoom lens. They agreed she would contact him again the following morning, once she had arrived in Buenos Aires, to give him a delivery location.

Jayne paused before hanging up. "Oh, there's one other thing." She went on to detail the other item she needed.

Finally, Jayne sent Johnson an encrypted text message.

Have thought over your proposal and have negotiated leave for next ten days. "Carolina Blanco" is leaving for Buenos Aires tonight. Arrive 8:15 a.m. tomorrow. See you there.

*   *   *

Frankfurt, Germany

The Cessna 340 had flown low and hard, steering a westward course north of Prague, then into Germany and past Bayreuth and Würzburg.

Now they were southeast of Frankfurt. Ignacio could see a number of large commercial jets, Boeings and Airbuses, circling the large international airport to his right and lining up to land.

But his pilot, Alfonso, had a different destination scheduled. He continued well south of the city until a much smaller airstrip came into view.

Frankfurt-Egelsbach Airport, around ten miles south of its bigger brother, had no scheduled services and was instead used by a variety of commercial and private aircraft, including business jets and helicopters, as well as flight schools.

For Ignacio, it was ideally placed: very anonymous and just a twenty-minute taxi ride from the main Frankfurt airport terminal where he needed to check in later for the Lufthansa flight to Buenos Aires, which was due to arrive the following morning.

He should have plenty of time for a shower in the airport lounge and to change out of his filthy clothes before the long-haul flight, he calculated.

Alfonso landed the Cessna safely on the 1,500-yard asphalt runway and taxied until he was just outside a hangar, where he brought the plane to a halt.

"There we go, safely down. You need to be careful coming into this airport. There have been a couple of nasty crashes over the past few years—planes hitting that forest we came over heading in from the east." Alfonso grinned. "No problems today though."

"Excellent, *muchas gracias,* Alfonso. See you next time, if there is a next time." Ignacio shook hands with his pilot, stepped down onto the tarmac, and climbed into a waiting black Audi.

"Frankfurt Airport, terminal one please, as quickly as you can," he told the driver in passable German, reflecting as he did so that it might have been the only useful skill he had ever learned from his father.

* * *

Wroclaw

After a long wait, Johnson and Fiona had discovered that flight options out of Wroclaw Airport were limited.

They were eventually told by the sales agent that they wouldn't be able to get to Frankfurt in time for the direct overnight Lufthansa flight to Buenos Aires, and in any case, the Buenos Aires flight was fully booked.

Instead, they were forced to settle for a tortuous route via Frankfurt and São Paulo that would get them to the Argentine capital only at 10:20 a.m. the following day.

Ironically, it was the same route that had been booked by Ignacio, prior to his no-show.

Johnson had just completed the payment when the text message arrived from Jayne. He blinked and had to read it twice. He hadn't really expected her to take him up on the offer, even if he'd hoped she would.

"Looks like we're going to have some assistance in Buenos Aires," he said.

"Who from?" Fiona asked.

"Jayne. She's taking some leave from work. She spent four years there with the SIS, knows the country, probably still has good contacts. She's going to be there a couple of hours before we are."

To his surprise, Fiona took the news positively.

Johnson tapped out a reply to Jayne.

That's good news. Please ask Carolina to head to Brenner's house and commence surveillance. We will join her.

He forwarded the text from Vic containing Brenner's address to Jayne. Then, almost by reflex, Johnson checked his e-mails.

There was a response from Ben at the HRSP. A cross-check with Brenner's SS file showed it included copies of the memos detailing the disciplinary action, promotion, and transfer to Wüstegiersdorf.

This was a critical development. The documents that Ignacio had sent were authentic. They would be admissible as evidence in court, of that Johnson was certain.

CHAPTER FORTY-SEVEN

Saturday, December 3, 2011
Buenos Aires

Ignacio arrived at Ministro Pistarini International Airport just before seven o'clock that morning and headed to his ramshackle house in Barrio 31, his journey under the Franzes Konigen alias having gone without a hitch.

Not entirely to his surprise, when he landed, he received a text from his girlfriend, Lucia. She'd written that she was leaving the city and was moving to Rosario.

Earlier, more in hope than expectation, he'd sent her a text to say he would be home shortly. But there had been no reply. He knew then that she was likely to have gone.

Sums up my life, more or less, he thought.

Ignacio walked over to the cupboard in his kitchen, reached into the bottom drawer, and picked up the friend he actually could rely on, his Glock.

He checked the weapon and put it in his small backpack together with extra magazines of ammunition.

After showering, he also put together a few other favorite belongings in a travel bag. A framed photograph of his two children, whom he hadn't seen for more than nine months, his collection of army medals, a silver hip flask, his laptop computer, credit cards, a leather bomber jacket, and a few other clothes.

That was about it. The sum total of his possessions.

Then he patted the inside breast pocket of the jacket he was wearing, just to reassure himself that the object inside was still there.

If his plan worked as he had envisaged, who knew when he would be back again. Or *if* he would be back again. Ever.

* * *

Buenos Aires

Feeling far better than she had expected she would, Jayne pulled her rented silver Toyota Hilux pickup onto Ombú, the upmarket, oval-shaped road in the Recoleta barrio, at around 10:15 a.m. A solid six hours of sleep on the overnight flight was more than she normally achieved on airplanes.

Returning to Buenos Aires was almost like coming home. She recalled attending a party hosted by an American embassy official in a luxurious town house just round the corner from Ombú in August 1996, only a few weeks after her arrival in the Argentine capital. She had drunk and flirted too much and then regretted it the next morning.

Now she parked under a tree on the opposite side of the road and about fifty yards away from Brenner's house.

She settled down to wait and watch through the dark-tinted windows of the double cab Hilux, which she had rented in the name of Carolina Blanco. The manager at the car rental company, just like the customs and immigration official, didn't give her passport a second glance, its shabby scratched cover adding to its authenticity.

The state of Brenner's house came as a surprise to Jayne, with its peeling paint and loose-hanging shutters. It was definitely the shabbiest on the street.

Ombú was quiet. Occasionally a car pulled up next to the curb. Their occupants, mostly casually dressed but clearly well heeled, appeared to be mainly either taking children somewhere or returning from shopping trips.

Jayne sent a text message in Spanish to Carlos, telling her where she was parked for delivery of the items she had requested the previous day.

> *Hi Carlos. Arrived safely. Road is Ombú. I'm sitting in a silver Hilux, registration GVA 076. Can't miss me. Just tell whoever brings it to be subtle. I'm on a house watch. Jayne*

Half an hour later, there came a quiet tap at Jayne's driver's side window. A man dressed in a black jacket and pants pulled out a police ID card from his pocket and, after giving Jayne a look of utter incredulity, handed her a brown paper package and disappeared.

She opened it. Inside were two Berettas and six spare magazines, together with a black plastic box about the size of a cigarette pack, with two chunky circular magnets attached to it and a sheet of paper with some instructions.

Jayne sat back in the driver's seat and chuckled. Nothing had changed in Argentina. It wasn't about *what* you knew in this country but *who,* and how you greased their palms.

At just after eleven, an old dark blue Peugeot parked carefully in a spot on the other side of the road about forty yards away, near Brenner's house.

Jayne watched, her left elbow propped on the windowsill

and her hand cupping the side of her chin. Nobody got out. Instead, she saw the driver wind his window halfway down, and then a white curl of cigarette smoke floated out, to be swiftly whisked away by a gust. After the driver finished that cigarette, Jayne noticed he tossed the stub onto the road and immediately lit another.

Interesting. The guy was clearly watching and waiting for someone.

There was a ping on her phone as a text message arrived. It was Johnson, saying his flight had been delayed by more than three quarters of an hour, but he now had landed. He would head over to her as quickly as possible.

Then at ten past eleven, an old black Mercedes pulled up outside Brenner's house, and a white-haired old man, stooping and carrying a walking stick, emerged from the gate.

That must be Brenner. Jayne leaned forward, fascinated to get a glimpse of what he looked like. He climbed stiffly into the back of the Mercedes, which then drove away.

Instantly, the driver of the blue Peugeot started his engine and also drove off, following the Mercedes at an unobtrusive distance.

Jayne swore out loud. Surely he wasn't tailing Brenner as well? She too started her engine and pulled into the road, keeping well back from the Peugeot while at the same time trying to keep an eye on where the Mercedes was heading.

The black car made its way along the long, straight Avenue Coronel Diaz, until it came to a crossroads with five exits. There it parked outside Café Nostalgia, on the corner. Brenner eased himself out of the car and walked into the café. Jayne smiled to herself. Another old haunt—she had several times met one of her agents for a clandestine late-evening drink at Nostalgia.

The driver of the blue Peugeot had also stopped and took a space across the road, next to a police car.

Jayne drove around the corner and parked her pickup out of sight behind a large delivery truck being unloaded in front of a fruit shop. Then she grabbed the props she had bought at the airport: a newspaper, a pack of cigarettes, and a lighter. She rarely smoked but had found that in the field, and especially in Argentina where many people smoked, cigarettes were a very useful tool for breaking the ice with contacts and as cover when carrying out surveillance.

She strolled into the café just in time to see Brenner sit down at a table in the corner opposite a middle-aged man in a black jacket, who was sipping a coffee.

The man shook Brenner's hand and appeared to introduce himself. Brenner nodded, and then Jayne watched as the man immediately pulled a fat brown envelope out of a briefcase and handed it to Brenner, who very swiftly put it straight into his inside jacket pocket.

Jayne sat at a table on the other side of the aisle to Brenner, unfolded her newspaper, lit a cigarette, and ordered a latte in fluent Spanish.

Then the man in the black jacket handed Brenner a small dark-blue booklet, which he also tried to place into his inside jacket pocket.

However, the old man, in his haste, missed the pocket; the booklet slipped down between his jacket and his shirt and onto the floor, where it lay for a few moments until he bent to pick it up again.

There was no mistaking what it was. Jayne had seen many of the blue booklets with embossed copper-colored lettering and a coat of arms on the front. It was a Chilean passport and was clearly in pristine condition.

Brenner quickly looked around, but by then, Jayne was pretending to concentrate on her phone.

The implications of what she had seen were clear. Jayne briefly considered intervening right there and apprehending

Brenner solo at gunpoint; she couldn't afford to let him slip out of the country with a new identity. But she almost immediately ruled that out: the location was too public, there were police outside, and it would guarantee a major diplomatic row. She would have to wait for Johnson's arrival and make a more calculated plan.

After only a few minutes, Brenner left and was driven back to his house, still tailed by the man in the Peugeot. Jayne, careful to avoid being seen, maintained a suitable distance behind.

Back on Ombú, Jayne parked farther away from Brenner's house than she had previously. She then walked around the oval road until she spotted the black Mercedes, which was parked a couple of hundred yards away from the house, underneath a tree.

Jayne wandered toward the Mercedes. Then, as she drew level with the black sedan, she let the cigarette lighter she was holding fall to the ground and into the gutter, right next to the car.

She bent down to retrieve the lighter. As Jayne picked it up, she simultaneously and with lightning speed reached underneath the Mercedes. There was a loud clunking noise.

Jayne quickly stood, appearing to check her lighter. Then she lit a cigarette and sauntered back to her Toyota.

CHAPTER FORTY-EIGHT

Saturday, December 3, 2011
Washington, D.C.

David Kudrow poured himself another coffee. It was his third in the space of two hours, and now the volume of caffeine he was consuming was becoming counterproductive.

To compound that, he got only a minimal amount of sleep the previous night. He had been up until midnight talking to Philip and his lawyer over the wording of a press statement, in case *Inside Track* or another news site decided to publish a story about his family's finances.

He'd been working so hard for the Republican nomination and for so long that the thought of it ending in a family disgrace was too much to contemplate. Worse, what if it turned out there was some link to Nathaniel's death in all this?

He was now sitting next to a speakerphone, with Philip in the chair in front of his desk, waiting for his father and uncle to join him on a conference call that had taken him more than a day to organize. His father had been busy helping his uncle Jacob, who was still in the hospital after his heart attack.

There was a beep from the speakerphone. "Hello, David? Are you there? It's your father here in London."

"Yes, Dad, I'm here," David said. "Philip's joining us for the call, and he's aware of everything, so don't censor yourself. I needed help managing this."

"Good morning. I'll just be listening in, Mr. Kudrow," Philip said.

"Okay, very well," Daniel said. "I'm in Jacob's hospital room with him. He's not meant to be talking to anyone, but he's insisting, so what could I do? The good news is he's doing all right and doesn't need an operation. Sorry if I sound a bit tinny, we're just using my phone on speaker here."

"That's good to hear," David said. "Glad you're okay, Jacob. You really shouldn't be worrying yourself about all this and doing conference calls. The consultant there would go nuts if he knew."

He swiveled around on his chair. "Look, I've been thinking this through. The bottom line is, if this story breaks —whether it's by this *Inside Track* journalist, Heppenstall, or someone else—then I will have to pull out of the campaign. You all obviously realize that."

David could hear Jacob coughing, so he stopped speaking.

Then Jacob spoke, softer and slower than normal. "David, look, yes, we know all that. It's difficult for me, but I have changed my thinking. This investigator Johnson wants to nail Brenner, right? Wants him in court. I know you won't like this, but the way I'm now thinking, I'd like to see that happen."

Jacob coughed again, then continued. "Okay, we've screwed him over the years, had our revenge, had our entire lifestyle built on it. Maybe it's an old-age thing here, maybe it takes something like a heart attack to make you see things differently, but it's about more than us, isn't it? Others want to see justice done too. Johnson and Heppenstall are the last chance to put him behind bars, as I see it. I've had a plan where that would happen eventually in any event. If I'm now nearing my end, then . . . " His voice trailed off and he coughed again.

David felt his anger building. He looked at Philip, whose face had completely shut down. *Keep calm, slow down. The old man's in his hospital bed.*

"Take it easy, uncle. My point is, that's fine, for your generation. You've had your future already, your dream. What about me? My dream's the White House. You're telling me you're going to rob me of that just to put a sad ninety-year-old in prison? If you were going to do that, you should have done it five decades ago. The truth is, you were too greedy, and now you're too late. And it's not fair to me that I get ruined in this belated pursuit of justice."

David swiveled his chair again. "I don't know how that Johnson guy and the journalist got hold of all this information in the first place. How did they know about the gold? Philip believes there was a leak from somewhere. We're working on that. But you two in London have made it worse. Why did you have to give Johnson so much more? You've served it all up on a plate for him and for the journalist."

David stood and did a lap of his office, his right fist pushed hard into his pocket as he walked. There was complete silence on the call.

Then Jacob's voice crackled through the loudspeaker again. "You've got to also think it through, David. If you *did* get to the White House in November, what would happen if it all came out then? Stepping down then would be much worse."

David shook his head. He could feel the tension building

in his face and neck. He paused and took a few deep breaths, remembering the advice of his psychiatrist.

"What do you think, Dad?" So far his father hadn't said a word. *Typical.*

Daniel's voice sounded distant, as if he had moved some distance away from the phone. "Don't forget, Johnson also rescued our Oliver here from a very nasty situation. I mean, if he had gone as well as Nathaniel, how would we all feel? He's going to take a while to recover from his injuries." Daniel paused, and David felt his chest rise and fall at the mention of his brother and cousin.

"But, thinking aloud," Daniel continued, "there *is* maybe something we could do. I mean, neither Johnson nor Heppenstall have exactly been on the right side of the law, have they? Breaking into our warehouse, into our safe, stealing papers. I could go on. I mean, what view would Johnson's clients or Heppenstall's publisher take if they knew what they've been doing, or if there were a police investigation? Someone might make an anonymous call or two to tip certain people off, if the course of events doesn't quite go in the right direction. You know what I mean? It could be quite damaging to both of their career prospects. It's worth thinking about."

For the first time that morning, a trace of a smile crossed David's face. But it didn't last long. He knew how the media operated.

"Trouble is though, once a story starts leaking a little, it's like trying to shove toothpaste back into the tube," David said. "If they don't run it, somebody else probably will."

He sat back down and faced Philip, then continued. "Heppenstall will probably tip off one of her friends at *The Washington Post* or something. You know, quiet chat over a glass of wine, a nod and a wink. Then it'll go completely *viral.*

The problem we've got is, we can't deny it, can we? That's the bottom line."

Philip pressed his lips together and rubbed his chin with his forefinger and thumb. For the first time since the start of the call, he spoke. "Of course we can deny it. Truth is one thing. Proof is another. Do they have proof? If they don't have it, we can deny it. Still beats me how this story got out in the first place."

* * *

Buenos Aires

Ignacio drove his white Renault Mégane around Ombú toward his father's house, passing a silver Toyota Hilux pickup heading in the opposite direction.

He parked next to the curb outside his father's house, grabbed his small backpack, and went to the front door, where he let himself in with his key.

Ignacio stopped still for a moment, a strange feeling in his stomach. After years of suffering at his father's hands, he knew that now was the time to turn the tables.

He walked through the hallway into his father's living room, where Brenner sat in his favorite black leather armchair.

Ignacio stopped near the doorway and stared at his father. "I'm back."

Brenner gazed back at him for several seconds before he replied. "Yes, I can see that. You're back earlier than I expected. I thought you were returning next week?"

"I thought I'd surprise you and come early. Why are you sitting there with your jacket on?"

His father didn't answer.

Ignacio looked around. Then he noticed a small suitcase next to the sofa. On the coffee table was a brand-new blue Chilean passport, an air ticket, and his father's phone.

Ignacio picked up the three items and flicked through the passport until he came to the photograph. "What the hell's this? You planning on going somewhere?" His head jerked back to look at his father.

He examined the air ticket. "Santiago, eh?" Ignacio straightened and folded his arms. "Are you going on holiday or a business trip? Looks like I got here just in time. I'll take care of these." He pocketed the passport, ticket, and phone.

Brenner's eyes widened. For the first time in his life, Ignacio saw a trace of fear flit across his father's face. He grimaced.

"You know something," Ignacio said. "When I was in Poland, I must have retraced your steps—the ones you took during the Second World War—into the tunnels of the Riese complex, where you used to work."

Brenner twitched in his chair, his fingers tapping on the arm rest. "What do you know about that?" he asked.

"SS *Obersturmführer* Erich Brenner, who ran concentration camps at Auschwitz and Gross-Rosen. No surprise you've refused to discuss your younger days with your son, is it?" Ignacio spat.

"I don't know where you got that information from, but it's completely false," Brenner said. "I worked as a jeweler's apprentice, not an SS officer."

Ignacio shook his head. "I've seen the papers. *Hauptsturmführer* Karl Beblo wasn't happy with you when those Jews escaped from the train, was he, way back in '44? You didn't impress your boss then, did you? And you've not impressed your son, either. I don't think you've treated me much differently than some of your prisoners."

A flicker of resignation crossed Brenner's face. His voice

rose. "You've stolen my papers from the attic. It's the only way you could know that. You're going to regret this."

Ignacio ignored the threat. "I've got a friend who's coming around shortly," he said. "You know him. Luis Castano, my old army colleague."

"I remember Luis," the old man said. "What's happening with him?"

Ignacio paused. "What's happening is that we're going for a little drive. And you'll be coming with us."

He saw his father swallow hard. "You want me to come with you for a little drive? When?" the old man asked.

"I don't know yet," Ignacio said. "Probably tomorrow morning. I've got to make some calls to set a few things up first."

"What's this all about, Ignacio?"

Ignacio gave a thin smile but said nothing.

Brenner gripped the side of his armchair and looked at his son.

"Sit in that wooden chair over there," Ignacio said, pointing to a large, heavy wooden piece of furniture near the door.

His father didn't move.

"I said sit there," Ignacio repeated, taking a threatening step toward Brenner.

The old man slowly got up and walked to the chair, then sat down.

"Put your hands down the side, against those wooden struts," Ignacio said.

When his father complied, Ignacio took some gaffer tape and fastened his father's wrists and legs to the chair. "I don't want you going anywhere, and I don't want you picking up any of the weaponry you've doubtless got hidden in the house somewhere. That wouldn't be good for either of us," Ignacio said.

He left his father and climbed the stairs. As he went, he took his phone out and tapped in the number for a good ex-army friend, Manuel Lopez, who ran his own security company in northern Argentina, Lopez Seguridad.

"*Hola*, Manuel. It's Ignacio."

"It's been a long time. How are you, *mi amigo*?"

"All good. Listen, I was wondering if you could let me have two of your armed guards for a day or so, starting tomorrow. Your best guys. And there are a few other things I may need help putting in place, too."

Ignacio went on to outline exactly what he needed.

* * *

Jayne got back into her Hilux, feeling satisfied with her few minutes of work, and drove back around to the other side of Ombú, where she parked in exactly the same spot she had left when Brenner had been driven to the café.

She surveyed Brenner's house. Now there was an old white Renault Mégane parked outside it.

Then she saw some movement at a window on the third floor, the top story right in the eaves of the house. A face looked out—that of a thickset, fair-haired man. He was only there for maybe thirty seconds, but Jayne was good with faces, and she had plenty of time to recognize him from the photograph that her colleague at SIS had obtained from Argentine passport records.

It was Ignacio Guzmann, the old man's son. She assumed the white Mégane was his: he must have arrived and gone inside in the few minutes she was attending to the black Mercedes.

Jayne cursed. That was bad news, given that Ignacio was the biggest threat to Johnson's plans.

She clearly couldn't go into the house herself. Instead, she toyed briefly with calling Carlos again but then dismissed that idea; it would open a huge can of worms.

Work it out, Jayne.

Before she could think any further, the man in the blue Peugeot swiftly got out of his car and marched up the street to the front door of Brenner's house, his cell phone clamped to his left ear, a large bag in his right hand, and knocked.

Jayne shot up in her car seat; her stomach felt as though it had flipped over.

There was a pause. Then the door opened, and the unmistakable figure of Ignacio appeared. He shook the man's hand, and they disappeared inside.

What had grabbed Jayne's attention was the bag the man from the blue Peugeot had been carrying in his right hand.

It looked at first glance like a businessman's briefcase.

But the initials on the side, UTG, gave the game away.

Jayne had a similar one under her bed at home.

It was a large pistol case.

CHAPTER FORTY-NINE

Saturday, December 3, 2011
  Buenos Aires

Johnson and Fiona were sitting in one of Buenos Aires's ubiquitous black and yellow taxis, driving the thirty-five kilometers from Ministro Pistarini International Airport into the city, when his phone rang. It was Jayne.

Before Johnson could speak, Jayne cut in. "Joe, I hope you're nearly here?"

"Yes, en route in a taxi right now. We'll be another twenty minutes, I think. What's happening?"

"I'm just down the road from old man Brenner's house. His son's inside the place. I've just seen him open the door to let in another guy with a pistol."

Johnson swore. His shoulders tensed, as if they had been locked solid.

"Okay. Not good. I suggest you sit tight and stick with them if they move before I get there."

Johnson was already glad he had Jayne on hand for this job.

"How do you know the guy had a pistol?" Johnson asked, lowering his voice. "And did you manage to get a gun for me?"

"He was carrying a pistol case," Jayne said. "I assume it wasn't empty. And yes, I've got two Berettas."

She gave Johnson the number and description of her hired Hilux. "When you get here, best if you park on the other side of Ombú from Brenner's house, then work your way around to my car on foot. I don't want a taxi dropping you off in full view of the house. I'll see you soon."

Johnson agreed and ended the call. His phone vibrated again as an e-mail arrived. It was from Clara in Berlin. She was pleased to help him, she wrote, just as much as she had always helped him "in other ways" when they were together as students.

Long, carefree days with nothing to do but drink, talk, and @*%@!!! Wish we were back there again.

Johnson smiled and held the phone out of Fiona's line of sight. But getting to the point, Clara said; she had been to the *Deutsche Dienststelle*, and Brenner's records were there. He had suffered a shrapnel injury to his right knee while fighting with the Third SS Panzer Division *Totenkopfe* near Kharkov in March 1943 and had been in the hospital for six weeks.

That would explain the limp.

Given Watson's interest in Brenner, Johnson was ultrasensitive to any sign of surveillance. He assumed Watson would have briefed someone in the Buenos Aires station. Using his fluent Spanish, Johnson instructed the taxi driver, who like many of his ilk looked streetwise, to watch carefully for any sign of a tail.

The taxi, a Citroën, was heading down the General Pablo

Ricchieri highway toward the city when Johnson noticed the driver adjusting his rearview mirror with his right hand.

That's the third time he's done that.

"Is someone following us back there?" Johnson asked.

The driver looked again. "Not sure. There was a big Lexus that has more or less mirrored everything I've done since leaving the airport. He's hanging back now."

Johnson resisted the temptation to twist around and look through the rear window. "Okay, see if you can lose him," he said.

At the next junction, the taxi driver suddenly swung right onto the off-ramp at the last possible moment and exited the highway, past signs to the central market.

He then flung the Citroën right, then left, down a couple of side streets in a rough-looking area with smashed-up concrete blocks and litter strewn across the shoulders. Then he made another left onto a road with several half-finished cinder-block houses.

The driver accelerated hard. A couple more turns and he was back on the highway they had left only a few minutes earlier.

"Think we're okay now," the driver said.

After another fifteen minutes, they pulled up in Ombú. Johnson squinted through the windshield. There was only one silver Hilux in view, about seventy yards in front of them. He paid the driver his fare, plus a tip, and he and Fiona got out.

Fiona noted that if they used the cover provided by a combination of the natural curvature of the road, a few tall 4x4 trucks parked at the curb, tall trees growing in the sidewalk, and bushes in certain front gardens, they could reach the Hilux without coming into anyone's line of sight from Brenner's house.

To Jayne's undisguised relief, they slipped into the Hilux a few minutes later without further alarms, Johnson in the front, Fiona in the back.

"Thank God for that. I was having visions of handling this solo," Jayne said. She gestured down the road. "That's Brenner's house there, the tatty white one with black shutters. I think that white Renault is his son's car. I'm certain Brenner is still inside."

Johnson opened his pack of cigarettes and lit one, inhaling deeply as he sank back into the front passenger seat and listened as Jayne gave full details of events so far.

"Sounds to me as though Brenner was planning to run if he's just acquired a new Chilean passport," Johnson said. "It may be that Ignacio's turned up and intercepted him."

Then Jayne jerked up in her seat and pointed. A large black Mercedes idled slowly around the other side of the oval and parked outside Brenner's house, next to the Renault.

"That's Brenner's Mercedes," Jayne said. "He used it to go to the café."

Johnson had just taken a second cigarette from his pack. Before he could light up, the black front door of Brenner's house opened, and two men emerged through the metal gate onto the sidewalk.

At the front, upright but frail looking, was a white-haired old man carrying a silver-topped cane. He was limping noticeably.

Johnson realized he was holding his breath.

"That's Brenner," said Jayne, unnecessarily.

Behind Brenner was Ignacio. Another dark-haired man jumped out of the driver's seat of the Mercedes and walked over to them.

There was an argument going on. The old man appeared to be pushed from behind by his son. He stumbled and almost fell, and as he moved forward, Johnson caught a clear glimpse of gun metal in Ignacio's hand.

The other man leapt forward and grabbed Brenner by the coat, preventing him from tumbling.

When he recovered his balance, Brenner turned and said something angrily to his son, waving his stick in the air. There was a furious exchange of words, too far out of earshot from the Hilux.

The two men bundled Brenner into the back of the Mercedes, and Ignacio climbed into the other rear seat. The other man then ran back into the house, picked up a couple of bags, threw them into the trunk, and got into the driver's seat.

A second later, the black Mercedes shot off down Ombú with a squeal of tires.

Jayne quickly started the Toyota's engine, let out the clutch, and followed. "The circus is on the move," she said, flicking on the sat nav.

She had difficulty keeping up with the Mercedes. It flew around the corner, onto Avenida Figueroa Alcorta, and accelerated through a set of red traffic lights at a junction near the Galileo Galilei planetarium and through an underpass with an array of messy political graffiti scrawled on the concrete side-walls in letters more than two feet high: *No Layoffs, No Job Cuts. General Strike Now!*

Jayne rammed the Hilux into fifth and overtook a Porsche on the inside as the Mercedes sped onto the four-lane ring road, heading northwest.

"Have you got those Berettas you mentioned?" Johnson asked.

"Yep. They're in the glove compartment." Jayne was staring intently at the traffic now, concentrating hard as the Mercedes surged forward. Without taking her eyes off the road, she picked up a map from between the front seats and gave it to Johnson. "Just use that and the sat nav and keep an eye on where we're going. I remember a lot of these roads, but it's been many years since I've lived here, so I can't recall all of them."

Johnson took the map, then opened the glove compartment and removed one of the Berettas. "Nice," he said.

He removed the magazine and racked the slide back, ensuring there were no live rounds in the chamber. Then he checked the magazine was full, put it back in, and clicked the safety catch off, then on again. "It'll do the job. Thanks." He repeated the process with the other Beretta.

"So, where exactly did you get these?" Johnson asked.

Jayne told him about Carlos, throwing in a few stories for good measure about his antics while operating as her agent in the late '90s.

In the back seat, Fiona chuckled away at a tale about how Jayne had persuaded Carlos to act as the middleman in a transaction whereby a naval mine was smuggled out of the Argentine naval base at Río Gallegos, at the southern tip of the country, and taken to Britain.

"You obviously won't mind if I report those stories," Fiona said.

Jayne grimaced. "You can try," she said, "But I warn you, Carlos has a long reach."

After a while, the Mercedes moved onto an off-ramp, this time moving onto National Route 9, a six-lane sprawling river of traffic, still heading northwest. Mile after mile of residential suburbs flew past: Boulogne, El Talar, followed by the industrial units of Ricardo Rojas.

While the traffic was heavy, Johnson wasn't worried that Ignacio might spot them. There were too many cars on the road, and Jayne was driving in textbook fashion, keeping a reasonable distance between the two vehicles.

But then, as the buildings began to thin out near the outer suburbs and green fields appeared to the right of the road, the traffic lightened and tailing became trickier. The Mercedes accelerated again. Johnson checked the speedometer, which showed 150 kilometers an hour.

"Just hang back," Johnson said. "Give him several hundred yards now." He knew it was going to be difficult to avoid being spotted, but without the advantages of an organized CIA-style operation, with multiple vehicles and communication between them, the chances of being noticed were higher the further they went out of the built-up city suburbs.

"Do you have binoculars?" Johnson asked.

To his surprise, Jayne told him to look under his seat, where he found a pair of powerful Carl Zeiss 20x42 optics. "Was that Carlos as well?" he asked. She nodded.

With Johnson manning the binoculars, they felt confident enough to drop back even farther behind the Mercedes.

Jayne wiped her hand across her forehead. "Good thing I refilled with diesel beforehand. Who knows where this is going to end up," she said.

At the small city of Campana, the Mercedes veered across three lanes and down an exit leading to National Route 12. Jayne followed.

Soon they were on a seemingly never-ending suspension bridge spanning the vast brown waters of the Paraná River. The river was busy with oceangoing container and cargo ships mostly heading east, where Johnson assumed they would join the River Plate and then make their way to the Atlantic.

Two enormous towers stood in the center of the river, from which an array of tree-trunk-size steel cables supported the bridge running beneath.

Beyond the riverbanks were flat green expanses of fields crisscrossed with huge electricity pylons and cables. "These all carry power to Buenos Aires from the hydro schemes," Jayne said.

She glanced at the river. "I sailed up and down here in '97 with some visitors from New York. Drank gin and got pissed with them and kept telling them it was South America's second longest river, over and over. They got irritated as hell."

Johnson smiled. He remembered well how Jane loved to share facts and history when plastered. He'd always thought it rather endearing, actually.

"I'm sure they did," he said.

Jayne chuckled. "I may have given them a bit of a lecture on the story behind the dams and hydroelectric projects farther upstream, as well."

In the back seat, Fiona was on the phone with somebody. It sounded as though it was her editor, judging by the scraps of conversation Johnson could hear over the noise of the car engine screaming, the wind whistling outside, and Jayne's conversation.

He tried to listen to what Fiona was saying without making it obvious to Jayne. He didn't want to make her any more aware of the journalist and the exposure that came with her than she probably already was. Fiona mentioned something about proof and documents. His ears pricked up. She was arguing; that much he could make out.

Johnson clung to the passenger door handle as Jayne swerved into the outside lane to pass a slow-moving truck, cutting off a speeding motorcyclist as she did so.

He was starting to become concerned about Jayne. Had she slept at all? "Are you okay?" he asked. "I can take a turn driving if you need a rest."

"Yes, good idea. Thanks," she said, braking to a halt so they could switch.

The sky, which had been cloudless when they had set off, had become completely overcast. Now high, light-gray clouds were starting to give way to lower, much darker ones, some of them practically black.

Johnson could see it was going to take all their effort to keep up with the powerful Mercedes and ensure it didn't turn unnoticed off the main highway. Now that it was getting darker, the binoculars were of less help.

Jayne's phone rang. She clamped it to her left ear. "It's Carlos," she muttered to Johnson, who was now focused on the road.

"Hello, Carlos! . . . Thanks for your help with all the, um, equipment. *Perfecto* . . . No, we're not still in the city. We're about 140 kilometers north, trying to keep up with the guy I told you about . . . God knows where we're heading . . . Yes, we'll be way up north if we keep going like this . . . Brazil? I hope not . . . What weather forecast? Ah, well . . . sounds bad. Just one other thing. If you can do what you can to ensure we don't get held up by police checkpoints, that would be helpful. Thanks. I'll keep in touch."

She ended the call and looked at Johnson. "This guy's driving like he's on drugs. He's doing 170 now, at least. I hope we don't blow up this Toyota. Oh, and Carlos says there's an awful weather forecast for up north. Rain, lightning storms, and high winds, all blowing down from Brazil. There's already flooding up there. Possibly tornadoes, too." She sighed. "Just what we need."

CHAPTER FIFTY

Sunday, December 4, 2011
Posadas, Argentina

The bad weather held off for much longer than Carlos had predicted. In fact, the rain stayed away until they had been driving north for nearly nine hours.

But when the rain did start, it was torrential. Lashing jets of water drove hard into the windshield of the Hilux, forcing Johnson to slow the truck to below forty kilometers an hour.

It was difficult to concentrate behind the wheel for long periods in such conditions, so Johnson and Jayne traded spots fairly frequently.

Now, with the darkness and the rain, Johnson agreed with Jayne that they should get much closer to Brenner's Mercedes. That meant the risk of being spotted was higher, so Johnson could only hope that Ignacio was not carrying out proper countersurveillance. There had been no obvious sign of it. But even though they were driving closer, visibility of the Mercedes was still poor, which made Johnson nervous.

Jayne, by contrast, seemed relaxed about the risk of losing sight of the Mercedes. When Johnson mentioned this, she simply shook her head.

"Don't worry, all under control," she said. "I have a plan B —we won't lose him." She reached for her phone, which she had mounted on the dashboard, tapped on an app, and showed Johnson a map on the screen. In the center were two dots—one green, one blue—that were moving slowly along a road.

"The green one," Jayne said, "is the Mercedes. There's a magnetic GPS tracking device which *mysteriously* became attached to its undercarriage. Don't ask me how. We're the blue dot. We won't lose him."

Johnson managed a smile for the first time in several hours. "You could have mentioned that before. You got that gadget from Carlos, I assume?"

"Correct. He's expensive but he's first class."

There were other vehicles that continually appeared and reappeared during the long journey north, too. Johnson and Jayne, working as a team across the rearview and side mirrors, kept a close eye on them, the thought of a tail working under Watto's or the Mossad's instructions at the forefront of Johnson's mind. But each time, Johnson could tell they were genuine tourists, locals, or businessmen. There were no vehicles or faces that caused him concern, even among the occasional repeats that popped up, and no evidence of coverage, which surprised him.

The road started to resemble the Paraná River, a short distance to their left, the path of which they now seemed to be following to the north.

The red, mineral-laden earth that formed the subsoil of the entire region was being washed across the road in streams as the gutters failed to cope with the runoff from the rain.

"Rivers of blood. Let's hope the weather's not a metaphor

for what's going on in that Mercedes," Fiona said from the back seat.

Huge rolling thunderclaps barreled across the countryside as jagged forks of white-hot lightning jerked down from a dark sky.

Johnson took another turn behind the wheel, while Jayne shifted to the passenger seat. They both declined Fiona's offer to take a turn at driving. "Best that we drive for this kind of surveillance operation," Jayne said.

The unspoken understanding was that Fiona simply wouldn't have had the training to achieve the right blend of distance, speed, and position to best blend into the background and avoid detection. As it was, Johnson felt he was operating at the outer limits of his somewhat rusty skill set, especially operating as a solo car, and Jayne, deskbound for so long, was similarly out of practice.

Apart from staying awake, Johnson quickly realized that one tricky issue was refueling.

The Mercedes had been the first to pull into a gas station earlier that afternoon after about five hundred kilometers, and Johnson, not wanting to risk stopping at the same place, told Jayne to continue driving until she got to the next station, which was thankfully a short distance later.

"We need to be as quick as we can, like a pit stop," he said.

After filling the Toyota with diesel, Johnson went with Fiona into the small shop to buy a few snacks and sandwiches. Jayne followed, adding a pack of high-strength caffeine tablets to their basket. "Looks like we're in for an all-nighter. We'll need these," she said.

Now, at just before ten o'clock in the evening, with the trip meter in the Hilux showing 920 kilometers, fuel was running low again. After another stop near Posadas, the capital of the Misiones province, which sat on the eastern bank of the Paraná, they were off again.

Before they'd gotten back on the road, Jayne took both Berettas and the spare magazines from the glove compartment, lifted the rear seat, and stashed the guns and ammunition in a concealed storage compartment underneath. She removed her holster, took Johnson's, and put them with the guns.

"Police checkpoints?" Johnson guessed, as she climbed into the passenger seat.

"Yes," Jayne said. "North from here—they're notorious. Unless things have changed, they'll take a couple of hundred dollars off us at each one, since we're foreigners. I don't want to give them an excuse to make it more. We're supposed to have permits and paperwork for these guns. Lots of people don't bother, but hopefully they won't do a thorough search. They're usually too lazy, and anyway, I've asked Carlos to smooth our path."

Jayne swallowed two of the caffeine tablets and accelerated out of the gas station.

She checked the tracker app on her phone. "It looks like those guys are heading for Puerto Iguazú now," Jayne said. "That's my best guess."

"How far?" asked Johnson.

"I did this journey a few times in the '90s," Jayne said. "Normally four hours heading north from here, about three hundred kilometers. But in this storm, I think it'll be a lot longer. We'll struggle to move much faster than forty or fifty kilometers an hour on these roads and with this amount of water."

Johnson looked at her, his bottom lip hanging at the prospect of an all-night drive. "Three hundred kilometers? What is Puerto Iguazú anyway?"

The driving rain battered the windshield hard now.

"It's a small city tucked in next to the Paraguay and Brazil borders," Jayne said. "A big tourist center for the Iguazú waterfalls. But the underworld's in charge there; there's no real border controls, and it's all about drug trafficking, people trafficking, terrorists, and organized crime. You name it. The police are corrupt and do nothing. I did a report on it for the SIS because we were worried about weapons being smuggled from there into Northern Ireland."

"Sounds all a bit Wild West," Johnson said.

"Yeah, that's one way of putting it. One of the big illegal activities is fake jewelry, watches, and so on, which get sold to tourists visiting the waterfalls. Mafia-type gangs have it all carved up."

Jayne became quiet and concentrated on the road through the pitch black and the driving rain. At least the road was smooth blacktop. But there were no white line markings, and at times it was hard to see where they were going.

To add to their problems, large numbers of heavy trucks crawled in both directions through the storm, making it almost impossible to pass, apart from when they hit the odd section of two-lane divided highway.

"This is ridiculous. We need to get a move on," Johnson said. "I'm worried that even if Ignacio doesn't kill the old man, someone from the Mossad will appear and do it, or the CIA will come and spirit him away."

Fiona stuck her head between them. "I'm surprised that if the Mossad or the CIA were planning to do something, it hasn't happened yet."

"Who knows what's going on behind the scenes," Johnson said. "What I've learned with the likes of them is we're never really in control. There's always some higher being pulling strings. And I don't mean God, I mean Watto."

Johnson suspected that Watson ran a variety of unofficial

operations outside the scheduled CIA ones he was responsible for.

He glanced behind him at Fiona, who nodded. He felt tired now, but he couldn't switch off and sleep. His thoughts wandered.

Was Brenner dead, lying by the roadside? Had they passed him somewhere in a ditch? The GPS tracker couldn't tell him that.

As they drove, the green dot on Jayne's phone screen gradually pulled farther and farther ahead of them.

CHAPTER FIFTY-ONE

Monday, December 5, 2011
Wolf Trap, Virginia

Watson sat in the study of his gray brick house and, through the gray light of dawn, looked down the garden toward the thick woodland that ran on either side of Difficult Run River.

The CIA veteran remained still. All he could hear was the tiny gurgle of hot water circulating through the radiators and pipes of his central heating system. There were no other sounds in the house; indeed, there was nobody else there to make a sound.

Watson glanced at the papers lying at the side of his desk. There was an invoice from his gardener, another from his cleaner, both of whom were indispensable. He had to admit, the six-bedroom property, in Wynhurst Lane, Wolf Trap, was far too large for someone living by himself.

But it was private and not too far from Langley. In any case, he needed to demonstrate that he was using his six-figure CIA salary for some tangible purpose. Watson viewed property as a good long-term investment, and the house, bought for more than $1.5 million five years earlier, would be his daughter's one day.

His mortgage statement, which he had just filed away, stated that $171,549 remained outstanding. But that was just for appearances' sake. Watson's fortune, like the bulk of an iceberg hidden below the waterline, remained mainly invisible. Indeed, he had gone to extreme lengths to ensure the vast majority of it, quietly accumulated from a handful of side ventures in different parts of the world, would never come under the penetrating scrutiny of his CIA colleagues.

Nearly all of it was stashed in numbered accounts in various tax havens, but principally Switzerland.

One of his Swiss accounts, in Zürich, was where Peretz had channeled the annual bonus paid unofficially to Watson in return for keeping a close eye on Brenner and ensuring that nothing happened to disrupt the status quo that had suited everyone—apart, perhaps, from Brenner—for so many years. Over the years, it had added up to almost $2.3 million: very significant for someone on a CIA salary.

There were other accounts elsewhere, too, containing significantly more money from other long-running projects. Although Watson sometimes found it frustrating that he was unable to make use of the money now, it would be there, ready for future use, when he no longer worked for the U.S. government.

He was increasingly unclear when that day would come; not everything was going to plan. In particular, he felt increasingly anxious about the way things were going with Brenner. He knew that his intermediary in Miami, Simon, had given a thorough briefing to Agustin Torres, the CIA case officer who was their main asset in Buenos Aires.

But Simon had just told Watson that the plan to get Brenner out of Argentina and into Chile had failed. The old man hadn't shown up for his flight to Santiago the previous evening, nor had he made the expected check-in call to Miami.

Even more worrying, the GPS tracking technology that Watson used told him Brenner's phone was on the move. It seemed to be in a vehicle heading north from Buenos Aires toward the borders with Paraguay and Brazil. And presumably, the old man was moving with it.

Simon, not knowing Brenner's current circumstances, deemed it too risky to call the phone, and Watson agreed.

Watson tapped on the screen of his encrypted cell phone and dialed a number in Argentina for Agustin, a longtime CIA employee within the Latin American Division whom he had dealt with several times over the years on operations spanning both their divisions.

"Hello?"

"Agustin. It's Robert Watson here."

"Robert. You're calling about VANDAL?"

"Yes, I know Simon's briefed you, but I'm just checking on things. I can see VANDAL appears to be heading north."

"Yeah. Plan A didn't work, unfortunately. I assume the son's got him and is going to do the necessary. VANDAL's company has a business unit in Puerto Iguazú—which is another story. But my bet is the son's taking the old man there."

Watson scratched his chin. "Right. Yes, but ideally, I don't want the son to do the necessary, as you put it. I'd like VANDAL out of there intact. But the most important thing is that Johnson doesn't get to VANDAL, or our friends in Tel Aviv will have a fit. You know how critical that is."

He thought for a second. "You're going to have to get up to Puerto Iguazú yourself, Agustin, and sort it out. We're still obligated to VANDAL, so I want you to find a way to exfiltrate him. I'm relying on you."

Agustin groaned. "I'm crazy busy here, Robert. We've got Operation SNOWCAP due to start next week: cross-border into Chile, very complex, involving six agents who I need to coordinate. I mean, VANDAL's in his '90s now. How important is this?"

"Just do it. I can't take any asshole-fashion excuses on this one."

There was a silence on the other end of the line. Then Agustin said, "Okay, okay. I've got a high-level police mole, Carlos Campos, who's on our payroll. Simon knows about him. Carlos tells me Johnson's traveling with two women, and they're well behind VANDAL. So that gives us a little time."

"*Two* women? You sure he said two?"

"Yes. One of them is an American journalist, Fiona Heppenstall. Carlos says he hasn't got a clue who the other is."

"Hmm. How far behind VANDAL are they?"

"Not sure. Couple of hours would be my guess," Agustin said.

"I want you to delay him further. Is there a way of doing that?"

"There's a police checkpoint heading up toward Puerto Iguazú," Agustin said. "I can get Carlos to pull a few strings."

"Yes, that'll do. Good. And you need to get a plane up there, fast as you can." Watson said,

"There's a flight in an hour and a half. If I move, I'll make it," Agustin said.

"Yes. Make sure you're on it. And I'm authorizing you to do *whatever* you need to do to keep Johnson away from VANDAL. That's an order. Just do it—no need for any more clearances from me. Keep me updated. Understood?"

"Okay. Will do," Agustin said.

"Thanks." Watson ended the call.

Two women? Who's the second, then?

CHAPTER FIFTY-TWO

Monday, December 5, 2011
Puerto Iguazú, Argentina

Johnson, now taking another turn behind the wheel, banged on the dashboard in frustration. He slowed to a crawl up a long, curving incline behind a massive logging truck loaded with tree trunks.

A steady flow of trucks came from the opposite direction, making it impossible for Johnson to pass.

Thankfully, dawn was starting to break, but the rain continued to beat down hard.

Then, just as Jayne had predicted, there were two police checkpoints along the way that cost them a total of four hundred U.S. dollars.

The second of them, not far from Puerto Iguazú, delayed them for nearly an hour. When they had driven a few hundred yards up the road, Johnson quietly uttered a single word, "Bastards."

Jayne folded her arms. "Never had that before. Not an hour. Usually it's five or ten minutes, if that, and a quick money exchange. Something's going on. I specifically asked Carlos to sort that out for me, given I'm paying the bastard. He's useless."

She checked the GPS device. "The Mercedes stopped moving some time ago. It's southwest of the city, I think a couple of kilometers out at least."

At a T-intersection, they took a left toward Puerto Iguazú. The road to the right led to the city's airport. As they turned left, they were almost deafened by the noise from a large passenger jet that roared low over their heads, descending as it prepared to land.

"That'll be the morning flight up here from Buenos Aires," Jayne said.

They passed the entrance to an army base, marked by a large, disused armored car complete with a rocket launcher on the top. An Argentine flag stood behind it on a pole, lying limp in the morning sunshine.

Now they were on the fringes of the city. There were a couple of hotels with rough homemade signs, a half-built restaurant, crumbling houses, and abandoned cars.

Then, as they went further into the center, the buildings gradually became nicer, the houses more upmarket. A sign reading Hilton Iguazú Golf and Resort pointed to the right.

Johnson, his head now feeling foggy from lack of sleep and overdoses of caffeine, pulled in outside a supermarket near the point where the Paraná and the Iguazú Rivers met.

Jayne checked the GPS app again. The green dot was still in the same place, out of town to the southwest. She pointed across the River Iguazú. "That's Brazil across there, and that's Paraguay there to the left. You can see why the underworld likes it here. They can just move across the borders in a blink."

She looked at the sat nav again and began to give Johnson directions.

"We'll need to make some sort of plan," Johnson said. "We can't just barge in, wherever they are. They probably think they're in the clear, but they must know we're trying to find them. They could have set a trap."

He accelerated down the road, heading southwest through a grid-like network of increasingly rough, potholed roads, all of them tinged red from the iron-rich dust that lay everywhere, its particles covering homes, cars, and sidewalks.

Soon, the blacktop road gave way to an unsealed red-dirt track. They drew nearer to the green dot, which still blinked away on Jayne's phone screen, unmoving.

Now the occasional houses were no more than shacks, roughly built from different colored planks of scavenged wood and with roofs made of mismatching pieces of corrugated iron. Old tires and bits of scrap metal lay at the side of the road.

Here the ground was dry. It appeared the rainstorm which had hit them further south had bypassed the city altogether.

The Hilux bounced across one hump and then another, tossing up puffs of dust into the air behind it and sending Jayne and Fiona lurching in their seats.

The green dot was now, by Jayne's calculations, no more than half a kilometer away, farther down the track.

Johnson promptly started to feel butterflies fluttering in his stomach. His chest tightened.

To the right, the Paraná River swung into view, wide and brown. On the other side of the water lay Paraguay.

A little farther on, an area of gravel lay behind some trees that provided some natural screening from the road.

"There, I'll park behind those trees," Johnson said. "I don't want to alert them with the engine noise. We'll walk from here."

"Just making sure, but you know I'm going with you," Fiona said. "Don't try and persuade me otherwise. I need to be there when we get to Brenner."

Johnson glanced at her. She meant what she said. Jayne was looking at him for a decision. Fiona was his responsibility in this case. He said nothing but pulled up and switched off the engine, then got out of the pickup and looked down the track.

Jayne cast him a disapproving look but shrugged, as if to say he could make the mistake if he wanted.

There was silence apart from a few birds singing and insects humming. Now the air felt hot, humid, and sticky. Johnson could feel himself begin to sweat.

Just visible down the track, past a clump of trees, was the red-tiled roof of what looked like a large outbuilding, and behind it was another roof.

Johnson peered at Jayne's phone. The green dot was flashing away, right where the buildings were.

Jayne retrieved the two Berettas from their hiding place underneath the rear seat and handed one to Johnson, along with a spare magazine. Thankfully the police hadn't done a thorough search of the vehicle but had only wanted to waste their time.

"Thanks," Johnson said. He strapped a holster to his hip and put the gun in it, noticing his right hand shook a little as he did so. "Let's think this through. I'll go with Fiona, given she's so insistent. You'd better hang back here and wait. You can give me some cover, which I might need if the worst happens. Just keep your ears open. See what happens. They don't even know we're here, I'm assuming."

Jayne nodded. "Yeah, makes sense. I'll cover you. I think they must be half expecting us."

She made her way to a thick clump of bushes, twenty yards left of the dirt road, where there was plenty of cover.

To the left, through the trees, Johnson could now see the buildings more clearly. Nearest to the track stood a rough brick structure with a large green garage door at the front and a small side door.

Behind that was a run-down single-story house, its white paint peeling and walls stained green and gray with mold in places. One front window was boarded up.

There was a ten-foot-high wooden fence running to the right and left of the house at the rear, forming what looked like a compound. On top of the fence was a continuous loop of tightly coiled razor wire. The roofs of several smaller buildings were just visible over the top of the fence.

A large, neatly painted sign stood on a plinth outside. Its message, in large red letters, was unmistakable.

SolGold Argentina
Propriedad Privada, Prohibido Pasar

Underneath it was the ubiquitous red circle with a white horizontal line across it. No entry.

SolGold. So it's part of Brenner's jewelry business, Johnson thought to himself. *What a bizarre location.*

He took a couple of steps, with Fiona right behind him. Then he heard the faint sound of music drifting from the direction of the large garage. It sounded like a chorus to a marching beat, backed by an old-fashioned brass band.

They inched closer, crouching behind a short brick wall that had been half demolished to allow vehicles to enter an area in front of the house.

Now the music that came from inside the garage was clearer. The singing was in a foreign language that Johnson recognized immediately.

It's in German. A Nazi marching tune.

The green garage door at the front of the building was

shut, but a small pedestrian door at the side was open a fraction. Johnson hunched over and signaled to Fiona to do likewise. Then they ran across a short section of grass and flattened themselves against the garage wall next to the pedestrian door.

Up close, the music was now much clearer, though somewhat crackly. An old recording, then.

Johnson applied his eye to the tiny crack where the door was ajar and drew an involuntary, sharp inward breath at what he saw. There, sitting on a wooden chair in the middle of the garage, a large red Nazi flag draped around his shoulders, was a white-haired old man.

Erich Brenner.

The white circle and central black swastika on the flag lay across the middle of the old man's chest. His eyes were half closed. Black bindings held his wrists to the arms of the wooden chair.

But to Johnson's relief, he could see Brenner was alive. His chest rose and fell with each breath.

What the hell?

The music came from a portable CD player that stood on an old wooden table.

The garage was filthy, with oil stains, grime, and mud all over the concrete floor and cobwebs on the rough brick walls. The building was lit by a bare fluorescent light attached to the wooden beams.

Johnson grasped the Beretta. There was no car in the garage, and there had been no sign of the black Mercedes outside, either. Yet the GPS signal was definitely coming from this spot.

Was this Ignacio's bizarre way of preparing his father for some sort of ceremonial execution, or was it simply a trap?

Johnson signaled to Fiona to remain outside the small garage door. He edged backward and stepped lightly to the farthest corner of the garage, then peered around. There was nobody in sight.

There was a momentary lull in the music as one track finished and the next began. During the gap, Johnson was sure he heard the faint sound of women's voices coming from behind the wooden fence at the back of the garage.

He moved cautiously down the side of the garage toward a small window at the far end. Then he crouched below the windowsill and lifted his eyes until he could see inside.

There was Brenner in his chair, but there was still no sign of anyone else. No noise. No movement.

Johnson found himself of two minds. His quarry was sitting a few yards away, there for the taking. If there were nobody else in the garage, he knew he could slip in, grab the old man, and frog-march him down the road to the Hilux. *A big if . . .*

He couldn't risk leaving Brenner there to be executed. He had to make a decision. There seemed only one option.

Johnson crept back around the outside of the building to the door and indicated with a nod of his head to Fiona that they were going to enter. He raised his Beretta, pushed the door open a fraction, and took a cautious step forward, preparing to sweep the room.

CHAPTER FIFTY-THREE

Monday, December 5, 2011
Puerto Iguazú

Johnson had no sooner pushed the door open enough to walk through than it slammed back toward him, knocking him off balance and into the opposite wall.

As he recovered his balance, the voice came from behind the door, level, calm, and menacing in heavily accented English.

"Drop it. Drop the gun. Now. And you, woman, stand next to this *idiota,* and don't move."

Ignacio stood there pointing a semiautomatic Glock at Johnson's head.

Johnson briefly tried to calculate the chances of getting a shot in. Out of the corner of his eye he saw Fiona step forward until she was beside him.

He realized he had no choice and let the gun fall.

"Ah, *Señor* Johnson. Nice to meet you at last, after coming close a few times. I have to say, you're persistent, chasing me across two continents. But anyway, you're just in time to see the denouement. *Perfecto.* Put your hands on your head and stand against the wall."

Patronizing bastard.

Johnson didn't move for a moment. His carefully thought-out plans, what he would say to Brenner, how he would present the "proof of the truth," how he would secure him and drive him back to the U.S. embassy in Buenos Aires, and how he'd have him extradited—they all evaporated like steam from a kettle.

"Quick, come on, move. Against the wall, now! You too, woman," Ignacio's voice rose in pitch by a few notes.

Johnson moved and placed his back to the wall, hands on the top of his head like a naughty child in the corner at school. Fiona did likewise next to him.

"Okay, Luis, check their pockets. I'm covering you," Ignacio ordered, keeping his gun trained on Johnson's head.

The dark-haired figure of Luis Castano emerged from the shadows of an alcove at the back of the garage. He picked up the Beretta from the floor and placed it on the table next to a couple of phones. Then he walked to Johnson and delved into his deep trouser pockets. He removed his phone and put it on the table, too.

"Clear, *jefe*," Luis said. Then he searched Fiona and removed her phone.

Ignacio scowled. "I assumed you would turn up here once I found that," he said.

He nodded toward the table where, alongside the phones, lay a small black plastic box, roughly the size of a cigarette pack, with two circular metal discs attached to it.

"Your tracking device," Ignacio said. "Very clever. Quite remarkable that you were smart enough, crafty enough, to stick it under our car without being seen."

He thinks I put it there. So he doesn't know about Jayne.

Ignacio walked over and stood near his father, who sat helplessly and silently; thick bands of Velcro bound the old man's wrists to the arms of the chair, and his ankles were similarly pinned to the chair's legs, preventing him from moving.

"Before I deliver the coup de grâce, as you might call it, there is something I need to show you both," Ignacio said. "It will explain everything. Come with me. Luis, you stay with the Nazi here."

Ignacio signaled with the barrel of his gun that Johnson and Fiona should walk toward the back of the garage, where another pedestrian door stood half open.

"Go through," he ordered.

Once through the door, Johnson and Fiona were faced with a wooden archway covered in roses, which led to the single-story house Johnson had seen from the road.

Attached to the archway, on a carved semicircular board, was a slogan, written in Spanish.

Ignacio stood behind him. "Recognize that slogan?" he asked. "You should. In German it's translated as *Arbeit Macht Frei*—work sets you free. It was written by the SS above the entrances to Dachau, Auschwitz, and other concentration camps during the Second World War. And you might know of Gross-Rosen, the camp where my father worked. 'Big roses,' it means. So here we are at Kleine Rosen, 'little roses.' Walk in, go on. Prepare yourself."

He poked Johnson in the back with the barrel of his Glock, pushing him onward. Johnson stumbled as he took a quick step forward. Fiona followed.

They moved through the open door of the house. A straight corridor with a wood block floor led to a hinged gate made of thick steel bars, which was just in front of a wooden back door.

"Open," Ignacio shouted.

A guard with a long black moustache, wearing a badge that identified him as a Lopez Seguridad employee, appeared from a room to the right and unlocked first the metal grill and then the wooden door, swinging both open.

Johnson took two steps forward, then stood rooted, struggling to take in the scene before him.

Inside the large compound formed by the wooden fence were several long wooden huts.

Most of the huts were old and decrepit, apart from two at the back, which were much newer. Between the huts were areas of concrete on which stood steel tables.

Working at the tables were dozens of emaciated women, all dark-skinned Latinas. They were dressed in ragged old T-shirts, jeans that were frayed and covered in stains, and shorts with holes where the stitching was coming apart. Most were wearing flip-flops or crude sandals.

Piles of wristwatch cases, straps, mechanisms, and other components were spread on the tables, which some of the women were assembling under the gaze of men standing nearby.

Other women at the end of the tables were sliding the finished products into plastic sleeves and small branded boxes and then packing them into larger brown cardboard boxes.

All the men carried wooden truncheons that hung from loops tied to their belts. Johnson noticed that frequently, if one of the women stopped working, one of the supervisors would step forward and speak angrily to them.

Sometimes they would take out their truncheon and threaten the women.

In the center of the compound was a water tap on a stand, with a couple of metal cups chained to it that clinked together as they moved in the breeze. Occasionally one of the women would walk to the stand, fill a cup with water, and drink.

Johnson took a couple more steps. He could see the watches and the boxes carried the names of famous brands: Rolex, Girard-Perregaux, Omega, Jaeger-LeCoultre, and others.

Ignacio spoke from behind him. "All fakes, mostly for sale to tourists in this country and elsewhere. And these people are all trafficked in from other countries around here: Paraguay, Bolivia, Chile. They are all slaves, basically. They are kept in this compound, they live and work in these huts, and they're not allowed out. They don't get much food, and what they do get is rubbish—restaurant leftovers and so on."

Johnson glanced at Fiona, who stood next to him. She was gaping, wide-eyed, at the women.

Ignacio walked around in front of Johnson, still pointing the gun at him. "And this is how my father has been making his money for decades. Trying to make up for the losses on his gold purchases from our *friends*," he hissed the words out, "the Kudrow brothers."

Johnson tried to process what he was seeing. What really struck him was how thin, filthy, and haunted the women looked. None of them spoke to the others. It was unnatural: Johnson assumed they had been threatened with punishment if they did so.

Some of the girls were very young, in their mid-to-late teens, and none of them looked much older than thirty, but it was difficult to tell because of their physical condition.

This was the sort of thing Johnson may have expected to see in some backward, third-world state. But in South America's second largest economy? He swore under his breath.

"It's outrageous," Johnson said, turning to Ignacio, his concern over the gun aimed at him temporarily overridden by his indignation. "This is a concentration camp. He's re-created one right here."

Ignacio continued, "You're right. It is outrageous. My

father's legacy. I only found out about this place a few months ago. Oh yes, Argentina signed up for the United Nations protocols on human trafficking and all that political crap— sounds good, doesn't it? But in reality, you find bastards like him running businesses like this all over the country."

Ignacio spat on the ground. "The police do nothing in return for a few bribes here, a roll of pesos there, sometimes a little favor or two. It's the same all over South America, for that matter. Here. Look at it."

He gestured with his hand at the compound, then indicated to one of the women. "Just a *girl*, isn't she? Yes, she might look older than her fifteen years, but she is just that —fifteen."

She had come from Bolivia, Ignacio went on, and it had probably cost his father only eighty dollars or so to buy her. The manager would keep her here for maybe five years, ruin her life, then let her go, Ignacio said.

"Where will she go from here? I don't know. Maybe prostitution, if she's lucky. The manager will find another. There's plenty where she came from."

Johnson heard Fiona swearing under her breath.

"You might think I'm a hypocrite," Ignacio said. "Well, fair enough. Everyone's a hypocrite in this country. But this was how he treated me as a kid, more or less." Ignacio said. "Not much different, really, except I was fed. He locked me in cupboards if I misbehaved, beat me, verbally abused me, told me I was never going to do *anything* with my life."

Ignacio took a breath, then continued his rant. "That's why I left home and joined the army to fight against the arrogant British in the Malvinas, at Port Stanley and Goose Green.

"But anyway, here we are. Now it's time for justice to be done. A little late, some may think. You do realize I was lucky to catch him, don't you?" He jerked a thumb back in the direction of the garage behind them where his father was. "He was on the point of disappearing again. When I arrived at his house, there was a new Chilean passport on his table, a new identity, and he had a bag packed and was ready to go. He even had his coat on. I was just in time."

Johnson refrained from responding.

Ignacio waved the Glock in Johnson's face. "The way of legal justice, that's your way. It's no good to me. It won't repay what he's done to *me*. Nor to any of these women here, for that matter."

He fell silent.

Johnson looked at Ignacio and knew he had to try to make him see the other side.

"He . . . that man through there, your father . . . *tortured* my mother. In Gross-Rosen. He whipped her and left her in the boiling sun all day with no food or water. He left her on the brink of death. She was lucky to survive—extremely fortunate. Most of the others in that place weren't so lucky. They didn't get out. There were thousands of others. Justice for all of them needs to happen in court, in a fair trial where living witnesses can give solid evidence and a fair sentence can be passed. Then, and only then, will justice for all be achieved."

Johnson scanned the women working in front of him. "The justice you've got in mind, *that* is kangaroo court justice of exactly the same type that he and his Nazi thug brothers handed out to Jewish prisoners all over Europe. Let's put to one side the way he's treated you. Don't go down the same road. And the financial justice of the type that the Kudrow brothers have given out is hardly better. It does nothing for the thousands of other victims. It has only benefited them. Don't make the same mistake. I'm asking you to turn him over now for the only true type of justice: that which an international criminal court can provide, based on evidence of the kind that you yourself e-mailed to me."

Ignacio's eyes were wide, but he seemed to ignore most of what Johnson had said.

"Your mother? Really?" Ignacio asked. "Well, that explains a lot. All I can say is, now's your chance for revenge, for your own justice. I'll do it for both of us, then. Come on, let's go."

"No, that's not the way," Johnson said. Fiona shot him a look, clearly terrified he'd further incite Ignacio when he had a gun in his hand.

With some effort, Johnson kept his voice even in an attempt not to further anger the Argentinian. "That's your justice. It's just personal. It's not justice for all those he killed in Poland and their families. He must appear in a court where he gets the opportunity to acknowledge what he's done wrong and accept he must pay a price."

Ignacio shook his head. He signaled with his Glock that Johnson and Fiona should go back the way they had come.

But Johnson stood looking at one girl, ten yards away, behind a steel table, her long hair matted and unwashed. What struck him first was her shirt. It was a red Portland Sea Dogs baseball tank top, the kind he saw baseball fans wearing everywhere back in his hometown.

But this shirt was ripped down the side; it was covered in what looked like oil stains, and all the buttons were missing, apart from one. He realized it must have been a long-discarded charity shop item that had somehow ended up being shipped to wherever it was this girl came from.

The second thing he noticed was the girl's eyes. They were glazed, unfocused, and dead. Although she momentarily looked at him, Johnson could tell her mind was a million miles away—maybe on some long-lost family, a home village, or an estranged sister. Who knew. The girl's hands moved robotically as she assembled a necklace, and she continually shifted her slight weight unconsciously from one bare foot to the other.

"Move!" Ignacio barked behind him, snapping him out of his trance.

Johnson turned and followed Fiona back through the doorway and the metal grill, Ignacio coming behind. The grill clanged shut, followed by the sound of a key turning as the moustachioed Lopez Seguridad guard locked it again.

Walking back into the filthy garage, Johnson noticed that Luis was no longer there, although there was another guard, this one with a shaven head and also wearing a Lopez Seguridad badge, standing near Brenner and carrying a gun.

CHAPTER FIFTY-FOUR

Monday, December 5, 2011
Cataratas del Iguazú International Airport, Argentina

Agustin Torres pushed past an old lady at the bottom of the aircraft steps, almost knocking her over, dodged around a family of four, and sprinted across the airport apron and into the small, two-story red brick terminal.

By the time he got through the terminal, the modern interior of which belied its 1980s house-like appearance, the thirty-one-year-old CIA case officer's white long-sleeve shirt was blotched with sweat. He slowed as he passed through the doors that led to the passenger pickup zone and looked for the new black Ford Ranger double-cab truck he had been told would be waiting for him.

After a few minutes of searching, he spotted it heading into the zone, ran over, and jumped into the passenger seat.

He didn't bother to greet the driver but instead barked an order in Spanish.

"We need to move. It's going to take at least half an hour, maybe forty-five minutes to get there. Go."

The driver of the Ranger was a man who Agustin had used a couple of times before on previous visits to Puerto Iguazú. However, on those occasions, Agustin had a far more leisurely agenda, making routine visits to sources who kept him in the loop on the criminal underworld in the region.

Now the driver's skills were about to be tested. Agustin, who had seven years of CIA service under his belt, prepared himself to take control of the Ranger if the man proved to be not up to the job.

"Your gun's in the glove compartment. Browning as requested. Loaded and good to go," the driver said tersely.

Agustin clicked open the glove compartment and took out the semiautomatic. He strapped on a holster and put the gun into it.

Agustin took out his phone and tapped on a secure maps app that he used to track the location of phones that had been triangulated by technical experts at the National Security Agency at Fort Meade in Maryland, northeast of Washington, D.C.

The last recorded location for the phone he was chasing, belonging to VANDAL, was on the western fringes of Puerto Iguazú, down a dirt road near to the Paraná River, although he noted there had been no update in the previous twenty-five minutes. The vehicle he had been told to look out for was a silver Toyota Hilux.

Agustin gave the best description of the location he could to the driver, who nodded. "*Si, si*, I know the road—it goes right down to the river."

The Ranger's 3.2 liter diesel engine growled as the driver floored the gas pedal and sped out of the airport toward the city.

Agustin knew his corrupt police chief friend Carlos had

arranged for police at a checkpoint near Puerto Iguazú to delay the rented Toyota Hilux in which Johnson was traveling by an hour. But Carlos wasn't prepared to push for longer, despite Agustin's offer of more cash. Carlos wouldn't explain why but just said it was difficult. And that meant that Agustin would be lucky to get to VANDAL's location first.

Clearly, much was at stake. Agustin didn't have the full suite of background information, but if the chief of the Near East division in the CIA's Directorate of Operations was giving him carte blanche to do whatever was necessary to prevent the investigator, Joe Johnson, and his journalist colleague from reaching VANDAL, then he'd give it his best shot. However, he wasn't relishing the prospect of having to carry out an exfiltration of the old man single-handedly.

Agustin sat silently as the driver weaved in and out of the traffic, pulling off several risky overtaking maneuvers with greater skill than Agustin had expected.

Before the Ranger reached the built-up area, the driver, his face tense, mouth pulled tight, swung a sharp left across the oncoming traffic, cutting right in front of a large red municipal bus, which provoked an extended, angry horn blast.

The driver accelerated hard, taking his speed up to more than 140 kilometers an hour as he forked left onto a red dirt road.

Agustin grasped the edge of his seat as the Ranger barreled toward VANDAL's last known location.

* * *

Puerto Iguazú

Johnson stood and stared at Ignacio, who continued to point

the Glock at him, his eyes flicking between him and Fiona. Was he bluffing or not? Probably not. There was a deadness, a hardness, in the Argentinian's dark eyes.

It was then that Johnson had a moment of suspicion, recalling a TV crime reporter's comment about Nathaniel having traveled extensively, including South America, and that police were investigating links between those trips and his death.

"Nathaniel Kudrow," Johnson said. "Was that you?"

Fiona's head whipped round toward him in surprise.

Ignacio moistened his lips. "I warned him."

"But why?"

"He came to Argentina and arranged a meeting with me, saying he'd found out about the gold sales to my father," Ignacio said. "He wanted to know if it was true, because he didn't believe it. He couldn't ask his family. He said he was planning to expose the whole thing. He thought it would be in my interests too. I warned him repeatedly not to, as I had other ideas; I told him to back off and shut up, or I'd take action. But he seemed determined. An ex-military intelligence friend and I tailed him for a week in Washington, so I knew about his discussions with her." Ignacio nodded toward Fiona.

Johnson decided to let Ignacio talk, if he wanted to talk. He was clearly trying to justify himself now, and if he did have doubts about what he was doing at the back of his mind, maybe that was a weakness that could be exploited. The longer Johnson let this run, the better. There was an irrational, obsessed quality about the man. *Maybe it's in the genes.*

"I told him to keep his mouth shut," Ignacio said, "but he was on a mission to expose it all. Stupid. I never understood why. Unfortunately, I was probably too late with him."

Ignacio turned and pointed at Fiona. "However, now that she's here, she's gonna be useful. I'm gonna make her write the story about why I'm going to dispose of my father so the world knows what he did to all those Jews and to me. Has she read those documents I sent you?"

Fiona cleared her throat. "Yes, I've seen them, and I fully intend to write the story about your father. But you don't have to kill him, like Joe says. We can take him to court."

Keep him talking, Fiona.

"And there's another thing," Fiona continued. "There's a story about to break. David Kudrow's stepping down shortly. I had a text message from his campaign manager earlier."

She looked apologetically at Johnson, who raised his eyebrows, feeling suddenly irritated that she hadn't mentioned it before.

"They're issuing a press statement in Washington this morning announcing he's pulling out of the race," Fiona continued. "The reality is he's realized that at some stage, *Inside Track* is going to run the story about his finances and the gold, and it's going to go viral, so he's stepping down first. But he's going to say it's due to personal reasons: the campaign is too much of an intrusion into his family time. Prospect of the presidency is too much. He has a business to run, et cetera, et cetera, you know the routine."

Johnson could tell she was nervous—understandably so, given Ignacio's threats—by the way she was tripping over her words. But he needed to keep the conversation going.

"So all the detail about the Kudrows reselling Hitler's gold? That'll now go in the story about him quitting, I assume?" Johnson asked.

She shrugged. "I don't know what my boss will do about that. The problem is, we still need actual physical proof of what they've done, don't we? That's why I wanted photographs from the tunnels. Yes, we've seen invoices of sales to Argentina from years ago but nothing to show what was actually sold, let alone where it came from. Services—

that's all it said on the invoices. David would just deny it all."
She cast a tentative glance toward Ignacio.

Johnson scratched the nick in his right ear. "Don't tell me
we've wasted our time. Why did Nathaniel do it, leak the
story I mean? Was he just pissed that he didn't get any benefit
from the gold, while his brother did? Was it a jealousy——"

"That's what I wanted to know," Ignacio interrupted. "I
never found out."

Johnson heard one of the cell phones lying on the table
ping as a text message arrived, followed by another, and then
yet another.

Fiona took a step toward the table, but Ignacio pointed
the gun at her. "Leave that phone alone. We've done enough
talking. It's time to finish things off in here now. I've waited
long enough."

Johnson cursed inwardly. From outside, he thought he
heard a faint thud and then a groan, but nobody else seemed
to notice.

Ignacio grabbed a wooden chair from behind the table
and put it next to the one in which his father was sitting.

Then, he aimed his gun at Johnson.

"You, Johnson, sit here. Now. I can't afford to take any
more risks with you. You're going to have to go, as well. You
and your pathetic *justice*." He almost spat the words out.

Ignacio reached behind him, eyes still on Johnson, and
took a small cardboard folder from the table. A couple of
sheets of paper fell out of it. Johnson could see they looked
like the originals of Brenner's SS documents, from which
Ignacio had e-mailed scanned pages to him.

The old man Brenner then spoke for the first time since
they had entered the garage. "Where did you get those from?
Tell me. And where are my guards who work here," he said in
a faint voice, almost a whisper.

"Never mind where I got the papers. I'm going to give

them to our reporter Fiona here so she can tell the whole world what you did—so they will know why you've had a bullet through your evil, wrinkled head," Ignacio said. "And my two guards are working here now. I've sent yours away."

Johnson still hadn't moved.

Ignacio stepped toward him, his face contorted, his eyes narrowed, his lips pressed tight . . . with what? Johnson didn't know if it was just rage, frustration, or disappointment. Then Ignacio said in a lower, threatening tone, "Move. Sit down." Johnson noticed that Ignacio's right hand, which held the gun, shook a little.

Johnson put his hands up and shuffled to the chair, then sat.

Ignacio walked a couple of paces and stood in front of his father, his back to the smaller garage door. Johnson sat in front of him to his right, his hands still raised.

Ignacio held out his pistol, the barrel pointing at Johnson.

Out of the corner of his eye, Johnson saw a shadow creeping forward along the narrow beam of sunlight shining through the partly open door. It moved behind Ignacio, and then Johnson began to see the outline of a person's head and shoulders. Then, at one side, the shape of a raised hand.

Jayne.

Ignacio was in full flow now, spitting hatred in Spanish at his father, oblivious to what was happening around him. "This is for *you*, for what you did to me and to all the others you've killed and tortured. It's for those *women* outside. This is the point where the *dog*, as you called me, the dog returns home, tail between his legs, then turns and rips his owner's throat out."

He lowered the barrel until it was pointing at his father's head.

At that moment, the shaven-headed Lopez Seguridad

guard must have noticed the shadow at the door. "Ignacio, watch out, behind you," he yelled.

Ignacio turned.

From behind him came a deafening gunshot, a pause, and then another; they echoed around the garage. Then three further shots, at least one of which zinged into the plastered ceiling, bringing down a large chunk of it with a flurry of debris.

Ignacio gave an agonized scream as he stumbled forward. The gun fell from his hand and clattered to the floor in front of Johnson.

Blood spurted from Ignacio's right shoulder onto the floor, instantly turning his shirt crimson. Two round black holes punctured the material. His right arm fell uselessly by his side, and he clutched his shoulder with his left hand. His mouth hung open and his eyes bulged.

Suddenly Fiona shouted, "Joe, the guard. His gun."

Johnson turned his head and saw the shaven-headed guard raising his pistol. "Jayne, dive," he shouted. Johnson threw himself off the chair and onto the floor as the guard pulled the trigger.

As he did so, Jayne fired off more rapid shots at the guard from her now-prone position on the floor. The first two caused more plasterwork in both the ceiling and the walls to explode into the air.

The third shot flung the security guard back, and blood sprayed behind him as Jayne's round struck him somewhere near his right collar bone.

Johnson rolled under the table. In the same moment, he saw Fiona hit the floor.

There was a loud revving and a squeal of tires from outside, and then behind Ignacio, the two large garage doors burst open as the rear end of a Jeep smashed through the woodwork and came to a halt a couple of yards into the garage. The moustachioed guard sat at the wheel.

One garage door swung back on its hinges at high speed and crashed into the garage wall; the other one splintered into two pieces.

In a flash, Ignacio ran to one of the rear doors of the car, opened it, and jumped in, blood spurting from his shoulder, leaving a crimson trail behind him.

"Hit him, Jayne," Johnson shouted. But he could see Jayne desperately trying to replace the magazine on her pistol.

The Jeep's engine revved loudly, the doors slammed, and with a squeal of tires spinning on concrete, the vehicle shot out of the garage and down the road.

Johnson turned and, just a few feet away, saw Fiona lying on her side on the floor, her back facing him. He yelled at her as he got up. "Fiona, you okay?"

But she didn't move. Johnson reached out and pulled at her shoulder.

It was only when he rolled Fiona onto her back that he saw blood pulsing from a bullet wound at the top of her left arm. She also had a large red gash and bruise on the side of her temple.

She lay there faceup, arms and legs spread wide, her head lolling sideways.

CHAPTER FIFTY-FIVE

Monday, December 5, 2011
Puerto Iguazú

Johnson stared at Fiona for a second or two, struggling to take in what had happened. He put both hands to his forehead, momentarily torn between his instinct to stay by Fiona's side and help her and his desire to stop Ignacio before he disappeared.

The roar of the Jeep's engine from outside decided it for him. He grabbed his Beretta, which still lay on the table, and ran out, closely followed by Jayne, who had slotted a fresh magazine into her gun. But by then, the Jeep was already fifty yards away and accelerating down the red dirt road.

Speedily, Johnson flicked off the safety, leveled the gun, and fired two quick shots at the vehicle. The first bullet crashed into the bodywork at the back, and the second shattered the rear window; but the vehicle kept going, and by that time there was so much dust flying up behind it that his third shot, together with two fired by Jayne, missed altogether.

The Jeep flew around a bend, behind some trees, and down the slope toward the river, leaving a trail of red dust that floated gently in the breeze.

At the bottom of the hill, next to some rocks where there was a small inlet off the main river, a boat waited, its two outboard motors throwing off exhaust fumes.

Jayne looked distraught. "Sorry, I just couldn't reload fast enough. It's my fault. Quick, let's get after them. I'll fetch the Toyota."

Johnson grabbed Jayne by the forearm and held on. He stared into the distance. "There's no way we're going to catch them. They'll be on that boat in a minute. It'll take us too long to get the Hilux. We've got no chance."

He turned quickly and headed back toward the garage. "Fiona's hurt in there. Better go and check on her."

Johnson entered the garage, followed by Jayne, and went straight to Fiona. She groaned and opened her eyes, then closed them again.

"Okay, Fiona, don't move," he said and held her wrist for a few seconds. "Pulse feels fine. I think she'll be okay, but we need to stop this bleeding. I think she banged her head when she fell down. Look at that gash on her temple."

Johnson grabbed a couple of cushions from a chair in the corner. He put one behind Fiona's head and ripped the cover off the other. Then he took a penknife from his pocket and cut the sleeve off Fiona's shirt. It appeared the round had gone straight through the soft flesh of her upper arm but had thankfully missed the bone. It had left a messy, ragged wound that was bleeding heavily. Johnson hesitated for a second and then pressed the material hard against the bullet wound. "I don't think there's much else I can do. The hospital will have to sort it out."

He scanned around the garage and spotted a roll of brown

sticky tape on a bench. "There, get that tape," he said, "I'll bandage her up best I can. Not ideal."

Jayne fetched the tape, and Johnson wound it tightly around Fiona's shoulder and upper arm so it held the cloth firmly in place. "That's the best I can do."

Fiona opened her eyes again. She had turned very pale and was clearly in a lot of pain, but Johnson could see she was breathing steadily.

Johnson turned and walked to the Lopez Seguridad guard who Jayne had shot. He lay groaning on the floor at the rear of the garage and bleeding heavily from a wound to his shoulder, which Johnson inspected briefly. It seemed as though the round had shattered his collar bone.

Johnson turned back to Jayne. "This is going to be difficult. Here's what I suggest. We'll get out of here now, before the police come. We'll call an ambulance for this security guard, and we'll drop Fiona off at the hospital. I don't want to leave her, but she's obviously going to need to stay in the hospital. We have to get this old bastard Brenner back to Buenos Aires somehow. And we need to be quick. You can bet the Mossad and probably the CIA will be on to us. If we can just get him into the U.S. or British embassy, we've got a chance. How about if I talk to the U.S., you speak to the U.K., and then I'll call the war crimes authorities. We'll need to work out a process. I just hope Argentina cooperates."

Johnson tried to mentally check through what else he needed to do before they left. A first priority was to collect evidence. He bent over and carefully picked up the originals of Brenner's SS documents, then replaced them in the folder, which he tucked under his arm. He walked to the table and looked at the four phones that lay there. One was his, one was Jayne's, which he handed to her, and another was Fiona's.

Johnson scrutinized the fourth device. A quick check of the

phone's address book, mostly consisting of SolGold staff members, told him it was Brenner's. Johnson stared at the former Nazi, who still sat secured in his chair. The sight triggered an image in his mind of his mother being whipped and caused a slight involuntary gagging reflex in Johnson. He felt bile rise inside his throat, which he quickly held back, swallowing hard.

It suddenly struck Johnson that amid the chaos, he hadn't yet spoken to Brenner. He felt an urge to deliver some kind of speech outlining exactly why he was going to turn the old man over to the judicial authorities and make Brenner remember the way he had tortured his mother. But the thought dissipated quickly, partly because it seemed superfluous, partly because he knew they needed to get out of the area, and fast. In any case, he knew Brenner wouldn't remember her. Why would he?

Instead, he just held the former SS officer's gaze. The pale blue eyes that Johnson imagined had once burned bright with venom and racist fervor were almost milky and pathetic.

He turned to fully face the old Nazi. "Just for the record," Johnson said quietly, "I'm Joe Johnson, a war crimes investigator. I'm going to make sure you go back where you came from, to Germany, so the Central Office can deal with you, like they dealt with John Demjanjuk earlier this year. We are going to take you to the U.S. embassy in Buenos Aires, and we'll move on from there."

He was referring to the Central Office of the State Justice Administrations for the Investigation of National Socialist Crimes, Germany's main agency for investigating Nazi war crimes. Demjanjuk, an auto worker in Cleveland, had been deported from the U.S. in 2009 and, at a trial in Munich in May 2011, had been found guilty of being an accessory to murder at the Sobibór death camp in Poland, where he was a guard during World War II.

Brenner stared back. "I know who you are."

Johnson simply shook his head. He removed the SIM card and the battery from Brenner's phone and tucked them all into his pocket. He assumed the CIA or the Mossad were tracking the SIM card.

Johnson walked back out of the door, followed by Jayne. In the distance he saw the Jeep containing Ignacio and his guard pull up at the bottom of the hill next to the boat.

The distant, tiny figures of the two men climbed out and boarded the boat.

As soon as they were on, the boat's engines roared, and it swept out into the river in an arc, heading upstream toward Paraguay on the opposite bank, leaving a large white wake frothing behind it.

Just outside the garage, Luis lay unconscious on the ground next to a short wooden pole. "What happened there, with this guy?" Johnson asked Jayne as he felt for Luis's pulse.

Jayne pursed her lips. "Well, I saw him looking around in this area near the garage. I got the feeling he was checking for any backup you might have. When I heard voices rising inside, I thought I might be needed. So I sneaked up behind him and hit him with that pole. He never saw me. I obviously didn't want to use my gun because everyone inside would have heard it."

Johnson gave a thin smile. Jayne had been, literally, a life-saver on this trip.

"Well, he's still alive," Johnson said. "We'll tie him up, and the ambulance can deal with him as well."

Johnson stood. "I owe you one, Jayne. Ignacio was definitely going to kill the old man and me. It was a bad situation in there."

He glanced at Fiona's phone. There were several text messages showing, which he scrolled down quickly. His eyes widened. "What the *hell* . . ." he said, as he digested the contents.

"What's that?" asked Jayne.

"These messages on Fiona's phone. Looks like they're from one of her *Inside Track* colleagues."

Johnson read on. "Apparently there's a warrant out for the arrest of a very senior Democratic Party executive suspected of making an unauthorized multimillion dollar payment into a numbered account in the Bahamas—which belongs to Nathaniel Kudrow."

He scrolled down further, then read the details from the next message. "The FBI thinks it's five million bucks. The guy's gone missing. They think he was on a plane this morning heading for Paraguay. Apparently the FBI tapped his line, and he was overheard saying something about payments to Nathaniel in return for engineering David Kudrow's withdrawal as Republican candidate. The first payment went through the same morning Nathaniel was stabbed to death but before the body was found. They found the cash in one of his bank accounts. They also uncovered text messages between the executive and Nathaniel referring to payments, including one from Nathaniel saying he'd done the job and the first transfer should be made. They're asking if Fiona can call them urgently. It says her website hasn't run a story yet, but it will."

Johnson shook his head. His mind worked overtime as he processed the information. So *that* was why Nathaniel had leaked the story. Philip's words about Nathaniel at the Republican fund-raiser almost a month earlier came back to him.

He was the one who suggested I put you on the guest list.

No doubt he'd put Fiona on the guest list, too.

Jayne's bottom jaw had also dropped a little. "He's betrayed his brother for five million bucks," she said. "Are you sure you read it right?"

"Looks that way. If we can get Fiona patched up, she's got two world exclusives here."

He knew that despite Fiona's earlier comments about needing "more proof," there was more than enough to satisfy any editor or media lawyer, while publishing a big story about Brenner would make it much more difficult for the CIA or the Mossad to somehow secretly exfiltrate him.

"Of course," Jayne said. "Huge stories. The last Nazi, probably. You must be feeling as though you've done it for your mother. I remember what you told me she went through."

Johnson met her gaze and nodded. "Yes, thanks to you. But this game's not over until we get Brenner out of here and out of Argentina. We also need someone to contact the United Nations and the human rights organizations about these poor women in the compound here. Can't trust the local police to do it, obviously. Maybe Fiona can write a story about them as well."

"I can get a couple of embassy staff whom I still know to help," Jayne said. "They can start things moving at the U.N. to get these women out of the compound as well."

She set off to fetch the Hilux while Johnson tied up the injured guard, who had slipped into unconsciousness, using lengths of rope he found in the garage. He then did the same with Luis, who also remained unconscious.

Once Jayne returned, they transferred Brenner to the rear seat of the Toyota, using Ignacio's original Velcro bindings around his arms and legs. The old SS officer put up no resistance.

Then they carefully carried Fiona and placed her in the front passenger seat. She looked weak, but despite the large patch of blood showing through the makeshift bandage on her shoulder, her pulse was strong and Johnson was reassured by the look of determination on her face.

Fiona preempted Johnson's concerns about leaving her at the hospital. "I'll be fine," she said, wincing heavily. "I'm

going to need an op to sort this shoulder out. And I'll talk my
way out of it with the police. Don't worry—you concentrate
on getting Brenner out of here. I'll be okay."

Johnson nodded and gave Fiona her phone back. "I'm
more worried about you getting those stories written and
published," he joked.

He climbed into the driver's seat, but then noticed that
Jayne had wandered off toward the concrete strip next to the
house. She was bent over, peering into the dust like an old
lady looking for a dropped dime.

"Come on, Jayne, we need to get out of here," Johnson
shouted. He was feeling increasingly agitated at the delays.

Jayne picked something up and returned to the Hilux,
where she climbed into the rear seat opposite Brenner.
Johnson let the clutch out, and the Hilux sped back up the
single-track dirt road.

Farther up the road, in the distance, Johnson saw a cloud
of dust being thrown up by a vehicle that was clearly traveling
at a high speed toward them.

His instinctive thought was that it seemed extremely
unusual for a vehicle to move at such speed in a rural location
down such a poorly maintained dirt road as this one. In that
moment, Johnson had a gut feeling and acted on it.

To his right, the road forked into a bay that was separated
from the road by bushes, grasses, and trees. Johnson braked
hard and pulled sharply into the bay, coming to a halt behind
a dense tussock of eight-foot pampas grass.

"What the hell are you doing," Jayne asked. "I thought we
were in a rush?"

Johnson pointed silently toward the road. Less than a
minute later, a shiny black Ford Ranger pickup sped around
the corner, affording Johnson a quick glimpse of the vehicle
before it passed behind the other side of the pampas grass.

It accelerated past the passing bay and disappeared out of

sight behind them. Once he was certain it had gone, Johnson pushed the Hilux back into gear and drove back onto the road.

"I don't know who that was, but it definitely wasn't a local in a truck like that, not from this poor area," Johnson said.

He turned and glanced at Fiona, then over his shoulder at Jayne in the back. "What did you pick up outside the SolGold workshop back there?" he asked Jayne.

She leaned around the driver's seat and held an object in front of Johnson.

"This," Jayne said. "I saw something metal bounce out of Ignacio's pocket when he was running to get into the car. It landed on the concrete."

Johnson glanced down at the rectangular piece of yellow metal that Jayne was holding. On the front of it was an engraving of a swastika and an eagle. Below were the words:

Deutsche Reichsbank
   1 kilo Feingold
   999.9

EPILOGUE

Monday, December 12, 2011
Portland, Maine

The first heavy snowstorm of winter was still raging across the Portland area as Johnson opened the envelope and spread the newspaper clippings out on his desk.

He stood staring at them for a few minutes, then he picked one up, sat down, and began to read.

"Nazi Mass Murderer to Face Trial After 67 Years on the Run," ran the headline in large type. Below it was a subhead, "SS Killer, 91, Runs Replica 'Concentration Camp' in Argentina."

There was a color photograph of Brenner, together with a black-and-white one of the Wüstegiersdorf concentration camp taken in 1944 and another of his jewelry manufacturing site in Puerto Iguazú.

The story below it detailed how Brenner had been tracked down. It included quotes from Johnson about the

Kudrows' London workshop, the tunnels in the Riese complex, and the car chase north to Puerto Iguazú.

Some of the other cuttings included scans taken from Brenner's incriminating SS documents.

Johnson picked up another clipping, this one a printout from *Inside Track*—which had managed to break the story first, despite Fiona's injuries. She had filed the piece in great pain from her hospital bed, with the help of a nurse who typed as she dictated and then e-mailed it for her.

Fiona's story was headlined, "White House Hopeful Kudrow Steps Down in Nazi Gold Funding Scandal." It also had a subhead: "Jewish Camp Survivors 'Blackmailed' SS Torturer."

The story, like most of the coverage, condemned the way the Kudrow twins had plundered Hitler's stolen gold and used it for their own ends, yet sympathized with their mission to wreak revenge on their Nazi torturer.

Another article from Fiona's website reported, "*Inside Track* Journalist Wounded in Gun Battle As Nazi Is Captured." Thankfully, the hospital in Puerto Iguazú had been able to repair Fiona's shoulder, although she would require extensive rehab work with a physiotherapist once the wound had healed. She had flown back to Washington, via Buenos Aires, three days after her surgery. Johnson still felt guilty at leaving her in Puerto Iguazú while he headed south with Brenner, but in reality, he had little choice.

Commentators and pundits across all the media outlets had struggled to work out what the Kudrow twins might be charged with—if anything—and which country should carry out any investigation.

Johnson was sure of one thing: if the Kudrows wanted to emerge from the saga with their credibility intact, they would have to agree to identify Brenner, first to have him extradited from Argentina and then again in court in Germany.

A viable identification would probably require the elderly twins to pick out an unlabeled photograph of Brenner as he was in the 1940s from an array of several different Nazi officers, using images taken from Brenner's and other SS personal files so they were all of similar sizes and styles.

Another story read "SS Chief's Documents Are 'Smoking Gun' Evidence." Well, yes, and copies of the papers were in Brenner's SS personal files stored in Berlin and Washington.

But the Kudrows would need to be prepared to go into some detail, both in statements and in court, about the background to the tunnel collapse, their escape from the train near Gluszyca, and the shots they heard as their fellow prisoners were murdered. All of that would corroborate the SS disciplinary notice issued to Brenner.

Could the two old men do all that, and would Jacob's ailing heart cope with the strain of the process and a court appearance? Johnson was confident the Kudrows would do it, based on a five-minute phone conversation he had the previous day with Daniel, who was still in London and had promised he and Jacob would do the right thing.

Daniel had been stunned into silence by news of the concentration camp set up by Brenner in Puerto Iguazú and Ignacio's line that Brenner had done it to try and make up for the financial hit taken from the Kudrows' long-running blackmail. But he had ended the conversation with a comment that Johnson found hard to disagree with. "The man is pure evil; he would have done it anyway."

There were several other major media stories focusing on the $5 million payment to Nathaniel's bank account by the Democratic Party official, who was now facing an FBI investigation for trying to influence the course of an election and had still not been found. He was believed to be in hiding in Paraguay or possibly Chile.

Most of the stories detailed how Ignacio was now the subject of an international manhunt: wanted in connection with the murders of Nathaniel Kudrow and Keith Bartelski and the attempted murder of his father. Police had already questioned Luis, now recovered from his concussion, several times.

But none of the media had mentioned Jayne. She had insisted on that and had returned to the U.K. without anyone from SIS appearing to have realized what Carolina Blanco had been up to. Nor did the media reference the CIA or the Mossad. Johnson had decided to leave them out of the briefings he had done with various journalists, and as he had expected, neither of the two intelligence agencies had subsequently raised their heads above the parapet.

Without concrete proof of wrongdoing by Watson, Johnson felt it was a high-risk strategy to accuse him of anything at this stage. But he had a strong feeling that biding his time would pay dividends. Watson, he was certain, had his finger in a number of pies that contained rotten ingredients. There would be another opportunity.

One of the reports mentioned Johnson had swapped vehicles twice as he and Jayne spirited Brenner eight hundred miles south to the U.S. Embassy in Buenos Aires. Johnson gave a thin smile on reading it. The report was true. He had paid cash for a black Mitsubishi pickup in Puerto Iguazú, where they had left Jayne's rented silver Hilux behind after dropping Fiona at the hospital. Farther down the road, they had done another swap, this time exchanging the Mitsubishi for a red Ford pickup in Concordia.

The trick had worked. They hadn't been pulled over by local police, nor had they been caught by the CIA or the Mossad. Johnson was still waiting for feedback from Vic on what Watson's reaction had been to the course of events.

The door opened behind Johnson. He turned around to see Carrie enter the room, closely followed by Cocoa, who was wagging his tail vigorously.

Johnson checked his computer screen and pulled at the hole in his right ear. It was only 10:20 a.m., and already six e-mails had arrived that morning inquiring about his availability for work assignments in the United States and abroad. Many others had come in during the days following Brenner's arrest and the surge of global media coverage that had followed from Fiona's initial exclusive report.

He glanced at his daughter, then stood up and walked over to her and gave her a silent hug.

After a minute, he stepped back and put his hands on her shoulders.

"You did a good job, Dad. Look at all those headlines. Grandma would have been proud of you," she said. "Sounded risky, though. More than Peter or I imagined."

Risky?

"Yes, well, I wasn't really expecting it to turn out the way it did, honey, that's for sure," Johnson said. He smiled at his own understatement.

And was it worth it, he asked himself, to finally catch Brenner? That was a big question.

"I'm just remembering something your grandmother wrote me," Johnson said. "Tracking down Brenner means justice for her and for the thousands of others who suffered and died all around her."

"You think you will? Is there enough proof?" Carrie asked.

"Oh yes, there's enough proof. Documents and eyewitnesses. That won't be a problem," Johnson said. "That's why it was worth it. Maybe if that discourages Brenner's present-day equivalent, someone else who's about to commit a war crime, maybe in Africa or Syria or somewhere, the world becomes a tiny bit of a better place. Like she said, these people can't run and hide forever. She suffered, we've persevered, and now there's hope."

He turned back to his computer, selected the first of that day's e-mails, and pressed reply.

UPDATES AND OTHER BOOKS IN THE JOE JOHNSON SERIES

I am keen to build a strong relationship with my readers. As part of this, I'm planning to send occasional email updates containing details of forthcoming new books, special offers, and perhaps snippets of background information on the research I've done, on plots, and on characters.

For example, I sometimes join together with other authors for promotions where we might offer a selection of our books at a discounted price — or even free.

If you would like to join my Readers' Group and receive the email updates, I will send you, FREE of charge, an ebook 'box set' containing the first five "taster" chapters of the next two books in the Joe Johnson series, *The Old Bridge* and *Bandit Country* (it includes *The Last Nazi* which you already have.)

You can sign up for the Readers' Group and get the free box set at:

www.BookHip.com/HGFSHT

The second book in the series, *The Old Bridge*, is another war crimes investigation. It is set in Bosnia, Croatia and the US in 2012, with flashbacks to the Yugoslav civil war of the early 1990s. Most of the action is set in Dubrovnik, New York City, Split, Mostar, and London. It can be found on Amazon at:

Amazon US: www.andrewturpin.com/amazonus-theoldbridge
Amazon UK: www.andrewturpin.com/amazonuk-theoldbridge

The third book in the series, *Bandit Country*, is set in Northern Ireland in 2013, with flashbacks to 1984. It dives into the murky depths of historic conflicts between British security forces and the IRA, as well as the illegal US-based fundraising and weapons smuggling operations that armed the terrorists. Most scenes are in Belfast, south Armagh, and Boston, Massachusetts. It can be found on Amazon at:

Amazon US: www.andrewturpin.com/amazonus-banditcountry
Amazon UK: www.andrewturpin.com/amazonuk-banditcountry

Andrew Turpin, St. Albans, UK.

IF YOU ENJOYED THIS BOOK – PLEASE WRITE A REVIEW

As an independent author with my own small publishing business, The Write Direction, I am very dependent on readers writing honest reviews of my books. This is the most powerful way for me to bring them to the attention of other potential readers.

As you will realize, unlike the big international publishers, I can't place advertisements in the newspapers or on the subway.

So I am committed to producing work of the best quality I can in order to attract a committed and loyal group of readers who are prepared to recommend my work to others.

Therefore, if you enjoyed reading this novel, then I would very much appreciate it if you would spend five minutes and leave a review—which can be as short as you like—preferably on the page or website where you bought it.

You can find the book's page on the Amazon website by typing 'Andrew Turpin The Last Nazi' in the search box. Once you have clicked on the page, scroll down to 'Customer Reviews', then click on 'Leave a Review.' Remember to sign into your Amazon account.

Reviews are also a great encouragement to me to write more.

Many thanks!

THANKS AND DEDICATION

First, I would like to thank everyone who reads *The Last Nazi*—which is my debut novel—and my future books. You are the reason I began to write in the first place, and I hope I can provide you with entertainment and interest for a long time into the future.

I would also like to thank those who helped me through the long process of research, writing, and editing and who encouraged me to keep going when the road ahead seemed uncertain.

A special thank you to my brother, Adrian Turpin, who patiently read through endless early rough drafts of the book and provided a lot of valuable ideas, feedback, and encouragement as I inched my way slowly toward the finish line, often doubting whether I would ever get there. Others, such as David Cole, Martin Scales, and Colleen Jacobs, did likewise at slightly later stages.

My parents, Jean and Gerald Turpin, showed great tenacity in getting to grips with using Kindles for the first time, at the ages of ninety-two and eighty-seven respectively, in order to read early drafts and provide very welcome encouragement. They were the ones who instilled in me a love of story, reading, and writing in the first place, and without that, I wouldn't have even started.

Adrian also helped enormously with setting up my website, especially the photography and artwork. He runs his own professional photography, lighting design and cinematography business, The Light Direction, based in Kendal, Cumbria, which can be found at www.thelightdirection.co.uk.

On the editing side, I had two main advisers. Katrina Diaz Arnold, owner of Refine Editing, which can be found at www.refineediting.com, consistently and enthusiastically provided great suggestions for improvements to the book at both the structural and the detailed levels, while Jon Ford's fantastic eye for detail and ideas for improving the authenticity of the project lifted it very significantly and meant I was able to eliminate many errors. I would like to thank both of them—the responsibility for any remaining mistakes lies solely with me.

I also had valuable input from a research historian at the U.S. Department of Justice, who wishes to remain nameless, which enabled me to improve the characterization of my protagonist, Joe Johnson, as well as give a better feel for the sources and methods a war crimes investigator might draw on.

I would also like to thank the team at Damonza for what I think is a great cover design.

Finally, a thank you to my children, Alexa and Ross, who have both been very patient while this book was being written and edited.

AUTHOR'S NOTE

Much of the historical backdrop to **The Last Nazi** is factual, including the details of Hitler's Project Riese in Lower Silesia and the extensive complex of tunnels that was built in the area in and around Walbrzych. This includes the tunnels underneath Książ Castle and in the Owl Mountains.

The Sokolec group of tunnels was one of seven such structures within the Riese complex, including Książ Castle.

However, I have taken poetic license in describing the layout of these tunnels, including the existence of emergency exit tunnels.

The Gross-Rosen concentration camp, including the Wüstegiersdorf subcamp, was built to provide the labor that dug out the Riese tunnels. Most prisoners held there were Jewish.

There has been a lot of speculation about the storage of gold and other treasures looted by the Nazis from across Europe during the Second World War, including gold bars taken from various government reserves and smaller gold items stolen from Jewish prisoners as they arrived at concentration camps, including tooth fillings that were forcibly extracted. For example, a large volume of gold and jewelry was found in a mine at Merkers, Germany, by American soldiers in 1945.

The tunnels of Project Riese, some of which have not yet been explored or which remain blocked due to rock falls, are believed by many to have been a storage location for some of this Nazi gold, but none has so far been found. I have therefore been creative in describing how gold bars were stored in the Sokolec tunnels.

As my protagonist Joe Johnson is from the United States,

and most scenes are from his point of view, it seemed to make sense to try and use American spellings and terminology wherever possible, rather than my native British.

BACKGROUND READING AND BIBLIOGRAPHY

As I did my research for this book—a task which despite lasting many months, unsurprisingly never felt complete—I came across many interesting and valuable books, articles, documents and videos.

For those who enjoy digging into history and might be interested in the worlds of organizations such as the CIA and the Office of Special Investigations, I am listing below just a few examples of the many sources I used.

I have been particularly inspired by the work done by the OSI, part of the United States Department of Justice, to track down and prosecute war criminals many decades after the original atrocities were committed. This organization, which since 2010 has been rebadged as the Human Rights and Special Prosecutions section of the DoJ, has been tenacious and incisive in its research, led by its team of historians who have delved into files hidden in the darkest corners of archives across Europe to unearth the evidence they require.

A 617-page internal history of the OSI, entitled *The Office of Special Investigations: Striving for Accountability in the Aftermath of the Holocaust,* was written for the Department of Justice by Judy Feigin. A copy is available at https://www.justice.gov/sites/default/files/criminal/legacy/2011/03/14/12-2008osu-accountability.pdf

This document provides great insight into the OSI's operations and into some of the high-profile Nazi cases it pursued during the period after it was established in 1979. Since then, the OSI has won cases against 107 individuals living in the U.S. who took part in Nazi crimes of persecution. The document also illustrates how the United States provided a safe haven for hundreds, possibly thousands, of Nazis who fled after World War II, some of them assisted by the CIA in exchange for intelligence about the Soviet Union as the Cold War escalated.

Journalist and author Eric Lichtblau wrote an article for *The New York Times* in 2010 which summarizes Judy Feigin's report, and is available at http://www.nytimes.-com/2010/11/14/us/14nazis.html?partner=rss&emc=rss.

Lichtblau's book, *The Nazis Next Door*, about the war criminals who took refuge in the United States after World War II and the efforts of the Office of Special Investigations and others to track them down, is a fascinating read. In particular, the chapter detailing OSI historian Mike MacQueen's hunt in the Vilnius archives for evidence of crimes committed by Aleksandras Lileikis, a Lithuanian security police chief who collaborated with the Nazis and subsequently lived in Massachusetts for thirty-five years, makes compelling reading.

An article on the CIA's website explores this theme further, and is found https://www.cia.gov/library/center-for-the-study-of-intelligence/csi-publications/csi-studies/studies/97unclass/naziwar.html.

An in-depth profile of Eli Rosenbaum, director of the OSI until 2010, can be found in Harvard Law Bulletin, at https://today.law.harvard.edu/feature/never-forget/

The Simon Wiesenthal Center's *Annual Report on the Investigation and Prosecution of Nazi War Criminals,* which was first published in 2001, has made consistently interesting background reading. The report for 2016, and previous reports, can be found at http://www.wiesenthal.com/site/apps/nl-net/content2.aspx?c=lsKWLbPJL-nF&b=9356941&ct=14848993 and also at the Operation Last Chance website http://www.operationlastchance.org/

The author of this report, Dr. Efraim Zuroff, wrote in the 2015 edition, "Despite the somewhat prevalent assumption that it is too late to bring Nazi murderers to justice, the figures clearly prove otherwise, and we are trying to ensure that at least several of these criminals will be brought to trial during the coming years. While it is generally assumed that it is the age of the suspects that is the biggest obstacle to prosecution, in many cases it is the lack of political will, more than anything else, that has hindered the efforts to bring Holocaust perpetrators to justice, along with the mistaken notion that it was impossible at this point to locate, identify, and convict these criminals. The success achieved by dedicated prosecutors, especially in Italy, Germany, and the United States, should encourage governments all over the world to make a serious effort to maximize justice while it can still be obtained."

For details of life in the Gross-Rosen concentration camp system 1940-45, I would recommend the book *A Narrow Bridge to Life*, by Bella Gutterman, which is a harrowing read but provides a real insight into the daily struggles that prisoners faced simply to remain alive in the face of ceaseless brutality by their SS guards.

Another graphic account of life in the camps, *If This Is A Man*, by Italian Jewish writer and chemist Primo Levi, describes the year he spent incarcerated in Auschwitz. (The U.S. edition is called *Survival in Auschwitz*).

More detail on Project Riese and the Gross-Rosen concentration camp complex which provided the labor to build it is available on a number of websites, including the Gross-Rosen website at https://en.gross-rosen.eu/ and also the Project Riese website http://www.riese.krzyzowa.org.pl/?lang=en

From 2015 to 2016 there were extensive efforts to locate and excavate a train rumored to contain gold and jewelry that was supposedly abandoned and buried by the Nazis in a secret railway tunnel just outside Walbrzych at the end of the war. Attempts to locate this train have so far proved unsuccessful. There was a fascinating BBC documentary about this in October 2016, *Hunting the Nazi Gold Train*, by historian and broadcaster Dan Snow, which provided much rich detail on Project Riese. It is still available on YouTube at https://www.youtube.com/watch?v=sQasnhDKxPU

The flight by hundreds, or more likely, thousands of Nazis to South America after World War II is well documented, although there is disagreement among some historians about the numbers and methods used to engineer their escape routes. In particular, Uki Goñi's book, *The Real Odessa: How Perón Brought the Nazi War Criminals to Argentina*, gives a well-researched insight into how the relationship between Hitler's Germany and Juan Perón's Argentina facilitated this.

Another similarly well-researched book is Guy Walters' *Hunting Evil*.

There are a number of novels which have also provided me with inspiration and useful background material. Of these, one of the best-known is Frederick Forsyth's *The Odessa File*, which detailed the Odessa escape network established by some SS officers at the end of World War II. Some historians, such as Guy Walters, have downplayed or even denied the existence of a network by that name.

Human trafficking and forced labor remains a significant problem in Argentina, including the Misiones province, where the border city of Puerto Iguazú is located. The U.S. State Department 2016 Trafficking in Persons report, available at https://www.state.gov/j/tip/rls/tiprpt/countries/2016/258713.htm, makes clear that Argentina still has a long way to go to tackle this issue.

The human rights organization The Protection Project published a country report on Argentina that also details the extent of human trafficking and can be found http://www.pro-

tectionproject.org/wp-content/uploads/2010/09/Argenti-
na.pdf. A report in *The Guardian* newspaper, albeit a few years
old, focusing on these issues in Puerto Iguazú specifically can
be   found   at
https://www.theguardian.com/world/2006/dec/20/argentina.brazil

ABOUT THE AUTHOR AND CONTACT DETAILS

Andrew has always had a love of writing and a passion for reading good thrillers. But despite having a long-standing dream of writing his own novels, it took him more than five decades to finally get around to doing it.

The Last Nazi is the first in a series of thrillers which also pull together some of Andrew's other interests, particularly history, world news, and travel.

Andrew studied history at Loughborough University and worked for many years as a business and financial journalist before becoming a corporate and financial communications adviser with several large energy companies, specializing in media relations.

He originally came from Grantham, Lincolnshire, and lives with his family in St. Albans, Hertfordshire, U.K.

You can connect with Andrew via these routes:
E-mail: andrew@andrewturpin.com
Website: www.andrewturpin.com.
Facebook: @AndrewTurpinAuthor
Twitter: @AndrewTurpin

Please do get in touch with your comments and views on the books, or anything else for that matter. Andrew very much enjoys hearing from readers and promises to reply.